CHILDREN
OF EARTH
AND SKY

CHILDREN OF EARTH AND SKY

GUY GAVRIEL KAY

HODDER &
STOUGHTON

First published in Great Britain in 2016 by Hodder & Stoughton
An Hachette UK company

1

Copyright © Guy Gavriel Kay 2016

The right of Guy Gavriel Kay to be identified as the Author of the Work has been
asserted by him in accordance with the Copyright, Designs and Patents Act 1988.

A CIP catalogue record for this title is available from the British Library

Hardback ISBN 978 1 473 62810 6
Trade Paperback ISBN 978 1 473 62811 3
eBook ISBN 978 1 473 62812 0

Printed and bound by Clays Ltd, St Ives plc

Hodder & Stoughton policy is to use papers that are natural, renewable and recyclable
products and made from wood grown in sustainable forests. The logging and manufacturing
processes are expected to conform to the environmental regulations of the country of origin.

for

GEORGE JONAS

and

EDWARD L. GREENSPAN

who belong together here

dear driends, lost

we were still at that first stage, still
preparing to begin a journey, but we were changed nevertheless;
we could see this in one another; we had changed although
we never moved, and one said, ah, behold how we have aged, traveling
from day to night only, neither forward nor sideward, and this seemed
in a strange way miraculous . . .

LOUISE GLÜCK

And all sway forward on the dangerous flood
Of history, that never sleeps or dies,
And, held one moment, burns the hand.

W.H. AUDEN

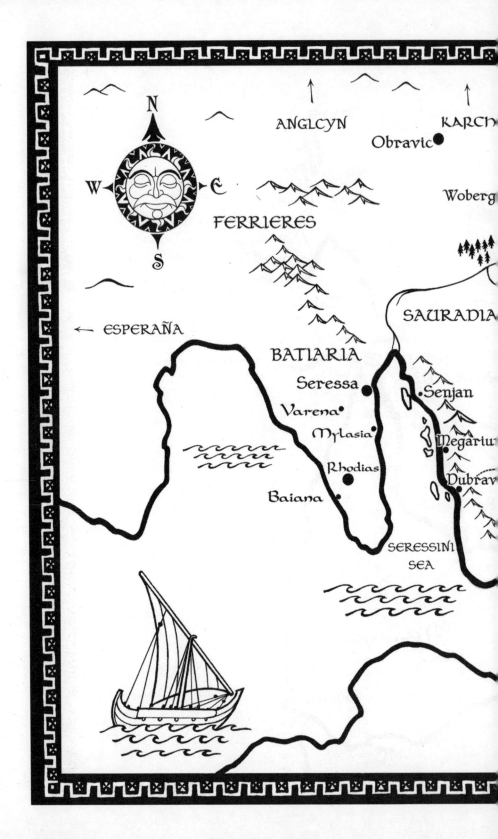

PRINCIPAL CHARACTERS

(A Partial List)

In Republic of Eressa and Elsewhere in Batiara

Duke Ricci, head of Seressa's Council of Twelve

Lorenzo Arnesti
Amadeo Frani } members of the Council of Twelve

Pero Villani, an artist, son of the late Viero Villani, also an artist
Tomo Agosta, his servant
Mara Citrani, subject of a portrait by Pero

Jacopo Miucci, physician
Leonora Valeri, a young woman passing as his wife

Count Erigio Valeri of Mylasia, Leonora's father
Paulo Canavli, her lover in Mylasia

Nelo Grilli
Guibaldo Ferri } merchants from Seressa
Marco Bossini

The High Patriarch of Jad, in Rhodias

In Obravic

Rodolfo, Jad's Holy Emperor

Savko, Imperial Chancellor
Hanns, principal secretary to the chancellor
Vitruvius of Karch, in the chancellor's service

Orso Faleri, Ambassador of Seressa to Obravic
Gaurio, his servant

Veith, a courtesan

In Senjan

Danica Gradek, a young woman
Tico, her dog
Neven Rusan, her maternal grandfather

Hrant Bunic, a Senjani raid leader

Tijan Lubic
Kukar Miho   } Senjani raiders
Goran Miho

In the Republic of Dubrava

Marin Djivo, younger son of a merchant family

Andrij, his father
Zarko, his brother

Drago Ostaja, one of their ship captains

Vlatko Orsat, another merchant
Elena and Iulia, his daughters
Vudrag, his son

Rastic Matko, another merchant
Kata Matko, his daughter

Jevic, a guard at the Rector's Palace

Giorgio Frani of Seressa (son of Amadeo),
    serving Seressa in Dubrava

Filipa di Lucaro, Eldest Daughter of Jad
    in the holy retreat on Sinan Isle
Juraj, a servant on the isle

Empress Eudoxia of Sarantium

In Asharias

Grand Khalif Gurçu ("the Destroyer")
Prince Cemal, his older son
Prince Beyet, his younger son

Yosef ben Hananon, the grand vizier

In Mulkar

Damaz, a trainee in the ranks of the djannis, the khalif's infantry
Koçi, another trainee

Hafiz, commander of the djannis in Mulkar
Kasim, an instructor in Mulkar

In Sauradia

Ban Rasca Tripon ("Skandir"), a rebel against the Asharites

Jelena, a village healer

Zorzi, a farmer in northern Sauradia
Rastic, Mavro, and Milena, his children

PART ONE

CHAPTER I

It was with a sinking heart that the newly arrived ambassador from Seressa grasped that the Emperor Rodolfo, famously eccentric, was serious about an experiment in court protocol.

The emperor liked experiments, everyone knew that.

It seemed the ambassador was to perform a triple obeisance—two separate times!—when finally invited to approach the imperial throne. This was, the very tall official escorting him explained, to be done in the manner of those presented to Grand Khalif Gurçu in Asharias.

It was also, the courtier added thoughtfully, how the great eastern emperors had been approached in long-ago days. Rodolfo was apparently now interested in the effect of such formal deference, observed and noted. And since Rodolfo was heir to those august figures of the past, it did make sense, didn't it?

It did not, at all, was the ambassador's unvoiced opinion.

He had no idea what this alleged *effect* was supposed to be.

He smiled politely. He nodded. He adjusted his velvet robe. In the antechamber where they waited he watched as a second court official—young, yellow-haired—enthusiastically demonstrated the salutations. His knees hurt with anticipatory pain. His back hurt. He was aware that, carrying evidence of prosperity about his midriff, he was likely to look foolish each time he prostrated himself, or rose to his feet.

Rodolfo, Jad's Holy Emperor, had sat the throne here for thirty years. You wouldn't ever want to call him foolish—he had many of the world's foremost artists, philosophers, alchemists at his court (performing *experiments*)—but you needed to consider the man unpredictable and possibly irresponsible.

This made him dangerous, of course. Orso Faleri, Ambassador of the Republic of Seressa, had had this made clear to him by the Council of Twelve before he'd left to come here.

He regarded the posting as a terrible hardship.

It was formally an honour, of course. One of the three most distinguished foreign posts a Seressini could be granted by the Twelve. It meant he might reasonably expect to become a member on his return, if someone withdrew, or died. But Orso Faleri loved his city of canals and bridges and palaces (especially his own!) with a passion. In addition, there were extremely limited opportunities for acquiring more wealth at Obravic in this role.

He was an emissary—and an observer. It was understood that all other considerations in a man's life were suspended for the year or possibly two that he was here.

Two years was a distressing thought.

He hadn't been allowed to bring his mistress.

His wife had declined to join him, of course. Faleri could have insisted she do so, but he wasn't nearly so self-abusive. No, he would have to discover, as best one might, what diversions there were in this windy northern city, far from Seressa's canals, where songs of love drifted in the torchlit night and men and women, cloaked against evening's damp, and sometimes masked, went about hidden from inquisitive eyes.

Orso Faleri was willing to simulate an interest in discussing the nature of the soul with the emperor's philosophers, or listen as some alchemist, stroking his singed beard, explained his search for arcane secrets of transmuting metal—but only to a point, surely.

If he performed his tasks, both public and secret, badly it would be noted back home, with consequences. If he did well he might be left here for two years! It was an appalling circumstance for a civilized man with skills in commerce and a magnificent woman left behind.

And now, the Osmanli triple obeisance. To be done twice. Good men, thought Faleri, suffered for the follies of royalty.

At the same time, this post was vitally important, and he knew it. In the world they inhabited, good relations with the emperor in Obravic were critical. Disagreements were acceptable, but open conflict could be ruinous for trade, and trade was what Seressa was about.

For the Seressinis, the idea of peace, with open, unthreatened commerce, was the most important thing in the god's created world. It mattered more (though this would never actually be *said*) than diligent attention to the doctrines of Jad as voiced by the sun god's clerics. Seressa traded, extensively, with the unbelieving Osmanlis in the east—and did so whatever High Patriarchs might say or demand.

Patriarchs came and went in Rhodias, thundering wrath in their echoing palace or cajoling like courtesans for a holy war and the need to regain lost Sarantium from the Osmanlis and their Asharite faith. That was a Patriarch's task. No one begrudged it. But for Seressa those god-denying Osmanlis offered some of the richest markets on earth.

Faleri knew it well. He was a merchant, son and grandson of merchants. His family's palace on the Great Canal had been built and expanded and sumptuously furnished with the profits of trading east. Grain at the beginning, then jewels, spices, silk, alum, lapis lazuli. Whatever was needed in the west, or desired. The caressing silks his wife and daughters wore (and his mistress, more appealingly) arrived at the lagoon on galleys and roundships voyaging to and from the ports of the Asharites.

The grand khalif liked trade, too. He had his palaces and gardens to attend to, and an expensive army. He might make war on the emperor's lands and fortresses where the shifting borders lay, and Rodolfo might be forced to spend sums he didn't have in bolstering defences there, but Seressa and its merchant fleet didn't want any part of that conflict: they needed peace more than anything.

Which meant that Signore Orso Faleri was here with missions to accomplish and assessments to make and send home in coded messages, even while filled with longings and memories that had little to do with politics or gaunt philosophers in a northern city.

His first priority, precisely set forth by the Council of Twelve, had to do with the savage, loathed, *humiliating* pirates in their walled town of Senjan. It happened to be a matter dear to Faleri's own merchant heart.

It was also desperately delicate. The Senjani were subjects, extremely loyal subjects, of Emperor Rodolfo. They were—the emperor's phrase had been widely quoted—his *brave heroes of the borderland*. They raided Asharite villages and farms inland and opposed counter-raids, defending Jaddites where they could. They were, in essence, fierce (unpaid) soldiers of the emperor.

And Seressa wanted them destroyed like poisonous snakes, scorpions, spiders, whatever you chose to call them.

They wanted them wiped out, their walls destroyed, boats burned, the raiders hanged, chopped to pieces, killed one by one or in a battle, burned on a great pyre seen for miles, or left out for the animals. Seressa didn't care. Dead was enough, chained as galley slaves would do. Would maybe even be better—you never had enough slaves for the fleet.

It was a vexed issue.

No matter how aggressively Seressa patrolled, how many war galleys they sent out, how carefully they escorted merchant ships, the Senjani raiders found ways to board some of them in the long, narrow Seressini Sea. It was impossible to completely defend against them. They raided in all seasons, all weather. Some said they could *control* the weather, that their women did so with enchantments.

One small town, perhaps two or three hundred fighting men inside its walls at any given time—and oh, the havoc they wreaked in their boats!

Complaints came to Obravic *and* to Seressa, endlessly, from the khalif and his grand vizier. *How*, the Asharites asked in graceful phrases, could they continue to trade with Seressa if their people and goods were subject to savage piracy? What was the worth of Seressini assurances of safety in the sea they proudly named for themselves?

Indeed, some of the letters queried, perhaps Seressa was secretly *pleased* when Osmanli merchants, pious followers of the teachings of Ashar, were seized by the Senjani for ransom, or worse?

It was, the Council of Twelve had impressed upon Faleri, his foremost task this autumn and winter. He was to induce a distractible, erratic emperor to surrender a town of raiders to Seressa's fury.

Rodolfo needed to understand that Senjan didn't *only* raid over the mountains against godless infidels or seize their goods on ships. No! They rowed or sailed south along their jagged coastline to Seressini-governed towns. They went even farther south, to that upstart marine republic of Dubrava (the Seressinis had issues with them, too).

Those towns and cities were Jaddite, the emperor knew it! In them dwelled devout worshippers of the god. These people and their goods were not to be targets! The Senjani were *pirates*, not heroes. They boarded honest merchant ships making their way to sell and buy in Seressa, queen of all Jad's cities, bringing it wealth. So much wealth.

The vile, dissembling raiders claimed that they only took goods belonging to Asharites, but that was—everyone knew it!—a pose, a pretense, a bad, black joke. Their piety was a mask.

The Seressinis knew all about masks.

Faleri himself had lost three cargoes (silk, pepper, alum) in two years to the Senjani. He wasn't any worshipper of the Asharite stars or the two Kindath moons! He was as good a Jaddite as the emperor. (Maybe a better one, if one considered Rodolfo's alchemy.)

His personal losses might even be, he suddenly thought, as the young, smooth courtier straightened from his sixth obeisance (six!), the reason he'd been appointed here. Duke Ricci, head of the Council of Twelve, was easily that subtle. Faleri would be able to speak with passion about the evil the Senjani represented.

"The emperor has received the gifts you brought," the tall official murmured, smiling. "He is much taken with the clock."

Of course he was taken with the clock, Faleri thought. That's why they had chosen it.

The clock had been half a year in the making. It was of ivory and mahogany, inlaid with precious stones. It showed the blue and white moons in their proper phases. It predicted eclipses of the sun. A Jaddite warrior came forth on the hour to smite a bearded Osmanli on the head with a mace.

The device made a steady ticking sound when properly adjusted. Faleri had brought a man with him who knew how to achieve that. He believed this man was also tasked with spying on him. There was always someone spying. There wasn't much you could do about it. Information was the iron key to unlock the world.

Orso Faleri felt as if the moments of his life were passing swiftly, to that ticking sound. His mistress was beautiful, young, imaginative, not celebrated for her patience. There were many back home who openly desired her, including two council members. At least two.

His unhappiness was extreme—and would need to be concealed.

The two great doors swung open. Servants in white and gold appeared, more tall men, standing extremely straight. The court official (he needed to begin remembering names) smiled at Faleri again. Another man appeared at the doors and greeted him. This, he knew, was the chancellor. A name they'd discussed back home. Chancellor Savko nodded his head. Ambassador Faleri nodded his.

They entered a large, long room together. There was a throne on a carpet most of the way towards the far end. There were fires lit, but it was still cold.

The clock had been placed on a table beside the throne. It was ticking. Faleri heard it when he rose heavily after the second set of obeisances. He managed to stand without help, which was gratifying, but he was perspiring under his heavy clothing, even in a chilly autumn room. It would not be seemly to mop his forehead at this point. His silk shirt under his doublet clung damply to his body. He worked to control his breathing.

If he had to do this every time he was presented for a year—or two!—it would kill him, he thought. He might as well die now.

Rodolfo was looking at the clock. He lifted a vague hand, in what might be construed as a greeting to the newest ambassador to his court. Or it could be a cautionary gesture to keep quiet. No one spoke. Faleri had not been introduced by anyone. He *couldn't* speak. He didn't exist here yet. A good thing, in a way. He needed to regain composure, and his breath.

The clock ticked loudly in a silent room.

Rodolfo, Jad's Holy Emperor, King of Karch, of Esperaña in the west, of the northern reaches of Sauradia, laying (disputed) claim to parts of Ferrieres, some of Trakesia, and diverse other territories and islands, Sword of the High Patriarch in Rhodias, scion of an illustrious (inbred) family, said thoughtfully, "We like this device. It divides eternity."

No one replied, though there were forty or fifty men in the room.

No women, Faleri realized. In Seressa there were always women at times such as this, adornments of life, often sublimely clever. He shifted his legs. His head was still swimming; the room wobbled and swayed like a child's top. He felt hot, dry-mouthed. They *would* kill him with these obeisances. He would die kneeling in Obravic!

The emperor was taller than expected. Rodolfo had the beaked nose and receding chin of the Kohlberg dynasty. He was pale-skinned, fair-haired. His hands were large, his eyes narrow above that nose, which made it hard to read their expression.

The chancellor finally broke the ticking stillness. "Excellency, I have the honour to present the distinguished emissary from the Republic of Seressa, arrived to take up his position among us. This is Signore Orso Faleri, who carries ambassador's papers attested by the seal of that republic, and who wishes the privilege of saluting you."

He had *already* saluted, Faleri thought grimly. Six times, head to marble floor. Was he now to crawl forward and kiss a slippered imperial foot? They did that in Asharias, didn't they? That great, triple-walled city wasn't called Sarantium any more, it had been conquered. It was where the khalif ruled. They had renamed the City of Cities since the fall, the terrible disaster of the age.

Twenty-five years ago. It was still difficult to grasp that it had happened. They lived in a sad, harsh world, Orso Faleri often thought. There was still money to be made, mind you.

The emperor finally looked at him. He actually turned from the ticking gift-object and regarded the ambassador of a power wealthier than he was, which lent him money, which was less beleaguered, and more sophisticated in almost all ways.

Well, good, thought Orso Faleri.

Rodolfo said, quietly, "We thank the Republic of Seressa for its gifts, and for sending Signore Faleri to us. Signore, it is our pleasure to see you again and to welcome you to Obravic. We hope to enjoy your presence here."

And with that he turned back to the clock. He did add, by way of explanation as he looked away, "We are waiting to see the man with the mace come out and strike the infidel."

He was, thought Faleri, said by many—including their last ambassador—to perhaps be going mad. It was possible. Faleri might spend two years of his life destroying his back and knees, burdening his heart and other parts of his anatomy at the court of a lunatic. There *was* madness in the imperial bloodline. All that intermarriage. It might have arrived again.

For one thing, Orso Faleri had never met the emperor before.

Our pleasure to see you again . . . ?

Was this a damaged mind, lost to alchemy and philosophies, or was it the empty pleasantry of a ruler not paying attention to what he said? Faleri might consider that an insult. On behalf of Seressa, of course. On the other hand, their gift had elicited approval. That was good, wasn't it?

There came a chiming sound.

Everyone regarded the clock.

A warrior of Jad, armoured in silver with a sun disk on his chest and bearing a golden mace, came forth on a curved track from doors on the left side of the apparatus. An Osmanli soldier, clad as one of the elite djanni infantry, bearded, wielding a curved sword, emerged similarly from the right. They met in the middle, in front of the clock face. Both stopped. The chiming continued. The Jaddite commenced to strike the Asharite upon his head with the mace. He did so three times. That was the hour. The chiming stopped. The warriors withdrew into the body of the clock, left side, right side. The doors closed, concealing them. There was ticking.

Jad's Holy Emperor laughed aloud.

LATER THAT AFTERNOON, as a cold rain fell, the chancellor of the Holy Jaddite Empire, a man greatly burdened by the demands of his office, closeted himself with two of his advisers in a fire-lit room.

The emperor was, at this moment, on a higher level of the palace—in a tower, in fact—where the latest attempt to alter the state of being of lead was underway under the auspices of a small, belligerent, untidy person from Ferrieres. There had been rumours of dramatic progress.

In this room the discussion was more prosaic. It concerned the Seressini ambassador. There was a vigorous dispute taking place. Chancellor Savko's tall secretary and the young man named Vitruvius, who held no significant official position but spent most nights in the chancellor's bed, were both of the opinion that the newest envoy from Seressa was a fool.

The chancellor pointed out that the Seressinis had not become the power they were by employing fools in important offices. He differed with their assessment. Indeed, he went further and chastised both—causing the younger one to flush (appealingly)—for being so hasty in formulating any opinion at all.

"Nothing about this," he said, lifting a necessary cup of warmed, spiced wine, "requires or is assisted by speed."

He drank slowly, as if to make a point. He set his cup down and looked out the streaked, barred window. Rain and mist. Red-roofed houses barely visible below, towards the grey river. "We have no *need* to form views about him yet," he said. "He can be observed at leisure."

"He asked about women," his secretary said. "Where the most desirable courtesans might be found. It could be a weakness?"

The chancellor made a note. "That is better," he said. "Bring me information, not judgments."

"What did you think of him?" his secretary asked.

"I think he is Seressini," Savko replied. "I think Seressa is always dangerous, always to be watched, and they sent this man to us. Did he say anything else?"

"Little," the secretary said. His name was Hanns. "A remark about pirates, the shared need to deal with them."

"Ah," said the chancellor. He had expected this. He made another note. "That will be about Senjan. He won't wait long before making a submission concerning them."

"What will we say?" his lover asked. Vitruvius was from Karch. He was pale-blond, blue-eyed, broad-shouldered, as many were in the north, and intelligent enough for his tasks. He was utterly loyal to the chancellor, which was critical at any court, and he knew how to kill people.

The chancellor tugged at his moustache, a habit. "I don't know yet. It depends on the Osmanlis, somewhat."

"Most things do," Secretary Hanns said.

He, as it happened, was too clever for his current position. There was a need to consider promoting him to a state office this winter. A useful man should not be allowed to become unhappy.

Savko favoured him with a rare smile. "You are right, of course," he said. "Pour yourselves wine, both of you. It is a miserable afternoon."

His mood, despite that, was benign. His foot wasn't hurting, for one thing, and he enjoyed minor mysteries of the sort this new envoy posed. He'd held office for fifteen years, half the emperor's reign. He knew he was good at what he did.

He'd kept a challenging emperor seated and secure, hadn't he? Well, largely secure. Money remained a vast, intractable problem, and the Osmanlis had been pushing forward just about every spring the last few years.

He'd be receiving the report on the state of their fortifications soon, since the campaign season had now ended. He wasn't looking forward to reading it. There was a probability the great fort of Woberg would be under siege again next spring, in which case repairs would be urgent, and expensive.

"I still think this new man is a fool," Vitruvius said, pouring wine.

"Let's set about finding out, shall we?" the chancellor said mildly.

He would think about the border forts when proper information arrived. A portion of his skill lay in not addressing matters until he had the facts he needed. He was endlessly aware of what he saw as a defining truth of the world: power almost always decided things.

Looking out the rain-blurred window as a wet evening descended, he gave quick, exact instructions concerning Orso Faleri, who appeared to like women, perhaps especially on cold autumn nights. This matter of a new ambassador he could begin to consider now. He'd done this before, many times.

IT WASN'T AS IF SERESSA was sunny and warm in late autumn. Indeed, if he was being honest he'd have to say his city on its lagoon could be colder than Obravic. Fog and damp that could find your chest and bones, even in a palace on the Great Canal. There weren't enough fireplaces in the world, Orso Faleri was thinking, to entirely ease a wet autumn or winter night back home.

Even so, even so. You felt the cold more when you were away. Men were like that, the world was. An unfamiliar house among strangers, darkness having descended to the sound of rain. Poets wrote about such things.

When he was younger he had done his share of travelling for the family, journeying east on their ships (his father's ships, then), enduring what came to a man at sea or in alien ports where, when bells rang, it was to summon Asharites to infidel prayers.

He had made a point of going once into the desert of Ammuz, an escorted journey inland from the port of Khatib, before sailing home with grain. He had looked up at the innumerable stars from outside a tent at night. He'd been bitten by a spider, he recalled.

If there was any pleasant aspect to growing older, it was that he'd reached a point where others made those journeys for him. He didn't regret tasting the wider world. A man needed, he thought, to know the bitterness of far-away beds and tables, danger and hardship and strangeness away. Spider bites in a desert night.

It made you appreciate what you had at home.

He was appreciating for all he was worth tonight. The after-noon's rain had not eased. He'd thought it might turn to snow, which would at least be delicate, white on the bare branches of trees, but it hadn't yet. It was just wet and cold in Obravic. Windy. The wind was from the north, winter in it. It rattled the windows.

They might have prepared a banquet for him, he thought. His first formal evening as ambassador, documents presented and accepted. They might have welcomed him properly. Of course they'd have been watching and judging him at any such feast, but he'd have been doing the same with those he met. That was what all this was, after all. Power assessing power.

Instead, he was in the ambassadorial residence, below the palace but on the same side of the river, alone except for servants. The clock-winder had remained in the palace. It seemed the emperor wished to have him housed among his men of art and science. That was all right. Faleri didn't trust the clock-winder. He wasn't one of his own men. He had only his manservant, Gaurio, with him. The others came with the house. They lived here, attending to whoever the ambassador was in a given year. Or two—may Jad defend his life and soul from that.

He had, however, enjoyed another passable meal. The cook appeared to know what he was doing. An unexpected blessing. He had drunk very good wine—his own. He'd brought three barrels of red Candarian with him, would send for more. There had been dreadful reports they mostly served those pale, sour Karchite wines in Obravic, or beer—and no civilized man could be expected to drink those for an entire year. Or two. (He needed to stop thinking about that.)

He was in a room furnished as a study on the ground level. A sturdy desk, a writing chair, daybed, south-facing terrace with a view of the river, for use in a better season. A good-sized fireplace, two more heavy chairs either side of it, a large table, storage chests with locks, Seressini paintings on the walls. One of these, an early Villani, was of the lagoon at sunrise: boats on bright water, the two sanctuaries, their domes gleaming, the lion pillars, the Arsenale just visible on the right. That painting was going to make him wistful, he thought.

Viero Villani was dead. Earlier this same year. Coughing blood, it had been reported, but not the plague. A good artist, in Faleri's view. Not one of the greatest, but skilled. He owned two of Villani's works himself. And tonight, looking at a painting (his own palace would have been just to the left of this scene), he morosely lifted a glass to toast the image and the man.

Not everyone could be a master. You could shape an honourable life somewhere below that level of accomplishment. It felt like an important thought. He had no one, he realized, with whom to share it.

He missed Annalisa already. She'd have seated him by the fire, poured another cup for both of them, listened sympathetically as he told of those six obeisances and the weak-chinned emperor clapping his hands like a child when their clock chimed and the warrior smote the Osmanli.

Then she'd have come upstairs to bed and unpinned her splendid hair and warmed him with the miracle of her youth while the sun god drove his chariot under the world and defended mankind from all that would assail it in the night.

Faleri drained his wine. Poured another cup. He wondered where she was tonight. If she was alone. He hoped she was alone. He heard a knocking at the door from out in the rain and dark.

FALERI SENT THE WOMAN home afterwards. It was difficult, as she had been warm and accommodating in his bed, but this was a game of courts, not desire, and those here were not to assume they had his measure so soon.

It was too transparent a device, in truth. Almost an insult, insufficient subtlety. Or perhaps just northern clumsiness. He had mentioned women to a yellow-haired man (and learned his name: Vitruvius) and—oh, see, astonishment!—a girl appears with an escort at his door that very night, scented, in low-cut green silk, which emerged as she shed a wet, dark, heavy cloak and hood.

Her name was Veith, she said. Yes, it was a bad night. Yes, wine would be much appreciated. She had a low, appealing voice.

He'd given her the wine in his bedchamber (best to get into the habit of not letting girls into the ground-floor room where there would be papers). He had taken his pleasure with her, and it *was* pleasurable. She simulated desire and gratification with practised, amusing skill. No northern clumsiness here. They'd spoken a little, afterwards, about autumn weather and importing silks, then he'd summoned Gaurio to take her back down to the front door where her escort would be—one dared assume—waiting under cover from the rain. She'd looked slightly disconcerted at being asked to dress and leave so expeditiously. That was all right.

He told Gaurio to be generous, though she'd have been paid by the court. She'd earned his coin, he judged, if not theirs.

He went to bed.

In the middle of the night Orso Faleri woke suddenly, even urgently, with a thought out of nowhere, or, more properly, out of the depths of a dream-memory.

He'd been standing with his father by the lagoon near the Arsenale. The slap of water against the stones. A great imperial ship was docked, a royal visit from Obravic. A herald presenting the republic's dignitaries to the previous emperor, including the well-regarded, prosperous merchant family of Faleri.

The previous emperor's oldest son, Rodolfo, was with *his* father. Walking behind him, hands clasped behind his back, looking about with curiosity. Faleri had been a boy, Prince Rodolfo a young man.

But they had seen each other that day. Almost forty years ago. *It is our pleasure to see you again.*

Faleri felt chilled, and not from the cold.

He adjusted his nightcap over his ears. It would be a grave mistake, he decided, wide awake in a black night, to decide that this emperor, however distracted he might appear, was any sort of fool. He would write that, encoded, in his first dispatch, he thought.

He hoped they'd make that sort of mistake judging him. It might be possible to behave in such a way as to encourage it. That could even be amusing.

The rain had stopped. It was quiet outside now. He wished he'd kept the girl, she'd have been warm. And the court might have drawn some conclusions about him. Not entirely false ones, he conceded, but it would be useful if they considered him only sensuous and incompetent.

He lay in bed and thought about the pirates of Senjan, the raiders behind their reefs and walls. His first task here. He was to induce this emperor—who had actually remembered him, glimpsed once as a boy—to allow Seressa to destroy them in the name of goodwill and trade.

He'd been authorized to offer money outright, not just loans. The emperor needed money. The Osmanlis would almost certainly be coming back against him in the spring.

CHAPTER II

She hadn't intended to bring the dog when she went out on a moonless night to begin the next stage of her life.

Problem was, Tico jumped in the boat while she was pushing it off the strand and refused to leave when she hissed a command at him. She knew that if she pushed him into the shallow water he'd start barking in protest, and she couldn't allow that.

So her dog was with her as she began rowing out into the black bay. It could have been comical, except it wasn't because she was here to kill people, and for all her hard, cold reputation in Senjan, she had never done that.

It was time, Danica thought.

The Senjani named themselves heroes, warriors of the god defending a dangerous border. If she was going to make herself accepted as a raider among them, not just a someday mother of fighters (and daughter of one, and granddaughter), she needed to begin. And she had her vengeance to pursue. Not against Seressa, but this could be a start.

No one knew she was out tonight in her family's small boat. She'd been careful. She was unmarried, lived alone now in their house (everyone in her family was dead, since last summer). She could come and go silently at night, and all the young people in Senjan knew how to get through the town walls if they needed to, on the landward side, or down to the stony beach and the boats.

The raid leaders might punish her after tonight, the emperor's small garrison almost certainly would want to, but she was prepared for that. She just needed to succeed. Recklessness and pride, courage and faith in Jad, and prowess, that was how the Senjani understood themselves. They could punish her and still honour her—if she did what she was out here to do. If she was right about tonight.

Nor did she find it distressing that the men she intended to kill were fellow worshippers of Jad, not god-denying Osmanlis—like the ones who had destroyed her own village years ago.

Danica had no trouble summoning hatred for arrogant Seressa across the narrow sea. For one thing, that republic traded greedily with the infidels, betraying the god in pursuit of gold.

For another, Seressa had been blockading Senjan, keeping all the boats pinned in the harbour or on the strand, and the town was hungry now. The Seressinis controlled Hrak Island, which was so near you could swim to it, and they'd forbidden the islanders, on pain of hanging, from dealing with Senjan. (There was some smuggling, but not enough, not nearly so.) They were bent on starving the Senjani, or destroying them if they came out. There was no mystery to it.

A good-sized overland party of twenty raiders had gone east through the pass into Asharite lands a week ago, but end of winter was not a time to find much in the way of food there, and there were terrible risks.

It was too early to know if the Osmanlis were advancing towards the imperial fortresses again this year, but they probably would be. Here in the west, the heroes of Senjan could try to capture animals or take villagers for ransom. They could fight the savage hadjuks in fair numbers if they met them, but not if those numbers were greatly increased, and not if the hadjuks had cavalry with them from the east.

Everything carried risks for ordinary people these days. The powers in their courts didn't appear to spend much time thinking about the heroes of Senjan—or any of the men and women on the borderlands.

The triple border, they called it: Osmanli Empire, Holy Jaddite Empire, Republic of Seressa. Ambitions collided here. These lands were where good people suffered and died for their families and faith.

The loyal heroes of Senjan were useful to their emperor. When there was war with Asharias they'd receive letters of praise on expensive paper from Obravic, and every so often half a dozen more soldiers to be garrisoned in the tall round tower inland from their walls, augmenting the handful usually here. But when the demands of trade, or finance, or conflicts among the Jaddite nations, or the need to end such conflicts, or whatever other factors in the lofty world of courts caused treaties to be made—well, then the raiders of Senjan, the heroes, became expendable. A problem, a threat to harmony if the Osmanli court or aggrieved Seressini ambassadors registered complaints.

These bloodthirsty savages have violated our sworn peace with the Osmanlis, the terms of a treaty. They have seized shipped goods, raided villages, sold people into slavery . . . So Seressa had notoriously written.

An emperor, reading that, needed to be more honourable, more aware, Danica thought, rowing under stars. Didn't he understand what they needed from him? Villages or farms on a violent border divided by faith didn't become peaceful because of pen strokes in courts far away.

If you lived on stony land or by a stony strand you still needed to feed yourself and your children. Heroes and warriors shouldn't be named *savages* so easily.

If the emperor didn't pay them to defend his land (their land!), or send soldiers to do it, or allow them to find goods and food for themselves, asking nothing of him, what did he want them to do? Die?

If Senjani seafarers boarded trading galleys and roundships, it was only for goods belonging to heretics. Jaddite merchants with goods in the holds were protected. Or, well, they were supposed to be. They usually were. No one was going to deny that extremes of need and anger might cause some raiders to be a little careless in sorting which merchant various properties belonged to on a taken ship.

Why do they ignore us in Obravic? she asked suddenly, in her mind.

You want honourable behaviour from courts? A foolish wish, her grandfather said.

I know, she replied, in thought, which was how she spoke with him. He'd been dead almost a year. The plague of last summer.

It had taken her mother, too, which is why Danica was alone now. There were about seven or eight hundred people in Senjan most of the time (more took refuge if there was trouble inland). Almost two hundred had died here in two successive summers.

There were no assurances in life, even if you prayed, honoured Jad, lived as decently as you could. Even if you had already suffered what someone might fairly have said was enough. But how did you measure what was enough? Who decided?

Her mother didn't talk to her in her mind. She was gone. So were her father and older brother, ten years ago in a burning village. They didn't talk to her.

Her grandfather was in her head at all times. They spoke to one another, clearly, silently. Had done so from the moment, just about, that he'd died.

What just happened? he'd said. Exactly that, abruptly, in her mind, as Danica walked away from the pyre where he and her mother had burned with half a dozen other plague victims.

She had screamed. Wheeled around in a mad, terrified circle, she remembered. Those beside her had thought it was grief.

How are you here? she'd cried out, silently. Her eyes had been wide open, staring, seeing nothing.

Danica! I don't know!

You died!

I know I did.

It was impossible, appalling. And became unimaginably comforting. She'd kept it secret, from that day to this night. There were those, and not just clerics, who would burn her if this became known.

It defined her life now, as much as the deaths of her father and brother had—and the memory of their small, sweet little one, Neven, the younger brother taken by the hadjuks in that night raid years ago. The raid that had brought three of them fleeing to Senjan: her grandfather, her mother, herself at ten years old.

So she talked in her thoughts with a man who was dead. She was as good with a bow as anyone in Senjan, better than anyone she knew with knives. Her grandfather had taught her both while he was alive, from when she was only a girl. There were no boys any more in the family to teach. They had both learned to handle boats here. It was what you did in Senjan. She had learned to kill with a thrown knife and a held one, to loose arrows from a boat, judging the movements of the sea. She was extremely good at that. It was why she had a chance to do what she was here to do tonight.

She wasn't, Danica knew, an especially *conventional* young woman.

She swung her quiver around and checked the arrows: habit, routine. She'd brought a lot of them, odds were very much against a strike with each one, out here on the water. Her bow was dry. She'd been careful. A wet bowstring was next to useless. She wasn't sure how far she'd have to aim—if this even happened. If the Seressinis were indeed coming. It wasn't as if they'd made her a promise.

It was a mild night, one of the first of a cold spring. Little wind. She couldn't have done this in a rough sea. She dropped her cloak from her shoulders. She looked up at the stars. When she was young, back in their village, sleeping outdoors behind the house on hot summer nights, she used to fall asleep trying to count them. Numbers went on and on, apparently. So did stars. She could almost understand how Asharites might worship them. Except it meant denying Jad, and how could anyone do that?

Tico was motionless at the prow, facing out to sea as if he were a figurehead. She wasn't able to put into words how much she loved her dog. There was no one to say it to, anyhow.

Wind now, a little: her grandfather, in her mind.

I know, she replied quickly, although in truth she'd only become aware of it in the moment he told her. He was acute that way, sharper than she was when it came to certain things. He used her senses now—sight, smell, touch, sound, even taste. She didn't understand how. Neither did he.

She heard him laugh softly in her head, at the too-swift reply. He'd been a fighter, a hard, harsh man to the world. Not with his daughter and granddaughter, though. His name had also been Neven, her little brother named for him. She called him "zadek," their family's own name for "grandfather," going back a long way, her mother had told her.

She knew he was worried, didn't approve of what she was doing. He'd been blunt about it. She had given him her reasons. They hadn't satisfied. She cared about that, but she also didn't. He was with her, but he didn't control her life. He couldn't do anything to stop her from doing what she chose. She also had the ability to close him off in her mind, shut down their exchanges and his ability to sense anything. She could do that any time she wanted. He hated it when she did.

She didn't like it either, in truth, though there were times (when she was with men, for example) when it was useful and extremely necessary. She was alone without him, though. There was Tico. But still.

I did know it was changing, she protested.

The freshening wind was north and east, could become a bura, in fact, which would make the sea dangerous, and almost impossible for a bow. These were her waters, however, her home now, since her first home had burned.

You weren't supposed to be angry with the god, it was presumption, heresy. Jad's face on the domes and walls of sanctuaries showed his love for his children, the clerics said. Holy books taught his infinite compassion and courage, battling darkness every night for them. But there had been no compassion from the god, or the hadjuks, in her village that night. She dreamed of fires.

And the proud and glorious Republic of Seressa, self-proclaimed Queen of the Sea, traded with those Osmanlis, by water routes and overland. And because of that trade, that greed, Seressa was starving the heroes of Senjan now, because the infidels were complaining.

The Seressinis hanged raiders when they captured them, or just killed them on board ships and threw the bodies into the sea without Jad's rites. They worshipped golden coins in Seressa more than the golden god, that was what people said.

The wind eased. Not about to be a bura, she thought. She stopped rowing. She was far enough out for now. Her grandfather was silent, leaving her to concentrate on watching in the dark.

The only thing he'd ever offered as an explanation for this impossible link they shared was that there were traditions in their family—her mother's family, his—of wisewomen and second sight.

Anything like this? she'd asked.

No, he'd replied. *Nothing I ever heard.*

She'd never experienced anything that suggested a wisewoman's sight in herself, any access to the half-world, anything at all besides a defining anger, skill with a bow and knives, and the best eyesight in Senjan.

That last was the other thing that made tonight possible. It was black on the water, only stars above, neither moon in the sky— which was why she was here now. She'd been fairly certain that if the Seressinis did do this they would come on a moonless night. They were vicious and arrogant, but never fools.

Two war galleys, carrying three hundred and fifty oarsmen and mercenary fighters, with new bronze cannons from Seressa's Arsenale, had been blocking the bay, both ends of Hrak Island, since winter's end, but they hadn't been able to do anything *but* that.

The galleys were too big to come closer in. These were shallow, rocky, reef-protected seas, and Senjan's walls and their own cannons could handle any shore party sent on foot from a landing farther south. Besides which, putting mercenaries ashore on lands formally ruled by the emperor could be seen as a declaration of war. Seressa and Obravic danced a dance, always, but there were too many other dangers in the world to start a war carelessly.

The republic had tried to blockade Senjan before, but never with two war galleys. This was a huge investment of money and men and time, and neither ship's captain could be happy sitting in open water with chilled, bored, restless fighters, achieving nothing for his own career.

The blockade was working, however. It was doing real harm, though it was hard for those on the galleys to know that yet.

In the past, the Senjani had always found ways of getting off-shore, but this was different, with two deadly ships controlling the lanes to north and south of the island that led to sea.

It seemed the Council of Twelve had decided the raiders had finally become too much of a nuisance to be endured. There had been mockery: songs and poetry. Seressa was not accustomed to being a source of amusement. They claimed this sea, they named it after themselves. And, more importantly, they guaranteed the safety of all ships coming up to dock by their canals for their merchants and markets. The heroes of Senjan, raiding to feed themselves, and for the greater glory of Jad, were a problem.

Danica offered a thought to her grandfather.

Yes, a thorn in the lion's paw, he agreed.

The Seressinis called themselves lions. A lion was on their flag and their red document seals. There were apparently lions on columns in the square before their palace, on either side of the slave market.

Danica preferred to call them wild dogs, devious and dangerous. She thought she could kill some of them tonight, if they sent a skiff into the bay, intending to set fire to the Senjani boats drawn up on the strand below the walls.

HE WASN'T GOING to say he *loved* her or anything like that. That wasn't the way the world went on Hrak Island. But Danica Gradek did drift into his dreams, and had done so for a while now. On the island and in Senjan there were women who interpreted dreams for a fee. Mirko didn't need them for these.

She was unsettling, Danica. Different from any of the girls on Hrak, or in the town when he made his way across to trade fish or wine.

You had to trade very cautiously these days. Seressa had forbidden anyone to deal with the pirates this spring. There were war galleys. You'd be flogged or branded if caught, could even be hanged, depending on who did the catching and how much your family could afford in bribes. Seressa almost certainly had spies in Senjan, too, so you needed to be careful that way, as well. Seressa had spies everywhere, was the general view.

Danica was younger than him but always acted as if she were older. She could laugh, but not always when you'd said something you thought was amusing. She was too cold, the other men said, you'd freeze your balls making love to her. They talked about her, though.

She handled a bow better than any of them. Better than anyone Mirko knew, anyhow. It was unnatural in a woman, *wrong*, ought to have been displeasing, but for Mirko it wasn't. He didn't know why. Her father, it was said, had been a famous fighter in his day. A man of reputation. He'd died in a hadjuk village raid, somewhere on the other side of the mountains.

Danica was tall. Her mother had been, too. She had yellow hair and extremely light blue eyes. There was northern blood in the family. Her grandfather had had eyes like that. He'd been a scary figure when he came to Senjan, scarred and fierce, thick moustaches, a border hero of the old style, men said.

She'd kissed him once, Danica. Just a few days ago, in fact. He'd been ashore south of the town walls with two casks of wine before dawn, thin blue moon setting. She and three others he knew had been waiting on the strand to buy from him. They'd used torches to signal from the beach.

It happened he had learned something not long before and—on an impulse—he'd asked her to walk a little away from the others. There had been jokes, of course. Mirko didn't mind, and she hadn't looked as if she did. It was hard to read her and he wouldn't claim to be good at understanding women, anyhow.

He told her that three days earlier he'd been part of a group supplying the war galley in the northern channel. He'd overheard talk about sending a boat to fire the Senjani ones drawn up on the strand. Bored men on ships, especially mercenaries, could grow careless. He said if it were him doing it, he'd do it on a no-moons night. *Of course*, she said.

He thought if she was the one he told she could reap the benefit of reporting the tidings to the raid captains and she'd be happy with him for that.

Danica Gradek kissed really well, it turned out. Fiercely, even hungrily. She wasn't quite as tall as he was. He wasn't sure, remembering

the moment, if it had been passion, or triumph, or the anger everyone said was in her, but he'd wanted more. Of the kiss, of her.

"Good lad," she said, stepping back.

Lad? That he didn't like. "You'll warn the captains?"

"Of course," she said.

It never occurred to him she might be lying.

SHE WAS PROTECTING the boy, she'd explained to her zadek. Mirko
wasn't a boy, but she thought of him that way. She thought of
most of the men her age that way. A few were different—she could
admire skill and bravery—but those often turned out to be the ones
who most fiercely rejected the idea of a woman as a raider. They
hated that she was better with her bow than them, but she wasn't,
ever, going to hide what she could do. She'd made that decision a
long time ago.

The heroes of Senjan, devoted equally to Jad and independence, also had a reputation for violence. That last, in the eyes
of the world, included their women. There were horrified, wide-
eyed stories told of Senjani women streaming down from hills
or woods to a triumphant battlefield at day's end—wild, like
wolves—to lick and drink the blood from the wounds of slain
foes, or even those not yet dead! Tearing or hacking limbs off and
letting blood drip down gaping throats. Senjani women believed,
the tale went, that if they drank blood their unborn sons would
be stronger warriors.

Foolish beyond words. But useful. It was a good thing to have
people afraid of you if you lived in a dangerous part of the world.

But Senjan didn't think it good for a woman, not long out of
girlhood, to believe—let alone seek to prove—she could equal a
man, a *real* fighter. That, they didn't like much, the heroes.

At least she wasn't strong with a sword. There was someone who
had spied on her throwing daggers at targets outside the walls and,

well, according to him she did that extremely well. She ran fast, could handle a boat, knew how to move silently, and . . .

Some reckless, very brave man, the general view became, needed to marry the ice-cold, pale-eyed Gradek girl and get a baby into her. End this folly of a woman raiding. She might be the daughter of Vuk Gradek, who'd had renown in his day, inland, but she was a *daughter* of a hero, not a son.

One of his sons had died with him; the other, a child, had been taken by the hadjuks in the raid on Antunic, their village. He was likely a eunuch by now in Asharias or some provincial city, or being trained for the djannis—their elite, Jaddite-born infantry. He might even one day come back attacking them.

It happened. One of the old, hard sorrows of the border.

The girl did want to join the raids, it was no secret. She spoke of vengeance for her family and village. Had been talking that way for years.

She'd openly asked the captains. Wanted to go through the pass into Osmanli lands on a raid for sheep and goats, or men and women to ransom or sell. Or she'd ask to go in the boats chasing merchant ships in the Seressini Sea—which they might actually be able to start doing again if this accursed blockade would only lift.

Danica knew the talk about her. Of course she did. She'd even let Kukar Miho watch her practising, thinking himself cleverly unseen behind (rustling) bushes, as she threw knives at olives on a tree near the watchtower.

This past winter the clerics had begun speaking to her about marrying, offering to negotiate with families on her behalf since she had no parent or brother to do so. Some of her mother's friends had made the same offer.

She was still mourning, she'd said, eyes lowered, as if shy. It hadn't been a year yet, she'd said.

Her mourning year would end in summer. They'd chant a service for her mother and grandfather in the sanctuary, along with so many others, then she'd need to think of another excuse. Or pick a man.

She was perfectly happy to sleep with one when a certain mood overtook her. She'd discovered some time ago that cups of wine and lovemaking could ease her on occasion. She closed off her grandfather in her mind on those nights, relieved she was able to do so. They never discussed it.

But being with a man by the strand or in a barn outside the walls (only one time in her own house—it had felt wrong in the morning and she'd never done it again) was as much as she wanted right now. If she married, her life would change. *End*, she was half inclined to say, though she knew that was excessive. A life ended when you died.

In any case, she'd told her grandfather the truth: she *was* protecting Mirko of Hrak by not reporting his information to the captains or the military. If the Senjani set a full ambush on the beach for a night attack, the Seressinis would realize someone had given their plan away. They were clever enough to do that, Jad knew, and vicious enough to torture a story out of the islanders. They might or might not arrive at Mirko, but why risk it? One guard out in a boat—that could be routine.

If she'd revealed Mirko's story she'd have been asked who told her, and it would have been impossible (and wrong) to not tell the captains. She wanted to join the raiders, not anger them. And the Seressini spy inside the walls (of course there was a spy, there was always a spy) would almost certainly learn whatever she said, see the preparations. They'd likely cancel the attack, if it was happening. If Mirko was right.

No, doing this alone was the prudent approach, she'd told her grandfather, choosing the word a little mischievously. Unsurprisingly, he had sworn at her. He had been legendary for his tongue in his day. She was developing a little of that reputation, but it was different for a woman.

Everything in the world was. Danica wondered sometimes why the god had made it so.

She really did have good eyesight. She saw a flame appear and vanish to her right, north, on the headland that framed that side of the bay. She caught her breath.

Jad sear his soul! What pustulent, slack-bowelled fucking traitor is that? her grandfather snarled.

She saw it again, quickly there and gone, moving right to left. A light on the headland could only be there to guide a boat. And to do that in these deadly waters you needed to know the bay and its rocks and shallows.

Tico had seen it too. He growled in his throat. She silenced him. It was a long bowshot to that headland at night. Too long from a boat. Danica began rowing again, heading that way, north, against the light breeze, but looking west as she went.

Quietly, girl!

I am.

Nothing to be seen yet. The Seressinis would have a long way to go past the island from where the galley blocked the channel. But that light on the headland was signalling a path through rocks and reefs. Swinging right now, then left, held briefly in the middle, then hidden, most likely by a cloak. It meant someone was coming, and that he could see them.

She gauged the distance, shipped her oars, took her bow, nocked an arrow.

Too far, Danica.

It isn't, zadek. And if he's up there they are on their way.

He was silent in her thoughts. Then said, *He's holding the lantern in his right hand, guiding them left and right. You can tell where his body is by how—*

I know, zadek. Shh. Please.

She waited on the wind, the small boat moving as the breeze moved the sea.

She was still watching two ways: that headland light, and where the channel opened, by the dark bulk of the island.

She heard them before she saw anything.

They were rowing, not silently. They were not expecting anyone out here and they were coming towards her.

Splash of oars in water, Tico stiffening again. Danica hushed him, stared into the night, and then it was there, clearing the dark bulk of the island, one small light. Seressinis on the water, come to burn boats on the strand. She was awake, this was not a dream of fire coming.

There was anger in her, no fear. She was the hunter tonight. They didn't know that. They thought they were.

I don't need to kill him, she said in her mind.

He needs to die.

Later. If we take him alive we can ask questions.

In truth, it might have been hard for her, killing that one on the headland: whoever he was, he was going to be someone she knew. She had decided it was time to learn how to kill, but she hadn't thought it might be a face she knew right at the start.

I ought to have realized they'd need someone to guide them in.

Might have been with them in the boat, her grandfather said. *Might still be someone with them. They tend to be cautious.*

She couldn't resist. *Like me?*

He swore. She smiled. And suddenly felt calm. She was in the midst of events now, not anticipating they might happen. Time had run, after almost ten years it had carried her to this moment, this boat on black water with her bow.

She could see the shape of the approaching craft, dark on darkness. They had one light, would mean to douse it when they came nearer to shore. She heard a voice, trying to be quiet, but carrying, if anyone was in the bay to hear.

"Over other way, he's saying. Rocks just there."

Speaking Seressini. She was glad of that.

Jad guide your arm and eye, her grandfather said. His voice in her mind was very cold.

Danica stood up, balanced herself. She had trained for this, so many times. The wind was easy, and the sea. She fitted an arrow to the string, drew the bowstring back. She could see them in the boat now. It looked like six men. Maybe seven.

She loosed her first arrow. Was nocking the second as that one flew.

CHAPTER III

"You don't like being inside me?"

Sometimes a girl likes to stay close in bed, after, be held, and Marin doesn't mind doing this. They have given him the gift of their intimacy, taking a risk. He may be a cynical man, but is not an ungenerous one, he hopes.

But this girl is getting dressed, briskly, as she asks her question, the curves of her body disappearing beneath clothing. There has been no lingering. She is young but hardly innocent. Quite a few of the well-bred girls in Dubrava, in his experience, lose their innocence early. It is not, on the whole, an innocent city.

He dresses as well. He crosses to the window, looks down. The sunset promenade has begun below her room above the Straden. If he waits he'll see her parents walk by. And his, of course.

He says, looking out, "I like it very much. I don't like the idea of something else growing inside you, after."

She laughs behind him. "Really, Marin. You think women can't count?"

He turns to look at her. She is coiling and pinning her hair. He has come to hate these moments when two people, having lain together, reassemble clothing and appearance, armour for the world. Even with courtesans, he doesn't like this. Intimacy, even a casual intimacy, ought to last longer, he thinks.

"I believe many women end up counting towards childbirth and ruin their lives. We are not as predictable as we like to think."

"Well, you certainly aren't, Marin Djivo."

He makes a face. "I do try not to be."

Her hair is pinned now, beneath a cap again. She looks at him. "Am I as . . . pleasurable as the girls on Plavko Street?"

"Easily," he lies.

She smiles, slyly. "I am so easy?"

She is clever. Men and women in Dubrava tend to be. The republic would not survive otherwise. He smiles back. "You were hard to conquer, then soft when you decided to be."

She laughs. Then an inquiring look again. "As skilled as the courtesans in Seressa, Marin?"

"Very much so." He is a good liar, as it happens.

"I don't believe you."

"Why not?"

"Because everyone knows what a good liar you are."

She won't know why he laughs aloud, but he sees it pleases her. He likes women; it is a matter of some regret that he finds himself growing tired of this particular dance. Maybe it is time to be wed, after all?

This is their third encounter up here. He is thinking it should be their last, for her sake, though he isn't vain enough to imagine he's the only man she's brought to this room. Dubrava is a wealthy city, an important port, but it is still small, risky for this sort of visit. She is eighteen, and their families have shared cargoes and ships and insurance for years.

She says, as if tracing the same path to a different port, "My mother spoke of you after sanctuary yesterday morning. Said you might make a strong marriage."

"I'm flattered," he says.

"I told her you had a terrible reputation. She said handsome men often do." She smiles.

He takes his leave a moment later, out a rear window on this upper floor, jumping across to the lower roof of the house beside then descending to the empty backstreet that way. He has done this before, other windows, other descents. You can call it exciting. Or not, after a certain number of occasions.

He walks west a little towards the harbour, then crosses to join the evening promenade. Friends call his name, fall into stride with him. Everyone knows Marin Djivo. Everyone among the merchants knows everyone. It is the way of things here.

He watches the others, his friends, their fathers, as they reach the eastern end by the gate and turn. It is said in Dubrava that as they do the evening stroll along the Straden—the wide street from the Rector's Palace to the landward gate—you can always tell who has a ship at sea.

Those men will invariably lift their heads from whatever conversation they are having when they reach the end of the street and turn back west.

They will be looking towards the harbour. They can't help themselves. Word can come at any moment: a ship returning, tidings of a ship lost, or taken by pirates. Messages of fortune or disaster arriving from the port behind the palace.

Who could *not* look to see if anything was happening, even if only a few moments had gone by since the last quick glance? A merchant who traded on the god's sea always had a part of his heart out on the wide waters. Imagination conjuring creatures from the deep, lightning storms, wild winds, Asharite corsairs in the open sea south, or Senjani raiders in these, their home waters.

There are so many things to fear when your life is bound, as with ropes, to the sea. So how should a man with a ship away from port not listen and look for a cry or commotion from the western end of a crowded street?

Marin Djivo, whose family owns three ships outright and often has goods carried on those of other merchants, has spent much of his life observing people in his small republic. He has seen this involuntary lifting of the head in friends (and not-quite-friends). He fights it in himself, as best he can, being the sort of man who dislikes being a slave to habit or fashion.

It is also too soon for tidings, he tells himself, bowing to the stylishly dressed wife and daughter of Radic Matko as they approach. It is early in spring and the *Blessed Ingacia* has gone a long way east, to Ammuz. The crew will have wintered in the port of Khatib there, awaiting the grain harvest among the small Jaddite colony permitted by the Asharites (with customs fees and bribes paid, of course).

Marin's father had established this routine years ago. One of their ships always winters in Khatib. It is a hardship for the sailors and captains and the Djivos pay them handsomely for it, but if that ship catches the earliest good winds of spring it can be back this way well before anyone else, with grain and spices, sometimes silk or wine, and being *before anyone else* is how fortunes are made.

Or lost, if the earliest winds of spring prove treacherous instead, if a late storm comes, winter's last gale. You gambled with cargoes and lives all the time, and prayed a great deal, as a consequence. It was said that an experienced Dubravae merchant was sensitive to *everything*, like a woman at a ball or dinner party assessing the subtle currents of the room.

The Matko girl, smiling as they pass each other, is soft and pretty. *She knows it, too*, Marin thinks. He is familiar with all the well-bred girls in Dubrava. And they know each man—older sons, younger sons, widowers. The families are not numerous, but no man or woman can easily marry outside their ranks. It makes for challenging domestic planning, but the women of the republic are good at this, of necessity.

Marin Djivo is thirty years old in a city where men of that age might wed and start a family. He is the younger son, however, with a brother in the earliest stages of marriage negotiations. It gives him a little time.

His father and brother are on both the Rector's Great Council *and* the Small, which means that the usual close-watching of each family ensures that the third Djivo, the clever-tongued one, is relegated to minor functions such as monitoring how the fire and quarantine regulations are observed, and duly reporting back to the councils.

He puts a good face on this but he loathes it with a passion that startles him sometimes. He is not a man naturally submissive to rules or regulations—or the monitoring of them. He spends as much time as he can on their ships, most often the short run northwest to Seressa. He has become skilled at trading there, his father trusts him among the Seressinis. You can hate and fear Seressa, but it is the best market in the world, and their own smaller republic always needs to acknowledge that.

Another mother with two daughters passes. He lifts his hat and bows again. He'd had encounters with the younger one last year, once coming close to being caught by the sister. One needs to be careful, but there are ways. Usually the women find them.

It had been with a true sense of discovery that he'd learned, when still young, that the well-bred women of Dubrava (married or otherwise) chafed under the formalities of social interaction and piety quite as much as the young men did.

A life-changing revelation, for a time. It has begun to pall. The pettiness of such encounters, the urgent furtiveness—exciting, then less so.

Kata Matko's eyes, holding his a moment as they passed, hint at much, as had Elena Orsat's, whom he has left upstairs just now.

Either is likely to make a handsome wife for someone soon. Indeed, it might be judged by their mothers that the younger Djivo son was due to be tamed into marriage a little more quickly than most, for everyone's good. Perhaps as soon as the older one was wed. He came from a very significant family, after all.

He will probably accept that, Marin is thinking on a pleasant evening in spring. There have been times when his dreams have been more encompassing, but there are only so many ways you can fight the world as it is given to you, and his will be far—very far—from a dismal fate or future.

He and his friends reach the inland gate. They touch the white stone on the right-side wall for ships' luck, and turn back. Everyone always waits until they reach the fountain nearest the wall, then they glance up towards the harbour. Marin does not. Small things. Small things you do to not be the same as everyone around you.

Then he hears the cannon, and of course he does look. The cannon is a signal.

Someone is running as fast as he can up the street, and Marin knows the boy: he is one of theirs. The runner skids to a stop before Marin's father, walking with others just ahead. The boy is speaking rapidly, gesturing, excited. Marin sees his father smile and then make the sign of the sun disk with both hands before his heart, in thanks and praise.

He strides quickly forward—and hears the tidings himself. You can be jaded, often bored, dream of a different life (with no clear idea of what that might be), but your heart will quicken at moments like this. Other merchants gather around offering congratulations, some hiding envy.

It seems the *Blessed Ingacia* has come home. First ship of the spring.

"It was *not* a girl!" Captain Zani shouted for the third time. He had a carrying, heavy voice, useful at sea, very likely. "My lords of the council, I deny that!"

The Duke of Seressa winced. He had discovered over the past while that loud noises increasingly irritated him, and he was already disturbed tonight.

Was it impossible, he wondered, for civilized men to discuss matters of state without raising their voices? When had everyone become so loud? He often had thoughts, lately, of withdrawing from his office—to prayer, and to quiet. It was proper for a man to guide his soul towards Jad as his days neared their end.

Duke Ricci had been elected nineteen years ago. Absent violence (not unknown), one was Duke of Seressa, heading the Council of Twelve, for life, or until choosing to step aside. He wasn't young, he hadn't been young nineteen years ago. But the divisions in the council were extreme just now. His departure, the voting for his successor, could plunge the republic into chaos.

He detested chaos.

"Your denial," he said to the loud, choleric man standing in front of him, "is hardly of weight, Captain, though it is certainly understandable, given that they were *your* men sent out and killed. We have evidence before us as to how they died."

He watched from his shadowed (cushioned) seat at the head of the table as this man, Zani, perspiring heavily, tried to draw himself up haughtily, and failed.

The man was too afraid. Captain Erilli beside him, the duke saw, was being careful not to smile. The deaths mattered, but so did the fact that both commanders had failed in their assigned task. Erilli would be swinging back and forth between pleasure at seeing the other man squirm like a hooked fish and his own apprehension.

The Council of Twelve of Seressa was very greatly feared, by enemies, and sometimes allies, and by their own citizens.

In this upper-level palace chamber they were all aware that
Seressa was mistrusted and envied, and they used this: the council
took strength and purpose from these truths when they swore their
oaths of office, and renewed these each spring in the Ceremony
of the Sea. Having enemies could concentrate the mind, rally
the heart.

Proud Seressa, on its lagoon amid canal-threaded, bridge-linked
islands, with no mainland toehold in Batiara to speak of any more,
was endlessly aware that its power rested on trade and wealth. And
so, ultimately, on ships and the sea.

There was nowhere like this city on Jad's earth, under his sky.
Dubrava, across the Seressini Sea (named so because men needed
to be reminded), might also be a republic, have a mercantile
fleet, survive by trading, but it was a fraction the size of Seressa.
Dubrava was no lion; it cringed and bowed in every direction. It
had no Arsenale, no war galleys to assert or defend power, no colonies. No great island like Candaria that it ruled.

The Dubravae were a pale, circumscribed, *permitted* shadow of
Seressa. Seressa was a light like the sun of Jad.

No man who understood the twinned worlds of commerce
and courts would compare any other place to this republic. You
marked yourself a fool doing so. Not that there weren't fools
enough in the world.

Right now, the war galley captains being interrogated, gently
enough (thus far), were proving themselves sadly deficient in intelligence. They might know winds and shorelines, but they were lost
in this room, the duke thought. He found himself remembering,
sadly, the great captains of his youth. That happened too often
these days.

Given the humiliating events at Senjan, the fear on display was
unsurprising. Fear made some people bluster, as if to outvoice
terror, the way men sang coarse wine-shop songs when passing a
burial crossroads at night.

Each captain was accusing the other of blundering. Each knew his career, if not his life, was at risk tonight. The council chamber was not a room one came to after dark happily. Their faces were lit by lanterns to either side of where they stood, while shadows obscured the expressions of the duke and council around their U-shaped table. Flame and shadow, in a room that terrified.

They'd had a long time in Seressa to refine their methods. Questions cast from darkness were powerful. And the palace prison, all knew, could be accessed directly from this room: through a door behind the duke, across a small canal by a high, covered stone bridge with iron-barred windows, then down steps of cold stone to cells of cold, wet stone and chambers where skilled men asked hard things.

Everyone in the city could see that bridge whenever they were near the palace and the great sanctuary. Reminders of power were useful. In a world replete with threats, including from within, no leaders could show weakness. They had a duty to the republic not to do so.

And yet . . . and yet it appeared that these two war galleys, sent at considerable cost at the end of winter to blockade and destroy one small town of pirates, had exposed considerable weakness in Seressa and its Council of Twelve, to a degree that might lead to mockery.

It was possible the council had erred in sending them. It would be preferable to blame the captains. Duke Ricci sighed. He was already tired, and they had matters to address after this one.

Both men had been speaking (sometimes at once) of the impossibility of the task they'd been assigned. Waters too shallow. Reefs. Rocks. A dangerous northeast wind. Eccentricities of the current. Orders not to land a force to approach overland because of the emperor in Obravic. The difficulty of enforcing a complete embargo of foodstuffs with no land presence. The eternal problem of mercenaries idle too long on ships . . .

These might even be true, all of them, the duke thought. It was certainly true they'd forbidden a landing. The vipers of Senjan lived (slithered!) behind their walls on lands governed by Jad's Holy Emperor. Seressa's new ambassador in Obravic had sent coded messages back in winter making it clear that Emperor Rodolfo, however eccentric he was, was not inclined (or his advisers were not) to permit the republic to attack a town he ruled.

They couldn't defy that. The raiders were an extreme, a considerable, an *infuriating* menace to trade, but they were not worth a war. The triple border over that way was its own dark, intractable problem. But even so . . .

Even so, the duke was thinking, the humiliation represented by a single person—a *woman*—killing every man in a boat sent out, however recklessly, on a night mission? They were to live now with the world knowing of this? Seven men had died on the water that night, and their long-time informer in the town had been exposed.

That one was in Seressa now, having come home with the galleys. He'd been allowed a chair before the council earlier today because of his condition. His condition was distressing. The barbarians had sent him back lacking both arms below the elbow. They had been cut off and cauterized. It was remarkable that he'd survived. There must be a competent doctor in that Jad-abandoned town, the duke thought, or else their man had simply been fortunate. Although, on reflection, *fortunate* wasn't a word readily applied to him now.

He'd need a small pension, the duke thought. Also orders to keep out of sight. His condition was a reminder of this sorry episode, it would be forever. Perhaps they could send him to Candaria. A good thought. The duke made a note. He preferred to write his own notes.

It was clear why their spy had been allowed to come back with the galleys. The Senjani *wanted* the tale told. It would be in Obravic soon, if it wasn't already, then in the gardens and courtyards of the grand khalif's palaces in Asharias. The duke winced again, picturing that. It would be in Dubrava already. The story would race to the king of Ferrieres, to Esperaña, Karch, Moskav . . .

It was too good a tale for the world not to tell, and laugh to hear. A woman, a woman alone, had detected a Seressini plot (shaped by those masters of deception and stealth!) and had killed every man sent out. Then she'd taken their boat and brought it ashore with three of the dead men on board, and the others dead in the sea.

When you were lions and there were other lions in the world mockery could be deadly.

They had ordered the war galleys home. They hadn't just failed in their task, they had done so on a level that brought new dangers. The duke tasted a bitterness in his mouth. He tried to remember what he had last eaten. He swallowed a little wine.

A small number of men killed on a night expedition ought to have been trivial in the balancing of the world's affairs. It might not, in the event, be so. It might be that the council really had erred in approving this plan to destroy the vipers in their nest.

Captain Zani, who'd sent out the boat, was still claiming there must have been a major ambush, boatloads of Senjani waiting in the bay. That what had happened was impossible otherwise, that their spy in the town *had* to have been mistaken in his report earlier today—all due credit to the man's courage and suffering, of course.

The other captain, in line with the duke's expectation, endorsed the spy's report and word emerging from Senjan. *He* hadn't sent any foolish boat out at night. He'd dutifully performed his assigned task, blockading the southern channel past Hrak Island.

It had been one woman, he agreed. Alone in a little craft. Arrows in the dark, as stated. Little more than a child, apparently. *A girl*, as some might say, had shamed Seressa. They would say that, the duke knew. They would be saying it already. There would be a need to address that aspect of this. But for tonight . . .

He still controlled his council. That hadn't been so for every elected duke of Seressa, but he knew how to maintain allegiances and becalm potential adversaries. It helped to know who those were. Who was most eagerly waiting for him to step down.

He cleared his throat. He lifted a hand, he spoke. His proposals were straightforward. The Council of Twelve took little time in ordering Captain Zani to be punished appropriately and for Captain Erilli to be confirmed in his captaincy and commended for proper conduct.

Together, these rulings served to limit responsibility to one person, which mattered. Any power could have servants who made mistakes. They were all mortal, in a world surrounded by the dark. The measure of leaders was what they did when they discovered failures.

The duke thought the rest of his devising tidy enough. It had come to him as he'd begun to speak. Captain Zani was to have both hands cut off, for grievous errors and the lamentable deaths of good men at the hands of savages. The duke did hope the captain would survive. This one *needed* to be seen or the point being made would be lost. His punishment was to balance and nullify what the Senjani had done, or tried to do, maiming the spy.

You might choose to set yourself against Seressa. It was not wise. That needed to be understood by the world, whether it worshipped Jad or the stars of Ashar, or even the Kindath moons. Whatever triumph you might find in a short run of events could turn and damage you terribly in less time than you might ever have guessed.

That was the message that needed to go from this room.

The two captains were removed, in opposite directions: one escorted from the palace into Jad's Square, the other through that small door behind the duke, across the bridge, and down. Both were blessedly silent. Zani in blank, desperate horror, stunned like a heifer by a hammer, the other man, very likely, in a cold awareness of what his own fate might easily have been. He would walk into a spring night and look up at the moons through clouds. He would probably go into a sanctuary and pray.

There was a pause in the chamber, low voices, release of strain. There were men on his council who would be thinking about what was to happen across that bridge with the barred windows. Around the table men stood up, stretched. The duke looked at his privy clerk.

The clerk signalled discreetly and doors opened to admit servants bearing food and more wine. The Council of Twelve didn't meet regularly at night, of course, but there were enough occasions that a pattern was established. They would eat before they ordered the next man brought in.

Unfortunately, according to the privy clerk, a whisper at the duke's elbow, there appeared to be a difficulty with that next man. He had not yet arrived.

The clerk whispered a suggestion: they might amend the order of business being attended to, bring in the other man who had been summoned.

More carelessness. The Duke of Seressa gathered displeasure about himself like a cloak. Unhappily, carefully eating olives harvested near Rhodias (where the best were grown), he accepted this amendment.

Nineteen years, he was thinking as he adjusted his papers to bring forward the notes on the doctor now about to enter. He put on his new eyeglasses again, fitting the irritating loops behind his ears. He gestured for a light.

He studied his notes amid the sounds of the council talking among themselves. Eventually he nodded and the servants began removing plates of food, though not the wine. Men took their seats. Chairs scraped. Another nod from the duke and the doors opened at the far end of the chamber. Two people were ushered in.

He'd forgotten there would be two. Careless. He wondered why the man in the other matter was not yet here. He didn't like it when the sequence of a night had to be changed. Was everything slipping? Was he?

Perhaps nineteen years is enough, he thought. Then he thought about his republic which, in spite of everything, he loved.

He knew, perhaps because he was old, what others did not always know, or admit to themselves, along the canals, in palaces, sanctuaries, warehouses, shops, in the bordellos with their music, the studios of artists making images of the city and the sea.

Seressa, on its silted marshland by the water, wedded to the sea as a bride, was dependent on it for everything. But the duke also knew that such an existence was transitory, precarious as wind, clouds, as a dream vivid and bright, and gone when morning comes.

An image in his mind, not for the first time: a small religious retreat, an old mosaic behind the altar, perhaps, an attached dwelling (good walls and roof, reliable fireplaces for winter), on one of the outlying islands of the lagoon. He saw a walled garden, fruit trees, a bench in summer shade, holy men surrounding him, leading prayers at proper hours, reading sacred texts together, discussing matters of faith and wisdom in voices that were never too loud.

ை

In most cities, painters tended to live and work in the less expensive districts, for obvious reasons.

Those overcrowded areas often lay where activities such as tanneries or dyeworks were located, the smells having a downward effect on the cost of a small room and studio. This was very much true in Seressa, which had never been the most pleasingly scented of cities in any case. Port towns rarely were, and Seressa in its lagoon was the queen of all ports.

On the other hand, those who bound and sold books—and Seressa was queen of that trade, too—were naturally unwilling to have their shops and binderies located where noxious odours could penetrate and infuse their product. They paid, of necessity, a higher rent to be in more salubrious districts.

Which was why the young artist Pero Villani was making his way home through dark streets on a windy night at the beginning of spring. He had been at the bookshop and bindery where he worked most days—to make a feed-himself wage, and for access to the books.

He'd been binding an edition of *The Book of the Sons of Jad* in red leather for a buyer from Varena. He had finished towards sundown, the shutters open and the light still adequate. After, he'd lingered in the shop, as usual, with the owner's permission (Alviso Sano was a good man), under instructions to lock up when he was done. He was studying the sheets (as yet unbound—they only bound them when an order was placed) of a new, magnificent text on anatomy.

An artist needed to understand the workings of the body, muscle and organ and bone, in order to render it properly on a canvas, or on wood or a wall. What lay beneath the flesh of a soldier lifting a sword or golden-haired Jad offering his open-palm blessing to mankind *mattered*. His father had taught him that.

His father was dead, his mother was dead. Their only son was too young to be established as a painter judged to be worth engaging. He could get a position doing backgrounds in the studio of one of those major artists who employed assistants. He might be forced to do that. It would be a surrender in his own mind. But the truth was, Pero had needed to be older, further along in his career, before his father was taken away from him, struggling to breathe, then not breathing at all.

Life didn't always (or ever?) allow you what you needed, in the way of time, or anything else. That was Pero's sense of things, at any rate. It didn't seem to matter if you prayed or if you didn't. Not a thought he shared.

Pero knew he had talent. His friends knew he had talent. They said so, often. Their opinion didn't seem to matter much to the world. Not if what you needed was the attention of those who could afford to buy paintings, so you could make a living with your art.

He'd had exactly two commissions since his father died. One was more or less a gift he'd offered another artist, a friend, and his wife—a sketch in charcoal of their new baby. He'd wanted to study an infant anyway. Most painters rendered children's faces as if they were adults done small. They weren't. Not if you *looked*.

That sketch was pinned to the wall in the Desanti family's crowded apartment next to his own, above where the baby slept in his basket. It wasn't framed. Frames were expensive. They'd insisted on paying him something, though.

His other commission, the real one, had never been framed either.

He'd been hired to paint a contessa on the recommendation of Alviso Sano, Jad bless his kind soul. The bookseller knew people. He sold extravagant leather-bound books to merchants and aristocrats who wanted the sheen of elegance and success it gave them to have such objects in their homes.

Paintings, especially portraits of themselves, had the same status. You were commissioned by contract to use so much ultramarine blue, so much gold—the most expensive colours. A painting was a sign, barely even coded, of how much you could afford. Sometimes the frames cost more than the art.

One of the Citrani family, the oldest brother, had commissioned the son of Viero Villani, said to be promising, to paint his wife. The wife, red-haired and green-eyed, was a celebrated beauty. She was older than Pero, much younger than her husband, elegant, and bored.

Sleeping with a young artist on winter afternoons, with a fire warming the small room where he was painting her, was a way to amuse oneself. Pero was young enough and she was easily compelling enough, in all ways, to make this an adventure for him. He was a little fearful, but that could add to excitement, of course. He wasn't the first artist, she wasn't the first wealthy woman . . .

His mistake was to bring his passion for his work into the affair: to paint her in oil on canvas, in his studio, the sketches pinned up around him, in a particular manner.

He'd carried it back, wrapped in cloth, to show her in the room where she'd posed, where they'd undressed each other by the fire, where he'd looked, very closely, at her face as she slipped him inside her, when she'd let him see she wasn't always bored.

As he'd leaned the finished canvas against the wall, she'd worn a rapidly changing sequence of expressions. He didn't see anger, nothing like that. Later, he would decide that where she'd ended up, sitting suddenly on the daybed, looking at herself as he'd painted her, was in regret, wistfulness.

He would have liked to have painted that expression, too.

"Oh, dear," was what Mara Citrani finally said. "Oh, my dear. Did I really look like that?"

She was clothed in his painting, of course, entirely properly, in the contracted blue gown trimmed with gold. Her hair was under a cap (green-gold, done with azurite), a few red strands coming free. She sat before an arched window, with a quince tree in a garden behind her and the lagoon beyond that. You could see a ship (her husband's—the family crest on the flag). She wore jewellery at her ears and throat, and a celebrated ring of her husband's family. All proper, conventional really (perhaps not the quince, which had its symbolism), but . . .

But her eyes as Pero had painted them were intense, and hungry. Her cheeks were slightly flushed, as was her throat. And her mouth . . . Mara Citrani's mouth in that portrait was the best thing Pero had ever done in his life. It embodied the knowing, intimate, sensuous look of a woman revealing desire, or gratified desire, or both.

A deeply private expression. One he knew only because she had invited him to that daybed and carpet with her, before the fire, and let him see how she could be when unclothed, touched, then touched again, then entered, then riding above him, hair unbound, aroused, in need—when not the haughty wife of a powerful man.

And so: "Oh, dear," Mara Citrani said again, softly. Then, after a silence, "It is wonderful, Signore Villani. *I* am wonderful in this! I would keep it by me all my life and look at it when I'm old. But . . . Pero, it has to be destroyed. You know this. He would kill us both."

There was a look in her eyes as she turned from the canvas to him, one he hadn't yet seen. He'd have liked to capture this, too. He heard an unexpected tenderness in her voice. She had never been tender, not with him. It was as if she saw him, suddenly, as young.

She'd kissed him that day, on the mouth again, but only lightly, as if saddened by the world, then she'd sent him away.

She told her husband, on his return from the family salt mine concession at Megarium across the narrow sea, that the painting had not pleased her and she'd destroyed it. She instructed him to pay the young man, nonetheless, since he had done his best, and sometimes a woman's needs were difficult to address. She'd smiled, saying that, made Citrani laugh knowingly.

The boy had simply been too inexperienced, evidently. It was no one's fault. Citrani commissioned someone else. He painted, by report, a perfectly acceptable portrait of the contessa.

The entire escapade, Pero understood, had been an example of his inadequacy with regard to such people. Yes, make love to a beautiful woman if she offered herself. Experience that world. Pray for forgiveness after, if you were inclined. But don't be lost to your art. Don't *show* her to everyone as she had been in the prelude or the aftermath of lovemaking. (It would have been interesting to know which of these people would have said the image was.) What was the *reason* to take such a risk?

There was no reason, except . . . except he didn't think any woman had ever been painted with that look in her eyes, and he'd wanted to see if he could.

You could die for wanting to see some things, Pero Villani thought.

No one knew what he'd achieved, no one would ever know, no one had even looked at it. Well, she had. She'd already been turning to gaze at herself on canvas again as he'd left the room that day. The story was simply that young Villani's work hadn't pleased the contessa. So good for a young artist's career, that was! He hadn't had a commission since.

It was likely he'd spend his life binding books. Or doing backgrounds of sea or hills for some shrewder artist's portraits, while dreaming of painting a soldier's properly rendered arm, or Blessed Victims, martyred variously, in procession across a sanctuary wall, or . . .

Or, his life could end tonight, Pero thought.

He wasn't running yet, but he was walking faster. You learned, in Seressa, to be alert after dark, and young men abroad in pursuit of prostitutes or wine at night had reason to become skilled at distinguishing the casual footfall of another night person from what might be someone following you.

No one would be following him with benign intent. Not at this hour. There were few lights here, only stray lanterns on canal boats in the distance. It was windy. He could hear water slap against stones to his left.

He had a cloak against the chill, and a short sword, since he wasn't a fool. Well, he might be a fool, since he was alone at night in a too-quiet district where he wasn't known. That was the problem with a place of work being so far from where he laid his head at night.

Villani was no stranger to prostitutes or wine shops, but of late it had been the excitement of those anatomy pages keeping him out after darkfall. He would finish whatever work Alviso gave him, then stay and study (burn a lamp, pay for the oil) and lock up and go home. Sometimes more oil used there, and a truly late night, as he sketched in his small room by the tanneries. You never really got used to the smell. You lived with it, if you were poor.

His father had had a good house—other side of the Great Canal, beyond the market. Viero Villani had had some status as a painter, a measure of recognition, and then debts.

The house had been an extravagance, an over-bold statement. It was gone, of course, the furnishings sold off. The elder Villani's belongings, including all unsold paintings, had been claimed by his creditors. In a city fixated on commerce, the law as to debts and inheritance was precise and the courts moved rapidly. His son had managed to conceal and keep two paintings, one a portrait of his mother. You could say he was a thief.

Pero Villani, after his father's sudden death, had found himself with nothing but a modestly respected family name, much desire, and what was judged to be talent—though only among others in his own situation, which is to say, those who meant nothing in the world.

The friends who knew his work were also drinking companions and would have been protection now had he been with them tonight. Had they all been making their way in a staggering group, singing, arm in arm down canal-side alleys, over bridges, under the two moons in and out of clouds.

There was more than one man behind him.

He was pretty certain he'd detected three footfalls. There might be four, and they'd sped up when he had. Thieves roamed Seressa at night, as they roamed any city. So did gangs of young aristocrats seeking the idle, vicious pleasure of attacking people at night to show their bravado, to prove they could. The law, so ardent in financial matters, could be slack in prosecuting sons of the powerful.

Villani suspected the second possibility, for the simple reason that any competent thieves would have sorted out by now that he wasn't going to have anything worth taking. Captured thieves were sent to the galleys, and there *were* night patrols. It didn't stop assault and robbery—hungry men needed to feed themselves, greedy ones remained greedy—but it did tend to mean that a thief would choose his target with a bit of care.

A threadbare artist carrying a sketchbook wasn't worth risking death chained to a rowing bench. He'd passed under lights in brackets on the walls of city palaces when he'd left the shop. The condition of his cloak could have been seen by anyone with a thought of robbing him.

He considered shouting that into the blackness, but didn't. If it was reckless sons of wealth behind him, it would only amuse and incite them. Of course, it could be no one. He could be agitating himself over some drunken cluster of friends, as his own would be, somewhere in their district.

Except there were no wine shops in this warehouse part of the city, and he'd heard this group come—quickly, not drunkenly—down a side street as he went by it, then turn to follow him.

Two more footbridges and one square—by the lovely Lesser Sanctuary of Blessed Victims—and he'd be on his own ground. He could find acquaintances abroad, working women he knew, who could shout or scream a warning; wine shops would be open.

He was sober and young. He ran.

Immediately he heard them do the same, which did answer any lingering questions or doubts.

He was in real danger. They had no particular reason to let him live. And if this was a pack of swaggering aristocrats they'd have even less concern about using a blade in the hidden dark—it might add to the glamour of their existence.

The walkway was briefly wider here. He stayed close to the canal side. There were posts at intervals for mooring boats. If he didn't crash into one himself, perhaps one of those behind him might. He needed to be careful, running this fast. It was easy to stumble on uneven stones, trip over a cat, a scurrying rat, someone's garbage not dumped in the water.

First bridge. Up one side of the curve and down. He liked this bridge, the smoothness of its arc.

A *really* trivial reflection just now, Pero thought.

Still no lights. This was a district crowded in the daytime with commerce and noise. Not now. He listened as he fled. The feet behind him were not receding. Pero had always thought himself decently fleet of foot but these men weren't slower, or . . .

One of them wasn't. The runners seemed to have separated themselves. One seemed to be ahead of the other two or three. He still wasn't sure of the number, but he did know that one man was keeping pace with him, even gaining, as the others fell back.

He did what he ought to have done before. You could overlook the obvious. His father used to tell him that about painting.

"*Guards!*" he shouted. "*Guards! Help!*"

He kept shouting as he ran. He didn't expect a patrol to materialize like saviours in the night, but there might be lights carried to upper windows by the curious, witnesses. People might pick up his cry. No one liked thieves. No one liked the bored aristocrats. The pursuers might have second thoughts.

It didn't happen. But just about then, nearing the second bridge, the one that marked his home district, Pero Villani realized that he was angry. Not a wisdom-inducing emotion, it almost never was, but it was there, it was in him. He was running for his life in his own city. His life was shabby and constrained. The one painting of which he was proud had been destroyed. Everyone thought it had been some incompetent's failure. He lived among stinking tanneries and dyeworks and he smelled of them.

It could make a man of any spirit at all just a little bit angry to also now be fleeing from whatever noblemen—who never smelled of dyeworks (who had probably never *smelled* the dyeworks!)—were pursuing him.

He took this route all the time to and from the bookshop. He knew the bridge he was sprinting towards. And he knew something else. There would be an empty wine barrel at this end: a blind beggar sat on it every day. He'd recognize people by their tread, call greetings, tell you gossip he'd heard if you stopped to talk. Pero would give him food when he had some, small coins if he'd been paid.

The beggar slept somewhere else, he wouldn't be here now.

The barrel would be.

Skidding to a halt, Pero reached out in the dark, clutched the upper rim, tilted and shifted the barrel into the middle of the cobbled street, which narrowed at the bridge.

Then, pretending to stumble, crying out, he went past it. He slowed on the bridge, as if hurt, swore loudly. Then he waited. And a moment later heard the extremely satisfying sound of his pursuer crashing—at speed—into a wine barrel in the street.

What he did next might not have been wise, either. He didn't feel like being wise. He had *reasons* for being angry. This was his city, he was a citizen of the Republic of Seressa, and whatever arrogant sprouts of overbred lineage these bastards were . . .

He dropped his sketchbook on the wooden planks. He drew his sword from beneath his cloak. If they were going to chase him, there would be one less man doing so. He'd never had swordfighting lessons, an artist's son didn't do that, but you didn't need expertise for everything. A blade was a blade.

He ran back, saw the downed man clutching with both hands at a knee, crying out in pain—and Pero bent and stabbed him in the chest.

His blade hit metal. It was turned aside.

You could be afraid, and then terrified. Not the same thing.

This was beyond frightening. If men wearing armour at night were pursuing him, they weren't thieves, nor were they noblemen looking for amusement. This was a soldier or a guardsman.

Pero fled. Again. His delay had allowed the lagging pair to draw closer, but the fastest man was down. He hadn't been killed, obviously. Pero didn't know if that was good or bad now. He didn't understand any of this.

He'd left his sketchbook on the bridge. No help for that. He continued to shout for help as he ran. He was on familiar ground now, cutting diagonally through the square in front of the Sanctuary of the Victims. He thought about dashing in, hoping a cleric was awake, begging protection, but, for good or ill, he kept running, trying to put distance between himself and those behind.

There were lights now, spilling from cheap wine shops he knew. He recognized two women on a corner. Had his pursuers been the sort of men he'd thought they were he'd have joined these two, taken them into a drinking place, been safe among a crowd.

Men in armour wouldn't care, he thought. It wouldn't stop them.

He knew these streets and alleys; the smell told him he was home. He could lose pursuers. He cut to his right up a leather-workers' laneway, the shops shuttered and dark, then left along a smaller, fetid alley as fast as he could, then out again at the far end into a little, untidy square where ramshackle buildings on all sides housed many of the indigent artists of Seressa, including the son of Viero Villani, currently being pursued.

And awaited.

There were many lights here, far more than there should have been. Torches in hand, half a dozen men in a livery he knew stood before Pero's own building. They looked at him as he burst into the square.

He stopped, breathing hard.

"What did I do?" he shouted. "*What did I do?*"

No answer. Of course, no answer.

In silence they came and surrounded him and took him away with them. A neat formation, well-trained guards, an artist in the middle. They took his sword. He didn't resist. What was the point of resisting? He was finding it difficult to breathe and not just because he'd been running. He hoped some of his friends were watching, at windows or in doorways. There had been none in the square. There wouldn't be, not with armed guards of the Council of Twelve here among them in the night.

CHAPTER IV

Some days—or nights—seemed to point themselves towards vexation, difficulty, obstacles, the Duke of Seressa found himself musing. He thought of images that applied: headwinds, lawsuits, dried ink clogging, burnt food, flooding, ambitious councillors, constipation.

Ambitious councillors causing constipation.

This windy night in spring was becoming such a time. Braced as he was for the unexpected after years in office, it was not especially startling to learn that the woman before them was quicker, and much more alert to what they were doing, than the man beside her.

The doctor, it appeared, was a step-by-step fellow. Perhaps useful in a physician but awkward just now. His grasp of matters appeared to be stuck like a gun-wagon on a road after heavy rain. (The duke was briefly pleased, he was arriving at excellent phrases tonight, if nothing else.)

The woman was otherwise. She had been investigated, interviewed twice, only then recruited to the service of the republic from one of the sequestered retreats of the Daughters of Jad. She was of an aristocratic family (from Mylasia down the coast), was obviously intelligent (too much so?), and sufficiently high-spirited as to have *required* being placed with one of the religious houses, for the usual reason. She'd delivered herself of an inconvenience there. It had been relocated to one of the foundling hospitals and then to some family somewhere.

She was now, it appeared, willing to accept an opportunity to leave the contemplative life for something more adventurous. Such women were rare, and could be important. Seressa had made use of them before, to variable effect. They could cause difficulties. Intelligence and spirit came with their own challenges.

"Why," Leonora Valeri was saying just then, "are we not doing more to simulate being married?"

The duke lifted his head, removed his spectacles, and gazed at her. The light, as always, was on those before the council. She was attractive, undeniably. Small, golden-haired under a dark-green cap, a good smile. He wished, briefly, that he were sixty again, in his prime. (That thought, too, amused him. A little.)

"What are you *saying*?" the physician asked, beside her. "What can you be—?"

"I am quite sure the Republic of Dubrava has people watching Seressa, just as we have men inside their walls. If someone merely checks sanctuary records or civic ones they can determine that we were married on whatever day we are going to say. Or they can discover that we weren't. It would be better, my lord"—she turned to the duke, offered that smile—"if the records reflected our union."

"But they won't. We didn't . . ."

Doctor Miucci was unhappy. He was said to be a good physician, had been courageous during the last plague outbreak, apparently. He was not well known, was new to Seressa, trying to build a practice and reputation. These were among the reasons he'd been selected for this. The council hadn't required imagination from their choice. Perhaps they ought to have.

The woman, it seemed, might have enough for the two of them.

"They can be caused to reflect such a happy state," the duke said. He favoured them both with a brief smile. "Signora Valeri is entirely correct. Details implemented or overlooked at the outset often determine success or failure before the end."

"Eloquently put, my lord duke," she said. She was flattering him, of course. She was also a little overexcited, he judged. Not a surprise, given the life she had left behind this morning.

"We will also, naturally, prepare in advance documents that will dissolve this temporary union upon your return, leaving you both as you are tonight, free citizens of Seressa—with the republic in your debt."

"But this cannot be!" said Jacopo Miucci with unexpected firmness. (A man accustomed to being decisive with patients?) "The good lady would be disgraced on our return! Married and then not so, merely for reasons of state?"

"But I am," the good lady murmured, "already disgraced, doctor."

Miucci coloured. You could see it by candlelight. It was amusing.

Leonora Valeri added, "Although, may I say I am touched by your kindness, thinking of my well-being already. It makes me trust even more that you will be kind when we are together."

One of the councillors coughed. The duke found it required an effort not to smile. The physician Miucci, it occurred to him, was likely to have an interesting time in Dubrava.

He wished, again, that he were younger.

He waited for silence. He said, in his decisive, concluding-a-matter voice, "We have an understanding, and it is to be recorded. Seressa is grateful to you both and will assuredly demonstrate as much. Doctor Miucci will be sent as our response to the Dubravae request for a new physician. We note their evident awareness that Seressa is where the best doctors are found. They have indicated they will, as always, house and recompense him, and they have been generous in the past with physicians we send. The term they request is the customary two years."

He took a sip of wine, looking closely at the two people in front of him. Miucci's expression wasn't precisely happy, but the duke didn't see anything alarming. They had reviewed a good deal of information on him. The man was a capable doctor from a respectable family, and not much else, it appeared. They didn't need much else. Compliance, competence, and an assumed marriage. The woman mattered more.

The duke added, to make this clear, "Doctor, you understand that you are truly there as a physician. You will not be requested or required to undertake any activities that jeopardize your status among the Dubravae."

"Except, my lord, to present myself as married when I am not, and to have my so-called wife engage in spying?"

Some asperity there. Perhaps the assessment had been made slightly too soon as to the man's possible difficulty. But Miucci was—the duke judged—being precise, not troublesome. The doctor *wanted* to go to Dubrava, it was a source of both income and status for a physician to do so. Some stayed on for another term. One, memorably, had married a Dubravae woman and proposed to settle there. A breach of understandings, of terms. He had needed, regrettably, to be killed. They had someone in Dubrava who did that for them, when necessary. You could not abandon the Council of Twelve so easily. Not when they chose you for your position, granted it to you, and had requirements. It had been some time ago, but the council was unlikely to forget: it was a reason they sent only married doctors now.

He nodded agreement at the man. "That is so, yes. She will do what she can for Seressa. Signora Miucci, as we must now name her, will use opportunities afforded by your role and stature to observe and converse. With women, and perhaps men, if she can do so without compromising your dignity. There is no present threat to us from Dubrava, you understand? But there are trade advantages to be gained from grasping their affairs, and you both know the other reason we need people inside those walls."

"Of course we do. The Osmanlis," the woman said. "Dubrava pays tribute to the grand khalif."

It was a presumption for her to be the one answering, but, the duke thought, she *was* the important person of the two, and diffidence wouldn't serve any of them well. He was beginning to believe diffidence was not a manner Leonora Valeri could readily assume.

He signalled assent. "Indeed. Dubrava sends information and bribes to Asharias, and trades there. As we do, of course. The road from their landward gate through Sauradia is a busy one. We live in precarious times. Whatever we learn, whatever we can know, helps ensure the safety of Seressa. It is," he concluded, "as uncomplicated as that."

"And if," the physician said quietly, "Signora Valeri is discovered in this gathering of information, will it be similarly uncomplicated?"

"You are unlikely to be killed, if that is what you mean," the duke said briskly. He was speaking a half-truth, of course. Half-truths, in his view, were all most people required.

There would never be any public accusation or trial, no formal punishment beyond sending them home, but accidents had happened to Seressinis in Dubrava in the past. The smaller republic was diplomatic, cautious, *crafty*. It watched the winds of the world. It was also proud of its freedoms. The people of Sauradia and Trakesia, all those over that way, had a history of violence and independence going back to when many of them were pagans in the days of the Sarantine Empire, when Sarantium ruled the world.

Sarantium had fallen. The duke remembered when word had come, twenty-five years ago now. Sense of a world ending. The city was named Asharias now, and the man who ruled there amid

gardens where silence was apparently the law on pain of stran-
gulation (the duke often thought wistfully about that) wanted to
rule the world. The Osmanlis and their intentions were very much
cause for concern for any Seressini spies.

"I don't expect to be discovered," the woman said, smiling
at the man she was to seem married to (and spend her nights with,
the duke thought). She turned to the head of the table. "It is an
honour to be trusted by the council."

Was it possible she was *too* poised? He wondered how old she
was. It would be in his notes.

"It is intended as an honour," he said gravely. "We place our confidence in you both. You will prepare your belongings and set what
affairs need ordering in such order. You will be advised as to codes
and contacts, signora. The doctor need only assemble his medical
equipment and make his farewells. The Dubravae ship that will
carry you is moored by the Arsenale now. It belongs to a merchant
family. One of their sons will welcome you aboard and escort you,
we have arranged for this. They wish to depart soon. They are waiting only for you, I believe, and perhaps one other passenger. You
may go now, with the council's thanks. Jad shine his light upon
you both. You will not regret undertaking this for the republic."

The doctor bowed neatly. A small, thin man, thinning hair,
stern-looking for someone still young. The woman sank to the
marble floor in salute with a grace that showed her lineage.

He wondered, suddenly, who had fathered her child.

He knew he couldn't make his last assurance—about their having no regrets—with any certainty. Life didn't allow for that. But
it needed to be said to people, he'd learned over the years.

He was tired but that could not be revealed. Not at this table.
He had his own dangers. He saw the privy clerk at the far doors
make a gesture, one he knew. Finally.

The duke put his spectacles on again and adjusted the papers
in front of him. The other matter for tonight appeared to be

upon them. The man had arrived—or been caused to arrive. He wasn't certain which. It mattered, as it happened. There might be delicacy required here. He wondered how he might broach the subject in a discreet fashion, subtly determine this new person's state of mind.

"HOW *DARE* YOUR GUARDS ACCOST ME! This is a disgrace! My lords, I am a free and honest citizen of the republic!"

Pero had decided at some point during the too-brisk march to the ducal palace that he was still angry, he was outraged, in fact, and he was not going to show fear. It helped, a little, that the guards hadn't handled him roughly. They'd even let him stop to reclaim his sketchbook on the bridge.

That was good, wasn't it?

"Careful," he'd said. "There is a barrel just ahead." They'd been carrying torches, didn't need the warning. None of them spoke, but two of them set the barrel back where it had been. Someone knew about the blind beggar, then.

Pero had no idea what to do with that particular insight. He was confused and, being honest, he *was* afraid. You'd be mad as a mountain hermit not to be fearful. The Council of Twelve could take anyone in this fashion, at night, and there was no assurance those who knew or loved them would see them again.

No one alive loved him, he thought. But perhaps his friends, the ones he hoped had been watching as he was taken away, perhaps some of them would ask questions in the morning?

They almost surely wouldn't. Seressinis, especially the poor, perhaps especially poor artists, learned, sometimes painfully, that the Council of Twelve didn't like questions being asked, or discussions taking place.

Seressa was a nominally free, extremely wealthy, cultured, powerful republic. The Seressinis' wealth and culture could be seen in their buildings and squares and monuments, in the endless activity by the port and in the Arsenale where the ships were built. They had no king or prince tyrannizing them. They elected their leaders (well, the wealthier among them elected themselves as leaders). Merchants had a status here they held nowhere else in the world. You could rise to influence from low birth more readily in Seressa than anywhere.

It was also, however, a mysterious, dangerous, frightening city. And that wasn't just about masks at carnival time or fog swirling about. One didn't walk up to the ducal palace on a spring morning and ask after the whereabouts of an artist friend who had—for some reason—been taken away in the night by the guards.

They'd ask your name. You didn't want that.

The guards had marched him across Jad's Square to a small side door of the palace. Two of them had escorted him up a back staircase, not the Stairway of Heroes with the giant statues of Seressa's founders on either side at the bottom.

Pero and his friends were of the view that the two bearded men rendered there might have been heroes but the sculptor had certainly not been. The carved figures were grotesquely over-muscled and absurdly expressionless. Their eyes were crudely done. It was also a matter of amusement among the younger artists that one of them, Seridas, appeared to have a partial erection beneath his tunic.

If it wasn't partial, one of Pero's wittier friends had declared one night, then the hero lacked heroism below, alas. The prostitutes in their neighbourhood began using the name Seridas to describe a man similarly unprepossessing.

It was all so amusing, in memory. It was also a world he seemed to have left behind step by step as they climbed the dark stairwell. No statues here. Damp stone walls, archer-windows, worn, slippery stairs.

The guard in front of him had stopped, so Pero did. The man opened a door with a heavy key. They'd come out into a handsome, well-lit corridor with tapestries along the walls.

More guards, and someone in very good clothing, conveying with his manner the disdain peculiar to higher-ranking civil servants.

"You are hardly in a condition to be brought before the council," he sniffed, eyeing Pero with impressive hauteur for a short, plump person.

"Fuck yourself," Pero had replied. "Or get one of these guards to do it to you against the wall here."

There had been no further conversation.

But he'd grasped an essential thing: he *was* being taken before the Council of Twelve. At night. People disappeared when that happened. It was madness. Pero Villani was no one who mattered at all.

He'd attempted, with complete lack of success, to imagine what they could want with him. His father's debts from last year? Paid! And the council would never descend to such a trivial matter . . .

The Citrani husband? No. Not that either. That one, if he'd learned what had happened, would have simply had Pero killed, or castrated, or bundled in a sack and placed on a galley—whatever aristocratic vengeance occurred to him. It would not have been done like this.

Whatever this turned out to be.

They came to a pair of doors. The arrogant functionary took another contemptuous look at Pero. He gestured, and a servant pushed them open. Pero Villani had entered the chamber of the Council of Twelve for the first time in his life.

He surprised himself. He hadn't expected to be bold here, but he was frightened and angry, and it seemed these emotions could make him behave in unexpected ways.

He stepped briskly into the room, head high. He strode past the functionary as the man paused to bow. Pero didn't bow. He stopped between two lamps on stands. He proceeded to upbraid the Duke of Seressa—gaunt, austere, face shadowed—at the head of the table. He did so with an aggression that wasn't really in his nature. Or so he'd always thought.

There was silence when he finished. In the stillness, Pero heard a door close, off to his right. He had a sudden image of himself being tortured underground, in a room lit by red and yellow flames so his pain could be observed and enjoyed.

JACOPO MIUCCI THE PHYSICIAN was happily leaving that audience chamber through a side door. He offered silent thanks to Jad it was not the door at the back that everyone knew led to the covered bridge and the cells. The woman was beside him. Right beside him, a hand on his arm, as if they were truly a couple. Married.

He was a long way from being able to deal with that. Or with, to be honest, the scent she had elected to wear. Daughters of Jad in their retreats did not wear perfume. They didn't marry. Or simulate that state. They served the god with prayer by day and night. They nursed the sick (after adequate endowments were offered, of course). They chanted invocations (also after donations) for the souls of the dead, that they might be gathered in light. They sheltered young women, invariably wealthy, who needed to be hidden away for the honour of their families. There were, of course, stories about other sorts of activity in some of the retreats, but Miucci had never been a man to dwell upon carnal anecdotes.

As they exited, he heard a loud, angry voice behind them in the room. The council's next visitor was—evidently—not best pleased to have been summoned. With alarming assertiveness he raised his voice in complaint.

"Wait," said Leonora Valeri, stopping. "This might be interesting!"

"It is none of our affair!" Miucci snapped.

She smiled at him. She was slim, fair, undeniably aristocratic. Full lips. Young. Scented. "But I am to develop my skills in this sort of affair, I believe."

"I am not," he retorted, and moved on.

She followed. The door had closed, in any event. They couldn't hear anything. Miucci had no idea who the man behind them was. He didn't care.

The woman fell into step with him, along the corridor and then down the Stairway of Heroes. She took his arm again, descending the marble stairs, the way a wife might do.

Miucci stole another glance at her. Her gaze was lowered now, either submissively, or watching where she stepped, or upon some private amusement. He was very much unsure which.

She said, eyes still down, "We had best become adept at walking this way, don't you think?"

He couldn't think what to say. He seemed to have agreed to present himself in Dubrava as married to a woman he'd never seen before this day. It was astonishing how a man could be drawn into something mad, at speed. So much speed! You didn't have any proper time to think. Perhaps that was deliberate. The duke and council pressed you so swiftly that careful thought was impossible. In his life, in his practice, Jacopo Miucci had greatly valued time to think.

But he wanted this posting. Of course he did. Every young physician coveted these positions. Dubrava paid exceptionally well for doctors. You could come home after two years with the money to buy a very good residence and practice chambers, and with your reputation made—as a physician the council had deemed worthy of sending across the water.

But you needed to be married to go to Dubrava now, since an unfortunate incident some time ago.

It seemed, therefore, that for the benefits the position offered he was to simulate the state of marriage. And the woman assigned to be his wife would have tasks for the council. It was dangerous, surely, whatever the duke said. It *had* to be dangerous. He ought to have refused. But then someone would have said yes, loyally aiding the republic, seizing the posting and all the good things that followed.

The woman had yellow hair under a green cap. He looked at her again, on his arm. They would be engaged in a profane violation of the Jad-blessed state of matrimony. His cleric back home would be aghast if he knew. So would his mother.

The cleric—and everyone else—would be caused to believe Jacopo had met and swiftly, unexpectedly, married this woman. Documents would reflect as much. She was from Mylasia, apparently. The story would have to do with his gallantly rescuing a transgressing woman from her sad state, after being called to offer medical services at a sanctuary.

It did happen. Not every aristocratic girl who'd borne an inconvenient child was suited to the life of a retreat, and since she could no longer marry among the nobility . . .

This particular transgressing woman said, a hand gripping his arm above the elbow, as if for balance and support, "I understand we are to spend tonight at your home. I am much looking forward to seeing it, and to learning more about you, Doctor Miucci."

Unmistakably, her fingers tightened on his arm.

Equally unmistakably, Doctor Jacopo Miucci, who had led a studious, unadventurous existence until this day and night, felt the stirrings of desire.

It was the perfume, he told himself. Scents had power. Doctors knew it. They could aid in healing, soothe the distressed . . . contribute to suborning the most disciplined of men.

Other aspects of the woman besides her perfume contributed to further suborning later that night after they reached his home.

He explained to his manservant when the door was opened to his knock that he had married that day and would be going abroad to work. No point waiting to say it. He presented his bride to his three servants. They were visibly taken aback. Astonished would be the better word. Of course they were. *He* was. Three mouths fell open, one man reached out a hand to support himself on the wall. Miucci supposed this could be seen as amusing. Leonora Valeri—Leonora Miucci now—laughed, but gently. She greeted the servants, repeated their names.

The night unfolded surprises, like a silken cloth opening, on display. There came a moment, after they'd dined and gone upstairs together, when Jacopo Miucci realized, in the darkness of his bedchamber, that he had surrendered fairly comprehensively to the idea that he and this woman were to be man and wife in Dubrava for the next two years.

It occurred when she whispered, with what appeared to be unfeigned pleasure as she caressed his sex anew, bringing it back to life, in ways only purchased women ever had, "Oh! How delightful of you, doctor."

SORROW IS ENDURING. It can define a life. Leonora had come to understand this through the course of a year. It could be deep as any well, cold as mountain lakes or forest paths in winter. It was harder than stone walls, or her father's face.

Her child had been taken away at birth. She has barely any memory of seeing it. The boy who fathered it had been killed by her family. She had moved through the days since then among the Daughters of Jad, waking or sleeping much the same to her, sunlight and rain much the same.

She'd been a girl, then a young woman, of spirit, laughter, cleverness. Sources of her trouble? They'd said that in the retreat. They'd said so at home. She needed to learn submission: to the god, the world. To her father's will, which had placed her there.

Her family were important in Mylasia, among the most powerful aristocrats. A grand palace in the city, a castle outside, a hunting lodge farther out. Her father enjoyed hunting. He had once enjoyed taking her with him, proud of her skill. The family's significance was another source of her trouble, of course: the Valeris are too prominent. Have enemies who would relish her disgrace. She'd been sent north, away. Entirely and eternally away until she died behind those walls. Removed from sight and memory.

They had probably told people she'd already died. Illness, they will have said: sent in search of a physician who could cure her. Seressa was said to have the best doctors. So sad, they will have said. A beloved child, even if a girl.

She will never know where her own child is.

She doesn't even know if it was a girl or a boy. They'd moved quickly, claiming it from her body. Someone else has named it, someone will watch it grow, laugh and weep, see the moons change and the seasons return.

Paulo Canavli, who had touched her heart and awakened her body, has no burial place. He had been cut into pieces and left for the wolves outside the walls of Mylasia. Her eldest brother had told her that, viciously, while bringing her to Seressa.

He hadn't said any other words to her on the way, or at the end. No farewell. Her father's orders, very surely. He never disobeyed their father. None of her brothers did. Erigio Valeri was accustomed to being obeyed, within and without his family. Her brother had taken her to the gates of the retreat and left her in the roadway there. He had turned and ridden away, towards home, to the richness life held for him.

Eventually, she had pulled a rope that rang a bell. They'd been expecting her. Of course they had. A very large sum would have been provided to ensure she was admitted—and never left. Leonora had gone in, heard an iron gate close behind her.

Time had passed in that place. Her body grew. A child was born and was taken away. There were prayers at dawn and sunset. Awake, asleep, seasons and sorrow.

The Council of Twelve sent two men to speak with her.

She hadn't been sure how they even knew she was there. Now, she is certain she is not the first woman brought to the retreat to have been asked to assist the council. Money will have changed hands for this, as well. The retreat is extremely wealthy.

She never asked about this, but it makes sense, and after that visit, after what was carefully hinted at then directly queried, she'd begun thinking in terms of what made sense in a life. Of choices and chances, decisions to be weighed.

The same two men had come back from Seressa a little later, after giving her time to consider what they offered—which was an opportunity to be in the world again.

She had accepted. She'd left the Daughters of Jad this morning at dawn. They'd had a horse for her. She was a Valeri, she had hunted from childhood, of course she knew how to ride. They'd known that, too. She'd looked back once in misty greyness: the stone walls, the sanctuary dome, the bell by the gate. The gate had already closed behind her.

And so now, that same night, she is in Seressa, away from that solitude and judgment and false sanctity, the pinched, fearful bitterness. Not all, to be fair—there were genuinely pious women in that place, kind ones. They had tried, but had been no help to her at all: she was never one of the bitter, she was simply claimed by sorrow.

And she doesn't want to live her days under the god's sun that way.

She'd needed to be out from those walls. And if her new path—offered by these endlessly subtle Seressinis—might, at its end, bring more shame upon her, upon her family, at least it *was* a path. It went somewhere. Her mind would be engaged, her spirit. And she wasn't going to spend a single morning, not the length of a dawn prayer, not a candle-flicker moment, dwelling on her family's pride or shame or her father's views about what she did.

Did she love Seressa? The republic she was now to serve? Of course not. She wasn't sure most Seressinis did, though she might be wrong about that.

They were proud of their independence, their republic. They valued power, wished to defend it and extend it, were aware of threats moving through the world. They were no worse than anyone else, she told herself, perhaps better than some. She could help them, in exchange for a gate unlocked. She would do that, and let no one judge her but Jad, who sees all with mercy and understands sorrow.

She had taken herself to that place in her mind, while preparing to leave the sanctuary.

And then, so unexpectedly, the doctor she was to pretend to have wed turned out to be a shy, decent man. She thought there might be kindness in him.

She was the one who was kind that first night. There were things she had learned (in joy) from the boy she'd loved and been loved by. These could be shared. It was necessary, what she did in the dark of Miucci's room. They were to pass as husband and wife, newly wed, and their assigned servants in Dubrava would be watching them, and listening. But Leonora discovered, with surprise, that eliciting gratitude carried a different sort of pleasure, and she permitted herself to feel that, accept it, a form of mercy after a shadowed year.

The sun would emerge from the sea on a different world for her. She would still wonder, then and every single morning when she rose with the god's light, where her child was that day, if it was alive, cared for, if it was loved, if Jad was good enough to permit that to be so.

JACOPO MIUCCI, PHYSICIAN, found himself experiencing many unexpected emotions in his bed at night beside a woman he had not even known in the morning—emotions over and above, well past desire. He was weary in the darkness but not sleepy, his mind shuttling from thought to thought, over-engaged. So much had happened. He had lived a very quiet life.

He found himself remembering that other man's voice, behind them in the council chamber, shouting fiercely: "How *dare* your guards accost me!"

That had been reckless. But it needed to be acknowledged that it was also a showing of courage in a room where it was difficult to be brave. Men could rise to courage. This was the thought that came to Miucci, in the dark beside a strange woman. He wondered if that other man was dead now, or progressing towards death in an underground chamber equipped with implements. He shivered.

He felt the press of the woman's body next to his. He was aware of her perfume, lingering. If he turned his head, his face would touch her unbound golden hair. He listened, lying very still, and from her breathing decided she was not asleep.

He said, softly, "I believe I understand what you have done, why you accepted the council's offer."

"Do you, doctor?" she murmured, after a moment. He couldn't see her, there was no light.

"I might . . . or some of why. But I . . . I am also of the view that they have not properly attended to you."

"Attended to me? Surely you just did that," she said, still softly. He could hear amusement—or the feigning of it. He wasn't sure.

He cleared his throat. "No. But I would like to, signora." A breath. "Is there a reason we cannot be wed in the morning, properly? I have little to offer a woman from a noble family but I—"

Fingers to his lips in the dark. When next she spoke he realized that she was fighting tears. It caught at his heart like a hook. He was not a man for whom such intensity had occurred very often.

She said, "It cannot happen. Thank you, though. Thank you. That is more generous than words can say. I . . . had no expectation of this at all. But no, signore. The council can ask us to simulate a marriage, ask me to work for them. But doctor, they cannot take my father's power from him. I cannot marry without his willing it."

"How old are you? If I may ask."

She was silent a moment. He thought he'd offended. Women were easy to offend, in his limited experience.

"I was nineteen in the winter."

He had thought older, she was so poised. That happened among aristocrats, he supposed. He'd had few dealings with aristocrats. He hadn't had a medical practice for long. He was hardly known in Seressa. Was that why they'd chosen him? He hadn't considered that. It might be so.

He said, "And he will not consent? Your father? He would not accept if I asked and affirmed truly that—?"

The hand to his mouth again. She left her fingers there, gently, then withdrew them.

Eventually he slept.

When he woke to sunshine through the shutters he was alone in the bed. He found her downstairs discussing with his servants (their servants) which belongings of his—books, clothing, instruments and compounds—would need to be packed for a sea voyage, and how this should best be done.

She greeted him with a kiss, like a bride.

ൟ

As the door closed behind the doctor and the spy, the Duke of Seressa turned his attention to the artist he'd had investigated, then summoned at night.

He had intended it to be discreet. Was there nothing done properly any more? Was that the way of the world in which they now lived?

He was tired and vexed, reminded himself to be careful this did not undermine their purpose here. He had thought to allow more time for this particular devising, but you couldn't always do that, and there was an opportunity worth seizing—if they could. A part of governance was planning ahead; another was responding to what was handed to you, however unexpectedly.

They had needed someone without ties, without reasons to refuse them—as had been the case with the Valeri girl and the doctor. This young man—Viero Villani's only son—was another such person. On the other hand, his entrance just now proclaimed him extremely unhappy. It was fair to note he had reason to be.

"Be silent until you are addressed!" Lorenzo Arnesti snapped at the artist from halfway down the table.

Arnesti was one of those here with ambitions. He wasn't troubling to mask them. A mistake. Too soon to be so transparent.

We don't wear masks only at Carnival.

The duke remembered his uncle saying that. Years ago. Time could run away from a man. He raised a hand now, a ringed finger lifted in admonishment. Arnesti looked quickly at him, then smoothed his features. Masked them.

The duke said, "The council apologizes for the manner of this, Signore Villani. There is a reason why your presence has been besought in this fashion. I trust you have not been injured and that you will permit us to explain?"

"Do I have a choice, my lord duke? May I turn now and leave?"

Perhaps a little too much bristling after a courteous greeting from power. The duke allowed his gaze to linger a moment before he replied. He marked, by the lamps to either side of the artist, that the pause did register.

"Of course you may go. Our hope is that you are at least curious as to the proposal we wish to make, and will listen before you leave us."

Proposal was the word that mattered. If the man was intelligent he'd catch it.

He was, he did. Duke Ricci saw Villani's son lower his gaze and take a moment to steady himself. His shoulders settled a little. He was quite young. It was a part of why he was here, of course. When he looked up it was with a different expression.

"Proposal?" he asked, as expected.

Men were, Duke Ricci thought, not difficult to control most of the time. You just needed to have been doing it long enough. And have power, of course. You needed the ability to have them killed. His uncle had said something like that, too. The duke's father had been one of those killed. Also many years ago.

He said, "Let me say first that the council were all admirers of your father's work, may Jad shelter him in light. In my own view he was a great master." Flattery was almost always effective.

Almost always. "Say you so, my lord duke?" said the younger Villani. "A great master? Such a shame that none of such a master's work adorns the ducal palace."

There was, even after all these years, pleasure to be derived from encountering spirit and intelligence. He preferred it in a woman, or he had, but it tended to matter more in men. He didn't have *time* for this tonight, but it did spark interest. He didn't recall the father, met two or three times, being like this at all.

"But one of his works hangs even now in our envoy's residence in Obravic," he said. "The Arsenale seen from across the lagoon." He was pleased with himself for remembering that. He doubted Lorenzo Arnesti would have.

Villani's son shrugged. "I know the work. It was part of the forced disposition of his property after death. Taken for a pittance. I understand the republic bought it for little more than that."

The duke managed a smile. He lifted a hand again, because Arnesti looked ready to interject. He said, "We Seressinis are well known for frugality in our purchases. But Signore Villani, I call your father to mind as a good man, loyal to the republic. Is his son the same?"

Sometimes direct questions worked best. They could also unsettle a man. He watched this one. They were committed to nothing here; this needed to be assessed.

"Emperor Canassus in Rhodias, in the early days of their empire, has a comment on that in his *Journals*," said Pero Villani to his duke, at night, in the chamber of the Council of Twelve.

The duke blinked. Then smiled again, more widely. "He does, indeed! 'The son grows next to the father's tree or seeks higher ground away from it.'"

He saw the artist was startled, in turn, that he knew the passage. Which was amusing. That *his* classical knowledge should surprise. He paused. This was enjoyable, but they did not have unlimited time.

He let his voice harden. "Which are you doing, Pero Villani? Staying close, or breaking away?"

PERO HAD THOUGHT to win a debating point with a quote. Which was about as foolish as possible, given where he was. Debating points?

The duke was fascinating and terrifying and old. There were so many stories. Some might be true. If all of them were, he was a monster. Actually, if all of them were true he had died long ago and the Council of Twelve was led by a demon from the half-world.

The flattery, patently insincere, had irritated him, however. It was true that two of his father's works had been bought from creditors by the republic, but they would have been saving money on art, not making a statement about mastery.

But it had become more difficult to sustain anger. *Proposal* had been unexpected—and a relief. He was here to be offered or asked something? But what? And why at night? Why seized in the street?

He made himself speak calmly. "I honoured my father in life and I do so in death. I pray Jad grants him light. What is it you want of me?" And then, as he heard those words in his own ears, how brusque they sounded, he added, "How may I assist the council?"

The duke's face was narrow, wrinkled, seamed. It was hard to discern its colour in the shadows there, but Pero imagined it pale like parchment. He saw the old man smile again. He wasn't sure what was amusing. Perhaps his bravado?

"Would you be willing to paint my portrait?" Duke Ricci asked.

Pero fought to keep his mouth from dropping open. It took some effort. He said, "You seized me at night to ask *that*?"

"Of course not!" snapped another of the council, to Pero's left.

The duke glanced coldly at the other man, then turned back to Pero. "The portrait of myself would be for this room, among the other ducal portraits. Done in due course, by way of a reward, with payment of eighty gold serales, if that is acceptable."

Acceptable? It was what the very greatest artists were paid for a major work. It was ten times what he'd received from Citrani. And for this room, the council chamber? As the formal portrait of the duke to hang among the work of masters on these walls? Pero felt faint suddenly. He needed something to support himself, or a drink.

"How do you even know my work?" he managed.

"I don't," the duke said frankly. He shifted papers in front of him, adjusted the spectacles on his nose. "But we have reports from other artists, and from," he glanced down, "a man named Sano, a bookseller, for whom it seems you work at times? He has paintings of yours?"

"Yes," said Pero. He was fighting dizziness. His own work? *In this room?* "Why did you seek reports on me?"

"Because we need an artist with two qualities."

Pero realized he was expected to ask, like words exchanged in an antiphonal litany.

He asked: "And these qualities are?"

"He must have talent and he must be young."

"Talent. Yes, well . . . yes. Why young, my lord?"

His heart was beating fast.

"Because our painter must appear too youthful, too eager, too ambitious for his career to be a spy. Although he will be one, of course."

Pero wondered if the others could hear his heart beating, if the room was loud with it. The duke, he noticed, seemed to be enjoying himself.

"A spy on what? Where?"

No smile this time from the tall old man at the head of the table. The council members were silent, watchful. The duke said, "We have been requested to send a skilled artist to someone. It is not without risk, but it is a rare opportunity for our republic. We need a man loyal, and with courage."

"And who is it who wishes a painter?" Pero asked.

There was a shifting, a stir of anticipation around the table.

Duke Ricci said, his voice thin but extremely clear, "The Grand Khalif Gurçu in Asharias. He desires his portrait done by a western hand. We wish, in turn, to send someone to do that. Signore Villani, will you go to the Osmanli court, for Seressa?"

CHAPTER V

With any luck and the blessing of the god, Drago Ostaja thought, they might leave for home in the morning. He wanted that very much. It did depend, a lot, on Marin, however. Drago respected his ship's owner, feared him a little, would deny that he loved him. He also knew he didn't understand Marin Djivo—but anyone who said they did would be lying.

Drago was ready to sail. He had been from the moment they'd pulled into the Seressini lagoon and moored at the foreign merchants' slip near the Arsenale, very early in the season, with wine, pepper, and grain to sell. First ship from the east at winter's end.

He didn't like Seressa. Never had, however many times he'd docked here with cargoes that brought Dubravae merchants like the Djivo family considerable wealth—and kept Drago employed as their captain.

There was no subtle reason for his unease. He didn't like Seressinis. Few did, really. Seressa was in the business of making money, not friends—they said that themselves. The two city-states were not at war—Dubrava could never go to war with the stronger republic. Dubrava didn't go to war with anyone: that was their way of life. War was ruinously expensive, and they weren't powerful enough, in any case. They were merchants and diplomats, watchers not warriors. Treaties, negotiation, concili-ation, bribes where needed, information shared in many direc-tions (another kind of bribe). An almost infinite shrewdness and caution (someone had called it a woman's attentiveness) guided policies in the Rector's Palace. Dubrava's walls had never been breached by catapults or cannon, their ships in the splendid har-bour never fired or sunk.

It was cleverness more than anything, Drago knew. And if a ship's captain born to a violence-prone people inland in wild Sauradia might dream of swinging a sword at a Seressini scion sniffing behind his handkerchief as he inspected goods, well, your dreams were your own, weren't they?

In truth, they were treated with arrogance here (everyone was), but fairly. The Seressinis worshipped money. If you brought them things they could buy, then sell for more than they'd paid, you'd be welcome in this lagoon. They would bid fiercely against each other for your cargoes, especially if you were early—and Drago Ostaja took pride in being an early ship. The Djivo family paid him well for it.

Beyond commerce, the two republics either side of the Seressini Sea shared the faith of Jad—the western liturgy and images, with its bright-haired, shining god-figure and High Patriarch in Rhodias.

Drago had grown up differently: his childhood village sanc-tuary in Sauradia bore images of Jad as dark, bearded, gaunt, suffering. There had also been the heresy of the god's beloved son.

He didn't talk about Heladikos, not since arriving in Dubrava as a boy with his parents, fleeing Osmanli advances. He had seen the sea for the first time and felt—so *decisively*—that he'd found his true home, out there among the bright ships riding the green-and-white waves of the harbour. Sometimes you just knew.

And your beliefs were your own as much as your dreams. Or they were if you kept your mouth shut and were seen chanting the western liturgy in the seamen's sanctuary or in Jaddite trading colonies among the Asharites in long winter months in the east, waiting for spring and a fair wind.

How you prayed in your head, what you whispered to yourself at night, especially before sailing, wasn't for anyone else. And sailors did often keep a place in their thoughts for Heladikos, who had fallen into the sea when he died, after driving his father's chariot too close to the sun.

The son's death was quietly seen by many mariners as a sacrifice, to protect those who sailed the wide, wild, deadly seas. It was a ship, sailors weeping for a young man's ruined beauty, that had collected his body from the waves, wasn't it? In the story.

And if you were among those who lived at sea, sometimes out of sight of any shore, well, you prayed to everything and everyone you could, didn't you? The sea might be where Drago Ostaja felt he belonged, but it was never less than deadly.

It had once been preached by eastern clerics that the god's gallant son had died bringing fire to mankind. Drago's mother had told him that tale. It wasn't a teaching any longer, not for hundreds of years. Heladikos bringing fire was heresy now, even in the east. They *burned* those who taught some old truths. Drago had never understood that. You didn't have to kill people because what clerics thought had changed.

But the newer teaching was better, to his mind, it made more sense: mankind couldn't have been fashioning metal weapons, cooking food, building ships, sailing, navigating, even collecting that half-mortal body from the sea, if they hadn't already *learned* how to use fire before Heladikos fell from heaven.

No, today's prayers in the east (not here, never here) were wiser: the god's son had died in that chariot trying to approach his father to petition mercy for Jad's suffering children below, living in pain and sorrow, dying too harshly of warfare and disease, childbirth and famine. Of so many terrible things. Storms at sea.

That was still how many people prayed in eastern Sauradia where Drago had grown up, and in Trakesia to the south, and in Moskav. Maybe Karch. Possibly other places he didn't know. It was a liturgy with a patriarch based in Sarantium until not long ago.

Sarantium was gone. The city was Asharias now, taken by a conquering khalif. The world was a different place.

Drago tried not to think about that too often: about the City of Cities on the day the walls were breached and Asharites poured through like lava from a volcano, bringing fire. There was always suffering in the world. There was little you could do about it.

There had been mighty forests in Sauradia once, much reduced now by the need for timber. Powers were said to have dwelled—or to still dwell—in those woods.

What you worshipped, Drago Ostaja believed, had to be determined by where you grew up. How else could anyone be an Asharite, or one of those strange Kindath praying to the moons? You worshipped Jad if you were raised where Jad was worshipped.

That wasn't a thought that needed sharing either.

At the moment his concern was filling and balancing the *Blessed Ingacia* with the cargo they were taking on. It was mostly northern woollens and cloth Marin had purchased, dyed over the winter in Seressa, to be sold east. A bulky cargo needed careful stowing, though they had been doing this for years and there was no mystery to it, just routine and prudence.

The mystery was Marin, more often. Second son of the family. The smart one, everyone knew, though not the more predictable, as everyone also knew. Not many shipowners took their reluctant captain with them, for example, to the most expensive brothel in Seressa and bought him the most expensive woman in the house for a night.

Marin had done it, Drago knew, to celebrate and reward his flying voyage from Khatib in the east to Dubrava, where they'd collected their owner (Marin) and raced on to Seressa. It had been a "pushing the season" trip, too early in spring for safety, but Drago had had a good feeling about the easterly that had sprung up, and had noticed that the fruit trees had already ripened. And, to be more certain, he'd consulted a Kindath sky-reader in a house on a lane he had come to know . . .

He'd heard what he'd needed to hear. The *Blessed Ingacia* had left the harbour of Khatib two days later, passing the ancient beacon light as the sun rose on their right (each man praying in his own way).

The clerics of Jad condemned sky-reading as heresy, magic. On the other hand, it was known that Emperor Rodolfo had such men at his court in Obravic, honoured for their learning. And Rodolfo was the Holy Jaddite Emperor, wasn't he?

A mariner heading to sea sought wisdom where he could, and the moons and stars were above the world every night, telling their tales to those who could hear.

They'd docked in Candaria to take on wine from their warehouse on the island and were swiftly back to sea, hurrying home on what turned out to be a glorious wind. They were the first ship from the east into the harbour at Dubrava. The cannon saluted them.

That, Marin had declared, after he'd come on board and they'd crossed the narrow sea to Seressa (no Senjani raiders, thanks be to Jad), was worth an extra captain's share *and* a silken woman at a place he knew. He'd offered two of the women, actually. Drago had quickly declined. One Seressini courtesan, at this level of sophistication, was daunting enough. He'd expected her to be disdainful, vexed at being assigned to the lowly captain and not the elegant shipowner.

If she was, Drago never saw it. He didn't want to know what that night had cost Marin, but he knew he'd remember it a long time. In a way, a woman like that could destroy you for others.

"I will have this pleasure again, signore?" she'd even asked, stretching on the bed like a cat when morning came.

Drago had grunted, pulling on his boots. He'd wanted to be back at his ship. There were goods to be stowed. "Maybe. If I set a record again crossing from Khatib," he replied.

"Khatib?" she said lazily. She had red hair. Her body was available to his glance even now, smooth, richly curved. "Tell me, handsome captain, what are they trading there this spring?"

Even the whores, he remembered thinking as he left the room. *Everyone* in Seressa was looking for information!

Which, he later thought, towards sundown the next day at sea, hugging the coastline past Mylasia, to the point where they'd angle across for Dubrava, ought to have made what Marin had said and done in the harbour less surprising.

Perhaps. Marin was Marin, though. He was going to surprise you.

IT WAS A VERY BRIGHT MORNING, which was unfortunate from Pero Villani's current perspective. He'd had a late night, as friends celebrated his sudden good fortune—and toasted his departure, extensively.

Once he'd agreed, three nights earlier in the council chamber, the secrecy about the portrait commissioned in Asharias had been immediately lifted. The painting *needed* to be announced. The duke (whom he was going to also paint when he returned!) had wanted discretion for that first conversation only. If Pero had declined, it would have been said that the invitation had never been made. If he'd spoken of it after saying no, they would have denied it, and he'd possibly have been killed for the indiscretion. No one had said anything like that, they were far too well-mannered, but Pero knew his republic.

But saying yes, as it turned out, meant going to the Osmanli court to do more than render an image of the grand khalif.

Painting a subject in the western manner required sessions of sketching, perhaps even doing the painting from life (if Gurçu the Destroyer could be induced to allow it). Pero Villani would have occasion to closely observe and perhaps even converse with the man who had taken Sarantium.

He was expected to remember these encounters and report them in detail when he returned. No one spoke the alternative phrasing aloud: *if he returned.*

It was suggested he take no notes, not even in code. A code would be seen as suspicious from a simple artist. The duke's privy clerk—more respectful the second time they met—advised him as to this. Signore Villani could confidently expect the Osmanlis to be listening to all his conversations. They would know his intimate preferences in bed after his first evening with one of the women they'd send to him.

"They will send me women?"

"Almost certainly," the man replied, amused. "But only incidentally for your pleasure. Much more for their information."

Pero remembered smiling. "How very like us," he'd said.

There were other matters on which he was prepared by the privy clerk. These were, it was made clear, only possibilities, he was not to dwell overmuch upon them. But if opportunity presented itself . . .

Pero made a decision to push these matters aside from the start. Opportunity, he decided, was unlikely to arise, and he didn't want it to.

It hadn't been difficult to make the decision to go. What did he have to stay here for? The only things ahead of him in Seressa were like the barrel he'd moved into the roadway to trip a man he'd almost killed. Obstacles.

That moment still bothered him this morning, even through a headache. He wasn't a violent man—or hadn't thought he was. But in his anger he'd come close to killing someone in the dark. If it hadn't been a guardsman wearing armour . . .

Sailing to Sarantium was the ancient phrase. One of his friends had quoted it last night, raising a cup. There was a new sorrow that came with the words, since there was no Sarantium any more. It used to mean that someone was changing his life, embarking on something new, transforming like a figure in a classical painting or mosaic, becoming something else.

He wondered if sailing to Asharias could achieve the same thing. Not just as a saying, but in reality, in the life that he, Pero, son of Viero Villani, was living. It could, he thought. It could change everything. He needed to paint well, earn respect from the khalif and his court, remember all he saw and heard, come home remembering. Unless the most secret, least likely part of his mission somehow happened. He had already decided he wasn't going to think about that.

Seressa was a cynical, calculating republic, but it paid its debts the way good businessmen did, to earn credit against the future. They'd owe him a debt if he managed this and returned. He'd be paid by the khalif for his portrait, and then be given a truly substantial sum to paint the duke when he came back. A commission to paint the Duke of Seressa? For the council chamber?

What young man, without wife, without family, without resources, would say no? You could die of plague at home as easily as anything could kill you on the road. Well, perhaps not quite as easily, but . . .

But he was going. It had been a simple matter to offer his room to a friend sharing someone's crowded space, and there was nothing to packing his clothing, since the privy clerk had undertaken to dress him in a manner befitting a representative of Seressa. That was what Pero was now. A representative of his republic, the Queen of the Sea. He had told them what he needed in the way of supplies for painting. They'd procured them.

Pero had paused for a moment by a window over the canal during the late, loud party last night to think about how his parents would have been proud. He'd realized that this chance, this sailing, would never have come had his father been alive, and the thought about pride went away, as if out the open window and over the waters below, where a boatman was singing a love song under the two moons in the sky.

As he approached the docks now, where the foreign ships moored, he caught sight of the *Blessed Ingacia*. Men were moving up and down a ramp and along the deck, loading cargo and stowing it. It was a trading vessel, good-sized. He supposed it was trim and ready and other important things, but Pero knew too little about ships to form an opinion. He had never been to sea. Had no idea if he was one of those who handled the waves easily or if he'd be vomiting and green for the duration of the crossing. On reflection, it might not have been wise to have drunk as much as he had last night.

His goods were with him, being rolled in a small cart along the dock. He was bringing his own supplies. Who knew what they had in Asharias? He had a servant, assigned by the council. It would have been inappropriate, it seemed, for the highly esteemed young artist he was now declared to be to travel east alone. The servant's name was Tomo. He was a small, slope-shouldered man, wiry and quick, no longer young. Pero knew nothing about him. Their first encounter had been this morning.

It was difficult to credit, what he was in the midst of doing. It could contort the brain, trying to grasp it. Also, there was the headache.

All the girls in the tavern had kissed him goodbye, some with a squeeze below for luck, and Rosina had taken him to her room for more than that and hadn't charged him for it. It had been a good farewell. He wondered if he'd see this lagoon again. Did sailors always wonder that? You almost had to, setting out to sea, let alone going onward, as he would be, overland from Dubrava to Asharias.

There was talk of war again, the Osmanlis marching and riding, wheeling their heavy cannon towards the fortresses of the emperor.

It was said that their new cannon master was a metalsmith from Obravic itself. It wouldn't be surprising. Men did that, moving back and forth across borders and faiths for gold. For a way to live. The High Patriarch pushed for holy war. Ordinary men pushed for themselves and their families.

The Osmanlis might be going north and west soon. Surely, Pero thought, they'd not harm an artist summoned by the grand khalif? He carried papers. Weren't there protections, immunities? Wouldn't a soldier have his skin flayed or some such if he did violence to a man the khalif wanted?

Some of his friends last night had offered this view; others had disagreed (Seressinis were good at that), suggesting that distances were too great and warfare too disruptive for discipline. With late-night, wine-fuelled concentration, they had debated the likelihood of Pero being castrated or killed on the road. They'd agreed he'd probably survive the short voyage to Dubrava. There was that, at least.

He had been told by the privy clerk to attach himself to any party of merchants going east. They would know the road, war tidings, other dangers. It was also possible an Osmanli official would be in Dubrava when Pero arrived. If so, he was to report to that person, present his documents, ask for an escort. Use his best judgment, in either case.

It was startling to Pero Villani that people believed he might have a best judgment in matters of this sort. It could have been amusing, but it didn't feel that way this morning, looking at the ship he was about to board.

It really was too bright. Sunlight was reflecting in dazzles and sparkles off the lagoon. The breeze was from the west, pushing high white clouds. He supposed that wind was good for the mariners.

He saw two men waiting by the ramp leading up to the *Blessed Ingacia*. One was burly, black-haired, a weathered face, full-bearded, wearing a red seaman's cap. He was watching the goods being wheeled and carried aboard, rasping orders.

The other was quite gorgeous.

He was better dressed than one needed to be for a ship's voyage, very tall, fair hair worn long. He wore an aristocrat's sword. He held his hat in one hand so that his bright hair gleamed in the unfair light. His beard was fashionably trimmed. He smiled widely as he watched Pero approach. His eyes would surely be blue, Pero decided, and confirmed it as he came up to them.

"Welcome! You will be the artist, Signore Villani?" the tall man said in flawless Batiaran. He sounded amused, for some reason.

"Pero Villani, yes." Pero bowed. "This is your ship?"

"My family's. Marin Djivo, eternally at your service."

"Eternally? More than I hope to need."

The other man laughed. "Indeed. I can be wearying over long periods, my friends often say. Our men will help yours stow your goods. You'll have to share a cabin with your servant or he sleeps on deck. Your choice, of course. I do apologize, but that is the way of things on board."

"I understand."

But Pero saw that the golden-haired shipowner's gaze had already moved past him, as if he was dismissed. Aristocrats could be like that. So much for eternal service, he thought. The man's smile grew wider. He had laughter-lines at the corners of his eyes, wasn't as youthful as he'd appeared at first glance. Older than Pero, certainly. Pero noticed the captain—the burly one—observe that smile, and wince. He turned to look.

A man and a woman, two servants with them and a larger cart than Pero's (carrying considerably more belongings), were approaching. One of the servants, a young girl, was holding a green-and-blue sunshade over the woman. Pero wished he had one of those shades.

These would be, he knew, the doctor and his wife headed for Dubrava on one of the contracts for physicians. The man looked sober and serious, as doctors usually tried to appear. If you were going to kill a patient you might as well seem thoughtful in the process.

His wife was small, young, genuinely lovely. She had her hand on her husband's arm. Her eyes were wide, head turning this way and that, taking everything in.

They weren't important to Pero at all; companions on a brief journey across to Dubrava, never to be seen again, most likely.

He wondered if the doctor had remedies for seasickness, should it arise. *Arise* was possibly the right word, Pero thought. He had friends who'd have laughed at that if they'd been here and he'd said it aloud.

Behind him, Marin Djivo did laugh, for some reason.

"Oh, Jad," Pero heard the ship's captain mutter. He glanced back at them. Djivo had spread his arms wide, one hand still holding the handsome hat.

"*Welcome!*" he cried again, more loudly this time. The word rang out over the commotion of the dockside. Men paused in their morning activity to look. "Be welcome, both of you! You must be this year's Seressini spies!"

"Oh, *Jad*," the captain repeated under his breath. "Oh, Marin, please!"

The physician stopped abruptly, and so his wife did, of necessity. So did the servants and the wagon. They remained like that, a dozen paces away. Pero felt a small but undeniable anticipation. This was unexpected. He looked again at the shipowner. Marin Djivo's smile seemed guileless, no hint of anything but pleasure in it, despite the words.

His captain looked anguished.

The doctor—his name was Miucci, Pero remembered—disengaged his arm from his wife's and came forward alone. He wasn't smiling.

He said, quietly, "Will I be dealing with further insults if I board your ship, signore?"

Djivo's smile wavered not at all. "So that you know, we say 'gospodar,' not signore, in Dubrava. Or 'gospar' will do for tradesmen and such."

The physician remained grave, but Pero could see anger. "We are not in Dubrava. Is it an uncivilized place, or is it just you?"

"Oh, dear. You feel insulted, doctor?"

"I do," said Miucci calmly.

Pero was impressed. He had no idea how he would have dealt with this himself.

The doctor added, "Dubrava has asked for a physician. I am acceding to that request. Your words suggest something very different. If I am unwelcome I have no desire to impose or intrude, or to spend two years with my wife in a place where we are not welcome. Please advise me. It is Signore Djivo, is it?"

"It is." The smile had gone. The man looked as serious as the physician. "How would you like to be advised, doctor?"

"Jacopo! I do believe Gospodar Djivo is amusing himself, no more than that." The woman came forward, leaving her servant and the sun-covering behind. "Amusements differ so much from city to city. Am I not right?" She smiled, the only one doing so.

There was a hesitation. Then Djivo said, "Also from person to person, Signora Miucci. It will be 'gosparko,' which means 'my lady,' when we reach our republic. And you are entirely correct. An observant woman, I note. I am a man whose friends are often unhappy with his notions of diversion."

"I can see that." Signora Miucci nodded towards the captain, whose face reflected his distress. "Assuming your captain is also a friend."

"Probably not in his own mind just now," Marin Djivo said, laughing. "Come, doctor. I jest too much and not always wisely. You *are* welcome on board, and I promise you will be pleased with your welcome in Dubrava."

"May I reserve the right to decide that?" the physician said. His pretty wife had taken his arm again, Pero saw. He was, he realized, enjoying himself, even with a steady pain behind his eyes.

"We always have such a right," Marin Djivo said.

Miucci nodded. "I also have no doubt you and your captain have been carefully observing Seressa while trading here, and every time before. That you will share your thoughts with each other and with the Rector's Council when we reach Dubrava. Would you suggest otherwise?"

Marin Djivo could look forbidding, Pero saw, not just frivolous. Tall men had an advantage in that way. The merchant said, "Your contention is that Seressinis in Dubrava can hardly not do the same?"

Miucci nodded again, briskly. "That is my thesis, yes. There are other cities with physicians—if you distrust Seressa."

"To be honest, doctor? The entire world distrusts Seressa."

To his great surprise, Pero saw Jacopo Miucci's face relax into a grin.

"With cause, I daresay. What shall I report in my first letter home about the merchant who took us across?"

Marin Djivo laughed again. You could see where the laughter-lines came from. Pero thought this might be a face worth sketching.

"That he had a wretched sense of what might amuse, but offered Candarian wine, kept back for his own use, to guests aboard ship."

"Very good," said the doctor, and "*Good!*" said his wife in the same moment. They looked at each other. The physician smiled; the woman laughed and squeezed her husband's arm.

They went aboard.

MARIN WATCHES THEM go up the ramp. He has a number of thoughts taking shape. He is also waiting on Drago. They've known each other a long time and, yes, his captain is his friend.

Or, he thinks of it that way. He suspects the other man might hesitate before using the word.

Drago says, not looking at him, eyes on the crates and sacks being brought past, "You had to do that?"

Marin puts his hat back on his head. He likes the hat. He just bought it here. It is a sunny day. Not hot, a brisk wind. A good wind, which is why his captain is pushing the crew; he wants to catch that breeze before evening if they can.

He says, "Do what, Drago?"

The other man swears. Marin laughs.

"Why do you need to complicate things?"

"I do that?"

"Yes!"

"You think I was being irresponsible?"

"Yes."

Marin sighs. The doctor and his wife are being helped onto the deck. The artist follows. He is quite young. Marin thinks about that, draws tentative conclusions.

"I wasn't, Drago. I wanted to test a few things."

The captain turns to him, his expression skeptical. "Is it so?"

"Yes it is. And I did."

"And what do you know from this testing?"

No harm in sharing. Drago Ostaja is both the best captain the Djivos have ever had and discreet as a statue.

"That the doctor is no spy, beyond the usual questions he'll be asked when he returns. But the wife has her own tasks. I have almost no doubt about it."

Drago swears again. He is inventive that way. "And *how* did you decide this?"

"Because I challenged them and watched. What you called being irresponsible. Miucci's anger was protective. He was thinking of her. Then she defused the matter so smoothly it just . . . went away.

Did you notice? It was impressive. She's better-born than him, knows courts from somewhere. Not Seressa, from her accent. We should find out where."

"*She* is the spy?"

"I'd say so. Nothing unusual, of course."

"Fucking Seressinis."

Marin grins. "As to that, I never did ask—how was last night?"

Drago flushes crimson, which is all the reward a man ought to ever need for a clever line. Unless he'd said it to a woman, perhaps.

His captain declines to answer, turning back to the ramp. "Easy with the crates, you! The sacks you can sling around, but not the crates!" He takes his time monitoring (unnecessarily) what is happening. They are nearly done, and this crew, Drago's crew, knows what they are doing.

Drago says, not looking back, "And the artist fellow?"

Marin considers it.

"Not our problem," he says.

PERO LET HIS SERVANT share his cabin. He wasn't some well-bred merchant prince like Marin Djivo or those on the Council of Twelve. He wasn't going to act like one. Tomo snored, it emerged, shouted out a couple of times, tossed on his pallet, but Pero had friends who were worse.

It seemed that he himself was all right at sea. No sickness.

He slept well into the mornings as they went south down the coast. Didn't hurry to be out of bed, there was nothing for him to do on deck. And so it was that he was awakened at dawn on the third day by urgent shouting from above, as Senjani pirates boarded them in the first pale light.

CHAPTER VI

Danica had made it clear from the start. She would come with her bow and arrows—and her dog. She would never go anywhere without the dog. Even on a raid. Even boarding a merchant ship, as they were doing this moment, off the coast of Batiara.

Yes, she'd told them, Tico would be fine at sea. There were often animals on merchant ships. Yes, she knew about sea air and salt and protecting bowstrings. She would do what needed doing. And in her view every raiding party would be well served by having someone who knew how to handle a bow. At sea, as by land. She had said that to the raid captains, when they'd summoned her to ask what she wanted as a reward for what she'd done in the bay at night.

She'd told them. If ever there was a time to ask again, it was the day after she'd brought a Seressini boat to the strand with dead men aboard.

Danica knew that if she was worth having on this raid—or any other—it was because of what she brought to a fighting party with her arrows and her eyesight. Maybe her knives, though others were good with those.

Until they'd actually set out, after the two war galleys had turned and gone home, she'd been unable to entirely believe they'd let her come. She had been sure permission would be revoked at some cruel final moment, right in the harbour, even, either because the clerics proclaimed it unnatural, or because some raiders didn't want a woman among them.

Many didn't. Some had been explicit as to what they thought a better use of her might be.

On the other hand, as she'd pointed out—sweetly at first, then less so—none of them had killed seven Seressinis in the bay, saving the boats from being set on fire in the dark, and exposing the spy in their midst. When he had achieved all those things, she'd said to one of the raiders, a Miho family member, loud and vulgar, he might be allowed to come calling at her door to discuss other matters. She'd evaluate him then, she said, and decide.

There had been laughter. It hadn't been a private exchange.

You may make an enemy, her grandfather had said in her mind.

I know. Did I do wrong, zadek? Is he dangerous?

He's a fool. It is all right. The others will honour your pride.

It was probably true. That was what happened in Senjan.

Silently, she'd said, *We're too much guided by pride, aren't we?*

What else is there to be guided by? he'd replied.

She'd thought about that a few times since.

Could pride alone carry you forward and up as you scrambled aboard a merchant ship flying the Dubravae flag? There was her cold, hard need for vengeance, but this raid wasn't a part of that. Dubrava wasn't her enemy. These were first steps on a journey.

Scaling the side of the ship wasn't difficult, even with the bow and quiver. (She'd changed her bowstring in the dark.) Tico was faster than any of them, a leap to an anchor chain, then along that to the deck as if he'd been doing this all his life. Danica reached the rail, pulled herself over, stood on the deck in the grey light. Most of the raiders were there before her. She needed to learn to be

quicker, she told herself. The crew had surrendered already, there
was no resistance. Some of the Senjani had already gone below, to
see what was being carried.

She hoped no one could see how frightened she was. A merchant
ship from Dubrava wasn't going to fight them, but she knew—
every one of them did—that they weren't supposed to board and
rob a Jaddite ship running from Seressa to Dubrava. It would be
hard to make a case that this was part of any war against infidels.

Not their fault that they'd been locked on their strand by
Seressa, unable to even trade with the islands. If you starved people, you left them no choice, right?

That was what their leader, a man named Hrant Bunic, had said
yesterday evening when they'd seen the sail and begun following
it. Senjani boats were shallow-bottomed, low to the sea, hard to
spot as they approached. Good at escaping into shallows, even up
rivers when they needed to.

It was early in the year for a Dubravae ship to have reached
Seressa and be heading home. If they'd caught it earlier, coming
north, Bunic said, they'd have reaped a harvest of goods from
Asharite lands, and had a claim to those—as heroes of the border.
The story they always told. And believed, mostly, Danica thought.
Now, it was going to be Dubrava-bought cargo from Seressa,
which meant Jaddite merchants selling to Jaddite buyers, which
meant they shouldn't be taking it.

With luck, maybe some Kindath goods, her grandfather said.
There is a district of them in Seressa.

And we war on the Kindath?

She knew he was trying to calm her. She'd taken up a position
towards the mainmast with two others, Tico beside them. The
other two held swords. Danica had an arrow to her bowstring, but
was holding the bow casually. There ought to be no need for violence. So Bunic had said, and her grandfather had said the same in
her head.

*The Kindath? Depends who you listen to. They deny Jad, after all.
And besides, after those war galleys you can take Seressini cargo and
claim it as a toll for what they did. Bunic probably will.*

The ship's captain, a broad-shouldered man with a black beard,
was facing Bunic now. His expression in the brightening light was
somewhere between anger and grim resignation.

"Early in spring for Senjani on this side of the water," he said,
almost conversationally.

"Took a chance," Hrant Bunic replied, also lightly. "We're in
some need, as you'll likely know. Early this way for the *Ingacia*,
too." Bunic smiled briefly. "From Khatib? Wintered there? You
made it back quickly then."

"We did. I don't think I know you."

"I don't think you do," Bunic replied. "You'll forgive us if we
check to see if there's anything from Jad-denying heretics below?"

"There isn't," said another man, approaching from behind the
captain. He was extremely tall, a neat beard, golden hair under a
hat, a polished voice and manner. "There is nothing but Jaddite
cargo. Check it and leave. Or take my word for it. I'm Marin
Djivo. This is my ship. You have no business being aboard, and
every cleric in the world will say as much." This one was controlling
anger, Danica thought.

"Not our clerics," Bunic said. "Ours were hungry this winter
and spring. Seressa was hanging islanders who traded with us."

"We heard that. We aren't Seressini. You don't hurt them if you
steal from us. We've paid them for what we're carrying."

"And you'll trade east with the Osmanlis, denying the god with
every coin you pocket."

Their usual argument in Senjan. Danica had never paid much
attention to Hrant Bunic before. She knew he was a leader of many
raiding parties, said to be calm and respected. She was impressed
with him just now.

The tall man laughed. "Ah. I have a devout man on my ship," he said.

"We all are," said Bunic quietly. "We are Jad's warriors on the border."

"Then go inland!" snapped Marin Djivo.

Tico growled, Danica gestured him to silence. Marin Djivo glanced at them, then back to Bunic.

"Fight east if the khalif's armies bring war. Do glorious battle for Jad and the emperor and Patriarch and leave honest citizens in peace! You don't need more enemies! And no thief can name himself a hero while boarding another man's ship. No one believes your lies about heroism."

"Bold talk for a man facing swords."

"Pah! I'll fight you alone to end this foolishness."

"What? To the death?" Bunic's tone was mocking.

"If you like."

There was a rippling of sound along the deck.

Bunic laughed. "A swordsman? Schooled in your youth by a rich man's fencing master?"

The tall man smiled. He tossed his hat away. "Can this be? A Senjani raid leader afraid of a merchant?"

Stop this now! her grandfather said abruptly. *This is no fight.*

Danica didn't understand, but she made herself move forward from the mast. She took off her own cap, shook out her hair. Everyone could see it now, and know she was a woman. "I'll fight you, rich man's son! Keep your sword, I have two knives. Just tell me where you'd like the killing blade to enter."

She was afraid of what Bunic might say, only relaxed when she heard him laugh again. "Yes. Fight one of our women, Gosparko Djivo! If you want to battle for your cargo, go ahead. You are all insured against raiders and storms. You think we don't *know* that?"

"I have no idea what the level of ignorance is in Senjan," Marin Djivo said icily. He was staring at Danica. "I am sure your girl can throw knives extremely well—or she wouldn't be here."

Danica was trying to breathe normally. What if he had accepted the challenge, what if the moment had forced him to? People could be trapped by pride.

Then she saw the merchant's mouth quirk. He said, in a different tone, "I've been scarred by women before, as it happens. Different reasons, but a wound's a wound."

There was laughter along the deck of the *Blessed Ingacia*. A change in the mood. Relief. No one, she realized, had wanted a fight, with what might follow. It was brighter now, birds wheeling and diving as the sun rose.

Well done. Her grandfather's silent voice.

I'm not sure what I did.

Saved a few deaths, it might be.

That merchant's?

Maybe after. If our men went wild. But Bunic dead first, I think. That pretty man can wield a blade or he'd not have challenged.

He'd beat a raid leader? She was startled.

Swords, one to one? Very likely. And if he killed our leader, then—

His voice in her head broke off. He was seeing what she saw.

What followed happened at speed. It was uncertain who might have stopped it, or how. Her own eventual action was a response, not a forestalling.

It was her first raid, after all.

"LOOK WHAT I FOUND!"

Marin turns and sees that the speaker, pushing someone before him, is one of the raiders. He is lean and long-nosed, hair shaggy like a wolfhound. And he has a hand gripping Leonora Miucci's elbow, thrusting her onto the deck through the hatch not far from where Marin stands. She wears only a light-blue night robe.

Her hair is unbound, which makes her look terribly vulnerable.

It is important, he realizes, to control anger now. He feels shame, though, which can engender fury. This is his ship, the woman is a guest. He is aware that Drago, behind him, will be feeling a murderous rage. Ships' captains take pirates personally; being boarded is an affront. But this is an old dance and they know the steps. The Senjani want money and goods. No one is looking for violence. This is a transaction for the raiders. They are conducting business, much as he does in the market in Seressa or their factors do in Khatib.

Nonetheless. This is also theft, and an assault on *his* ship, and he likes the Miucci woman, even if he is almost certain she's a spy. She is clever, attentive to her husband, attractive.

She looks more angry than afraid, he sees with renewed admiration. It cannot be pleasant having a man like that forcing her up here, barely clad. He is still gripping her arm.

There are two women on his deck now, impressive in different ways. The tall Senjani girl holds her bow with relaxed assurance. He has no doubt she can use it. The leaders of Senjan don't play games in picking their raiding parties, there is too much at stake. And Marin does know—everyone knows—what the Seressinis tried to do to Senjan this spring. There will be anger on their part as well.

A need to be careful, accordingly. He gives Drago a meaningful glance over his shoulder. He turns back and says, "It would be kinder to release her. No one is going anywhere."

"Kinder!" mocks the man who has dragged Leonora Miucci from below deck. "We are *kind* to Seressinis now?"

"I am from Mylasia," she says coldly, her voice suddenly as aristocratic as her bearing. With a twist she tries—and fails—to remove herself from the raider's grasp. Marin, fighting anger, is about to speak again when he sees the Senjani leader nod at his man.

With a shrug, the raider lets her go.

Partly the effect of her voice, Marin guesses. Men will deny it, but there is instinctive deference to the obviously well-bred.

Or they kill them. Or demand an extravagant ransom. That is how the world works. And ransom is what this is now about.

"Ah! Do forgive us, esteemed signora! Mylasia, is it?" The man beside Leonora Miucci rasps the words like a woodcutter's saw. He spits on the deck. "Will we split hairs like lawyers?"

"Be quiet, Kukar."

The raid leader is experienced, Marin can see it. He will want a fair return from this boarding—but not so much as to arouse fury in Dubrava. Then he'll be gone, north and east in their light, swift boats to their own waters and walls.

But a ransom is now in play for the woman. It might have been better if she hadn't used such an elegant voice, he thinks. He wonders why she did, after days of sounding much less high-born. It is interesting that she can do it, too.

She steps away from the one called Kukar, as if proximity offends. "If your quarrel is with Seressa I will not do. Sorry to disappoint."

The man grins. He looks her up and down. He is enjoying himself. "Haven't disappointed me yet, girl. We find other uses for the ones not ransomed, back home."

"Kukar!" The raider leader says the name again. But his man steps over and grips Leonora once more, on the arm above her elbow, higher, more intimately.

That one is vicious, Marin thinks. Some of them will be. Theirs is not a life conducive to civility. Hardship and fighting and faith, mostly. He looks at the leader again, sees distaste. Some do think of themselves as beleaguered heroes in Senjan. It might be amusing, except that their courage is well known, and they do fight the Osmanlis for the emperor, or on behalf of farmers and villagers on the border all the time. *And* they had sent men to defend

Sarantium before it fell, unlike most places in the western world. Including Seressa. Including Dubrava.

There is nothing tidy about the Senjani or their place in the world. Right now Marin doesn't want to be reflecting upon that. He wants them gone. He will lose some cargo; he needs to keep the quantity acceptable. And it will be a disgrace to let them take the woman.

She isn't Seressini, which helps, but her family will be wealthy, most likely, which doesn't. He wonders how she ended up married to a doctor. A physician and a Mylasian aristocrat? It doesn't square.

Marin leaves that for now. He is reconciling himself to negotiating a ransom on his deck, a price for the raiders leaving her behind. And then he'll need to hope her family reimburses his own. That will depend on many things, and is hardly a certainty.

But then everything becomes much more uncertain, because why should men be permitted certainty in life, especially at sea?

PERO VILLANI WENT quickly up the ladder to the deck. Later he would wonder why he'd moved so fast. It wasn't as if he could bring anything to a confrontation with pirates.

It had been clear what was happening. Strangers were striding about below deck, shouting, shifting and banging things. His heart was beating fast. You heard tales about piracy at sea. Seressa lived and breathed in fear of Asharite corsairs from the coastline below Esperaña, or these so-called heroes from Senjan across the narrow sea. The corsairs were worse. Men and women were taken into slavery by them. Almost never returned. Lived, died, on galleys or in Asharite lands. The Senjani just wanted ransom and goods.

Or revenge now? Because of those war galleys that had just come back after trying to starve them out. Bad luck, he thought, to be taken so soon after that failed adventure.

Was this to become his own failed adventure now? Ending before it began? He had no one to ransom him, was worth nothing to the raiders. Would they want paint pots and sketchbooks? Their portraits rendered in charcoal? Or—the thought occurred—would their well-known piety be offended if they learned he was going to Asharias to paint the grand khalif for coins and fame?

Perhaps best not mention that.

Up on deck he stayed by the rearmost hatch, conspicuously unarmed, a threat to no one. Hardly worth noticing, really. He had hurried into a tunic and trousers and pulled on his boots. His clothing, he thought, was much better than it was at home. Would they decide he had money?

Marin Djivo, whom he had come to admire, was speaking with the captain of the pirates when there was a commotion at the other hatch and Pero saw Leonora Miucci manhandled up to the deck by a raider. Her hair was unbound, exposed. She was barefoot, clad in an unbelted night robe.

Pero took an impulsive step forward, then remembered who he was, and where he was. This was not something an artist was going to be able to address. He swore under his breath. He had a sword here. It was below with his servant. He wasn't very good with it.

The man gripping Signora Miucci was skinny, sour-faced, with unkempt hair. Pero was *not* going to think him any kind of hero. It pained him to see this woman even touched by such a man. She twisted to escape. Then the Senjani leader snapped a name and she was released. She spoke, in a voice cold and cutting—and suddenly patrician. And she wasn't Seressini, it seemed.

Wouldn't matter. Pero knew enough to know that. What would raiders care about her birthplace? Her voice would say *money* to the Senjani. He realized that she was at risk of being taken now. He looked an urgent appeal at Marin Djivo. Read a hard anger in the shipowner's face.

There were about forty raiders on the deck, however. Four of their small boats surrounded the *Blessed Ingacia* like wolves around a solitary sheep. They were outnumbered here two to one, and they were seamen and merchants (and an artist and a doctor), not fighting men. This would need more than anger, Pero thought.

Then the doctor came on deck, and a mild morning turned dark.

IT WAS BRAVE BUT FOOLISH, and those two together, Danica thought, could get men killed.

The man who burst onto the deck of the *Blessed Ingacia*, behind Kukar and the woman, was holding a thin, bright surgeon's knife.

He said, a voice with some authority, in fact, "You will unhand her now, or you are dead now!"

Kukar Miho had been raiding since he was a boy. His father and grandfather and Miho men for generations had been Senjani fighters.

He turned towards the voice. He did let the woman go. Did so in order to draw his sword and run the physician through with it, in the belly.

He pulled the blade out, twisting, as you were taught. Blood followed. The gutted man's mouth gaped. He fell. The knife clattered on the deck.

It was too fast, too unexpected. They had been moving towards ransom talk, Danica was certain of it. That was what Senjan *did* with people like this woman. Ransoms negotiated and paid immediately, on the ship. Easier for everyone, no letters, no intermediaries, no time-consuming back-and-forth. They would take the coins and some of the Dubravae cargo, and go home. A successful first raid of the spring. Money for the town to buy food. Goods to resell up the coast . . .

Not now.

Oh, Jad! That limp-cock fool! she heard her grandfather snarl.

She saw the ship's owner, the tall man, stride forward, reaching for his sword. The other woman was screaming. Danica looked at Hrant Bunic, her leader. His face had gone dark with fury.

"*Kukar!*" he roared.

The merchant was halfway across the deck—sword leaving its sheath—towards Kukar, who had spied on Danica once outside Senjan's walls, thinking he was unseen, who was a crude, thought-less, *stupid* man.

She loosed her arrow. Targeted him. Kukar Miho. Her raid companion. It struck him in the chest, an easy, short flight. Killed him instantly. An arrow to the heart will do that.

HE WAS NOT HER HUSBAND. He was dead. Her life was over, with his.

Leonora knelt beside Jacopo Miucci whom she had met only days before, and who had been so unexpectedly decent and kind. She was amazed at how desperately she was weeping on the deck of a ship in bright sunlight.

There was blood soaking her night robe, she realized. The man who had killed the doctor lay beside her, on his back. He had seized her from their small room below, gripped her in an ugly, insinuating manner, his hand on her an intolerable insult. There was an arrow in the raider's chest. His mouth was open.

She couldn't stop crying. Jacopo Miucci, in death, looked startled, affronted. He had come rushing up to save her with a surgeon's knife—against raiders with swords.

It had happened at such speed, Leonora thought. A certain life was yours, it was unfolding, and then it wasn't and would never be again. How did men and women deal with that much fragility? Your existence under Jad could be knit tightly (if not perfectly), you could be sailing a springtime sea, and then . . .

Her grief was unfeigned, but they would not understand it. They would think her a woman wildly mourning the husband lying before her. It was that, yes, but in a way no one here could know.

Dubrava would send her back.

Of course they would. Why would she *want* to stay, in their minds? And in Seressa? What good was she to the council now? What worth did she have? Would they want to arrange a false marriage to a second doctor? Do it all again? They *couldn't* do that—she'd been on a Dubravae ship!

Perhaps they'd propose she become a state-employed courtesan, an elegant whore bedding merchants and ambassadors, wheedling what she could from them in candlelit pillow talk after offering subtle pleasures, or violent ones. And unless she agreed? Back behind the walls of the Daughters of Jad on the mainland, where her father had wanted her locked away. Leonora could almost hear the iron gate closing, the loneliness of the bell.

She wouldn't be a prostitute, she hadn't been born for that. It was not a path. But nor would she ever go back behind those high and holy walls. (They weren't guarding holiness. They were not!) Which left little in the way of choice, Leonora thought. Left nothing, really.

They were at sea. The waters would be deep here, cold this early in the year. Final. Silent. There were worse ways to die. The man she'd loved had been tortured by her brothers, castrated, his body left unburied in wilderness. And this other man, who'd seemed to care for her, astonishingly, was dead on the deck among strangers, his life ripped apart, ended by a sword.

You lay down to sleep at night, woke to noises in the morning . . .

A footfall. The Senjani woman who had killed her own companion walked up. She bent over the raider, gripped the arrow in his chest and twisted it out. Through tears, Leonora looked up at her. The other woman was tall, young, expressionless. Her fair hair was also down along her back.

"I'm sorry," the woman said in a brusque voice. "He shouldn't have done that. It was a mistake."

"A *mistake*?" Leonora managed. She wiped at her cheeks with the backs of her hands. "That is the word?"

"One of them," the other woman said.

Leonora became aware of a hunting dog pushing his head against her shoulder.

"Tico, gentle," the woman said. She added, "He won't hurt you. I think he feels your sorrow."

"The dog does? I see. What about the beasts who just killed my husband?"

"Said I was sorry. Kukar Miho doesn't represent Senjan."

"No? Just the ones among you who raid and kill?"

"Not those either," the woman said. "I'll leave you."

She turned and walked away towards where Marin Djivo was now speaking intensely with the Senjani leader. There was a different mood on the deck. Men had died.

"My lady, do you wish to go below?"

Leonora looked up again. It was the artist, Villani, his face so pale it was startling. "I will help you back down, signora."

"Am I even permitted? Aren't they planning to take me for ransom?"

"I, ah . . . I believe it is being negotiated. To be paid by Dubrava now, or by the Djivos."

"They are *bargaining* for me while my husband lies dead?"

It was beyond belief. Except that if the pirates *did* take her, there would be no ransom paid by her family. Seressa might offer something, out of shame, to preserve appearances. She had been presented to the world as a Seressini doctor's wife. It wouldn't help them to risk having that exposed.

"I believe they are. Negotiating. Yes," Pero Villani said awkwardly. "Let me take you down?"

It would be quieter there. She could be alone. She looked away, at the sea in sunlight.

"No," said Leonora Valeri, addressing herself as much as the man beside her. "No. That is not what happens now."

She stood up, ignoring the quick hand he extended to help. She wiped at her tears again. Blood had soaked her robe from the knees down. It was chilly in the spring air, but that didn't matter, not now. She took a breath and, head high, walked across the deck towards the railing and the rising sun, away from the men, a tight cluster of them, who were presuming to define her worth in silver and gold in the morning's light.

HE HAD BEEN READY to kill the ugly Senjani bastard who'd gutted the doctor. He'd been striding that way, knowing it might doom the ship, all his mariners, turn this morning into something other than it had been meant to be, make it an encounter defined by death.

Raids had a rhythm, a protocol (like trading). There was a *process*. Insurance and shared understanding guided them. Violence would normally be avoided. If there were no Asharite or Kindath goods or merchants on board when Senjan's raiders came you could limit the damage in terms of what they seized.

Even so, even knowing this, sometimes a man might deem himself to be less than he wanted to be if he didn't act, consequences be cursed to darkness. This, Marin Djivo had thought, seeing the doctor die, was such a moment for him.

He had been moving, drawing his sword. They might—many or all of them—have been sent to the afterworld, to darkness or light as Jad decreed, if an arrow had not killed the raider before he got there.

In the taut silence that follows, he looks at the woman who'd loosed that arrow. The one who had offered to fight him with knives. Her gaze meets his. She nocks another arrow without looking at the bow.

Marin lets his sword slide back into its sheath.

And seeing that, she nods, as if he is being granted approval.

By a female Senjani! Marin Djivo has enough wryness, and he does apply it to himself, to imagine that later he might find this moment amusing. Maybe.

Just now, nothing is. He breaks that exchange of gazes and crosses to the Senjani raid leader. This needs to be dealt with swiftly, properly. No one else should lose their life on his ship.

The leader seems to agree. The process resumes. They will take twenty bales of the fabric below, the Senjani says briskly. Marin knows the raiders cannot even carry that much. He offers ten, lets anger infuse his voice. In negotiating you use what you have—and his fury is real. He sees that the Senjani are unhappy, there is tension among them. One of them—a woman—has killed another. That will make for a pleasant journey home, Marin thinks. They'll also be aware that killing a Seressini physician contracted to Dubrava might rally two republics that dislike each other against Senjan.

It is never good when your enemies are allied.

Murdering Jacopo Miucci might even weaken the emperor's support for Senjan. Small things can affect larger ones.

Marin has a thought. He looks back at the woman with the bow. She isn't far away, standing with feet spread for an archer's balance, arrow to string, hair unbound.

Marin Djivo is a man who makes connections, draws conclusions. It is possible, it is even *likely*, he thinks, that this woman is the same one who . . .

Not a time to ponder that. And it hardly signifies right now.

The raid leader says they will accept fourteen bales. And six hundred serales for the doctor's wife. Otherwise she goes with them.

Marin lets his anger overflow. It is real and satisfying. A decent man, a *necessary* man, lies dead on his ship.

He snaps, "You will take your goods, fourteen bales, that is accepted, and leave us. You killed her husband! The goods are all you get."

"No, gospodar. Respectfully, they are not. You are not able to stop us from doing whatever we want, and you know it. I am extending a courtesy. Receive it as such. I have no idea what that woman's family will pay to have her back, but it is surely more than six hundred. It will be on your head, what follows, if you do not—"

"I had not taken you for a fool. You seize a high-born lady from Mylasia after murdering her husband and you believe the Holy Patriarch and the emperor will protect Senjan from the fury of the Jaddite world? Do you?"

He says it loudly. A tactic. He knows his words will register—and disturb the raiders, however well they hide it.

He pushes harder. "You killed your own man. Because you *know* what he did was a Jad-cursed wrong. Your task is to ensure that the world sees you are aware of it! Not to make it worse by abducting a grieving woman. Think, man! How much hatred can the heroes of Senjan survive?"

He lets mockery show in the way he says *heroes*.

You didn't become a raid leader by being easily outfaced. The other man remains calm, shakes his head. "That one, the doctor, was from Seressa. For what they did to us this spring we will be forgiven our own anger, I think. We will address the hatred of the world for a man slain by ill chance if we must. But six hundred serales for the woman, gospodar, or she comes with us."

Marin looks away, to where two men lie dead. And so he actually sees the moment when the woman stands up, small, golden-haired. The blood soaking the lower part of her robe disturbs him. It is so wrong.

He has duties. To her, to his ship, to those with cargo being carried. You are not permitted very often to give voice to what you feel.

He says, "Four hundred serales, fourteen bales. Go. I undertake to report that the man who killed the physician was immediately slain by one of your own, and that you expressed regret. You have my word on it."

A hesitation. Four hundred is much less than they might get if her family is truly wealthy, but it will take months, ships and messengers, and Senjan needs money and goods to sell for food right now.

"*No!*" Marin hears. The word is shouted. "No! Do not!"

It is the Senjani woman's voice, the one with the bow. He looks quickly over, sees what she sees.

And, "*No!*" he also cries.

LEONORA WILL NEVER understand why she stopped, one foot actually on the ship's rail, the green sea below her. It will come to her in dreams, that moment.

It had nothing to do with the voices crying out in horror. Of course they would be horrified to see her at the railing near the prow, preparing to step up—and go down to her release.

It had nothing to do with them. No, it was as if she suddenly felt *resistance*, pressure, a force of denial. It was as if she was being told she *could* not leap, that the sea was not—yet?—her home, her rest, an ending.

Something was pulling her back, a dragging weight, or perhaps it was more like a barrier, a wall—she could never shape a proper image, afterwards.

Confused, frightened, she stood at the rail, breathing hard. She hadn't been afraid. She had been so sure . . .

She saw the small Senjani boats below, saw sunlight on the sea. She looked up. A fair morning sky, thin high clouds, light breeze in the sails, seabirds around the ship. Brightness. The god's sun in the east, over water, over land she could not see. She had walked towards that light.

And had been stopped, somehow, from going over the side and down into the deep.

It was the captain, the burly, bearded, gruff man named Drago, who reached her first, running.

"My lady!" he cried. He extended a hand but stopped, not touching her.

Leonora felt strange. She probably looked it, she thought.

She said, clearing her throat around a difficulty, "I . . . am not doing it. I thought I would. But I find I can't." He wouldn't know what she meant by *can't*. He would misunderstand.

"Jad be thanked, signora. Please. They are not taking you. The pirates. You are staying with us."

"Why will that matter?" she asked him, unfairly.

Unfair, because he'd have no answer to give. How could he possibly understand her life? She was a deception on his ship's deck, and she had nowhere in the world to go.

The sea had seemed a destination.

The artist came hurrying over, still white-faced, more so now, in fact. Another sweet man? There seemed to be some of those. It didn't matter.

Leonora let him take her down below this time, to her cabin. Hers alone now. She closed the heavy door and sat on her cot, feeling the motion of the ship like a cradle. A child's cradle. Somewhere in the world there was a child in its cradle, there were many of them . . .

She did not weep. It was too strange for tears.

She thought of the water all around them. It was cold and deep, and would have been an answer.

ZADEK, WHAT JUST HAPPENED?

I don't know. His voice in her head was hesitant.

She was going over the side.

I saw. She changed her mind. It is a fearsome thing to do.

Did she? Change her mind?

She felt him hesitate again. *What do you mean?*

I don't know what I mean! But it looked, or, it didn't look as if . . .

Danica stopped. Her grandfather was silent. There was something different in him now, too, she didn't know what. She was frightened. It had been clear that the other woman had been ready to leap into the sea rather than be taken hostage or be bought back for coins—or even live without her husband.

Was that it? Could someone love another person so much?

And when she'd stopped, in the act of mounting the rail, it had seemed as if . . .

Danica turned her mind away from thinking about it. There was something difficult here and it disturbed her.

They were concluding the negotiations, Hrant Bunic and the ship-owner named Djivo. Danica looked around. She saw that the other raiders seemed even more uneasy now, carrying tension like a bow strung too tightly.

Some had been ordered below to bring up the goods they were taking. Fourteen bales of cloth. It was a large number. If the material was good they would sell it farther up the coast for considerable value. It probably was good. An early ship, the Dubravae would have had their pick in the marketplace.

Then something else fell into place for her—and a new fear came. She became aware that some of the other raiders were eyeing her, looking away when she glanced at them.

She went over to where she'd thrown aside her hat. She picked it up and put it back on, so she'd look more like a man, a boy, an ordinary raider from Senjan.

By the time she'd finished tucking her hair back, aware she was still being looked at by those she'd sailed and rowed beside, Danica had realized that her life was going to have to change. Right now.

She felt the thump of her heart like a drum hit hard.

There was no twisting away from this. She'd just killed Kukar Miho—whose family had been in Senjan since the walls were built, some said. He had five brothers and a powerful father, uncles, many cousins.

She had herself. Their family, three of them—mother and grandfather and her—had come to Senjan only ten years ago, and she was alone.

Sometimes you did certain things and everything altered. She straightened her shoulders. She walked over to Bunic and the merchant. They were standing quietly, the captain with them, negotiations were over, consequences being implemented. Goods and gold for Senjan, within reason, that the world might remain in balance.

They turned as she came up.

Danica said, looking at Marin Djivo, "You swore you would report we killed the man who slew the doctor, that we are sorry for it."

He had very blue eyes. He said, "I did, and I will. Are you the one who put arrows in the Seressinis in your bay?"

She ignored that, though it was surprising to be asked. She turned to Bunic. A breath. Some things you said, there was no going back, after.

"We'll need more than him saying it. Someone has to go to Dubrava and express our regret."

"What? Who would go there to be hanged?"

"No one. But I'll go, with assurances from this one that I won't be hanged."

"*Why?*" Bunic asked.

But he was clever, a good leader, and she could see that he was working it through, that he already understood, in fact.

"Because I killed Kukar," she said.

"So you come to us and apologize? So that we will see you are sincere?" the merchant asked. "I suppose that might—"

"No," Danica said. She was looking at Bunic, at the comprehension in his eyes, and an unexpected sadness. "No. I come to you because I'll be killed in Senjan by his family. I can't go home."

There was a silence. The ship's captain, the stocky, broad-shouldered one, cleared his throat. "Ever?" he asked.

"Who can speak to *ever*," Danica said.

Oh, child, she heard within. She'd been waiting for him.

Hush, zadek, or I will not be able to do this.

Child, he said again, then was silent.

She could feel his pain, though. And her own, heavy, a cannon-ball, an anchor going down and down into the sea.

Bunic said, "I will speak for you at home, Danica. You stopped a great deal of bloodshed this morning."

"Mostly theirs," she said. "Not ours. They will say that in Senjan. And you know the Miho family. Whatever you say, will it stop them?"

She had never seen Hrant Bunic look sorrowful. He did now, at the very edge of finishing a hugely successful first raid of the season.

"They would really kill her?" the merchant asked. He was looking at Bunic.

"I . . . it is likely," Hrant said finally. "We are a hard people."

"A hard people," Marin Djivo repeated without inflection. He turned to Danica. "You wish to come to Dubrava, to speak to the Rector's Council about Senjani contrition. And then?"

"And then I have no idea," Danica said.

Which was only the truth.

LATE IN THE DAY, towards sundown. It is colder. Marin is at the prow, wrapped against the chill. They are running southeast now, crossing towards home with the sails up and a good wind. There is always trepidation when a ship leaves sight of land, even in the home sea, but they do know these waters.

The raiders are gone, north towards Senjan. They took their slain man to bury him at home. Drago has overseen the wrapping of Doctor Miucci's body. He will be laid in Dubrava's cemetery outside the walls, then exhumed and sent back to Seressa if a request comes.

This has happened so many times, Marin is thinking. Their ships have been boarded, men have died in raids, they have often lost far more than they did this morning. Darkness awaits even the sun as it goes down. Change and chance are the way of the world, and more so for those living on disputed borders, or venturing to sea. And Dubrava—their small republic caught between powers— partakes of both these things. The borderlands and the sea.

So does Senjan, it occurs to him, but he doesn't linger on that thought. He isn't feeling kindly towards the heroes. Not today.

"Were you going to fight him?"

She has a silent tread. He turns as the woman—her name is Danica Gradek, he now knows—comes up beside him. Her dog is with her. A big wolfhound, not one you'd want angry with you.

He shrugs. "Did you kill those men in the dark this spring?"

He isn't sure why he's challenging her, but you don't always know why you do what you do.

She looks at him. "Why do you care? You want to hang me? Right in the harbour? Or hand me over to Seressa to do it?"

In the wind and the snap of the sail and with the birds crying, he has to strain to hear her. He remembers that her life has changed today—forever, it might be—as much as the other woman's has.

He says, "You have my word. I will say what happened, what you did, how it saved lives. I will swear it before an altar when we land, if you like."

"Men can lie at altars as easily as anywhere else."

She looks out at the sea. There is only the sea ahead and behind now. Waves white in wind.

After a time, he says, "My father told me of a saying once. That the world is divided into the living and the dead and those at sea. He didn't know where it was from."

She is silent. Finally says, "If I hadn't killed Kukar, and you'd fought him . . ."

"I was angry."

"I saw."

"Drago would have drawn his sword, then others."

"And our men. We'd have killed many of you."

"I am going to say all this to our council, Danica Gradek. Why are you . . . ?"

The birds around the ship are diving into the waves to emerge, wet and wheeling. He sees one with a fish caught, as it rises. Dive and rise, over and again.

She says, "I need a reason to have destroyed my life."

"You are too young to think that. You have altered your life. Not the same."

"Here's an arrogant man. To tell me what I've done or not done."

He smiles. He says, "Well, we're arrogant in Dubrava. Not as bad as the Seressinis, but . . ."

"No, you aren't as bad as them." She doesn't smile back. She says, looking at the sea, not him, "From the time I came to Senjan I wanted to be allowed among the raiders. Inland, though. Not this. I wanted to fight Osmanlis."

Another borderlands story, he thinks. He has heard these before. But everyone's story is their own, he also thinks. He wonders who died. Whose memory drives and aches in this woman. And how did she end up at sea? Are they raiding with women now?

He asks it. Why should he not, on his own ship?

She sighs. "This was my reward. They asked me what I wanted for saving our boats that night. I needed to be seen to be capable before I could go east. That won't happen now."

She's addressed his earlier question after all, he realizes. Although, in truth, it will be obvious to everyone when they land. A Senjani woman is known to have killed Seressinis with arrows, a woman took part in this raid, carrying a bow, killing a man with it . . .

Nonetheless. "Thank you for answering," he says.

She looks at him this time. After a moment she looks back out to sea.

He wonders what she is thinking. Doesn't ask. His own thought: it is likely she'll be killed after they reach Dubrava. Or handed to Seressa, as she's just surmised.

Sometimes there is nowhere to hide in the world.

The ship rises and falls. Marin looks at her profile while she stares at the slowly darkening sea, and that is the thought that comes to him, as if swooping and diving, swift and hard.

HE HAD LANCED a painful boil for one of the mariners the day before. Had been looking in on the man in the sailors' quarters at sunrise, a lantern held by another man. They had heard loud sounds above. Both seamen swore violently.

"Senjani!" they'd exclaimed.

Neither moved, even as boots were heard coming down and men began entering the holds. The Dubravae mariners gestured for Miucci to stay with them. He had understood this was not an occasion for resistance. He'd taken guidance from them.

Until he saw Leonora stumble past their doorway, protesting, still in her sleeping robe, a pirate's hand on her arm, forcing her with him.

You didn't plan every moment of your life, even if you were a man who tended to be organized, methodical, precise.

You didn't plan your death either, usually.

He'd run to their own room, seized the first blade he found in his instrument case, hurried up the rungs of the ladder to the deck. And died there, to his very great surprise.

There had been a moment of extreme pain, white, fierce, a sword plunging into him, withdrawn. Then no pain at all. Nothing, astonishingly.

His body lay on the deck, bleeding from the belly, his knife beside it. He was dead and he knew he was—and he was seeing it, seeing all of it, from beyond, from *somewhere*. Outside himself, as if floating, like a dandelion seed in spring. It was spring now. He remembered those floating seeds outside their home when he was young, watching them in wonder.

Leonora was on her knees beside his body. She was weeping. He didn't want her to be doing that. He didn't want to be dead. It was . . . disappointing. There were, Jacopo Miucci thought, so many things he still wanted to do.

He watched an arrow kill the man who'd killed him.

He felt, in some hard-to-fathom way, satisfaction, seeing that. He didn't know how he was seeing it. He didn't know where he was.

He seemed to be drifting higher, far above the deck, weightless, without substance. He was aware of sunlight but heard no sounds. He saw waves below, men below, himself lying below. It was extremely sorrowful, he thought.

Men were talking. The merchants, the pirates. He couldn't hear anything. He saw the Senjani boats. They seemed very small to have come all this way across the home sea to this western coast. He wondered who would miss him in the world now that he was gone, if anyone would. Leonora Valeri, for a little while, perhaps? Perhaps. She was crying beside his body. He saw her. He saw himself. He wondered what would happen to her now. That was a bad thought.

He drifted again. He was remembering those dandelion seeds, in childhood.

Stop her!

He had no idea who had said that. In his mind. How could he even hear? Who—?

Stop her! Now! She's going over the side!

Then he saw it. Leonora had risen from by his body and was moving purposefully across the deck. The men down there hadn't seen her yet, or realized what was happening.

Over the side? She was going into the sea!

How? Miucci cried (somehow). *How do I stop her?*

Tell her to stop! Help me hold her. Do something!

So he tried. He didn't want her to do this. *Tell her?* He called her name, shaped it in thought.

And saw her falter for an instant, then continue on. It gave him hope, impetus, urgency, seeing that. Sometimes, he had told patients, you needed only to take the first step towards walking again, after a broken bone had been set, for example, and then the next ones would come more easily. Only take the first step, he used to say.

He'd been a good physician. He knew it. He'd been on his way to becoming a better one. He was sure of that, too.

She was at the railing, and now he saw (high above) men turning to look at her, understanding belatedly.

Do something! That harsh voice in his mind.

Miucci tried again. He forced himself downwards from this drifting height. He tried to move whatever of him was left here in the morning air above the *Blessed Ingacia.* And, by the grace offered by Jad to his children (could you speak of that when you were already dead?), he saw the railing nearer, and Leonora there.

No, my dear! he said, in his mind.

He was right next to her now, above the sea, beside the ship, and he made whatever was left of him, whatever he *was* now, hovering here, dead on the deck, *push* as she lifted one leg to the rail. He felt another presence, that harsh one, pushing her from beside him.

The sea was below. He thought, for an instant, that if she jumped they would be together in death today, and then he drove that thought away and he said again, driving it at her, *No, my dear! Not yet, not this way.*

And he realized that she was aware of him, or of *something*, because she stopped. She did stop.

He saw—floating, hovering, dead—the moment when her bare foot came back down to the deck. She stood as if becalmed, adrift, lost, confused.

My dear, Miucci said again, gently this time.

He didn't know if she heard him. He saw that there were tears in her eyes, on her cheeks. For him? For her own lost future?

He didn't know. He couldn't know. He felt himself beginning to lift again, he couldn't resist it now, he was the one adrift (dandelion seed in a long-ago springtime). He heard, more faintly, *That was well done.* And then, a different tone, *I'm sorry.*

And then he was high, really high, and still rising, the morning sun seemed to be below him, the sea and the ships so far below, and then they were gone because he was gone.

PART TWO

CHAPTER VII

They hadn't castrated him.

They did that at eight or nine years of age to almost all Jaddite boys taken on raids. They waited that long to see which ones were bigger, stronger, showed signs of promise as a fighter. He had done that. They had left him intact and sent him to this barracks at Mulkar to be trained for the djannis, the elite infantry of the khalif, might his reign last forever and his name be blessed under stars.

He was fourteen years old now. You didn't usually join the army and fight until you were sixteen, but sometimes you did, if there was a major war, west or east, in a given year. He hoped that might happen for him.

Training could be boring, the same things endlessly, but he never complained the way some of the others did. He understood that this was what training was, over and over so you didn't have to think when it happened for real, you just did what you had to do. He knew this was the path to stepping forward. Possibly. Not everyone stepped forward into high rank, Kasim reminded them in his classes. You carried on with your life, even so. You still had a life.

He wanted more than just carrying on, though. He wanted to be on battlefields winning glory, his name coming to the attention (you could dream, couldn't you?) of serdars, and even the khalif in Asharias, as a fearless warrior, a hewer and slayer of infidels.

His name was Damaz. It hadn't always been, but he'd been four years old when they took him and renamed him, and he couldn't remember his Jaddite name any more.

All the djannis, without exception, were Jaddite-born—seized as boys in raids and raised in the true faith of Ashar. They owed everything—their lives, their chance at fortune, their hope of paradise—to the khalif. It was a good way to ensure a loyal core to an army.

Sometimes at night, dreaming, he had thought he was close to reclaiming fragments of his childhood, drifting towards faces and names, but those dreams were rare, defined by images of fire, and he didn't really need to remember such things. What would be the point? His life was here, and how could it be better, whatever it had been in some village on the borderlands?

The djannis—even the young ones—were a commanding presence in Mulkar, a garrison town south of the road between Asharias and the Sauradian coastline. Mulkar, too, had had a different name once, apparently. Damaz didn't know what it was. He supposed he could ask Kasim, who knew such things.

In their green coats and high boots and the tall, emblematic hats bearing the crest of their regiment, the djannis strode through the city as if they ruled it. There was a governor here, of course. He would not cross them. No man was keen to cross the djannis, no woman inclined to deny one of them, even the boys being trained—though you could be gelded or even executed for causing trouble for a woman of rank or birth, so you avoided those.

They paraded and drilled in regiments, they fought each other with spear and sword, they trained with their bows. They went days without eating. They marched out from the walls, in winter, too, and they tracked wolves and bears in snow and killed them if they found them. They had to stay outside the walls at night if they didn't find any. Some hated the hard bite of winter. Damaz wasn't bothered by it. He just disliked the waiting. All this delay. He carried within himself a feeling that time was rushing past him. He couldn't have said why he was in such a hurry.

He must have had a family but he had no images of them. He assumed they'd been killed in the raid when he'd been freed to come and train to be a djanni.

He had a mild aversion to fires, but he controlled it, and he didn't think anyone had noticed. It was a bad thing, to let others see your weaknesses.

They had done march-squares and turning manoeuvres this morning in a steady rain. Rain was bad. If the army was to set out for Woberg Fortress in the north they needed the roads to be good enough (and the rivers not in flood) for the great wall-smashing cannons not to bog down in mud.

Only the rain, the saying went, could forestall the grand khalif's designs. The rain hid the stars of Ashar, after all. It also blocked the sun and moons of the Jaddite and Kindath infidels, but that didn't signify.

Damaz wouldn't be part of this year's army, in any case. Whatever glory came wouldn't be his.

After the drilling the rain had eased. He'd walked from the barracks out to the marketplace in the city for a bowl of barley soup from a Kindath stall. Some of the infidels made good food, you needed to acknowledge that. There was a place for them among the star-born. The generous khalif tolerated infidels throughout his lands. They paid a tax to worship as they chose, and those taxes paid for soldiers and cannons, and gardens in Asharias. That had been Kasim again, explaining things.

When the bells for midday prayer sounded through the city, Damaz strolled to the nearest temple rather than back to the barracks. He left his boots and hat by the doors and knelt in prayer, invoking Ashar and the god who had given him his visions under the desert stars. There were stars painted on the temple dome, as there always were. In the wealthiest temples they might be made of metal, swaying from chains.

There was a new wadji here, younger than the last one. A thinner beard, a piercing voice as he led the chants. Damaz didn't give him another thought until later in the day.

It was then, on the training ground after afternoon sword work (he was good with a sword, bigger than most of the trainees, and quicker), that he overheard Koçi telling his friends—followers was more like it, really—that the new wadji at the market temple had made an indecent suggestion to him after sundown prayers last night, and how he, Koçi, was not inclined to accept that from anyone, let alone a false, vile man pretending to serve Ashar in holiness.

Relations between men and boys were hardly rare among the djannis. A friendship with the right officer had been the key to many a young man's rise. Damaz had never been approached by anyone of rank; he was too big, was his own thought, not pretty enough with his freckled features. But he knew—they all knew— that if it came from a man not within the regiments a proposition was an offence. And a young wadji new to a garrison city had no status at all. He could raise the shield of his piety, but he needed to actually be pious, and have friends.

Still, Damaz felt there was something wrong, not quite believable about the story. The wadji was truly just-arrived, would he be so reckless? Koçi could have reported the man immediately, right in the temple. He could have gone to his regimental leader, or one of their own wadjis here at the barracks.

Damaz was thoughtful in geography and history class. This was always late in the afternoon, after they'd worn themselves out with drills and might (sometimes) be able to sit and listen. The class was taught by Kasim. He had been an officer once, captured and mutilated by the Jaddites while scouting ahead of the army. He'd had his nose cut off by the savages and been sent west to the galleys to row until he died.

He'd escaped, instead, as a capable djanni could—and should. Had somehow made his way back. He didn't talk much about it, even when the boys asked, as they did, of course. He wore a silver attachment to hide his severed nose, affixed with silk ties that went behind his head.

He was, given the life he'd led, a thoughtful, composed man. The djannis had made a place for him as a teacher in Mulkar. They were all expected to be able to read and write in two or three languages, but the history and geography class was voluntary after you were twelve years old. Damaz never missed it unless they were outside the walls on a march.

They could all speak the Trakesian of today, but under Kasim a few of them were learning to read the writings of the long-ago city-states to the south. Poetry, dramas, he even gave them medical treatises to struggle through. Much of what their own doctors did today apparently came from Trakesia in its glory, two thousand years ago.

Ashar had not yet been born to have his vision in the desert night. There had been no star-worshippers, no Jaddites. The Kindath with their moons had apparently been present, along with other strange beliefs to the east, and the gods of Trakesia and those of Sauradia (where Mulkar was) had been a confusing diversity of powers.

Damaz usually enjoyed Kasim's classes, liked watching the young ones trying to look attentive and awake, remembering himself at that age, but he was distracted today. Kasim looked at him quizzically a few times, but said nothing. He was a teacher who waited for you to come to him.

Damaz didn't do that. He could have, but he didn't. Instead, when class was over and they all walked out into the cloudy afternoon, he did something reckless in the hour before they were called to prayer.

You couldn't spy easily on another regiment's sleeping quarters. For one thing, there were soldiers and officers mixed in with the trainees, and the regiments had an intense, sometimes violent rivalry for precedence and recognition. It wasn't as though you could linger by a window and listen.

Still, Koçi was boastful and vain, and of those in their year he was certainly one of Damaz's rivals for an early promotion into the ranks. Each spring, one, sometimes two of the fourteen- or fifteen-year-olds *might* (there were no promises, ever) be elevated into the army and go to war, where glory was. Where a life might be found, amid the dealing of death to infidels.

So Damaz would probably have admitted, if pressed by some-one like Kasim, that he had personal reasons for what he did in the darkening of late day, a breeze stirring the early leaves of trees. He walked towards the third regiment's quarters—Koçi's—and took a wide route to the back wall.

He looked around calmly, saw he was alone, and climbed to the flat roof. It was no achievement to get up a wall.

On the roof of any building here—they all knew this—you could place yourself near one of the chimneys and, if no fires were lit and smoking, crouch to listen to what was said inside. He was quiet in his movements. The room below was almost empty, but not quite. At the second of the chimneys he heard Koçi almost directly beneath him talking to a few others. It sounded like four voices.

You needed to be patient doing this, and lucky. Sometimes, they had been told, a spy in war might have to remain in place for days, knowing if he made a sound he might die. You voided yourself where you were, and hoped the smell didn't give you away. And if you were hungry you were hungry.

He didn't have to wait very long. They were talking about girls, insulting some. One boasted of a Kindath who'd smiled at him. Koçi made it clear that if such a girl wasn't bedded within a day or two it was a disgrace to the man smiled upon.

"And if a wadji smiles at you?" one of the others asked slyly.

"Fuck that," Koçi snapped.

"Oh, really?" a fourth voice taunted. There was laughter.

Koçi swore again. "Watch yourself," he said. "We're going to deal with him tonight."

"Did he really offer to bed you?"

"Course not. Wouldn't dare. I just don't like him."

On the roof Damaz blinked. He didn't move.

"He's a wadji!" the fourth voice said again, moving from taunting to doubt.

"Right? And no wadjis like boys?"

"But he didn't *do* anything, you just said."

"Didn't have to. Told you, I don't like him. We geld him, somebody better will come."

"Because we don't like him?"

"We're djannis!" said Koçi. "Who tells us what to do?"

"Officers," someone said.

"When they know," said Koçi. Damaz heard him laugh. "They don't always need to know. Are you with me? You don't have to be, but this is a test, make no mistake."

He had a forceful manner. The others were a year younger, one of them was twelve years old if the voice belonged to the one Damaz thought it did. They weren't about to gainsay Koçi.

It seemed he had been right.

To be planning an attack on a holy man spoke to boredom and viciousness more than anything else. The boredom he understood, the viciousness he had seen in Koçi, and some others, before. It wasn't an impediment in the army.

The wadji meant nothing to Damaz. Just another of the interchangeable faces of holiness sent to Mulkar, moving on after a time.

A nasal voice, not very musical. But from what he'd just heard there had been no incident. Koçi just saw a chance to confirm his power over other trainees. And if he was questioned by superiors, well, he had a group to support his story—which is what the conversation below now turned to.

There were many reasons to keep out of this, and no reason to interfere. Well, there might be. If any of them was going to move up to the ranks this spring Damaz wanted it to be himself. He was ready. And he truly didn't like the idea of a man being gelded so that a boy among the djannis could amuse and assert himself.

"YOU OVERHEARD THIS AT A WINDOW?"

Damaz looked at his teacher. He shook his head. This might have been a mistake after all, coming to Kasim.

"On the roof?"

He nodded.

Kasim smiled. He had lit a lamp to read by, was sitting beside it. They were alone in the room. Classes were finished for the day.

"We used to do that," the teacher said. "You can hear at a chimney when no fires are lit."

Damaz nodded again. He had told the story to the one man he could think to trust. Kasim had seemed the only choice if he was going to talk to anyone. Damaz wasn't sure if he'd been right. He felt even less certain with the next words.

"You shouldn't have gone up," his teacher said.

"I was trying to be fair. To be sure of what I believed."

"I understand. But, you see, now that you are sure you have a difficulty."

"I know that. That's why I came to you!"

Kasim smiled again but said, "A softer tongue, please."

"I'm sorry, teacher. I'm sorry about all of this. Tell me what to do."

Kasim drank from his bowl of tea. He hadn't offered any to his pupil. Teachers didn't do that. He looked at Damaz a long time, thoughtful eyes over the silver simulacrum of a nose. A man who had been to war.

EVENING. THE CLOUDS THINNING, a breeze from the west. Damaz could see the blue moon, with the white to rise later. The Kindath would attach a meaning to patterns in the sky, to this day, this hour. He saw a star, his first of the night. You prayed to that, a superstition, not any formal teaching of Ashar. Mostly the trainees prayed to be accepted into the ranks. Tonight Damaz prayed that he might live to see the morning and the last stars of night.

He was alone near the gates that led out to the city. He was waiting. Unless there was some sort of alert, djannis were free to leave the compound in the evening, the gates were open. There were always women just outside, also waiting—for them. Alcohol was forbidden to the pious, of course, but not every man was born to be pious, and women were forbidden to no one. The boys being trained had to be back in their barracks by the second night bells. The soldiers had no such restrictions in peacetime, though they were mustered at sunrise every morning and needed to be present for that.

All of which meant that Koçi and his followers would have no reason to hide themselves as they came towards the gate, heading out. Nor did they. Damaz saw them coming along the wide, smooth gravel path. They were laughing. It sounded nervous to his ears, but that might have been his own anxiety.

His teacher had put it simply.

"You made a decision, knowingly or not, when you went on the roof. If that man suffers or dies tonight it lies upon you."

"Not them?"

"Yes, them, too. Burdens fall in different degrees in a case such as this. But you *know* now, and that has meaning."

There were torches on tall stands along the path and lamps by the gate, with guards there and on the walkway above it. Damaz stepped forward so he could be seen.

He did know. *That has meaning.*

He called out, "Koçi, a word."

There were four of them. They stopped in front of him.

"A word?" Koçi laughed. "Damaz? You wish to know the word I have for you?"

The others laughed. They were young, it was important to remember that, and they'd surely be afraid right now. Damaz took a breath. He was aware that he could die here. He wasn't ready for that. He had a life he wanted to live, for the khalif, for Ashar, for himself.

He said, "My first word for you is *liar*. I have others. If you walk past me here, the next one will be *coward* and I will shout it so that everyone hears."

The laughter stopped.

One of the four coughed nervously. On top of the gate behind him Damaz heard the guards' conversation stop. They would enjoy a fight among the boys. Entertainment on a spring night.

"What kind of fucking fool are you, you northern savage?"

Koçi had been born in Batiara, some said in Rhodias itself, taken by corsairs from a ship. His parents had been killed, the boy brought east. It was rumoured they had been wealthy and the pirates chastised for not keeping them for ransom. Sometimes the need to kill Jaddites overcame good sense.

A djanni's earlier life was not supposed to matter at all. It was left behind—with his name—as if it had never been. This wasn't entirely so, however. You heard stories, sometimes they might be true.

Damaz said, "I did not report you to any officers. It is just me here. But I heard you earlier. You are not going out to do what you intend to do, not without fighting me first." He was careful, didn't name the action. He was giving them a chance.

Another nervous cough. Someone muttered, "Koçi, he knows!"

"Shut up," Koçi said quickly. "There are flies in your mouth."

"And in your brain, Koçi," Damaz said, lifting his voice. It mattered that he frighten the other three, that they realize the guards could hear. "You think *this* will give you a reputation for bravery?"

"He . . . I have my honour to defend!" Koçi declared.

"You do not. I heard you, remember? I heard all of you. And I have named you a liar." He squared his shoulders. "Do something about it."

"Koçi! He heard us. He was on the roof!"

"I was on the roof," Damaz agreed. "So I know Koçi lied, and that you three are going out also, knowing that. Which brave hero carries the gelding blade?"

That had an effect.

"Koçi, he'll tell the officers!"

"His word against four of us, idiot."

"But he *heard*."

Damaz smiled, though his heart was pounding. You didn't let others see anxiety in you, ever. "Last offer. I have told no officer in your regiment or mine. It is just us here and nothing has happened. You lied about that man and I cannot, in honour, let you pass, because I know."

"Honour!" scoffed Koçi. He was blustering and unpleasant on the edge of manhood and would likely be worse as a man, Damaz thought. He wondered if well-born people from Batiara were all like this. It was even possible these traits would *help* him as a djanni. Koçi had followers already, didn't he? On the other hand, he wasn't very smart.

"Guards!" Koçi called. "An impertinent trainee is blocking our path!"

Nothing had happened. Now something would.

Damaz could walk away. He wasn't going to do that. He wouldn't have been here if that was a possibility. The blue moon, waxing, was free of clouds above them now, the wind was in his face.

"Guards," he said, "these four trainees are carrying gelding tools to attack a wadji at his temple in the city. A disgrace for all the djannis. Please search them and confirm the truth of what I say."

"*Ashar's soul!*" one of the boys with Koçi gasped. And a moment later Damaz heard a sound he was listening for.

"One of them," he called out, "just threw a gelding blade to his right. Bring a lantern, you will find it."

"No need," came a cold voice from the cypress trees beside the path. "He almost hit me with it."

Men stepped from the trees into the light of the torches. Damaz felt himself going pale, even as he drew himself up as straight as he could and saluted, urgently. He was looking at his own commander of the fifth regiment, and at Koçi's of the third. Teacher Kasim was with them. A betrayal? It felt like one.

Because in front of those three stood the serdar of all the djannis in Mulkar. Their commander, whose voice was the one they'd just heard. One of the boys with Koçi, the youngest one, was gasping for breath, as if he'd been clubbed in the belly.

Damaz felt a little like that. He wasn't going to let it show. He looked at his teacher, who met his gaze calmly. There was, Damaz thought, a lesson to be learned here, if he survived this night.

"Bring lanterns!" the serdar said. His name was Hafiz, and he was feared by the young ones more than angry ghosts or plague or the figure of Death itself. In some compounds, it was said, you wanted to attract your serdar's attention. Not in Mulkar.

Damaz could hear the gate guards scrambling to obey behind him. This had become much more than a diversion. Several of them hurried up, bearing the demanded lights. Men began drifting towards them, attracted by the commotion. Soldiers would be going out into the city along this path. They'd stop now, to see what trouble the young ones had brought upon themselves.

"Which one threw away the blade?"

Hafiz, serdar of the djanni, never raised his voice. No one ever missed a word he spoke. With real pity, Damaz saw one of the boys step forward and salute as best he could while trembling.

"I did, serdar. It was unforgivable."

That was brave, Damaz thought.

"You were afraid?" the serdar asked.

The boy swallowed. "I was, serdar."

"Understandable. But you are correct, it is not forgivable for a djanni. Guards, take this one to the physicians. He is to be castrated and handed over, if he recovers, to the office of the eunuchs in the city."

Damaz's turn to swallow hard. He looked at Kasim and saw his teacher gazing back at him.

Neither of the regimental leaders had spoken. Both had faces like winter. The serdar said, "Who else carries a gelding knife?"

One of the other boys stepped hesitantly forward. Koçi had not moved. He was as rigid as Damaz, staring straight ahead. It was too dark to see his eyes.

"You did not throw it away," the serdar said.

The boy shook his head, then added, "No, serdar. I have it still."

"You were going to use it on a wadji in the city?"

What could a thirteen-year-old possibly say? "Yes, serdar. He . . . he offended one of—"

"Did he? The truth. Be very careful."

Damaz wanted to look away.

The boy took a shaky breath. "No, serdar. That . . . that is what we were going to say."

"And who decided you were to say that?"

Courage could appear in many different guises, Damaz thought. The boy—he didn't know this one's name—held his posture, and kept silent.

The serdar stared at him. He gestured at the third of Koçi's acolytes. "Step forward, trainee." The boy did so. His legs were shaking. "Who told you to say the wadji had offended?"

The serdar knew the answer, Damaz thought. They all did. But that wasn't the point of the question, was it? And this one, too, was brave beyond his years. His hair was so blond it was almost white.

"Serdar, it would shame my regiment for me to answer. Forgive me. Please."

Damaz closed his eyes for a moment. He opened them and looked at the white-haired boy. The serdar said, quietly as ever, "They are brave enough to be djannis, but it is not permitted to refuse an officer's request for information. Forty lashes. If they live they may be returned to the third regiment. Take them."

A guard from the gate spoke an order, men detached themselves. Damaz watched three boys led away, back up the gravel path, around where it curved, and out of sight.

He felt grief come into him. He had done this. Twenty lashes by a disciplinary officer could kill a man, and those two were younger than he was, smaller. And the third boy was going to be . . .

No time to think about it.

"The two of you," the serdar said. "Before me. Now!"

Damaz and Koçi stepped forward, as if on parade. They stopped before their commander. There was a good deal of light now, the torches and the lanterns.

There was also a crowd, extending into the shadows. The clouds were gone, a moon was out, the night was young as a maiden, there were pleasures waiting in the city. This was, however, a pleasure worth lingering for.

"Are you ashamed, as a djanni?"

The serdar was looking at him, not Koçi. Damaz stepped forward one pace, as required, holding himself as straight as he could. *You are a spear*, their drillmaster always said. *You are ready to be hurled forward by your orders.*

He said, "Serdar, I am not."

He heard murmuring.

"And why not so?"

"I sought wiser counsel, serdar. I hoped to stop an assault that would shame the compound. I came alone and I was prepared to die for our honour. I do . . . I do feel sorrow, serdar."

"Not a djanni's proper feeling, trainee."

"Even . . . if companions are to be lost, serdar?"

Another murmuring. He tried to breathe normally. The serdar's face was utterly unrevealing, even lit by the lantern beside him. He said, "If companions shame the djannis, they are not worthy to be mourned."

"Yes, serdar," Damaz said.

"Do you also regret climbing on that roof?"

Kasim had told everything, it seemed.

Damaz said, "No, serdar. I needed to be certain before I acted on what I thought I'd heard. In . . . in fairness, and in honour."

"You might have gone to an officer."

"Serdar, not without being sure. I . . . I still needed to go to the roof first. Then I did go to my teacher."

"After you were sure?"

Damaz nodded his head. "Serdar."

He thought he saw the faintest hint of a smile. A wolf might smile like that, he thought. "Not the commander of your regiment, or the officers in your barracks?"

Damaz realized his hands were beginning to tremble. He kept them pressed to his thighs. "Serdar, I had hoped this folly among trainees might be resolved by us, need not trouble those above. If this was an error, my regret is deep and . . . I should be punished for it."

"You thought four others would stop for you?"

Somewhere in the world, Damaz thought, people were happy in this moment. He said, "Serdar, I thought three of them might. And then it would be two of us."

You could hear the wind in the cypresses. The flames of torches bent and wavered, smoking.

"Trainee!" The serdar turned to Koçi, who stepped forward beside Damaz, another spear. "Would you have gone out alone to attack a wadji tonight?"

An impossible question, Damaz thought. It was all impossible, it had been from the moment that cold voice had been heard from among the trees.

He heard Koçi say, steadily, "No, serdar, I'd have fought this one for . . . for bringing shame to the third regiment to which I belong."

Clever.

Or not.

"No. No shame to us in what that one did," said a loud, clear voice, also cold. "Not standing alone, one against four of ours." It was Koçi's commander. Koçi didn't move.

The serdar of all the djannis in Mulkar said, "Very well. This is what will now happen. These two fight each other. Here, while we watch. The winner of that fight will be elevated to military rank in his regiment."

"Serdar, is that just?" It was Damaz's commander, his first words. "Our trainee acted with honour and upon counsel. The other—"

"We are soldiers, commander. Not judges or holy men. The other one persuaded three to join him. He is a leader and willing to kill. I can use such men."

"You say one is promoted to the ranks, serdar." It was Kasim. "And the other?"

The serdar looked surprised. "The other will be dead, Teacher Kasim. They fight with knives. Make a space and bring more light."

IT TOOK LESS TIME than you might have expected to clear a fighting ground, bring more lanterns, have a large number of men ring the gravel path, define an area with their excited presence.

Wagers, Damaz saw, were already being made. You could find women and wine in the city any night. Two boys fighting, with a death to come, was memorable.

He stood at one end of the oval space and listened to the sounds of men waiting happily for someone to be killed. The serdar had taken a position midway, with the two commanders beside him. Koçi stood opposite Damaz. He looked calm and assured, shifting rhythmically back and forth, weight on one foot and then the other.

Damaz stared at him through flame and smoke and realized something: the other boy *wasn't* assured. Damaz had a memory of Koçi before training battles, one regiment against another. He stood very still at such times, bigger than most, quicker than almost all, and with only wooden weapons used, where the worst you would likely suffer was a cracked bone.

They had each been given a soldier's dagger. They didn't train often with these. Damaz wondered if the serdar had chosen the weapons for that reason. Probably not. More likely the limited space here, he thought. Or maybe because knife battles were savage, and therefore exciting. Diversion was a part of what this was.

He shouldn't be thinking this way, he told himself. He should be thinking that his death might be here right now, waiting, that he needed to account for his days beneath the stars and be prepared to die. Or kill. He had never killed anyone. But he'd wanted to be moved into the ranks, hadn't he? To be a true djanni of the khalif. Killing men and women (and children?) was what that meant, didn't it?

He stared at Koçi and kept still.

"Serdar!" he heard. It was Kasim, who had betrayed his confidence and brought them all here. Kasim was standing behind Damaz. He hadn't seen him there. He didn't look back.

The serdar turned. Kasim said, "The boy of the third regiment will be carrying a second knife, because of what they were going out to do."

By lamplight Damaz saw the serdar's thin smile. "Then this one knows it. Combat in war is not about balancing weapons, is it?"

"It is not," said Kasim. "In which event, may I show the trainee of the third regiment that I am handing a second blade to this one?"

The voices around them had subsided, now they rose again. Damaz watched the serdar. Kasim was beside him. He didn't reach for the new knife yet.

They heard the serdar's laughter. "Someone ought to cut off your nose, Kasim!" he said, and those gathered—hundreds by now—roared approval. Their serdar had made a jest!

The serdar nodded his head. Damaz took the knife, smaller than the one he already held, and slid it into his belt. Some knew how to fight with a blade in each hand. He didn't.

"My thanks, teacher," he said.

"Don't thank me," said Kasim. "I didn't think it would happen this way."

"What man controls the world as it passes? Didn't you teach us that, from the Trakesians?"

He saw that his teacher was moved. "I shall be sorry if you die," Kasim said.

"I won't die," said Damaz, and stepped forward at the serdar's gesture, a blade in his hand, another in his belt, into the ring of men.

"HOW DID YOU KNOW TO DO THAT?"

Damaz looked at the teacher by wavering lamplight in wind. He didn't answer. He didn't know the answer. Everything was extremely difficult, even more than before, during the fight. Black smoke was blowing from torches. He was afraid he might be sick.

Men were carrying Koçi's body away.

Four of them bore him, two went with torches beside. The crowd was dispersing, most of the djannis continuing loudly out through the gate, as they had been before this distraction occurred.

The night was young, the white moon still to rise, the city waited for them beyond the compound walls. So little time had passed.

The serdar and the two commanders had already left. Damaz's of the fifth had stopped to lay a hand on his shoulder approvingly. It would be noticed, that was the point. It seemed he had brought honour and triumph to their regiment. The commander had never acknowledged Damaz's existence before.

It also seemed he was no longer a trainee. The serdar had proclaimed as much before departing. Damaz was now one of the beloved djannis of Grand Khalif Gurçu, ruling in Asharias by the grace of Ashar and the holy stars.

He had been preparing for this from the time they'd decided he showed promise and chose not to geld him.

They never trained formally with knives. Knives were not a true weapon for the djannis, though they all carried one, for mealtimes, cutting ropes.

But approaching the other boy in a ring of shouting men, beginning to circle each other, a thought had come to Damaz. A thought about the torch smoke now blowing from behind him (not planned, it was only chance that he'd been motioned to one side and had circled to the other), and about the fact that he had two blades now.

And so . . . so he had thrown the first knife he'd been given, the one in his hand, just as a curtain of black smoke blew from behind him, passing between, as he and Koçi drew near to each other.

Everyone played with knives. You threw at tree trunks and hanging fruit. You threw at birds on branches (and rarely hit them). You wagered in games against other boys. The loser cleaned the latrines.

Or died.

They weren't armoured in any way tonight. He'd thrown at Koçi's chest, and had been only a few paces away as they closed with each other, preparing to defend and slash. A big youngster,

Koçi, headed towards being a bigger man. He'd been an easy target. Much easier than a bird in a poplar tree. And the smoke meant
he didn't see Damaz's movement—arm going back and up instead
of forward—until it was too late (forever too late) to do anything
again at all.

Except clutch at his chest, his own weapon dropped, a high,
strange sound escaping his lips. A sound Damaz wondered if he
might now hear for the rest of his own days.

In a way, they had disappointed those gathered. It was over
so abruptly, one swift throw. Damaz had grabbed for his second
knife—Kasim's—and rushed forward, thinking to seize an advantage from wounding the other.

No need. He'd already killed the other.

He'd stood there, suddenly uncertain, lost, over the body of
a boy whose life he had ended between torches and lanterns and
under the blue moon. And abruptly, shockingly, he remembered in
that moment that his name as a small child in the west had been
Neven, and that he'd had a sister whom he'd loved.

CHAPTER VIII

*A*re you awake?

Her grandfather did that sometimes. Danica would hear his voice in her head and wake frightened. She was seldom afraid during the day; the nights could be different, and much had changed now. Since she'd killed Kukar Miho.

I am now, zadek. Was I shouting again?

No. No.

Then what . . . ?

They were still at sea on the *Blessed Ingacia,* would be reaching Dubrava today, the captain had said. More changes when they did that, and it was possible she'd be killed.

But what she'd said earlier remained true: she'd have surely died had she gone home. There were too many in the Miho clan, an angry, vengeful family. Senjan was locked to her. Like a tower, or a sanctuary gate.

It felt as if the night might be over, sunrise soon, but it was hard to tell down below.

She was sharing a cabin with the other woman now, the one whose husband had died by Kukar's sword. She'd tried to decline this, to leave the other one alone, sleep on deck with Tico beside her, but the captain wouldn't let her do that. A woman didn't spend the night in the open. Even a Senjani raider, he'd said.

The other woman had said nothing when Danica first came in to the cabin, nor after. She'd extended a hand to Tico, who had licked her fingers. A woman who knew dogs. She hadn't spoken to anyone since the doctor died three days ago. Had barely come out of the cabin at all.

Zadek, what is it?

Her grandfather made no reply.

Zadek, you woke me, what is it?

She was aware of him, she always was, unless she blocked his presence. He didn't reply. But now she was wide awake, and frightened. She didn't like it.

Zadek . . .

Your brother is alive, he said.

And her heart was pounding so hard.

What? We . . . truly? Zadek, we always thought he might be. They raise the children they capture, we know that!

Dani, I was with him. Last evening. It had *to be him, or . . . how else could I be there?*

I don't understand! Where? Where were you?

He was fighting. I could see it. Not clearly, but I could see.

Zadek, you are scaring me.

I know. I am sorry. But . . . he's alive.

And this fight?

He killed the other man.

Man? Neven is fourteen, zadek!

Other boy, I think. They had knives. I could see *it. There was smoke behind Neven, and they were very close.*

She said, *You made him throw a knife?*

Silence.

Zadek!

I couldn't make him, I can't make you *do anything. I . . . pushed a thought to him.*

And he threw it?

Dani, he did.

Oh, dear Jad. Where? Where is he?

I don't know where we were! Men were watching. If he had weapons I think this means . . .

It means he's a djanni! Or becoming one? And you saved his life!

Maybe. Maybe. Dani, I have no idea if he heard me, or felt me. I can't see him now. It was only for the fighting, then I was . . . gone. I was back here with you.

But you did see . . . ?

I saw him throw, yes. But . . . it was like looking through smoke. And there was real smoke.

But you know it was Neven?

Oh, surely it was. It had to be, girl.

"Oh, dear Jad," she said again, but aloud this time, and opened her eyes. He had been four years old. She had loved him with the unbruised heart she had carried within her then.

He was still lost, but it seemed he wasn't dead.

Her grandfather was dead, and talking to her. The world the god had chosen to make for them was a strange, frightening place. How did you even grasp what was possible, permitted?

Her brother might have killed another boy last night if this was true. She needed it to be true. It meant he was alive, even if it also meant he was in Osmanli lands, worshipping like them, becoming one of the khalif's infantry. The soldiers who came each spring to burn and kill. And sometimes take Jaddite children from the burning homes to become what he was becoming.

Her own worst dreams, always, were of fires.

"Oh, Jad, indeed," the other woman said, from her cot across the cabin. "I agree."

Danica looked over. It was very dark, black, really. Only because her eyesight was good could she make out the other woman's shape, lying there. Tico was scratching at the door now, he'd have heard her voice.

"I'm sorry. I woke you."

"I wasn't asleep."

"They tell me I talk in my sleep."

"You shout. Warnings."

"I know. I dream about raiders sometimes."

The ship rose and fell gently, creaking. It seemed to be a calm morning, if it was morning.

"Aren't you the raiders?"

What? Damn her for ignorant!

No, zadek.

She said aloud, "I grew up in a village that was burned by hadjuks. We fled to Senjan, three of us."

"I don't know what hadjuks are."

It was odd, but Danica was pleased the other woman was speaking, finally. It shouldn't have mattered, but they *had* killed her husband.

"Osmanli brigands. From the mountains, mostly. They come down and attack farms or villages, sometimes a long way west. They take people for ransom, steal livestock. Children are carried away."

"Ransom? How terrible," the other said, and the irony was unmissable.

Damn her!

She didn't reply to him this time. Aloud, she said, "We were starving in Senjan, signora. Winter is always hard, and you blocked the sea channels and forbade even ordinary trade with the islands. It was intended to kill us. Did you know?"

A silence. She went on. "You didn't, did you? Why should you know? Why should a Seressini woman care about children dying in Senjan? Or in some village in the borderlands?"

"I'm not from Seressa."

"So you said. Is that an answer? Or does everyone in Batiara just picture savages in Senjan and their women drinking blood?"

"I didn't know you drank blood."

First, faint hint of something else in her voice. You might call it wryness, even amusement. Danica realized she wanted to call it that.

"Eat severed arms, too."

"Just Osmanli arms, I dare hope." No missing the tone this time.

"Of course. Mylasians, down your coast, taste very bitter, or so I've heard."

"We do?"

Danica hesitated. "I meant what I said before, signora. So did our leader, Bunic. He should not have killed your husband, our man."

"Doesn't help much, knowing that. He's still dead."

"Even if we killed one of our own?"

"You did that—just your own decision."

"No. I did it for Senjan. For all of us."

"Truly?"

"Truly, signora."

"Then why are you here now, alone?"

Danica got up. She went to the door and opened it. Tico bustled in, large, shaggy, tail going fast. He pushed his head into her, then turned politely to greet the other woman, who was sitting up now. There was some light, coming down the near hatchway.

Danica said, "You may have heard us talking about it? Someone needs to explain in Dubrava. Apologize. We don't need to be hated even more. Your husband should not have died."

"But why is it you?"

A hard question, that one.

She said, "They all knew I did the right thing, there would have been bloodshed. The ship's owner was drawing his sword to fight Kukar. Everything would have become bad. That needs to be said in Dubrava."

"But that doesn't answer me. Your leaders know you did the right thing. Very well. But you are here, not going home. Dubrava might hand you over to Seressa. Or hang you themselves. Are you being sacrificed?"

A clever woman. More than expected. Did it even matter? This one would be on the next ship back to Seressa, probably with compensation paid by both cities for the dead husband. They might even be on the same ship, Danica in irons.

She said, "I couldn't go back. The man I killed has a large family. I do not. Doing the right thing doesn't always save you."

THE SENJANI, LEONORA THOUGHT, was more intelligent than expected. It occurred to her that she'd made some too-quick guesses about the other woman. It also occurred to her that if she was to deal with the world unprotected (and she was utterly unprotected), she'd have to be more careful about that.

She extended a hand to the dog again and had her fingers licked. She'd grown up with hunting dogs. This wasn't the largest she'd seen—her father had prided himself on his pack—but it was big. She had little doubt it would rip someone's throat out defending the Senjani woman. That assumption she felt safe making.

Her father had prided himself on his daughter in much the same way as his dogs, the thought came to her. Not a grief. Not any more. She was past that sorrow. There were newer ones.

Someone was shouting up above, then they heard cheering. In the muted light the two women looked at each other.

"That will be land sighted," the Senjani said. "We've crossed. They will pray on deck now, having survived the sea."

"Some survived," Leonora said, then regretted it. She didn't like that tone in her voice.

The other woman only shrugged. "Do you want to go up? Pray with them?"

She didn't, but she was tired of being in this close darkness. It would be morning above. She looked at the woman across from her. She said, "I have been unfair to you, I think. What happened to Jacopo wasn't your fault, and you did act, after."

"I acted for all of us."

"Yes, yes," Leonora said, feeling impatient. "So you said. But no one else did, did they?"

The Senjani woman smiled a little. "I had the bow."

Leonora found herself smiling back. "I suppose that's true. May I know your name?"

"I am Danica Gradek. I don't think you'll know me long."

"I have no idea. I'm Leonora Miucci. I *am* from Mylasia, not Seressa."

"I believed you. Why would you have lied?"

Later, she would try to understand what that simple question had done to her, why she said what she said. There was no easy answer. This was a young woman, as she was, among strangers and far from home, that was part of it. We don't, Leonora would eventually decide, always do what we do for obvious reasons—or a life might be very different from what it became.

"I didn't lie about that," she said. "But I've been lying since we came on board."

The other woman just looked at her, waiting. The dog turned from one to the other, tail still wagging, but uncertainly now. Something in the changed feeling.

"I am not . . . I was sent . . ."

Danica Gradek said calmly, "You were sent to spy for Seressa."

Leonora stared at her. "It is so obvious?"

"They do that. There was a spy in Senjan. There will be another soon enough. There will be Seressini-paid observers on the dock waiting for us in Dubrava. You are likely meant to report to them."

"No. Yes, I mean. But . . ."

Leonora stood up. She took a breath. She said, "I was never married to him. To Miucci. There are reasons why I agreed. But I will not, I *cannot* go back to Seressa. I am alone."

Danica Gradek was a tall woman. With the dog beside her it made for a crowded chamber. She smiled at Leonora, then she laughed.

"Alone? That's two of us, then. Shall we see what we can do?"

DRAGO OSTAJA WASN'T HAPPY with *any* of what had happened on his ship from the time they'd left Seressa and headed for home.

He hated pirates with a fierce intensity. Those raiders had been on his deck, down in his holds, taking goods entrusted to him. And he couldn't stop it.

It had happened to ships he'd captained before, and the sense of helplessness had left him feeling unmanned for a long time after. But they simply could not battle raiders, nor avoid them all the time.

Senjan existed as a kind of additional tax on trading ships, Marin had once said. They liked to call themselves the heroes of the border, Drago knew. He refused to allow them that in his own mind. And then one of them had killed a passenger on Drago's ship. He'd seen Marin draw his sword, start across the deck, and Drago had known he'd have to unsheath his own, and that they were likely to die on the *Blessed Ingacia*.

The woman had averted all of that with an arrow. She wasn't going to survive that in Senjan, Drago remembered thinking, even in the moment.

Then the other woman, the one Marin told him was a spy, had moved across the deck to the ship's rail, and Drago, turning too late, *knew* she was going into the sea, and he'd cried out and then . . . she didn't.

Something had happened there, by the railing.

The memory of it left him unhappy and afraid, days after. He kept thinking of his mother, and the wisewoman in the village where he'd been raised, and how no one could honestly say he understood all (or even most) of what happened in the world.

Leonora Miucci had not stopped at that railing entirely by her own choice, Drago believed. She had been going into the sea. He couldn't say why he was so sure, couldn't speak of it to Marin or any mariner or cleric he knew. He could have told his mother, but she'd been gone for years. He still missed her.

And now, to add to the cup of his distress, the women came up on deck, just as the ship approached the coast—and pretty much every mariner alive believed two women on a ship's deck could bring bad luck.

It had happened before, hadn't it? When the doctor and the raider died? Both women had been on deck.

Drago was prepared to treat this as a baseless superstition, but mariners were *always* superstitious. There was too much to fear on the water, and he didn't want his seamen frightened as they approached land, which had its perils.

He was bringing them in running south and carefully, even on a mild morning. So many ships wrecked right outside their home ports, too anxious to get back, careless of the sea as they left it behind.

There were rocks around Dubrava, both sides of the isles that sheltered the harbour. And even a sunny morning like this one could find and summon a wind in no time at all. He had seen it happen, had been part of desperate efforts to save cargo and drowning men. Had attended rites after amid the sound of weeping for those they hadn't taken ashore, or had brought home dead from the sea.

The women emerged from the forward hatchway just as prayers ended. The first time for Signora Miucci since the raid. She was elegant, composed. The other one was . . . a raider from Senjan, a bow and quiver and a dog at her side.

Drago liked the look of the dog, that was as far as he'd go in that.

The women were coming over to him. He cleared his throat, turned to await them, spreading his legs as if to ready himself for something. For whatever this was. He clasped his hands behind his back in what he hoped was a dignified pose.

"Gosparko," he said to the doctor's wife. He bowed. Had to unclasp his hands to do that, then he put them behind him again. He offered a nod to the other one, which was enough for what she was.

They were both young, both yellow-haired, otherwise nothing linked these two, by appearance or background, he thought. The Senjani was tall, moved lightly on her feet. Knew how to kill. The other one, the widow, was . . . well, Drago didn't use the word *delicate* often, but it seemed to fit. She was well-born, Marin had declared the first time they saw her. He was remembering her at the railing, her husband's blood soaking the lower part of her robe.

"Captain," said the Senjani, "I just realized something. I'm truly sorry. I'll go below. You don't need two women on deck making your men nervous before landfall."

Drago blinked. How did she know to say that? He saw Marin coming over. He glanced up at his sails. There was nothing there, at least, to stir alarm.

He said, dismissively, "That old tale? Do you pirates believe that in Senjan?"

She smiled a little. "No, but I know mariners do elsewhere. I wouldn't want to cause distress."

"I think," said Marin, coming up, "that you prevented more than distress. You are both welcome to watch us approach Dubrava. It is a beautiful harbour, if I am allowed to say so."

The Senjani woman smiled briefly. She was very young, Drago was thinking. And likely to never see her home again. Well, he himself had been younger, fleeing the Osmanlis here, and he would never see *his* village again, either. The world owed you nothing, Drago Ostaja believed.

"With the captain's permission," Danica Gradek said, "I'll go aloft then, and not down below. I can watch for weather west of us, if you like."

He'd been about to send a man up, of course.

"You know how to handle yourself above?" he asked.

She wasn't a member of his crew. She was a passenger on his ship, soon to appear before the Rector's Council. He was responsible for her.

She didn't answer. She unslung her bow and quiver, placed them out of anyone's way, behind ropes. She spoke to her dog. The animal lay down by the ropes. The woman walked to the mainmast and began to climb. They lived on boats in Senjan, of course, but none nearly this big, Drago knew, none with a mast and sails this high. It didn't seem to matter. She went up the mast, not the rigging; she'd have noticed the spikes, then, earlier.

He saw the artist emerge from below. That one, at least, was no trouble. Villani nodded politely, bowed from a distance to the doctor's widow, and made his way to the stern, to piss over the rail back there.

He'd done it into the wind and spray the first afternoon, trying to be modest, his back to the crew, occasioning mirth as he returned along the deck after, red-faced, clothing stained with his own piss. (It was common enough, they really should warn passengers but they never did.) Drago had no experience with artists, but he did understand the need for them, had admired some work in sanctuaries, and this one had no airs or pretensions to him. He would be carrying on east, apparently, all the way to Asharias, to paint the grand khalif. Better a man put a knife in Gurçu, Drago thought. In memory of Sarantium.

He looked at Marin. He was watching the girl climb, against the pale-blue morning sky. Drago looked around. The crew were gazing up at her as well. It could have been amusing, but it wasn't.

"Eyes on tasks, damn you!" he roared, captain of the *Blessed Ingacia*, bringing her safe home.

"I don't have a task," the other woman said softly at his side. She glanced at Drago, and then at Marin. "You will have to give me one, I'm afraid."

Marin smiled, Drago didn't. Two women on a ship's deck, he was thinking. And also about how many different forms trouble could take.

SHE HAD NEVER CLIMBED anything like this, the mast swaying as the ship did, and more, of course, as you went higher, gripping and stepping on spikes in the pine wood. But it wasn't difficult if heights didn't bother you, and they didn't.

It was wonderful up here, Danica thought, standing on the small platform near the top. You were still in the world, could see it spread below you, but from enough distance that no one could do anything to you for a little while.

Those on the deck looked small as a child's toys. She saw Tico lying patiently beside her bow and quiver. Voices drifted up. The Seressini artist (a slight, good-looking, gentle-seeming man) proceeded to the stern to piss at the rail, but she was too high to see anything interesting.

The captain and the owner (an even more handsome man, in truth) were still with Leonora Miucci. But she wasn't Leonora Miucci, she had just told Danica. Her name was Valeri, and her marriage had been a contrivance, leaving her no real choice but to take the next ship to Seressa, or have that unmasked.

"I won't go back," she'd said, before they'd gone up on deck. "I'll go into the sea first."

"Why didn't you, before?"

She hadn't known she was going to ask that until she did.

"I don't know," Leonora Valeri had said. "I intended to."

Danica had expected her grandfather to speak to her then, but he'd kept silent. She hadn't heard him since he'd woken her with the news about Neven.

Her brother was alive, and in the Osmanli army, among the djannis. And he had killed someone last night.

It was interesting: that she didn't doubt this for a moment. How could you doubt these things, when a man dead almost a year now was telling them to you?

Are you there? she asked, far above the deck.

I am. What do you need?

Just for you to be here, she said.

Look, Dani, he said. *Dubrava.*

She was facing the east but she'd been thinking hard, not seeing, until he spoke. Now she did look, and so saw that harbour and city for the first time, distant yet, but visible from where she was, as they came around a big, fortified island that sheltered it, the way Hrak sheltered Senjan.

But the city of Dubrava wasn't the town of Senjan.

Red roofs, sunlit, climbing steeply to north and south from the harbour, where a commanding structure stood beyond the moored boats. There was a large sanctuary north of it, twin domes. A wide street went east from the harbour. The city walls were massive, running all the way around. There was a guard walk along the top, curved towers at intervals, with cannons, and turrets for guns or arrows.

She knew Seressa was far bigger than this city, and Obravic, where the emperor reigned, and Rhodias. So many cities were bigger than this. She knew Asharias, which had been Sarantium, was even larger than these, had been called the City of Cities, glory of the world.

There was a line of islands, spring green vineyards, stone towers, stone fences, and nearest to the city a very small islet, almost in the harbour's mouth, a religious retreat visible from here. Then she was looking at the city again, and out of youthful pride (and she knew it was that) Danica tried not to be daunted, and failed.

Dubrava, approached from the sea on a springtime morning,

the sun rising behind it, was a glory. She shivered, felt a sudden strangeness. She might never go home, Danica thought, it was true, but there was a world out here to be found.

She realized something else. Belatedly, she cried, "There it is! City walls!" She was the one up top, the alert was hers to cry.

Responding cries below, the joyous sound of mariners after crossing open sea and coming home. Danica turned to look back west. That was why someone was always posted up here, to watch for changing weather from seaward as a ship approached land.

Blue sky, mild breeze. You could forgive yourself for feeling happy for a moment.

Did you ever see it, zadek?

Dubrava? No.

Look at the roofs in the sun.

I see them. Dani. The people living under those roofs will want you dead.

Not all. Surely not all of them?

Perhaps, he said.

HE IS BESIDE THE MAST as she descends. She is easy doing so. Mannish trousers and tunic, salt-stained boots to the knee, bright hair under a wide hat. They are past the nearest islands—Gjadina, Sinan—are in the harbour's mouth, their glorious harbour under the towers with their cannons. He can see a crowd on the quayside. There is always a crowd when a ship comes home, even if only from across the narrow sea. People are waving.

The sea is an interlude, Marin Djivo thinks, a space between life and life. The Senjani girl steps down to the deck beside him. She is flushed for some reason, he notes.

He says, "We should have a word."

She looks at him warily. Her dog comes over. A big dog. Nuzzles his head against her thigh. She rubs its ears absently.

"I'm better listening," she says with another of those brief smiles. "I would prefer to not be killed. Will I be?"

They can hear voices calling across the water now and their mariners are shouting back. Dubrava will begin to know that the *Blessed Ingacia* has been boarded by pirates, goods were taken, and the doctor they were bringing is dead. And they'll learn that one of the raiders is on the ship, delivered to them.

"I have a thought about that," Marin says.

DON'T TRUST HIM *just because he's a pretty man,* her grandfather said, as she made her way down to where Marin Djivo was waiting.

Danica felt herself blushing. She refused to reply. She thought of closing off her grandfather, as a punishment, but she needed him just now. Tico came over, wagging his tail as if he were some courtesan's pet dog, not a fierce and fearless hunter.

The shipowner nodded as she stepped down, his expression grave, which made her uneasy.

"We should have a word," he said.

Danica felt herself grimace. She said, "I'm better listening. I'd prefer not to be killed. Will I be?"

He looked at her as she patted Tico. A very tall man, quick on his feet. Her grandfather had said, before she'd put an arrow in Kukar Miho, that this one might kill a Senjani in a fair fight. Kukar didn't do fair fights, mind you. Or he hadn't done.

Djivo said, "I have a proposal about that."

She stared, trying to read his face. It was difficult. She didn't know these people, their world.

Careful! her zadek said.

I have to trust someone.

So she said, "Yes, I will accept employment as a guard to the Djivo family. Can you really protect me that way?"

She smiled, seeing his eyes widen. Enjoyed it a moment, then added, "It seemed obvious, gospodar. There is no other role I could readily take in any proposal you might make. I am . . . trusting your goodwill."

She was pleased to see him laugh. "Well," he said, "given that much quickness, we could use you as a business adviser."

"I doubt it," Danica said.

"Don't doubt till you meet my brother," he said. Then, "But the goodwill is real, Danica Gradek. You saved lives."

"Well, one life I ended. Which is why—"

"Why you aren't going home. You will be sheltered to a degree as one of our retainers. Drago will tell the same story I will."

"What do I do as a guard for the Djivo family?"

He grinned. He really was good-looking, she thought.

"Stay close to me," he said.

She couldn't think of a reply. Then she did remember something.

"What happens to the signora? The doctor's widow?"

He looked puzzled. "I imagine she'll be anxious to go home. The council will arrange it. I suspect they will authorize a payment, recompense. Her husband died coming to serve us."

"You are," Danica said, composure regained, "imagining and suspecting a great deal, aren't you?"

He said, "Is there something I need to know?"

He was, she reminded herself, a clever man. She felt uneasy again under his scrutiny. He was someone who lived in this world: balancing and withholding information. Hints, clues, guile. Senjan didn't prepare you for that. Senjan trained men (and one woman) to use a bow and sword and knives. To handle small boats at sea and perhaps, one day, to go through the mountain passes in search of Asharites, maybe even hadjuk raiders—and begin a long-desired vengeance.

She expected her grandfather to urge caution again, but he was silent. She said, "It isn't mine to tell."

"That she's a spy?"

That surprised her, but not as much as he might have expected. Danica shrugged. "All Seressinis are spies, no?"

"Perhaps. But not—if I am correct—with someone to report to and access to powerful people. She'd have had that access as the doctor's wife."

"She doesn't have it now."

"I was going to invite her to stay in our home."

Danica blinked. "I see," she said.

"My father and brother both sit on the Rector's Council. Powerful enough to help her. I'm the younger son, everyone ignores me."

She doubted that. She said, "Is it any kind of concern, if she is in your home?"

"And spies? It is all right." He grinned. "Even if she reports on the furnishings, I am not unhappy to have Leonora Miucci under my roof."

"I'm sure," she said.

He let his smile fade. "But what is it I need to know? You haven't said."

You needed to trust someone.

"She will refuse to go back to Seressa."

She'd startled him this time, it showed. "What? Why?"

"I don't know."

He smiled again, more gently. "You aren't a good liar."

"Maybe not. Makes me trustworthy, doesn't it?"

He shook his head. "Not if secrets are confided. I may need you to be able to lie."

"I can learn," said Danica. "But this isn't my story to tell. That's another kind of trust."

She saw him look to where the other woman stood watching Dubrava come nearer in the light.

"You think she was going to jump, before?"

That was unexpected. Danica said, "I do."

"But not now?"

"Not just now, no."

"And you won't tell me more?"

Danica shook her head. "She does need help, though."

"And you would help someone from Seressa?"

"She's not. You heard her."

"Yes," he said. "They aren't all born there."

Danica shrugged again. "I am only asking. I can't make you do anything."

But she wanted him to, she realized. She had more than her own life to try to secure here. She might even have a friend. Lacking family, exiled, that was next best, wasn't it? And you didn't reveal what a friend had confided: that she'd never been married to the man she'd been coming here with.

In the event, before the *Blessed Ingacia* berthed, amid gulls wheeling and questions back and forth, before the ramps slid out and down to the wharf, Marin Djivo had invited the lady Leonora Miucci to stay, during her time in Dubrava, at his family home, as a small, admittedly inadequate gesture of courtesy and regret for the loss of her beloved husband.

She was graciously pleased to accept.

CHAPTER IX

It was hardly necessary to explain to anyone how tidings came so swiftly to her at the Daughters of Jad retreat on Sinan Isle in the harbour of Dubrava.

The retreat was celebrated, hundreds of years old. There were mosaics in its sanctuary that attracted visitors (who made donations, of course). The degree of luxury here was her own achievement, however, since becoming Eldest Daughter.

She had spent a long time nurturing power and connections, lines of awareness reaching in many directions from the isle. And one of the things power meant was not having to explain what she chose not to explain.

Seressa valued that in her, and rewarded her for it, generously. Her name was Filipa di Lucaro. Or, rather, that was the name she used.

She had been here almost two decades, but knew from the eyes of men seeing her that she remained arresting and attractive. They also looked afraid, quite often. Another matter, and entirely good. She still had the appetites of the young, enough to be selective concerning the attributes of those men employed, variously, on the isle.

One of the gardeners, her current favourite, was a mute—his tongue had been cut out by corsairs after he was taken on a ship they raided. That enforced silence was among the reasons he was favoured, of course. He'd escaped an Asharite galley, she didn't know how, and she didn't actually care, in any case. He was a lover of considerable stamina and pleasing proportion. She occasionally wished he still had his tongue, but one couldn't have everything one desired (alas!). He had also been of use in other ways, when people needed to be discreetly killed, for instance, which did sometimes happen in this sad and challenging world.

Her own history no one here knew. She was thought to be from near Rhodias, born into a family stretching back centuries, which was what she wanted thought. Her value to Seressa would be lessened if it were known where she'd actually been born and what she'd risen from to be what she was.

She was Eldest Daughter on Sinan, the religious leader here. She was also called, by some of the women, the Snake Goddess. She wasn't supposed to know that but she did, of course. She didn't mind the name. Eliciting apprehension was useful in so many ways.

When the Djivo family's *Blessed Ingacia* appeared on a morning in spring, coming in past the isle, she saw it herself from her terrace.

She was out there in morning light after prayers, sitting with their venerable and honoured long-time guest. That guest, as it happened, was the one person she herself feared, but she believed she'd been successful in not letting it be seen by the older woman.

She was wrong about that, in fact. Her guest had her own subtlety and had nurtured it for longer and in more challenging circumstances.

She had inquiries made about the *Blessed Ingacia* in the city later that morning, and so they were, on Sinan, among the first to learn that an artist from Seressa had arrived, and a doctor's wife— but not the doctor, who was dead.

It was also reported by one of the Eldest Daughter's sources that there was a Senjani raider, a woman, on board the ship for some reason. She was rumoured to be the one who had killed Seressinis earlier this spring at Senjan.

This was interesting, all of it, and required thought. Filipa di Lucaro was a quick thinker, and not at all indecisive.

Invitations were conveyed.

She was surprised when the Senjani woman arrived three days later with the others, but sometimes the god was generous to those who served him in his holy places.

ೞ

Marin knows it can take weeks or even months to be received at the courts of Asharias or Obravic. Rhodias and Seressa are more expeditious in granting audiences, because the High Patriarch in the one feels beleaguered and the Council of Twelve in the other is aware that delay can cost money. He is less certain about other courts and cities. Would like to see them. His dreams sometimes involve being in places where he isn't known.

His own republic feels both beleaguered *and* conscious of commerce and speed and their relationship. He is unsurprised therefore when Danica Gradek is summoned to her audience before the Rector's Council (the full council, both his father and his brother will be sitting) only two days after the *Blessed Ingacia* comes into harbour.

The Senjani are an ongoing source of debate here, invariably angry. It is one thing for Dubrava to have shrewd ways to insure ships and cargoes, dividing risks. It is another to have a doctor they'd just hired be murdered on one of those ships.

Surviving by guile and craft (and bribery and a self-abasing diplomacy in all directions), Dubrava resents and sometimes hates

Seressa, the vastly grander republic in this world of monarchs and emperors and princes and a khalif—but they cannot afford to truly offend.

Seressa is their principal market. It is as simple as that. A truth that carries defining implications for a small city-state depending on trade and the sea. They do well here. But they can be destroyed at any moment if the balancing of the world (the balancing they try to shape in the world) changes.

On the other hand, the Senjani in their town to the north along this island-strewn coastline enjoy the protection and sometimes the praise of the Emperor Rodolfo, and Dubrava also sends bribes and gifts to that court. Not, accordingly, a place to cause offence, either.

There is, as a result, delicacy attached to this matter of the Senjani woman who has arrived here by her own choice, and has requested to be received by the Rector's Council.

It is entirely possible to have her hanged by their executioner, or handed over to Seressa. The Seressinis may have a particular grievance against this woman. She is alleged to have killed a number of them this spring, and the fact that she's a woman adds humiliation to anger.

Humiliation of Seressa isn't something Dubrava will regret, but the world is as it is, and that is not a view that can be voiced in public.

Marin Djivo would prefer to find all of this amusing, to regard it with cultivated detachment. He finds himself, escorting Danica Gradek to the palace, unable to achieve this state of mind.

Formally, she is escorting him. She wears Djivo crimson and blue, a paid guard of the family—his idea for keeping her alive long enough to get her to the council. Because where public execution might be compromised by politics, a quiet bit of murder has often been a solution, for some. Being one of the Djivo retainers is a measure of protection against that.

Danica carries her bow and arrows, as his guard. She'll need to surrender those at the palace. Marin realizes he's forgotten to warn her about that. This isn't someone who will have any experience of palaces.

With them are Drago Ostaja, their captain, to give his account if needed, and also the injured woman in this affair: the family's guest, the distracting Leonora Miucci.

She no longer seems disposed to end her life, at least. She has been quiet, and impeccably courteous, since they docked. She has made it clear to the Djivos (to go no further, as yet) that she will decline to return to Seressa which is what she *should* be doing—or what they should be doing with her. She also declines to explain. She is, therefore, another woman posing a diplomatic problem. And both are in the Djivo house. His mother is unenthused. The Rector's Council is likely to feel the same.

His father, normally not in the least distractible, seems to be smitten by the doctor's widow. Chastely and respectably, of course. His father and brother never do anything that is not respectable. The senior Djivo is genuinely pious; the older son is genuinely too frightened to transgress in any significant manner.

Marin often imagines himself living far away.

There are many people in the Straden as they make their way from the Djivo mansion towards the Rector's Palace by the harbour. Their progression is an entertainment, Marin knows.

It is a bright morning, the best of springtime weather. Summer in Dubrava is hot. People withdraw if they can from the city to the countryside along the coast, or the islands. They visit each other, drink wine cooled in cellars, awaiting the autumn harvest and cooler weather. Marin usually tries to be on board one of their ships going somewhere, anywhere.

Those they walk past stare with frank curiosity at the women— the raider with her bow rather more than the Seressini widow.

Their expressions are not welcoming. Leonora Miucci will not be unusual here, though younger women will be eyeing the cut of her black gown and considering changes to their own. Seressa shapes fashion in Dubrava even more than the courts do.

But the Senjani woman, with her long stride and straight posture, this one is worth staring at. She has killed at least one man, possibly many. She has also refused to change her raider's garb, wears it under the crimson and blue overtunic, though she has allowed the household servants to clean it for her, and has been extremely happy to bathe, twice already. Her hair is pinned up, and covered by a leather hat. Her dog is with her. Marin has come to understand that he always is.

The dog and the woman, he notes, are both alert as they walk. It would not be unheard of for someone to kill an enemy in the street, and Seressa might have made plans for her already. They know there are Seressini agents here, they have guesses as to some of them, but Marin's father has often noted that if they knew all the spies Seressa would be less than it was thought to be.

And it isn't, he always adds.

The Matko women are just ahead, he sees. They are on the street, enduring the sunlight for a better view of them. He looks at Kata, pretty and bright, and wonders, perhaps unfairly, if she is going to hurry off to order a dress made in the style worn by the Seressini woman while she still has the details in mind.

As they pass he nods politely at the three of them, mother and two daughters. He realizes that Kata's eyes are on him, not Leonora Miucci or the Senjani, and her expression is unexpectedly concerned.

Women in Dubrava tend not to do unexpected things, in his experience—once you accepted that some enjoy the company of men in their bedchambers. That this was not, in fact, to be seen as unexpected.

An intense gaze on a morning street is, however. It is likely that she and her mother have him marked as marriage material, and seeing him walking beside a young, suddenly widowed Seressini woman of undeniable appeal has unsettled her.

He is too much on edge this morning (though he doesn't like admitting that, even to himself) to be as amused as he might normally be. He has no idea what will happen before the council. It is entirely possible that Danica Gradek will be ordered executed. She raided a Dubravae ship, the raiders took goods and a ransom and killed a doctor coming here. You died for such things, or went to the galleys. They wouldn't send a woman to the galleys, they were not barbarians, but they could hang her and no one could ever say it was unjust or even harsh, despite the small redress she had made in killing one of her own.

He's been trying to sort out his own speech for this morning. He isn't uncomfortable speaking in public, but he's aware that these words may have a life suspended at the end of them, as on a rope. He also has no idea what Danica Gradek will say, he doesn't have any understanding of this woman.

Just then, to add to his joy this morning, she stops in the street. She looks back. At the Matko women.

They all come to a halt.

"What are you doing?" Drago mutters to her. "We're exposed here. You're a guard, remember?"

"I remember," she says. She is still looking back. Then she says, "Stay with Gospodar Djivo, keep your eyes open. Signora Miucci, will you be good enough to walk with me?"

And Leonora does so, unhesitatingly—leaving the men alone in the street.

"Did she just give me an order?" Drago says. His voice—and expression—would be amusing on any other day.

"I believe she did," Marin says. "Go ahead. Guard me. Wits about you, Captain."

He is watching the women as they go back the way they've just come. He sees them stop in front of the Matkos, mother and daughters.

He doesn't understand what this is about, at all. That rarely happens to him.

WHAT ARE YOU DOING?

Hush, please, zadek. Listen. Help me, but hush.

She didn't know cities, crowds like this at all, it was taking some effort not to let apprehension show. But *something* in the look of one of the three they'd just passed—a mother and daughters, she assumed—had sounded a warning for her.

As they walked back, she said to Leonora, "The younger one, we need her alone for a moment. Can you?"

"Easily," said her new friend. Her only friend.

Leonora smiled charmingly at the three women they approached. She stopped in front of the younger one, who was pretty and soft and had very good eyes. Leonora let her gaze go up and down the girl's dress. Danica had no thoughts regarding the dress. None at all.

Leonora said, "Might I trouble you for a private word, gosparko? I need guidance, and your lovely gown suggests you may be able to help me."

"Of course!" said the girl. She glanced at her mother, but not for permission. "Come this way, the arcade is quieter."

They went that way. The arcade was, indeed, quieter.

"How may I help, signora? And may I say how sorry we all are for your loss? Those terrible Senjani!" She looked at Danica for the first time, but it wasn't a look that said *terrible*.

"Might I know your name?" Danica said. They were alone. Someone would have to work very hard to overhear. "I'm Danica Gradek. They may decide to kill me this morning."

The woman looked at her.

What are you doing?

Zadek, what you know about women is nothing piled on nothing. Hush!

"I'm Kata Matko. I know they might kill you. But I also believe . . ."

The expression on her face spoke for her.

"It isn't just about that vote, is it—hanging me or handing me over. There's something you know?"

The girl was brave. Even a rich man's daughter in Dubrava could be brave, it seemed. She met Danica's gaze. They were about the same age, the three of them.

Kata Matko said, "Not just you, maybe." She lowered her voice, the other two women had to strain to hear.

What? What is she—?

Danica nodded. It was important, always, that others not see she was disturbed. She said, calmly, "Someone might appear to be attacking me and intend someone else?"

The girl's dark eyes widened. "How did you . . . ?"

"I've had a certain kind of life," Danica said, but kept her voice gentle. She looked at the other woman. "Gospodar Djivo? Marin? You don't want him dead?"

Beside her Leonora made a startled sound, and her grandfather made a similar noise in her head. People, men and women, could be wildly different and much the same, it occurred to Danica. They could be alive and dead and much the same, she thought.

"No, I don't," said Kata Matko, colouring. "He doesn't deserve to be. Not for this."

"Someone is unhappy with him? And you know of it, more than the men do?"

"Yes. A few of us do."

"This is to do with a girl? Her family?"

That was a gamble, a guess. Perhaps too much so.

"I didn't say it to you," the other woman said firmly. "And it isn't me or my family."

"You didn't," Danica agreed quickly. The woman hadn't denied the thought, though. Had confirmed it, really. "You have been generous. I lack the skills to put it better but I thank you."

"What are we to have been talking about?" Kata said, looking at Leonora. "My mother will ask. I can deceive her but . . ."

"But you need a direction." Leonora smiled briefly, she'd regained her own composure quickly. "I admired the cut of your dress. I need mourning clothes made. I wish to have them made well."

Kata Matko nodded. "Tamara, in Sule Street. First one north of here, halfway along. She is a Kindath, but is very good if you don't object to them. She makes all my clothes and has many fabrics. Tell her I sent you. Or . . ." She hesitated. "Would you like me to go with you?"

Leonora smiled again. "That would be lovely. It does depend on what happens this morning."

"Yes," said Kata Matko. She turned to Danica. Her colour was still high. "I would be happy if you were able to come with us."

"A Senjani raider?"

"Yes."

"For a dress?" Danica smiled, but her thought was, again, *This one has courage.*

Kata Matko smiled back. "Well, as our guard, then, if you don't want to look as pretty as you are."

She wasn't going to address that here.

They made their way back to the mother and the older sister, whose curiosity was amusingly avid, as was that of others nearby. One woman's mouth was actually hanging open. *Catching dragon-flies,* her mother used to call that.

Kata and Leonora sank down impeccably to each other. Danica bowed. To the mother as well, on impulse. She was thinking hard.

That was well done, her grandfather said gruffly.

A start. What do you think they'll do?

We'll need to see the council chamber. They won't let you keep your bow.

I can try.

AS MARIN HAD EXPECTED, they will not let Danica Gradek in with weapons. She is a Senjani, an enemy of the republic, whatever her reasons for being here.

As they approached the palace, she'd been crisp, speaking to him and Drago.

"If I can't keep my bow and quiver, I need them near me. I think there might be trouble."

"Of course there is trouble," Drago muttered. "Why else are we here?"

"No. Listen to me. Captain, please offer to keep my bow for the guards, then stay close to me, and . . . also near Gospodar Djivo. This may not be about me."

Which had been unexpected. There was no time for more. There are people all around them, entering the chamber; privacy is gone.

Marin needs to concentrate on what he is going to say. He sees his father and brother already inside. His father is never late for council.

"I am a guard for the Djivo family," Danica says to the man at the doors. They are proud of the new bronze doors to the Rector's Palace. Images in relief of the lives of Blessed Victims, done by an artist from Rhodias, paid extremely well.

"There are guards inside," the one at the entrance says. He's a senior man, in the rector's dark-green livery. He speaks courteously but he isn't about to be moved in this. The guard looks at Drago.

Who says, easily, "She's here of her own accord, Jevic."

"Perhaps also for her own reasons," the guard says, still politely. "No weapons. That includes the dog."

Danica Gradek nods. She speaks to her dog, a hand on his head.

The dog goes obediently to the shade near the entrance. He is impressively disciplined and formidably large. A weapon, any way you want to define those.

Drago turns to Danica. "Gosparko, this guard does have his duties, and only those approved may bear weapons, even ceremonial ones, here. I undertake to hold yours for you. You'll get them back."

"If they let me out without ordering me hanged," the woman says. She hands her bow and quiver to Marin's captain. The guard hesitates a moment, then nods to Drago.

"Knife?" the guard named Jevic says. He is performing a task. There is no malice here.

Danica removes hers from her belt. Hands it to Drago as well. She smiles briefly at the guard. "I have another in my boot." She bends down and pulls this one out, thin blade, thin hilt. Drago takes this, too.

"Always prepared, you Senjani," Jevic says. He seems close to smiling back.

"Not much choice," Danica replies.

Marin sees respect in the man's eyes. It surprises him. Jevic steps aside. They go in. The dog watches from the shade outside.

THERE ARE SIXTY-FIVE MEMBERS of the Rector's Council as of this morning. There should be sixty-six but one has recently died and not yet been replaced. It isn't a trivial process, replacing a councillor. There have been skirmishes, feuds, even deaths in the past.

There are other councils and committees governing Dubrava, smaller groups for day-to-day decisions. There are many decisions in a city-state with wide and varying needs, from quarantining some visitors against arrival of the plague, to dealing with information—or demands—from Asharias, to the need to arrange the remarriage of a wealthy widow, deploying her assets strategically within the circle of noble families.

There are night patrols against theft and disorder, monitoring of water quality in the fountains, defending their salt flats to the south. All have committees. The city governs several of the islands north of them (against Seressini pressure, always) and there is frequent unrest among the islanders at having to pay a land tax. There are those charged with controlling this unrest.

Public baths need construction and maintenance, as do, more importantly, the city walls and towers. Gifts and communications to various powers of the world must be carefully judged. Information is gathered and assessed and deciding where they share what they learn is an intricate challenge.

Medical needs are responded to, whether acquiring doctors (a renewed problem this morning), dealing with unwed mothers, or caring for the indigent. The sanctuaries of the god are to be preserved and, whenever possible, improved, to the greater glory of Jad and Dubrava.

Marriage among the noble classes is not a private matter. There is a committee controlling how large a dowry may be offered with a daughter. Competitiveness is an element in this. The republic allows wealth to be displayed, but excess is disruptive.

They frown in Dubrava upon that which disrupts.

They trade and survive in a world disinclined to allow them to trade and survive as an independent republic, and so extreme attention to many matters is always to be paid. They know their past and observe the present closely. A small city-state, among lions and the threat (or reality) of war, cannot do otherwise.

They pride themselves on being more observant of shifts in the winds of the world than others are. A younger son in Ferrieres named heir of valuable lands instead of his brother? That can ripple a long way. The daughter of the king of Esperaña rumoured to have inherited the Kohlberg dynasty's mental infirmity? Some will be glad to learn of this from Dubrava. A new cavalry serdar at the Osmanli garrison in Mulkar? Might have implications here, since their overland trade route to Asharias runs near there. Someone will be assigned to discover the new man's tastes in gifts. Everything matters.

Even Seressa with all its spies does not observe so obsessively, because Seressa is one of the lions. It has the power and scope to survive a serious mistake. The Dubravae believe that they might not.

The Rector's Palace has been rebuilt twice after fires. Fire is a matter for which there is a committee. It is the greatest fear, along with plague. A careless blacksmith or cook can destroy a city.

The current palace is new, a source of pride. High-ceilinged, with worked bronze bands around the perimeter inside and a ceiling fresco by another Batiaran master. There are sixteen red marble pillars, cedarwood benches for the councillors, and an upper-level gallery for visitors, from which some of the rector's guards observe proceedings below. The new windows are tall, handsome, with expensively tinted glass. The chamber on a morning in spring is airy and bright.

The rector sits in a handsome chair but not a throne. This is a republic—not always, but for two hundred years now, since the Seressinis and then the emperor in Obravic ceded control. Their rectors change every two years, rotating among the council members who are all, of course, from the nobility. They are expected to marry only each other. It is difficult for even the most successful merchants to enter this class.

These merchants are placated by being allowed to wear furs and expensive jewellery and to have handsome works of art in their homes. On occasion they are allowed elevation to the nobility. (It costs, of course.) There is, after all, a risk of excessive intermarriage, which their clerics frown upon. New blood is useful, in moderation.

The clerics also need appeasing, always.

This morning, two decisions face the council in the form of two women now entering the chamber—causing a predictable stir, since women are almost never here. One is comely and sympathetic, it is agreed; the other is Senjani. They represent very different dilemmas, though they are linked to a single incident on the Djivo family's *Blessed Ingacia*.

The charming one in black needs to be sent back to Seressa, and her family will be contacted with regard to assuming a portion of a ransom paid for her to Senjani pirates. Either that, or the republic itself will need to compensate the Djivos, whose clever younger son seems to have avoided a diplomatic incident by paying the raiders directly, keeping the woman on his ship.

In addition, this widow of a doctor they'd hired and who has died in their care likely has to be personally compensated. The clerics will urge this, and, frankly, the Seressinis will need to know it has been done. There will be little debate about this. The sum is another matter.

For merchants, it is always about the sum.

Unfortunately, it seems the widow of Doctor Miucci has made it clear, through one of their own number (the senior Djivo, Andrij, sitting in the front row with his older son) that her family will *not* reimburse any of the ransom paid for her. She has not explained why. Nor, she has also indicated, will she willingly return to Seressa. She has not explained why.

She intends to stay in Dubrava, it seems. Charming as the woman undoubtedly is, it is a difficulty.

The other difficulty is the other woman. Some in this chamber are prepared to enjoy watching her executed. There is, to put it more delicately than they would themselves, no love in this room for the so-called heroes of Senjan.

The rector seems to have finished the conversations he's been having. He can be seen moving towards his chair, slowly (the bad leg is from long ago, at sea). A well-built man in a green silk robe trimmed with fox fur. He uses a handsome walking stick, has a mane of still-dark hair, the envy of many much younger than him. He is not to be taken lightly.

LEONORA HADN'T THOUGHT any of this through. There hadn't been time. She was here under false pretenses. She knew enough not to tell them that. She *had* told Danica Gradek, improbably. Her first friend since being sent away from home turned out to be a tall, fierce woman from Senjan who carried weapons, dressed like a man, and had killed the raider who'd run Jacopo Miucci through with a sword.

What saddened her was that she was beginning to forget what Miucci had been like, after only a few days. She remembered kindness, and his gratitude in the dark. Both had been new to her. A gentle man.

But this morning in the Rector's Palace she needed to be clear and alert, and she wasn't feeling so. Clarity was beyond her just now. Or, rather, she was clear only on what she would not do— and had told them.

She had no idea what she *would* do with the life Jad seemed to have ordained for her, this unexpected path, so far from what she'd imagined as a child, daughter of a distinguished family. Loved. Or at least seen as valuable.

She didn't know how to attach value to herself now, and it needed to be done or they would send her back to Seressa. Andrij Djivo, Marin's father, had explained this over dinner the night before. He had assumed it would be what she wanted.

She had cried then, at their table, explaining that she could not go back. Actually, she hadn't explained it, only told them, and begged that they'd honour her privacy by not asking why. Pleaded that Gospodar Djivo might cause the Rector's Council to allow her to stay, at least for a time.

He'd shown great sympathy, the elder Djivo, along with per-
plexity. He obviously liked her, her appearance, manners, accent,
breeding. Liked her much more than Danica, of course.

She saw him standing now beside the older son, near the rector's
chair at the front, under the tall windows. He was talking to a man
with a walking stick. That one, in fur-trimmed green, would be the
rector of Dubrava, she guessed.

It was a handsome room. Not as large as the council chamber
in Seressa where she and Miucci had accepted their tasks, but it
was beautifully fashioned, and on another morning Leonora might
have paused to admire the windows facing the sea.

Just now she couldn't. She was too afraid. She stole a glance
at Danica. The other woman was scanning the room and upper
gallery. Danica was standing in front of Marin Djivo, who was
greeting one of the younger councillors.

She had already considered—and dismissed—the idea of
marrying here in order to remain. It was almost impossible. She
was in mourning, was not a member of their nobility, even though
she would certainly count as a good marriage. Or, she might have
done so if there hadn't been a child somewhere in the world and if
her father hadn't disowned her entirely.

And if the Council of Twelve across the water didn't hold her
life in its hands, like something easily shattered. They could make
her do what they wanted to. Or so they'd think.

Leonora had spent two nights trying to work it through.
If they revealed her false marriage they exposed themselves as
having arranged it. If *she* revealed it . . . she wasn't sure what
followed. But she'd be self-exposed as a spy, and also as the
sort of woman who slept with a man not her husband for a
state purpose.

A whore, it would be said.

"Go step by step," Danica had told her. "We can't know what is
to come. Do you think," she'd added, "that I expected to be here?"

Right now, Leonora thought, Danica might be thinking only as far as tomorrow. They had both seen the gallows and headman's block, just outside the city gates.

Nobles were allowed beheading and a burial. Common thieves— or Senjani pirates—were hanged and left to rot. Messages were sent that way everywhere in the world. There was no reason to expect Dubrava to be different.

It occurred to Leonora that death could be very close to a person, even someone young, as she moved under sun or moons, over a blue-green sea, along city streets or wilderness roads past forests with dark leaves hiding the god's sun, or between red marble pillars under tall windows.

DANICA KEPT LOOKING at the men gathered in the chamber and those still entering. The problem was, she wasn't trained for this. Simply being Senjani didn't make you a capable guard. On the other hand . . .

Zadek, help me, what do I need to see?

Be aware of the younger ones. And the gallery above. Watch that.

The gallery was a concern. There were guards up there, she saw some with crossbows. But what could she do if one of them . . . ?

She motioned to Drago Ostaja. He was still holding her weapons. The captain hesitated, obviously startled that she was ordering him about, but he did approach. Marin was behind her, talking to another man. She was trying to screen him from the gallery; he would be exposed if she moved.

She said quietly to Drago, "Stay in front of him, where I am now. I do believe there is danger."

"For Marin?" His tone was somewhere between dismay and anger.

She nodded. "Yes. That's what I learned in the street. From the girl. It may have to do with women, that is why they knew."

She left him, walking quickly back to the guard at the door, the one who had made her yield her weapons but had done so with courtesy, perhaps even respect. He also had a crossbow, against the wall beside him.

She waited for him to finish admitting three men, who eyed her with expressions that could not be called courteous or respectful. The guard—his name was Jevic, she remembered—turned to her.

"I need your help," Danica said briskly.

"Mine?"

"I am speaking as a guard for the Djivo family. I have reason to believe there is danger, or there might be." She was in a hurry to get back, had no time to make this easier.

"For the Djivos? In *here*?"

"I have reason to believe," she repeated. "I am not allowed my weapons. I understand. But may I ask you to keep alert? You don't want violence while you are on duty."

"Here?" he repeated. But he wasn't a stupid man, and Danica saw that he had already glanced past her towards Marin, with Drago in his red cap standing in front of him watching the chamber— she hoped.

She hesitated. "One more thing. A kindness. If . . . if they condemn me in here, put me in irons, I need you to kill my dog. He will go wild seeing that, there will be no way to stop him. People will be hurt. You'll . . . need to do that for me. For him."

Is that necessary, Dani?

Yes, she said shortly.

The guard's expression was odd. He looked outside to where Tico would be. Danica had stopped where her dog could not see her. This had become extremely difficult.

"I will do that," said the man named Jevic. He looked as if he'd say more, but people were approaching the doors.

She'd been away long enough.

"The galleries," she said. "There are weapons up there." She turned and started back.

What followed happened extremely fast.

You could go from nothing occurring to terrible danger in no time at all. It had happened on the ship, too.

Danica!

I see him!

She was already running. A well-dressed man (a young one) had begun moving too quickly, grim-faced, with a directness not that of a man strolling across a council chamber to have a conversation before a session began.

"*Drago!*" she cried.

But Drago Ostaja was a fighting man himself, and he'd been warned. He'd seen this man as well. He backed up a stride, body between Marin and the one approaching. Marin was turning, having heard Danica's cry. Leonora was a few steps away: too near, in fact, endangered, but you couldn't position every piece on a gameboard. Or maybe you could, if you were better at this than Danica was? She didn't know.

She did know that the man heading for Marin carried a sword, which meant he was a councillor, allowed that honour. And yes, he was drawing it now—and quickening to a run. Someone turned, bemused, as he shouldered past. Someone spoke a name, startled.

Drago, awkwardly holding Danica's bow and quiver, could only stand between this one and Marin—who was also weaponless, being only a younger brother, not a member of the Rector's Council.

You could get a warning in the street, Danica thought, but you still had to be able to *do* something with it—or someone would die.

She thrust her left arm up, on the run across the floor. Her tunic sleeve fell back. She claimed her third dagger from its thin sheath strapped to her inner arm and she threw it, running, and it buried itself (as if in ripening fruit on a tree outside Senjan) in the eye of the one who had drawn his sword.

Men cried out, in horror.

One man fell to a marble floor.

I am, Danica Gradek thought—coming to a halt beside Drago, breathing hard—*killing so many people this spring.*

None of them Osmanli. Not one. None of them any part of her life's sworn purpose. Grief took many forms, was her thought.

She glanced at Drago. She turned to speak to Marin.

"Above!" she heard. Leonora Miucci, pointing up and across the way—at the gallery.

Danica grabbed for her bow, knowing she was too late, that it would take her too long.

"Down, Marin!" she screamed.

She had the bow—Drago didn't fight her for it. She had an arrow, she was turning, nocking, pulling, looking up—

In time to see a crossbow fall between pillars to smash on the floor. A chip of stone cracked loose. And now—now there was a man falling, over the railing, both hands to his chest, making one slow turn in the air—to land on his back with a blunt, flat sound. Men scrabbled away in terror.

There was an arrow in his chest, Danica saw.

She turned, her own arrow still on the string of her bow.

She saw the man named Jevic calmly scanning the overhead gallery, a second arrow slotted to his weapon, and he was winding it again.

There was, given that this was a crowded room of frightened people, an extreme stillness.

It didn't last. Noise exploded like a fired cannon.

I don't believe there will be a third, granddaughter.

Why? Why not? She was trying to be calm.

I think the second was in the event the first one failed.

He did fail.

That was, her zadek said quietly, in her head, *a very good knife throw.*

I would have been too late to stop the one above.

Maybe. Djivo was shielded. By you, by the captain.

So one of us would have died? Then him?

Maybe, he said again. The room was so loud now. She saw Marin's father hurrying over, his face a book in which to read anger and fear. Her grandfather said, *We can't defend everyone, child.*

And she knew he was remembering the same fires she did, awake or asleep. When he called her *child* he was often back in their village on the night the hadjuks came.

HE HAS ALWAYS BEEN KNOWN as the clever son, if wayward. His brother has never appeared to resent this, although it is possible he does. Perhaps you need to be clever yourself, or value it, to be resentful. His father swings like a pendulum, even now, between a growing trust in Marin's judgment in business and suspicion of his views and behaviour in other matters.

But if you are thought to be intelligent—and feel that way about yourself—it can be disturbing to realize that you'd been unaware the target this morning was you, and that others had known it, or deduced it, which is the reason you are still alive.

There are two dead men in the Rector's Palace. There is chaos. Marin sees his father hurrying towards him. His face might have been diverting at another time: it conveys fear and anger and confusion, chasing each other. His brother, standing back, shows only the last of these.

He tries to school his features. He looks at Drago, and then at Danica Gradek. She's in front of him, bow to hand now, scanning the tumult of the chamber like—well, like a raider, or a guard. Both of which she is. She's the one who just saved his life, it seems. In his mind, that thrown knife is still flying.

He is pleased to discover that his breathing appears normal enough. He has faced down danger before. But all the other times he had *known* a threat was present. Abroad alone one night in

Khatib, recklessly. In Seressa among the bridges and canals, also after dark. Three times on a raider-boarded ship (just a few days ago, one of those). Other nights, fleeing a room where he ought not to have been.

This morning, walking here, he had been oblivious to everything, missed any threat entirely. He'd thought the Senjani woman might be a target, though had decided it was unlikely before the council judged her. Why kill someone who might soon be hanged?

Belatedly, he understands why the two women had turned back on the Straden and walked off with Kata Matko. Something women would know first, before the men? And now he considers the fact that it was the oldest son of Vlatko Orsat who just rushed across the floor, drawing a sword and snarling Marin's name.

He believes that when they identify the man who has fallen from the gallery he will be a guardsman of the Orsat family, who slipped in among the other guards up there. He thinks, *Someone will be punished for allowing that.* He thinks . . . he is having difficulty arranging his thoughts.

Vudrag Orsat, lying with a knife blade in his eye (in his eye!), had been a friend since childhood. And he had been coming to kill Marin just now. There is no avoiding it. The sword lies beside him.

He looks towards the guard by the door—who has just killed the man in the gallery—and he now recalls Danica walking back that way as well. The man is still alert, another crossbow arrow slotted and wound back. All the guards bristle. Swords are drawn.

Men have been killed, with the rector and much of the nobility of the republic present. Alertness seems called for, yes, on the whole.

"I think it is over," Danica Gradek says, over the noise, though she continues to face forward, her back to him. "I think it is all right."

"No, it isn't," Marin says.

And steps forward from behind her, because now Vlatko Orsat is also approaching, catching up to Marin's father, and those two have known each other all their lives and this is not going to be *all right* in any great hurry.

"*You killed my son!*" the elder Orsat cries. His face is purple with rage—and grief, one must assume. He looks from Danica to Marin.

"Our guard did so, yes," Marin says. He is pleased to be controlling his voice, but he feels a growing fear. Not for himself. "He was coming for me, sword drawn. You can see it there. Gospodar, why would Vudrag do that?"

There is no answer. Which means no denial.

Marin continues, keeping his voice low. "And a man of yours was about to fire a crossbow when he was killed by one of the rector's guards. The doctor's widow cried a warning. She may have saved my life. Did you also notice that, gospodar? He's lying right there. Beside his weapon. Look."

A slight risk, that *a man of yours*, but Orsat isn't denying this either.

"What happened?" his father gasps, visibly bewildered. "What can this mean? Vlatko, what did . . . ?"

Marin is gazing at Vlatko Orsat, the big, grey-bearded, familiar face distorted by emotion. He remembers when that beard was black.

"Yes," Marin says, "what can this possibly mean, gospodar?" Then adds, "You might keep your voice quiet when you tell us." Because he believes he knows the answer to the question.

"Keep quiet? Why would I do that?" Orsat snaps.

Marin shrugs. "You will do what you like. It was a suggestion."

"With my son *dead*?" Vudrag is—was—the principal heir. Already a member of the council. Which is why he'd had a sword.

No, this is not over.

"Your son was about to commit murder," Marin says, his own voice still low. There is someone to protect, he is thinking. But it may be too late.

He realizes that Danica and Drago have positioned themselves to give the three of them space, not let anyone near. The guard from the doors has also come over. The noise is beginning to subside.

"You cannot prove that!" Orsat says.

"You deny it, Vlatko?" Marin's father seems to almost want a denial. Marin can understand that. Andrij Djivo is looking at the sword by the dead man.

But Vlatko Orsat, after a moment, says only, "Sometimes honour demands we do certain things. Children die, we die."

And so Marin's fear becomes sorrow.

"What does that mean?" his father says, clearly lost.

"Yes," Marin says. He is not lost. "What does it mean?" Out of the corner of his eye he sees Leonora Miucci listening closely. Her face is pale. He adds, "Tell us, gospodar. Say what it means."

Orsat's blue eyes are cold. He says, "A man of our class has life-and-death control over his children."

"*What?* Who says that?" Marin rasps. His heart is pounding now. "Are we in Rhodias a thousand years ago?"

"I know exactly where and when we live," Vlatko Orsat says. A man Marin has known all his life. "As I know the value I place on our family's honour."

"I think," says Andrij Djivo, "that you may be called to account as to that honour, Vlatko. What have you done?"

But he's asked the last question of his son, not the grey-bearded man beside them.

Marin ignores the question, which he doesn't often do with his father. He is staring at Orsat. He says, almost whispering, "No. What have *you* done, Gospodar Orsat?" And then he says it: "Please. Is she all right?"

The room has grown quiet as men become aware of this confrontation. So Marin hears the small sound Leonora Miucci makes.

"My children are entirely within my disposition, Marin. You have no right to ask questions."

No right to ask questions.

"*Where is Elena?*" Marin hears his voice crack.

He wants to kill now, but carries no sword. He is not a member of the council. This man is. Vudrag was. His father and brother are. He is only a younger son. He is heart-poundingly afraid.

Then he hears Vlatko Orsat say, with surprise, "*Elena?* In the street with her mother, likely buying things."

Marin closes his eyes.

He opens them. Pain and sorrow and fury, and now an image of Iulia Orsat comes to him. Elena's sister. Dark eyes, dark hair— whom he scarcely knows, and never has.

He says, snarling it, "You are a great and savage fool. You have betrayed your family, not defended them. Just what is it you think I did?"

Something in his voice arrests the other man. Orsat's expression changes. He glances away, at his dead son. Blood is bright on the marble by Vudrag's head. A knife is in his eye. He had been alive, vibrant, young in this chamber moments ago.

Vlatko Orsat turns back to Marin. He clears his throat. He whispers, "You were seen! Climbing down our wall at night in winter. More than once, I was told. And three days ago Iulia confessed to me that she was . . . she told us . . ."

"*Oh, Jad!* She was with child, and confided in her father, in trust. Did you kill her, you barbarian? *Did you do that?*"

It is Leonora Miucci. She is weeping, but her hands are clenched as if she, too, could commit murder now.

"How dare you speak to me that way!"

"No. I believe you need to answer her, Vlatko." Marin's father, his voice grave. "Or answer me, because I am now asking the same question."

"Wait," Marin says.

He draws another breath and says slowly, "Vlatko Orsat, I swear it by the god and on my family's honour—if I lie may all our ships go to the bottom of the sea—I have never been with your daughter Iulia. I am innocent of her and she of me. Holy Jad, man, why did you not find the man and marry them to each other? *That is what we do!*"

Vlatko Orsat's eyes are different now. But he shakes his head again, stubbornly. He says, "Whatever your Jad-denying generation believes, my family's pride is still mine to defend."

It is suddenly too much. Marin steps forward and slaps the older man across the face. There are cries of shock in the room. He snaps, "Good, then! Defend your god-cursed pride! Challenge me. Now! Choose anyone you like to fight for you!"

"You think that is how—?"

"*Fight me!*" He is trembling. He forces his voice lower. "I never touched Iulia in my life. Did you just kill your daughter—as well as your son?"

Beside him Leonora Miucci is still weeping, which he doesn't entirely understand. Danica hasn't looked around, neither has Drago. They are watching the room. Marin hears his father say, "This was entirely wrong, Vlatko. You shame the republic."

"*I do?* You, who bring a Senjani killer into this chamber and—"

And amid all of this, there is laughter.

Danica Gradek, who is the one laughing, finally turns. She says to Vlatko Orsat, "No one *brought* me. I came of my own choice to bring a message to your rector and council. The man I killed on the *Blessed Ingacia* was one of our own. It seems you have done the same." There is contempt in her eyes.

Marin's father also has a different look now, one his son knows. He has proceeded from confusion to an understanding—by his own lights—of what needs to happen.

He raises his deep voice to carry. "Rector, I wish to lay formal charges before the council against this man. I want him judged."

"How dare you! I have every right to deal with my own family—"

"No, Vlatko! I charge you with trying to have *my* son killed. Or do you forget?"

"You say this to a man whose son lies murdered by a Senjani!"

Marin's palm is stinging. Orsat's cheek is red. Marin is trying to picture Iulia Orsat—whom he really does scarcely know—Elena's younger sister.

"Your son is here. Where," says Leonora Miucci, "is your daughter?"

A painful silence.

"Yes," says Marin's father. "Vlatko, what have you done?"

And finally they hear, "She is on Gjadina. Our estates on the island. I . . . I would not kill her. I would never do that. He . . . Andrij, your son was *seen* climbing down our wall!"

Marin's father looks at him. Marin says, "I did so, yes. Many nights this winter." There is relief in him now. The girl is not dead. Orsat would not lie about this. "Gospodar, you have erred at terrible cost. I was bedding your wife's new maidservant. Forgive me for that grave sin against your family honour."

"Her *servant?*"

"Her servant, gospodar. Is it a killing offence? Shall I go across to the sanctuary and beg forgiveness of Jad? If so, what forgiveness will *you* seek?"

"I believe," comes a different voice, "that it begins with the council's and the Djivo family's forgiveness for what has happened here. And it will not be inexpensive."

"Rector," says Andrij Djivo.

He bows. Marin does the same. He sees Vlatko Orsat hesitate— actually, it is less a hesitation than what seems an inability to move normally—before he also bows to the rector.

"He will *buy* his way free of this?"

It is Danica Gradek. Her face under the wide hat seems genuinely shocked.

"That is what we do here," says the rector of Dubrava, speaking gravely, leaning on his stick, and Marin hears his own words to Orsat echo back to him.

The rector turns to the guard named Jevic. "You did well. It has been noted. Have these bodies removed. Identify the one from above. Be respectful. Take them to the Orsat house, but send a man ahead to give warning, please. A mother will be greeting her dead child."

He is looking at Vlatko as he says that.

Marin sees Orsat's face crumple. A shaking hand covers his eyes. Marin looks again at the dead man on the floor. Vudrag. They'd played "Hunt the Osmanli" as children with wooden swords. Learned to handle small boats from the pier on Gjadina in summers gone. Later slept with island girls in vineyards after harvests on autumn nights.

The father is weeping now, he sees, and trying to both hide it and stop. It is difficult to watch. Marin sees Danica Gradek looking on. There is no sympathy in her features. *She's young*, he thinks. *Senjan*, he thinks. *The life they live there.*

He feels tired now. He suddenly has a startlingly vivid image in his mind: open sea far from land, from the councils of men, a ship running before the west wind into a rising sun, and then it is as if he sees Heladikos falling from high, from his father's chariot, into the white-capped waves.

We are always falling, Marin Djivo thinks. *Even if we are the children of a god.*

CHAPTER X

One of the two women Leonora had feared for this morning—someone she had never seen—was not dead, after all. The other, her friend, was apparently not going to be executed.

Danica, coming out of an inner room back into the council chamber, had looked briefly at her and nodded her head slightly. Leonora, standing with Drago Ostaja under the tall western windows of the palace, had found herself fighting tears again.

In truth, earlier today she hadn't fought them.

She had hated the blustering aristocrat who had led them to believe he'd killed his daughter because he *could*, because she had shamed him by conceiving a child.

Was it any wonder that story had knifed into her so hard? Leonora Valeri of Mylasia thought. Any wonder at all? Should she have knelt in desperate gratitude back home that her own dear father had let her live? Had only killed the man she'd loved, and packed her off to a religious retreat?

She could picture the two of them together, Vlatko Orsat of Dubrava and Erigio Valeri of Mylasia. Imagined them downing cups of wine somewhere after a hunt, lamenting disgraceful daughters and some lost, false dream of honour.

But the other girl—Iulia—was not dead. *I would never do that*, this father had said, beside his dead son and red blood on marble.

Leonora had found no pity within her. Not then, not now, seeing him come out of that inner chamber with Danica and the Djivos and the rector and his clerks.

These people had tried to kill Marin. Danica—her friend Danica from Senjan—had killed the younger Orsat. Second time she'd ended a man's life with Leonora right there.

Were the women all like this in Senjan? she'd asked on the *Blessed Ingacia* at sea. Apparently not. The stories of Senjani women severing enemy limbs and drinking the dripping blood were only that—stories. Useful ones, Danica had said from her cot in the darkness.

Nor could they control the winds or tides. Or feed their children during a blockade, she had added bitterly.

In the council chamber now, as order was gradually achieved, the rector of Dubrava moved briskly through a number of matters. The council had reassembled in their seats. They were still disturbed, afraid—and not a little excited, Leonora Valeri thought. Men were like that. Women, too.

She had the sense the rector was trying to restore calm with a dry precision. She doubted he'd succeed. Not with two deaths, and word of them surely rolling like waves through the city.

Issues were addressed, nonetheless. A secretary recorded. Probably very much as matters were handled by the Council of Twelve. She was hearing the rector of Dubrava speak, and she was one of the reasons they were assembled on a spring morning.

Danica Gradek, he said, late of Senjan, now residing in their republic, was to be fined one hundred Dubravae silver serales. Her offence: carrying secretly and using a weapon in the council chamber.

It was a large sum. But this was balanced and offset by an immediate commendation spoken from that handsome chair. Danica was praised for quick-wittedness and skill saving her employer's life. Dubrava, the rector said, owed her thanks that murder had been forestalled. There was murmuring at that.

Two of their noble families, the rector said, had resolved unfortunate differences. He didn't say anything about Iulia Orsat, which was good.

It became almost entirely about money after that. The Orsats had agreed to pay a large sum to the Djivos for the attack on Marin.

The rector spoke of gambling debts, two young men at odds over a wager. That would be the story, Leonora thought. All they needed was a story, it didn't have to be a convincing one.

The rector stopped. Andrij Djivo stood up. He said that the Djivos would gladly pay Danica Gradek's fine on her behalf. He spoke about her saving his child's life. He said *child*. Marin, across the chamber, was expressionless.

The older Djivo turned to Leonora and bowed and said the same of her. That she'd saved Marin's life. She was the one who had seen the crossbow above, he said. Both women in this chamber had the gratitude of the Djivo family. He expressed sorrow for the Orsats' loss, spoke about the evil of gambling. He said he would be talking to both his sons about that. The older son looked indignant. Marin smiled thinly. The father thanked the council, took his seat.

The rector addressed Leonora. She faced him with a lowered gaze, wearing black. He spoke of their sorrow concerning her husband and a firm intention to do right by her. He asked, almost apologetically, if it was acceptable that they write her father regarding the ransom paid to the raiders. It was hoped her honourable family (that word again) would address this, realizing that the ransom would have been demanded of them had she been taken, and that she'd have been in great peril.

"Of course you may write my father," Leonora said gravely.

What else could she have said?

Other matters concerning her, the rector indicated, would be dealt with in due course. He trusted she was comfortably housed with the Djivos?

She was, Leonora said. They had been gracious beyond measure at this sad time.

Plans for a service for Vudrag Orsat, a member of the council, were discussed. Council members, the rector advised, would be informed as to when it would take place. Civic functions and meetings would be suspended at that time, except those related to security.

They left the chamber. All of them spilled out into the midday-bright square and street. Leonora walked home with the Djivos and Danica and the captain on a day in spring.

She didn't linger at the house. She asked for an escort. She had her instructions from the Council of Twelve and needed to follow them until some way to be clear emerged. If it emerged.

The Djivos sent a guard with her.

It was too soon to declare in public that she would not return home. Or rather, not return to Seressa—which was not her home and never had been. *Home* was lost. She'd talked to Danica about it the night before. Then expressed the thought she was being hopelessly self-absorbed, asking her friend to advise her when the other woman was to be tried tomorrow, with a hangman waiting.

Danica had smiled. She had one smile that conveyed no real happiness or pleasure at all. She had a different one, Leonora had noted, one that could warm you, but was rare.

But today had become a brighter day. Danica might owe her life, Leonora thought, to the Orsats attacking Marin Djivo. A person's fate could change in such a way. Men and women could live or die randomly, the way dice fell in a tavern game. She thought about Jacopo Miucci. She was still trying to hold on to his face in her mind.

She was guided along the Straden, then up a narrower street of stone steps. The guard knew where they were going. She didn't, only the name of the house she'd given him.

She wondered if she'd ever see that promised compensation for Miucci's death. Almost certainly not. It would surely be sent to the Council of Twelve, to manage in their wisdom for the doctor's young widow.

Men died, money squared accounts. Vlatko Orsat had proposed a sum for his son's attempt at murder and Andrij Djivo had accepted it. He seemed a rigidly virtuous man. It might be difficult to be the son of such a person, Leonora thought. But there were worse things.

She'd expected Danica to have to speak for her life this morning. Leonora had been prepared to tell what she'd seen, what had been done on the ship to the man she'd called her husband—and then to the raider who'd killed Miucci.

Marin had been there to do the same, and Drago (a man she liked) had been ready to do so. That one would rather face pirates or demons from the darkness below the world than make a speech, she'd decided.

None of it had happened. It was not even mentioned that Danica had been one of the raiders boarding a ship, seizing goods, killing a man, extracting a ransom for that man's wife.

No testimony had been required. Leonora remembered relief in Drago Ostaja's face.

Her own relief had also been real. They'd seen crows on the gibbet outside the gates, and rotting bodies. Crows took eyes first, unless there were entrails spilling. They'd had gibbets in Mylasia.

The steps of this street continued climbing north, but her escort now turned to the right along another street parallel to the Straden. Then he stopped outside a door.

Leonora looked at a handsome building and went in.

EARLIER THAT AFTERNOON the artist Pero Villani had also learned, with more relief than he'd have expected, that there would be no execution of the Senjani raider.

He was Seressini, judged important, and was given the news personally. He believed they expected him to be unhappy, hearing it. He kept his expression noncommittal.

He had stature now for the first time in his life, because of his mission to Asharias. He was residing above the Straden in the handsome residence for prominent Seressinis. Tomo had a place in the servants' quarters.

An official appointed by the Council of Twelve managed here and assisted travellers, with the aid of a sizable staff. The official was, apparently, the son of a member of the Council of Twelve. Pero found it an exceptionally comfortable place. Of course he had been living in a room above a tannery only days before.

The *Blessed Ingacia* had carried a letter advising the Seressini officials about him. It had made for some flurry and fluster since there had been no advance word, but these were well-trained men. A short time after having his goods carried up from the harbour, Pero was assigned a room and having a drink by the fire with the man in charge, a smooth-featured personage named Frani.

He found it difficult to judge whether Frani, a man of effusive gesture and speech, considered him brave or foolish regarding the journey he was undertaking. He claimed to have known of Pero's father. It might be true. He asked questions about the dramatic events on the *Blessed Ingacia*. Pero answered as best he could. Giorgio Frani smiled often, clasped his hands thoughtfully, nodded. He was partial to a floral scent.

Pero took a walk in the afternoon then dined with some merchants and another artist that night, and then the next, in the Seressini residence. Tomo ate with the servants downstairs.

At times they heard laughter from down there. At times Pero wished that was where he was.

The other artist was an older man painting frescoes in a sanctuary near the landward gates. He was at pains to establish seniority to Pero. He mentioned distinguished colleagues, other commissions. One in Rhodias.

Everyone was senior to Pero, really, but he was the one chosen by the Council of Twelve to go to Asharias to paint a portrait of Gurçu, ravager of Sarantium, grand khalif of the Asharites.

It caused them to regard him differently.

That journey could make someone's fortune and name—if he survived it. Pero could see how an older artist might chafe and bridle, meeting him. He didn't say a great deal or rise to any challenges. He promised to come see the frescoes before going east. Frani, scented, declared them magnificent.

They had been told over dinner that the Rector's Council was to meet on the third morning after the *Blessed Ingacia* arrived, to make decisions concerning the women who had come on the ship. Pero supposed he ought to have endorsed, as the others did, the idea of hanging the Senjani raider. The word of choice at the Seressini residence seemed to be *maggots*.

He didn't. Support the idea, that is. Danica Gradek had impressed him from the moment she'd loosed an arrow at one of her own, and he'd seen that Leonora seemed to trust her, and he was urgently in love with Leonora Valeri by then, so his views were affected by that.

This matter of being in love was not anything he'd expected to encounter on the road to Asharias. Or anywhere, at this stage of his life. It was one thing to desire a woman, whether you paid for her or she was a friend, or an aristocrat looking for amusement. This feeling was a world away from such things. From everything, really.

He had already decided that it was not anything he could ever speak to her about. She'd be going back to Seressa. Her husband had been killed, her life thrown into chaos and grief.

Money was involved. Giorgio Frani had expounded on that. He liked talk of money, it seemed. The matter of her ransom would be delicate, Frani had observed with enthusiasm. Did Signore Villani have any knowledge of her family, their circumstances? Signore Villani regretted to say he did not.

What he did know was that Leonora Miucci didn't need an unknown artist paying court to her, now or ever. He *couldn't* pay court to her. He had no social position at all. The very notion—given what had happened to her—was an insult, ill-bred. Unthinkable.

It was surprising how easy it was to think about the unthinkable if you'd had a few glasses of wine on a spring night.

She was intelligent, graceful, clearly well-born, and in his dreams and reveries Pero could unfortunately still hear the sound of her urgent voice through the thin walls of the ship's chambers in the nights before her husband died.

The wine in Dubrava was quite good. The best was pale, slightly sweet, from the island of Gjadina, he'd been told. They'd passed the island on the way into the harbour.

It was early on the third afternoon now. The Rector's Council had met this morning. There had been confused word of violence in the chamber. Tomo, back from the square, told Pero there had been weapons used, that men were dead. The officials here were waiting for clearer tidings with excitement and eagerness. Violence made some people eager, Pero thought.

Frani came and reported to him, shortly after, that the Senjani woman was apparently not to be hanged. A disappointment, he said.

Pero took another walk alone, along the street and then down the steps to the Straden. He turned left towards the sanctuary on the square near the Rector's Palace. There were white clouds west, beyond the ships in the harbour. A light breeze blew. The square was crowded in the sunlight. He heard a rise and fall of intense conversation. More eagerness.

He pushed through the crowd and entered the sanctuary, which was quieter. He made the sign of the sun disk and he knelt and prayed—for ease of mind and heart, for safety on the road ahead, for success at the end of that journey and a safe return.

He was painfully aware, amid everything else, that he was expected to paint the portrait of the ruler who could fairly be called the most important man in the world. Pero's only formal portrait of anyone significant had been burned by his subject so her husband would never see it.

He was also expected to spy. He had heard tales of what the Osmanlis did to spies if they were discovered. There was another thing he'd been asked to do. He tried not to think about that.

Before rising he prayed, as always, for the souls of his mother and father, that they might be with Jad in light. He could have used his father's counsel now, he thought. It was sometimes diffi-cult to accept that he was alone, deemed a man in his own right.

It was time, however, Pero thought. You had to grow into your own significance—or come to terms with the lack of it.

He had immediate tasks here. He was to find merchants plan-ning a journey east. His instructions were to join such a party for the security it would offer. Frani and his officials at the residence knew of no groups assembling yet, but their role was to aid him, and this was one of the things they did. It might take some time or it might not, Pero had been told.

He'd asked last night if any Osmanli officials were in Dubrava (he'd been instructed to do that as well). None were, it seemed. They might arrive at any time. He had been offered more of the good pale wine and reminded that it was early in the season.

Information as to Osmanli military intentions had not yet reached Dubrava. War, if it came (it probably would come, was the prevailing view), was likely to take place again in and around the emperor's fortress of Woberg, far to the north of the road from Dubrava to Asharias. But war was a wild beast and never predictable. One of his drinking companions last night, a round-faced trader in optical instruments, going no farther than Dubrava (and glad of it, he'd said), had put it that way.

Pero signed the disk, rose, and left the sanctuary. He crossed the Rector's Square again and strolled the length of the Straden to the gates.

Dubrava was not Seressa, but it was a handsome city, and no street in Pero's own was as wide and straight as this one was. The canals and the necessary bridges precluded that back home. He walked past solidly built homes of three or four storeys, mercantile rooms, warehouses, several wine shops. Red roofs everywhere, a signature of Dubrava.

He passed three fountains, people gathering at them as they did at fountains everywhere. Mostly women, filling pitchers and buckets, sharing tidings and laments. Laughter. The women watched him pass, appraisingly. The street would fill up at day's end, he knew. That also happened everywhere as people came out to see and be seen at sunset.

The walls were impressive. Forbidding and in good repair, defensive towers at intervals and a wall-walk all the way around for guards to patrol. The republic had never been taken by a foe. They boasted of that (he'd heard it already), but Pero judged that there was anxiety in that bravado. If Asharias or the Emperor Rodolfo or Seressa ever truly wanted to they could take this small republic.

Holding it, after making sense of the cost and distance of maintaining a siege, would be another matter. Which was—for all their celebrated diplomacy—probably where Dubrava's true safety lay, as much as in these walls.

He saw the hangman's gibbet outside the open gates at the Straden's end. It had been entirely possible this morning that Danica Gradek's body might swing there. There were two rotting bodies now. His mind turned from imagining it. He had seen a

206 Guy Gavriel Kay

sufficiency of executions. Would they really hang a woman in Dubrava? He'd been told it had happened.

In a laneway running south he saw a girl in light green smile at him, then tilt her head in inquiry. He considered it. He was young, disturbed by dreams and desire, far from any of the women who cared for him even a little, those who had said their goodbyes at his farewell party.

He smiled at her but went the other way again along the wide street. He thought briefly of going to see those frescoes, but they weren't really a temptation.

He felt a not-unpleasant strangeness, an awareness that he had begun a journey that could change everything in his life. At the very least it *was* a journey. He wasn't binding books to pay rent while failing to find painting work and living in a crumbling, odorous room in the cheapest district of Seressa. He was *moving* now.

No one here knew him. What would they see, watching the Seressini artist Pero Villani walk by? A youngish man, slight, blue eyes, brown hair, long fingers. A thin beard that needed to be heavier—but what could you do about that? A pleasant face, surely? No harm in it. Some intelligence revealed? Perhaps. He thought: *No one will know my name in any wine shop here.* There was something exciting about that.

He went into the next one he came to. He took a table, ordered a flask of the island wine he now liked and a plate of grilled octopus. The proprietor brought him a dish of olives. There was no one to share any of it with but Pero realized, with surprise, that in this moment he would have to say he was happy.

He began to think for the first time about the details, the necessary craft of what he was journeying to do: about *how* he might paint the khalif. It really was true: there were artists who would kill for the chance to do this. Or a man might be killed on the way to doing it, or for saying the wrong thing, for saying *anything* in some parts of the palace compound in Asharias. It was reported that only mutes were allowed in the innermost quarters. He didn't know if it was true. He was going to find out.

Pero wasn't just a traveller on the roads of the world, not just another spy for Seressa, he was an artist, as his father had been, and he had a commission of great significance. He might not deserve it, but did every man receive what he deserved, for good or ill?

He sat in a Dubravae wine shop on a spring afternoon, enjoying his food, and he thought about portraits he had admired. He wondered what the khalif looked like. Tall, he had heard. Pale. A prominent nose.

You could be afraid, facing this sort of challenge. You might charge wildly towards it like a mad cavalryman into a line of pikemen. Or you could try to be mature, thoughtful, aware that Jad (and the Council of Twelve) had given you a gift—or the chance at a gift—and it needed your fierce attentiveness.

He paid the reckoning and went back into the street. Late afternoon now, the sun towards the sea and the clouds that way, the street and shaded arcades beginning to fill with people. Pero walked back west then up the steps, looking at the mountains beyond the walls and towers. Then he turned again to the Seressini hostel.

Leonora Miucci was there when he arrived.

Attentiveness to his art and journey and destination became considerably diminished.

Pero was self-aware enough to find it amusing, but only a little bit. He hesitated in the doorway of the reception room, looking at her.

She was dressed in black, a black hat covering pinned-up hair. She was sitting with Giorgio Frani, whose role was to advise the important citizens of his republic when they came through. She would be one of those, of course. Decisions involving money and travel would be being made concerning her. Perhaps they had already been finalized. Pero wouldn't know, he had no reason to know.

Her mouth, he thought, shaped words beautifully when she spoke.

I am an idiot, he thought.

Frani was behaving like a high-ranking functionary, which he was, of course. He could be ingratiating or imperious at a moment's notice, depending on who you were. He was being obsequious now. Pero didn't like him. Liked him less when he saw how solicitously close the man had pulled his chair to that of the doctor's young widow.

He tugged at his surcoat, smoothed his expression, walked into the room. He bowed.

"Signora Miucci," he said.

She looked up at him. She smiled, then glanced down quickly, modestly. "Signore Villani! I had hoped to find you."

She had hoped to find him?

Pero achieved a clearing of the throat. "I am at your service, signora."

She said, "Would it impose too greatly upon your kindness to ask you to walk out with me? I have a matter upon which I would value your thoughts."

He was fairly sure he managed a reply to this. Surely he must have, since they seemed, moments later, to be outside in the sunlight. That meant he'd said something appropriate, didn't it?

On the street she spoke to her guard from the Djivo residence, instructed him to return home and say that Signore Villani would escort her back. Signore Villani nodded vigorous agreement.

"That appalling man!" said Leonora Miucci, as they went down the stone steps. "Frani. He needs to be doused in a fountain to get rid of the scent he wears. Faugh! Forgive me. It was overwhelming. I needed a reason to get away!"

"Ah," said Pero sagely. Then, "Yes." And then, "Ah. Scent. Yes. He wears much of scent."

Much of scent? He desired to strike himself in the head.

"Doused in a fountain," she repeated.

"Doused!" he agreed happily. They reached the Straden. He saw a fountain, couldn't think of a witticism.

She smiled at him. "Have you been inside the sanctuary by the palace yet?"

"No," he lied.

"Shall we visit it? I would like to pray—for Jacopo, and in thanks for Danica's life. And Marin Djivo's. And my own, I suppose."

"I can pray for all of those things," Pero said, perhaps a shade too enthusiastically. She smiled again, lips together, eyes downcast.

There were more people inside the sanctuary this time. A rustle of prayers being spoken, men and women talking, almost certainly about what had happened this morning across the square. A balding cleric was arranging candles on either side of the altar for the evening service. A boy came running towards him from a side door, carrying an armful of white candles. He slowed at a glance from the cleric, walked the rest of the way.

They signed the disk, found a place to kneel beside each other, a little removed from others. Leonora Miucci wore no perfume (her husband had just died!) but Pero was painfully aware of a scent to her hair and a too-vivid presence. He felt dizzied and happy, both.

She finished her prayers, opened her eyes, remained kneeling by him. "You heard what happened this morning?"

"Some of it," he said.

She told him the story. But people were not to learn, she said, that the Orsat girl was the reason her brother had been coming for Marin Djivo.

"I am trusting you," she said. "And perhaps you can help me. I would like to visit the girl."

"Why?" Pero asked, surprised.

She glanced at him, not smiling this time. "Because I doubt visitors will be allowed. She'll be alone. But her family may have difficulty saying no to me."

Pero thought about it. He shook his head. "If she is with child and has been sent away to conceal it, her family will have no trouble declining visitors, signora. Especially strangers from Seressa."

She sighed. "I was afraid you'd say that."

"I am sorry."

She shook her head. "No. I need truths told to me."

"I will do that," said Pero. He restrained himself from adding, *always*. But then, after a moment, he said, "I did lie earlier, signora. I was here today. But since you wanted to see it, I . . ."

She laughed softly. Someone glanced over at them. She bit her lip, lowered her head decorously. She murmured, "A gentle lie then, Signore Villani."

"I am permitted those?"

She didn't answer.

They rose and walked out. They turned, without speaking, towards the harbour. He badly wanted her to take his arm but she did not. The crowd was behind them, walking the other way from the Rector's Square, along the busy Straden as the sun began to set. See and be seen, the evening promenade on a day when there was so much to talk about.

The two of them went down to the stone dock and then along it towards the *Blessed Ingacia*, rocking by its pier, tied down with thick ropes, sails lowered, empty.

They stood in silence. They were alone.

Pero cleared his throat again. He said, "Look how the sunset lights those clouds. They are exactly where we need them to be for that effect."

She looked for a long time. She said, "Did you ever think that 'sunset' is an inadequate word for how much beauty it can hold?"

And with that, with all of this—her presence, the evening's graceful light, the salt in the breeze, the sea and the ships and the seabirds, the world given to them—it became too much more than his capacity for silence.

"I love you," Pero Villani said. "I am sorry," he said. "I will never embarrass or afflict you. You have my oath, on my parents' graves."

She flushed immediately, he saw. Looked at him then quickly away at the reddened clouds in the west and the beautifully darkening sky.

His heart was thudding, his mouth was dry.

She said, "You cannot love me."

"I understand!" Pero exclaimed. His voice was odd, scratchy. "I mean only to tell you so that you know. Not to expect—"

"No. You *cannot* love me, signore. You do not know me at all."

The hammer of one's heart.

He said, "We can know someone for years and never nearly love them, and know another for days and be theirs for life. I am . . . that is what I am with you."

She looked at him again. He saw tears.

He tried again. He said, "Signora, please, this is not to be a burden for you. I understand your terrible loss. I understand how presumptuous my words are. But please believe my respect for you. I only—"

"No," she said again. "No . . . you cannot understand."

The breeze off the water lifted and blew back strands of her hair under the black cloth hat she wore in mourning.

Pero Villani thought: *These are the most important words I will ever speak.*

He said, "I know there is a story here. I . . . signora, you are obviously from a noble family. You told us as much. And . . . forgive me, my lady, such women do not wed physicians from northern towns, to end up in Seressa. Or Dubrava."

She had been flushed before, now she became very pale. White-faced, in fact. She stared at him in horror.

I have ruined my life, Pero thought.

"Is it so obvious?" she asked. Whispered it. She wiped at tears on her cheek. He wanted to do that for her.

He shook his head. "No! I have been . . . I have thought much about you, signora. I believe the Council of Twelve may have . . . that they may be a part of your life now?"

She was crying, soundlessly.

"I have no life," she said.

He was remembering her walk to the railing of the *Blessed Ingacia*. He had known—she had been so fierce, so purposeful—that she meant to go over the side into the sea.

Fierce, he thought. One of the things she was.

"My lady, there are moments when we can believe that," he said. "Then Jad, or fortune, or our own decisions can change everything."

She looked up at him. A small, elegant woman in the black of mourning. He felt like apologizing again—for presuming to speak any words at all. He kept silent, waiting.

She wiped at her cheeks again. Behind her, far down, three children appeared on the dock. They glanced at the two of them, and Pero imagined the annoyed, disdainful look children could reserve for adults in a place where they were used to playing. He watched them walk then run the other way, farther along. Another ship was moored down there, its cargo had been unloaded, a few mariners were dealing with the last stages of tying the sails. The sun slipped behind the lowest line of clouds. It was chillier now.

Leonora Miucci took his arm.

"Come," she said.

They didn't go far. She walked him only to an empty wine barrel sitting against the stone breakwater. She let go of his arm, turned, and neatly pushed herself up on it. Pero had an incongruous memory of his blind friend by the bridge in Seressa, sitting in just this way.

Or, not quite this way.

"I have never been married," she said calmly. "My name is Leonora Valeri. I was sent to the Daughters of Jad outside Seressa to bear a child. The father was murdered by my family. They took the child from me when it was born. I have no idea where it is. The Council of Twelve offered me a way out of that terrible place if I would spy for them, pretending to be wed, since doctors must have a wife to serve here. I agreed. I agreed, Signore Villani. And now I am lost, I have no honest position, no proper life. But I will *not* go back to that retreat or be an instrument for the council somewhere else, as I expect they will now demand. You cannot even respect me, Signore Villani, let alone . . . anything else."

"I HAVE NEVER BEEN MARRIED," she heard herself saying, by the water, not far from the boat that had brought them here. And then she said more. She told him so much. And there was such a strange feeling of relief, release, to not be lying to this man. Even if it meant he would walk away from her now, she thought.

She did not believe he would become hard, an enemy, any kind of predator, but he would surely turn and go—so that he, a kind person, might step free of the darkness she seemed to carry with her.

Both the men who had cared for her had died, after all.

She looked at Villani: his manner seemed younger than his years. His eyes were blue and his fingers beautiful. This was an artist, she reminded herself, on his own long journey now. He would do best to walk her home then set about pursuing his fortune and fate.

She lifted her chin defiantly. *Hold to pride*, she told herself. She felt cold, not just the breeze, but also . . . altered by what she'd said. Freed by truth.

Pero Villani said, gravely, "Now I see why the Orsat girl disturbs you, signora."

He had not yet turned away. His long brown hair was moving in the wind off the water. She nodded, not trusting herself to reply.

He said, "Perhaps we will find a way to visit with her. Let me think on that."

We?

"Have you even heard what I said?" Leonora demanded.

"All of it," Pero Villani replied. He smiled. Women will have liked that smile, she thought. "I will still grieve for Doctor Miucci, but I am happy you are not his widow."

She shook her head. Men could be, they often were, so innocent.

"To the world I am. I must be. Seressa is humiliated if anything else is believed. I am *bound* to the Council of Twelve. They control my life. I have to go across to that isle tomorrow, to the retreat. There is a woman there to whom their spies in Dubrava report."

She could see Sinan Isle from where they were, right in the entrance to the harbour. Gjadina, the larger one, was out of sight to the north.

He smiled again. "I know about her," he said. "I have an invitation as well. More a command, I suppose."

"You do?"

He looked at her. "Do you think Seressa would send a man to Asharias, to stand in the presence of the grand khalif, and not give him duties beyond painting?"

"That is . . . that is dangerous," she said, after a moment.

He nodded. "They did tell me I could decline."

"And you didn't."

"I have very little at home." He thought a moment. "But . . . as to tomorrow. No one here knows the woman on that isle is Seressini. How will she explain your coming to her . . . ?"

Leonora made a face. "The Daughters of Jad extend care and compassion to all women who are alone. They wish to console me, offer spiritual guidance while I am here."

"Indeed," he said, drily.

"Yes. In the eyes of the world I am the grieving widow of a cruelly slain doctor. A good man, I will add. He was kind. He told me he wanted us to be truly wed."

"And you said?"

He had been looking at the isle, now he turned to her. His manner was thoughtful. He had seemed nervous before. He didn't now. As if truths told had calmed him.

"I told Jacopo Miucci I could not marry without my father's consent and he would never give it. Nor would I burden any man with my shame."

"And if a man were to say it is no burden but an honour to have you at his side?"

"I would say he was foolish and childlike. Especially if he was on his way to Asharias."

His face fell.

She said, "You cannot care for me that way, Signore Villani. I have trusted you, though. And I will be grateful to have you as a friend while you are here. I only have the one."

"Danica Gradek?"

She nodded.

"A good friend to have, I think."

"You don't hate her? As a Seressini?"

"She is your friend, signora. That is what matters now."

Again she said, exasperated, "Have you heard nothing I've said?"

And he replied, again, "All of it." Then added, "I am not an inconstant man, I should warn you."

Leonora's thought, unexpectedly, was, *He is telling me the truth.*

"I AM NOT AN INCONSTANT MAN," he heard himself say.

And the realization came with the words, the speaking of them: *This is true.*

He had never considered himself in such terms, but he thought of his mother and father, still loved, and of friends known—and kept—all his life, and Pero thought again, *Yes, that is what I am.*

It happens this way sometimes, we can discover truths about ourselves in a moment, sometimes in the midst of drama, sometimes quietly. A sunset wind can be blowing off the sea, we might be alone in bed on a winter night, or grieving by a grave among leaves. We are drunk in a tavern, dealing with desperate pain, waiting to confront enemies on a battlefield. We are bearing a child, falling in love, reading by candlelight, watching the sun rise, a star set, we are dying . . .

But there is something else to all of this, because of how the world is for us, how we are within it. Something can be true of our deepest nature and the running tide of days and years might let it reach the shore, be made real there—or not.

"Will you take me home?" she asked.

He did so. At the doorway of the Djivo city palace the guard outside—the one who had been with her before—looked relieved, Pero saw.

He nodded to him, bowed to her. He watched her go in. He turned back west, then up the now familiar stone steps and along the higher street to the hostel.

As he entered, Signore Frani approached at speed from the sitting room, beaming. He stopped, squeezed Pero's arm, reported that a ship from home, just arrived, had brought Seressini merchants intending to travel overland to Asharias.

Frani had taken the liberty of suggesting they might include an important artist in their party and they had happily acceded.

When would they be leaving? A matter of days, it appeared.

Signore Villani was a man greatly blessed by fortune, evidently. Frani smiled again. Pero managed a smile.

CHAPTER XI

Facing death in the morning can change one's day.

Marin Djivo has remained at home with wine (a second flask now), passing up the evening promenade. His father and mother have gone out and his brother is seldom far from their father, so Marin has the house to himself except for the servants, and their business employees closing up in the front rooms, and the guards. Danica Gradek is likely among that last group, in their quarters.

She is under instructions to stay inside today, perhaps for longer than that. There is still a real potential for violence. She'd killed a Dubravae nobleman this morning. Yes, with cause, yes, doing her duty to the equally noble family that hired her. But even so . . .

He had given thought to walking out, being seen in the Straden. He can hear the noise out there now, there will be *intense* conversations. But even though it might be important to present an illusion of normality, he'd decided his parents and brother could manage that for the family this evening, and his father had not disagreed.

His father had looked at him oddly once or twice, but hadn't said anything. It is possible to imagine him feeling emotional about what almost happened. His mother has been expressionless, but she always is, except when praying, eyes closed, hands wrapped tightly around her sun disk.

Marin pours more wine. It is early to be having so much, but it is also . . . it has been a difficult day. He can't stop thinking about Vudrag Orsat, who is dead, and about the Orsat sisters. Elena, the older one, had bedded him half a dozen times last winter in her bedchamber. It wasn't, in fact, the mother's serving girl he'd been climbing down the wall from visiting. He'd lied about that. Some lies are important, he thinks.

Marin is remembering his own words in the Rector's Palace about her sister, Iulia: *Why did you not find the man and marry them to each other?*

It could have been him being married now, he thinks, had Elena Orsat decided he was the husband she wanted, and chosen a way of ensuring it. They wouldn't have been the first well-born couple in Dubrava to be joined in such circumstances. Nor was she a bad choice, if he is to marry among the noble families—and of course he is. What else is there? Really?

He could join the Sons of Jad in a holy retreat. He could do that.

He drains the cup. His father will know he's been drinking. Will say nothing. Not today. His father is a . . . he is a good man, with definite views on many things.

He wonders who the father of Iulia's child is. Why the Orsats haven't done this the obvious way. Probably she had refused to tell.

He hears the Miucci widow come in and go up to her room. The fourth and the ninth stairs creak. You learn these things in a lifetime of slipping out at night.

That woman has also played a role in saving his life. Warning of the crossbow above. His father already admires her extravagantly. It is amusing in a way, but there is something about Leonora Miucci that nags at Marin. It has been there from the first time he and Drago saw the doctor and his wife approaching along the dock in Seressa. He feels sure she is not what she seems to be.

Only with a great deal of wine, or fatigue, or sometimes love-making, can Marin Djivo suppress a questioning turn of mind. This woman, he thinks, is too sophisticated. She has to be more than a doctor's wife . . . or widow, he corrects himself.

It doesn't matter. She is only about money now. Ledgers and transactions following violent death. It might take time, but these things unfold predictably, like the progression of mile markers on one of the old highways.

She'll be gone soon. She has told the Djivos she doesn't want to go back to Seressa, but that will change, he imagines, and it isn't really her choice. Women have, he thinks, a limited number of choices in their lives.

One might be to get pregnant by a man they want.

One might be to kill a fellow raider on a ship. Though that decision—which meant exile—might not have been carefully worked through.

His family will be home soon. Then they will dine. His father is particular about meals and mealtimes. His mother will ask them not to talk about this morning, will say it distresses her. His father will raise the matter of the ship that has just arrived. His brother will know its cargo and the merchants' names and intentions. His brother has little insight but is good at gathering information. Marin has never disliked Zarko at all. Finds him easily anticipated, pallid. His brother fears and mistrusts him—from childhood, and still. They are past an age where that will change, he thinks.

He hears the ninth stair's light creak, then the lower tone of the fourth. The door to the study is open. Leonora Miucci appears there. Her hat has been removed. Her bright hair is coiled and pinned. Marin stands and bows.

"Gospodar," she says.

"Signora," he says. "May I offer you wine?"

She shakes her head. "Thank you, no. But I have a request, if I may."

"Ask," he says. "You saved my life today."

She looks away. "I did not."

"*The one who shouts the warning is blessed*," he quotes.

She looks at him. She has dark eyes. "A folk saying here?"

"It is. Not all are true, of course."

She smiles a little. "We say, *A false warning can bring a true death*."

Marin smiles. "There was nothing false in yours."

She looks around the room before answering. He knows she is clever. He also knows she carries some sorrow within her. The complicating thing is, he had thought this before her husband died.

She says, "I have been invited to Sinan Isle tomorrow. I am not certain why."

"To the Daughters of Jad?" He thinks about how much to say. "I'd imagine they'll have heard of your husband's death, and wish to offer comfort."

She shrugs. "I have seldom found comfort in such places."

"But you wish to go?"

"It would be ungracious to refuse."

He considers it another moment, then does say, cautiously, "The Eldest Daughter is a woman named Filipa di Lucaro. From Rhodias. She is . . . a subtle woman."

"How can I matter to her?"

"I have no idea," he says frankly. "But I'd be careful nonetheless."

She nods. "Thank you. May I ask for a boat? I have been told that Signore Villani is also summoned. We can go together."

The artist being called to the isle seems odd for a moment, then Marin remembers something. "He won't have been invited by the Daughters, I suspect."

"No?" She looks surprised. "He said someone there has asked to see him before he goes east."

"East" is Asharias, of course. Which unlocks one small puzzle. Marin always feels happier when mysteries are solved, even trivial ones. He doesn't feel up to explaining it to her, who this other person is, how she came here. They will find out tomorrow, and it is the artist's affair, not hers—or Marin's. He realizes he is feeling the effects of the wine, after all.

He says, "We will happily offer a boat to carry you over and bring you back. I'll ask Drago to take you."

"Isn't he . . . doesn't he have much to do?"

"In the city? He hates it on land, signora. He'll be pleased to do this."

"May I also take Danica Gradek, please? For the day. I feel safer when she is with me."

"I can understand that," Marin says, with some feeling. "Of course you may. It seems a good idea."

It isn't, in fact, a good idea.

They know some things here in Dubrava, in this household, but they don't know enough. They aren't the only clever people, and being decent by nature can be a disadvantage in some circumstances.

The door to the street opens, there are voices.

"We will dine now," Marin says. "The table will be ready. The servants start moving as soon as they hear my father home from the promenade. Do you need to go upstairs first?"

"Am I acceptable?" she asks. A faint smile. The words, that wry look, seem like a glimpse of someone from before. He doesn't expect to ever know her story. Some stories, Marin Djivo thinks, we never learn, or tell.

"Of course you are," he says.

At dinner he is careful with the wine. His father is watching (and his brother, of course) and he doesn't want either of them to think he is drinking because he's afraid.

They discuss, as expected, the ship in the harbour. The *Silver Moon* of the Hrabak family (they live two houses east) has carried a number of Seressini merchants, Zarko reports, importantly. They intend to head overland immediately. Word is they carry gems and goldsmiths' work, but he isn't certain.

"So, with those, all the way to Asharias?" Andrij Djivo says.

"The court is always best for precious goods," Marin says.

He is utterly uninterested, but he also knows it is best not to reveal that, and he also knows his father relies on him, more and more. It occurs to him, mortality having impinged upon them this morning, that Andrij Djivo can't be said to be in the prime of life any more.

He looks at his father, but not too intently, or for long. Prime or otherwise, the older Djivo is still sharp as a tailor's needle in most ways. He'd know if he was being scrutinized.

Grey now, however, his younger son thinks. His father's beard and hair are even white in places. Still a full head of hair, mind you. A firm voice and a strong laugh. And there are occasionally sounds from the parental bedchamber at night that can embarrass grown sons living in the same house.

It is almost certainly time for those sons to be married, starting with the older one. He knows his mother thinks that way.

He excuses himself as soon as it seems acceptable. He could plead fatigue, but he's not in the habit of explaining himself. He rises and bows. He creaks at the fourth and ninth stairs, walks the high-ceilinged, lamplit corridor to his room, and enters.

The servants know his habits and they like him, which always helps. There is a fire going, and a lantern by the bed with another by his reading chair. There is a wine flask on a table beside the chair. No glass or cup, however. An omission. He turns, feeling a breeze.

Danica Gradek is sitting on the window ledge with the window and shutters open to the night. Stars can be seen behind her. She holds a glass of dark red wine.

"It wasn't the servant girl, was it?" she says. "In the Orsat house."

DANICA COULDN'T HAVE SAID why she climbed the outer wall to his room, entering through the too easily opened window. She had gone properly up the main stairway (two of the steps creak) to Leonora twice since arriving. She was a family guard, not required to move in secrecy, even after dark.

She was in a strange mood this evening, however.

What are you doing? her grandfather asked, irritated, as she went out the back door to the quiet street behind the house. She looked around to be sure she was alone, and began to climb.

Not sure, was all she said, at first. And then, *I think I'd like to be by myself for a little, zadek.*

Be careful, child, and—

She closed his presence down in her mind. He hated that, and she didn't like it either, but there were times . . .

She continued up the wall. She knew which room was Marin's. She knew where everyone slept by now. She was a family guard and a Senjani.

Well, she had been a Senjani for a few years. She wasn't now. Did some time there, mostly as a child, make you one of the heroes of Senjan? And another fair question: why *was* she doing this now, climbing?

Partly a mood? This morning had affected her. More than it should have? But how could you judge that, Danica thought.

Last night she'd been lying on the pallet in the room they'd given her in the guards' quarters, and had closed her eyes on the thought that she could be hanged as soon as tomorrow and so end a small life without meaning.

The shutters outside his room were hooked back against the outside wall. She pulled open the window, slipped inside, seated herself on the ledge to wait. She reminded herself to talk to the house steward about proper latches and locks for all the windows and shutters.

She saw the wine they'd brought in for Marin. It amused her to claim the glass, pour for herself. She thought of taking the chair by the fire, but went back to the window and sat there again.

She didn't have long to wait. She might not have stayed if she'd had too much time to think about this. The door opened, he came in, saw her. She made a comment about his visits to the Orsat house. She had heard him say the other sister's name this morning. *Elena.* It wasn't difficult to figure out what he'd been doing, what he'd initially thought was happening in the council chamber.

She hadn't meant to say that, though. She wasn't thinking very clearly. She hoped he couldn't see that, and then she realized another part of her hoped he might, and would make this easier. All of it. That *someone* could do that.

"SHALL I CALL for another glass?" Marin asks, sounding more calm than he feels, seeing her framed in the window with night behind her.

"We can share," she murmurs. "That happens on raids."

"Is that what this is?"

She smiles briefly. "I don't think so." A pause. "I'm not a Senjani any more."

He looks more closely at her. She has no weapons except, probably, for the concealed knives. Nor is she wearing her hat. Her hair is unpinned, past her shoulders. This is not a small, aristocratic lady from Batiara. This is the extremely capable person who saved his life today.

"I know you aren't," he says. He crosses, takes the glass from her hand. "It must be difficult. I'm happy to share, but I do need a drink. I was restrained at dinner."

"So you wouldn't be seen to be disturbed by what happened?"

He looks at her again. "Yes," he says.

He fills the glass, drinks half, hands the wine back to her. She drains it. He takes it and goes to the flask again.

"Were you?" she asks. "Disturbed?"

He nods. There is no reason to deny it, he thinks. "Vudrag was a friend, among the other parts of this."

"I'm sorry," she says, unexpectedly.

He looks at the wineglass and decides—also unexpectedly—to slow down. He says, "And you? How do you feel tonight?"

"I'm not sure," says Danica Gradek. "Not sure why I came here, either. And this way."

"Neither am I," Marin says.

She laughs, then stops. She says, "The window was too easy to open. They all need locks."

"We aren't normally in much danger here."

She is silent a moment, then says, "I have killed nine men this spring."

Unexpected, again. He comes back to the window, hands her the wineglass. She drinks, just a little of it this time. He says, "You never did, before?"

She shakes her head. "Of course not. I was a child. And whatever you've heard about Senjan we don't go around killing people. Nor do the women drink blood."

"I hadn't heard they did. Or, not from anyone intelligent." He is thinking hard. They are quite close now. There is a long-legged, fair-haired woman sitting in the window of his bedroom at night. He says, "They weigh on you? These deaths?"

She bites her lip. "Maybe. But that isn't it," Danica Gradek says. "It is that none of them, not one, was Osmanli, and they are my revenge. *They are*, not Seressinis, or my raid companion, or some foolish nobleman here."

"I see," he says, after a silence.

"Do you?" She glares at him. "Do you?"

He shakes his head. "Probably not. Not yet. I am willing to try."

She looks away then, towards the fire. Then she puts the wine-glass carefully down beside her. She pushes herself off the ledge, stands in front of him.

"Try later," she says, almost angrily.

She puts her hands behind his head and draws it down and she kisses him slowly. Her mouth is soft. He hasn't expected softness.

"Try later," she says again. "Not now."

By then his arms have closed around her. He is ferociously aroused, hungry to taste her, made more so by feeling the hunger in her, in the way her fingers tighten in his hair.

"I wanted you on the ship," he says, pulling back for a moment.

Her eyes are very blue. "Of course you did. Men are like that."

"No. Well, yes, they are. We are. But it wasn't only because—"

"Stop talking," she says. Her mouth takes his again.

AND NOW, FINALLY, she does acknowledge why she's here.

You need to try to be honest with yourself, Danica thinks, although thinking has become a challenge. But lovemaking is how she has been able to (at times) bring herself entirely into a given moment, night, hour before sunrise—not be enmeshed in the hard sorrow of memory, or imagining what might redress remembered fires.

She has never been with someone this experienced, however. The realization arrives with its own power. The young fighters of Senjan, or boys from Hrak Island, were never so . . . aware of her? Nor has she ever lain in a room, on a bed, like this. Her clothing is gone, with astonishingly little effort (she cannot recall her boots coming off, nor either of her knives). The firelight and the lamps play upon his body, and hers. His hair is reddened by the firelight, hers must be the same. She closes her eyes. She is only here, in this room. Now. It feels like a gift.

"Which would please you? My fingers or my mouth?" Marin Djivo asks, and pauses in what he is doing. That pause becomes a kind of agony. She suspects he knows it. She is sure he does. She could hate him for that, she thinks. She arches her hips, involuntarily.

She says, a little breathlessly, "Need I decide?"

And hears him laugh before his mouth returns to the great astonishment of what it has been doing to her. She hears herself say, as if from far away, "If I must choose . . . That is, if I . . ."

Not a sentence she ever finishes. She looks down at him, along the bed, his bed, exploring her, and it is as if she's exploring herself with him in the moment. Not wrapped in sorrow, not raging. Not just now.

Danica reaches down, tugs his hair.

"Up," she says. "Come up by me."

And a little later she is the one who says, laughing inwardly, suspecting he can hear it in her voice, "My fingers or my mouth, a preference? Will you tell?"

"Oh, Jad! All of you," Marin Djivo says. "Please."

"Greedy?"

"I am," he manages. It is mostly a gasp, which pleases her. He says, "I have decided not to . . . make distinctions . . . as to parts of your body, Danica Gradek."

"I see," she says.

And shifts above and on top of him, in need. She mounts him, sheathing his sex in hers. Time is running as it always runs, carrying them, carrying everyone. The silver moon will reach the window, rising through stars. Two men died violently this morning. She did not die, he did not. They are in this room, this night. He is in her.

She rides him, rising and falling, awareness of life like a pulse-beat within her, and he meets her urgency with his own. He turns her over, staying inside, and they are fire to each other, but also shelter, a place to hide tonight. And there is also tenderness before they are done and lying back on the bed, sweat glistening on two bodies, and they do see, through the open window, a silver half moon shining above the rooftops of Dubrava.

HE ALMOST FEELS to be in danger, lying in his own bed with a woman's head on his chest. Not danger like this morning's (he hadn't even grasped that in the moment, it was over too quickly) but the sensation is real, and so Marin is unwontedly hesitant.

He says, "You said I should only try to understand later. About those you've killed. Do you remember?"

"I remember," Danica Gradek says softly, not moving her head. He suspects her eyes are closed.

"I would like to. Understand."

She stirs a little. Her hair is across his body. Her scent surrounds him.

"It isn't later enough," she says.

Her voice is low, satiated. Normally, he'd feel pleased with himself. Taking pleasure, giving it. He has had enough encounters with expensive women to know how to do both.

But tonight he wants to understand something that has nothing to do with lovemaking. Or, perhaps it does for her. Perhaps, he thinks, that is why she came up here. Desire cresting and fulfilled, to make something go away for a time.

He says, "You told me you were a girl in Senjan? You came there from . . . where?"

"Oh, dear. Are you a talking sort of man? After?" He likes this laziness in her voice.

"Sometimes I want to know where I am, where those beside me are."

"Easy enough. They are beside you." She moves her head and bites one of his nipples. He winces, tugs at her hair. She laughs, still softly.

They are silent. She breaks the stillness, surprising him. "You did lie with the other sister? You thought this morning's attack was about her, didn't you?"

"Yes," he says. "I didn't know Iulia at all."

"They made it very public."

"I hope not. I don't think people heard much."

"Maybe, but they did want the attack on you to be seen."

He's been dealing with that thought all day. "Yes," he says.

"You think the brother I killed is the one who bedded her?"

He is shocked, genuinely so. "What? Why would you . . . ?"

She shrugs, her head still on his chest. It is darker in the room, the fire has settled, embers. "They accuse you, they kill you, once dead you cannot deny being her lover. That becomes the story the world knows."

Marin shakes his head. "More complex than it needs to be. She is with child by someone she won't name, probably someone not of her class. They can't arrange a wedding. And someone evidently did see me climbing down their wall in winter."

"From the maidservant's room?"

He sighs. "I had to say that. For Elena."

"Yes," she says. "Very courteous. The servant will be dismissed now, though."

He hadn't thought about that. "I will arrange a position for her if that happens."

"It will happen," Danica Gradek says. And then, after another silence, "Hadjuks raided and torched my village. Killed or captured almost everyone. They killed my father and my older brother, took my little brother away with them."

"Oh, Jad," Marin says.

"Jad wasn't there."

The voice isn't lazy any more.

He says, carefully, "And so it is Osmanlis, Asharites, you have set yourself to kill?"

She moves her head up and down on his chest. She still hasn't looked at him.

"I'm not doing very well at it," she says.

He is trying to think of something to say to that when she glides a hand down his belly and finds the slackness of his sex. She begins, as if carelessly, to play with it, and it isn't slack after a little while.

"I believe you wish to say something comforting," Danica Gradek says. "That isn't what I want."

Marin offers her again what it seems she does want from him tonight, and takes his own disturbingly intense pleasure doing so, seeing her respond, listening, sharing.

He sleeps after.

He is alone in the bed when he wakes towards dawn. She's closed the window behind her and the lamps and fire are out.

When he goes downstairs later, having tumbled back into sleep again, she is gone from the house, and so is Leonora Miucci.

Drago had come for them not long after sunrise, a servant in the dining room reports. Marin had forgotten that the doctor's widow had been summoned to Sinan Isle and had asked for Danica as a guard.

He'd meant to warn Danica about the Eldest Daughter there, how no one trusted her. And to mention the other woman they might meet. It was good, in his experience, to have as much information in advance as possible.

He is unhappy with himself for neglecting this. He thinks about taking another of their boats and going across, following them. That would be, he decides, a strange thing to do, and he hasn't been invited.

His mind keeps circling back to last night. Unsurprisingly, on the whole.

His father offers a new thought at their morning meeting, an interesting one. It concerns the ship that has just come in and the merchants headed east. It requires, Andrij Djivo says, more reliable tidings than they currently have as to the khalif's plans for war. Marin undertakes to see what he can discover in the city. He does try to do that, later, with little result beyond gossip and rumour. It is too early in the spring to know, everyone says.

He remains uneasy about the two women. Even walks down to the harbour at one point, looking across at Sinan. The isle is close enough that one can see the dome of their sanctuary.

Drago is there with them, he reminds himself, and there is reason to believe Danica Gradek can take care of anyone she's asked to guard.

Still, he isn't entirely surprised by what they learn later, and he does blame himself.

CHAPTER XII

It had often occurred to her how desperately hard it was for a woman to make her own way in the world—and how rarely it happened.

One possibility was to marry someone who went off to war and died conveniently, leaving a business, property, valuables. Widows, depending on where they lived and on their families, might shape a little freedom. Most often they were forced to marry again quickly, and not someone of their choosing.

You needed to be fortunate, and extremely determined.

She had been both, Filipa di Lucaro thought, waiting on Sinan Isle for her visitor on a springtime morning. Choosing faith, the path of the god, was no assurance of controlling your destiny. Unless you were an aristocrat and arrived at a retreat preceded by substantial gifts, the religious course left you with arrogant superiors and surrounded by frustrated women. The struggles for trivial advantage in a closed-off, overwrought retreat could create hatreds and rage fiercer than on a battlefield, and they festered like untreated wounds.

Of course, if you were truly devout, genuinely envisaged yourself as a servant of Jad, lived to comfort the sick and the grieving, to pray six times a day clutching a worn-smooth sun disk, were wrapped in thoughts of the god from sunrise to nightfall when you lay alone on a narrow pallet—well, how pleasant for you. Different assessments of what made for a good life applied to different women.

Filipa di Lucaro, Eldest Daughter of Jad on Sinan for a long time now, ruling like a queen in this retreat in the harbour of Dubrava, was not one of the devout.

She had freedom and power, both. She corresponded with the Council of Twelve—and the Duke of Seressa, privately. She received letters from around the Jaddite world: from Ferrieres and Karch and Anglcyn, from the mad emperor's court in Obravic, or all the way west in Esperaña. She played a *role* in the world. She chose her own lovers. She chose whom she wanted killed—usually for Seressa, discussed in coded messages, but not invariably.

She had that dearly prized, almost impossible thing for a woman: independence.

Her only significant, ongoing trouble was that she had arrived on Sinan to find a *real* queen here before her. More than a queen: an empress.

She was not someone with any desire to be Eldest Daughter on the isle, or even take the vows of the god, but Eudoxia of Sarantium had been here for almost twenty-five bitter years now, and she was—there was no gainsaying it—an enemy.

Enemies could often be killed. Not this one. She'd tried.

Filipa had vivid memories of that. She'd essayed two poisons in the year after coming into power here and realizing that the older woman was going to be an impediment. Neither poison did anything at all, though both were considered infallible, one slow, one very swift.

And shortly after the second attempt had come the morning in this room when the empress-mother of Sarantium (which was no more) had told her why the poisons had failed, then told her certain other things.

It seemed that in the court of Sarantium in the last turbulent, frightened decades, when the threat of the Osmanli Asharites was matched by savage rivalries within the palace compound, it had become customary for the imperial family, even the children, to take small doses of most known poisons, to build protection against them.

There were, of course, lesser-known poisons, but the empress had made something else clear on that long-ago morning. She had, it seemed, sent out three copies of a letter, to be opened on her death. One was with the rector of Dubrava, one with the privy councillors of the High Patriarch in Rhodias, and one was in a location she did not reveal.

She had shown a fourth copy of this letter to Filipa that morning. It stipulated, in neatly written Trakesian, that if the empress-mother died it was due to poison administered by the Eldest Daughter in the retreat where she had taken shelter after the great calamity.

Further, it indicated that Filipa di Lucaro was not—as she had put forth to the world—from a good family near Rhodias, but was Seressa-born, an artisan's daughter, and had been guided by the Council of Twelve through a long, deceitful route here, to serve as the most important Seressini spy in Dubrava.

Communications from Seressa to her, this letter went on, with precision, were routed through Rhodias or from another retreat near Seressa, appearing to discuss matters of faith and administration. In secret ink would come her instructions from the Council of Twelve. Her replies to them were sent by the same routes.

Every detail, down to the way the ink was made, had been correct.

She could remember the words Empress Eudoxia had spoken to her that morning (also a springtime): "You are a child among children if you believe your shallow intrigues can touch what Sarantium knew. When I die, however I die, you are destroyed. Take good care of me."

"Why? Why do you hate me?" Filipa could remember asking with horror rising like a wave in a wind.

"Aside from your trying to kill me, you mean?"

No good answer to that, then or now.

The empress-mother had smiled that morning long ago. Her smile had frightened Filipa from the beginning, those bleak, enraged eyes. She had said, "I despise you for pettiness and greed. For killing because you can, not for need. And because your eternally accursed Seressa left its fleet in its harbour when the City of Cities, glory of the god, was allowed to fall."

"I didn't do that! I was barely out of childhood!"

"And now you aren't, and you serve them, masked in faith. I see you clearly, I know you very well. Take care of my life. Yours ends when I die."

So many years ago. Her life bound since that day to that of this implacable woman, locked in undying rage.

Filipa di Lucaro had reason to believe she could get that sealed letter retrieved from the Rector's Palace. Some people owed her a great deal, one member of the council wanted a night with her very much. His retrieving a document and handing it to her still sealed would be a fair price for her body and she would pay it gladly.

She even thought she might be able to have someone find the letter in Rhodias, with help from the Council of Twelve who would—surely!—not want a valuable person exposed, along with their own secrets.

But there was no true *surely* when it came to Seressa.

They might be childlike in intrigue for the dreadful woman in Filipa's own rooms (*always* in these rooms—in an armchair in the shadows, day after day, year after year) but they might as easily disown her, dismiss her, *expose* her if they saw benefit in doing so.

And there was that abominable third letter, and she had no idea where it had been sent.

She was trapped, in the midst of the power and ease and pleasure of her life. And that life would come to an ugly end when a vicious old woman died.

There truly were no easy—or safe—paths to control of her own fate for a woman, even if you thought you'd found one on an isle in the bay of Dubrava.

Hatred, however, a hatred so large it filled the retreat and the isle—that you could carry within yourself.

"At least," she had said more than once to the old, vile woman in her rooms, "my husband did not throw away an empire in slack folly, and my son did not die uselessly on the city walls. Remind me, what *did* the Asharites do with his head after sticking it on a spike? I confess have forgotten!"

No reply to taunting. Never. Not once. The blackness of that gaze, those eyes.

On this morning in springtime, word came to both of them that their guest had arrived. Guests, it appeared. Filipa heard the man's name for the first time as he was presented to her. Of course she'd read about him in the letter from the Twelve. So had the other woman, that was part of their arrangement. Eudoxia kept silent, remained alive, had access to anything she wanted. The empress-mother had sent her own invitation to this man, for whatever reason. She did that. She did what she chose to do.

What neither of them had expected was the third person who entered behind the other two.

THE RETREAT ON THE ISLE was beautiful, perched on a rise of land, views in all directions. Terraced gardens sloped south and west, with a vineyard beyond. They'd come up from the dock along a path shaded by cypress trees. Drago remained outside, near the entrance to the complex.

"I won't be far," he'd said.

The Eldest Daughter of the Sinan retreat was also beautiful, her skin pale and perfect, cheekbones high. Her welcome to Leonora Miucci and Pero Villani was courteous, formal, regal. There was something cold in this room, however, Danica thought, watching from a few steps behind. From Rhodias, Drago had said this woman was, on the isle a long time, and—

Her thoughts were interrupted. But not by anyone who was speaking.

She'd seen someone. Her eyesight had always been good.

Drago had told them about the older woman who lived on Sinan Isle. Pero's command to visit had come from her. On the way across in a morning breeze the captain had spoken of the mother of the last emperor—Valerius XI, who had died, and been beheaded and mutilated in the final assault on Sarantium. The empress-mother had made her way here not long after. She had been sent from the city by her son before the siege began. The last siege.

She wasn't just on the isle, however. The Empress Eudoxia was, Danica realized, in this room with them.

She was in shadow, an alcove to their right, in a high-backed chair with wide arms. A small woman, face difficult to make out there. But Danica knew who this was, and where the truly regal was therefore to be found here, so far to the west of where she belonged.

Do you see her?

I do, her zadek said. She could feel his emotion. *Child, I never thought to ever . . .*

I know.

Danica surprised herself. Sometimes you did that. She crossed the tiled floor, moving from where sunlight fell from a wide stone terrace, into a shadow like shadows of the past.

She knelt, aware of how insignificant she was, how little she could bring to this woman. She said, hearing a huskiness in her voice, "My lady, permit me, please."

And she kissed the slippered foot of the woman sitting here, so far from glory, from shining, from what had been, by all accounts there were, brighter once than anything the world knew.

"You are permitted," the old woman said, a thin, clear voice. Then, "You are . . . ?"

Call her "your grace."

"I am no one, your grace. My name is Danica Gradek, once of Senjan, now serving in Dubrava."

"Serving?"

"The Djivo family, as a guard, your grace."

"Ah. You are the one who came in on their ship."

"Came in? She *attacked* that ship!" It was the Eldest Daughter, the beautiful one. "A murderous Senjani joins us. How interesting."

Murderous? Danica, be careful.

But how can I matter to her?

I don't know. But there is malice there.

I see it. Surely not towards me. Not from Rhodias!

I think it is, child.

The old woman looked at the younger one who ruled here and it was impossible to miss the malice there, too. This morning might not proceed, Danica thought, as they had imagined it.

She stepped back, because Leonora and the artist had both come to do exactly as she had, in turn.

"The Senjani," said the woman who had been empress of the eastern world, "was first to know and salute us. It is worthy of note."

"Is it?" said Filipa di Lucaro. "An appeal for clemency?"

"Why," said Leonora Miucci, "would Danica need clemency here?"

The Eldest Daughter looked briefly disconcerted. She hadn't expected quickness, or a challenge, from the young widow, perhaps.

"Really? Are you unaware of what Senjan does to Seressa? To Dubrava?"

"Hardly unaware. I was also in the council chamber yesterday when she saved a life, and on the ship when she avenged my husband's death. She is owed gratitude. The rector said as much."

"He did say that. It has been reported. What do you say?" asked Pero Villani, looking at the First Daughter.

"A Seressini asks me that?"

"He does," the artist said. "And the High Patriarch you serve has commended the Senjani as loyal servants of Jad on our border with the Asharites."

A moment of stillness.

"There were also Senjani who fell on the walls of Sarantium." It was the old woman who had been an empress.

"Even so," Filipa di Lucaro replied, "they deny the god and despoil his faith. Fighting Asharites is one thing, but stealing from—"

"How dare you!" said Danica.

Oh, child. Be careful.

No!

"You speak to me like that?" The cheekbones seemed even sharper now, Danica thought. "In this place, where I am armed with the will of the High Patriarch and the sanctity of Jad?"

"Are you?" Danica said. "You heard Signore Villani. The High Patriarch, may he be blessed in light, has defended and commended us."

"We understand," said the old woman from her shadows, "that this is true."

You could hear cold pleasure in her voice.

"And," Danica added, "Senjan *did* have men die at Sarantium. They sent eighty all the way east from a town of several hundred souls, and every one of them died for the emperor and the god. Were any of *your* family there when the love of Jad died? Where were the Rhodian soldiers, or Seressini ships and men? Singing love songs on canals? Making money among Asharites in Soriyya?

And you denounce us? Name as barbarians those *still* fighting and dying for the god's faith?"

Child, you have an enemy now.

She was an enemy when she knew me. I don't know why. Unless . . .

What?

Unless she isn't from Rhodias.

Oh, Jad. Don't say—

But she did. Because if she was right, it explained why Leonora had been summoned here. Not to be given comfort, but for instructions.

She didn't feel like being careful, suddenly.

"Are you even from Rhodias?" she asked the woman who ruled here. And heard, from behind, dry laughter from the older woman who had sat a throne in a greater realm.

"What? Of course I am!" said Filipa di Lucaro. "Do you want my family's lineage? To know if they are worth pillaging?"

"I'm certain they are," said Danica. "We don't require much." There came another chuckle from the shadows.

And unexpected laughter—from the Eldest Daughter herself.

"I deserve that, I suppose," Filipa di Lucaro said. She smiled. She had a very good smile. "I believe I have let my dismay at the death of Doctor Miucci in a Senjani raid overcome my duty to guests. Whatever else, that *is* what you all are. I would be grateful if we might begin anew, with wine on the terrace here."

"That might indeed be better," Leonora said.

Danica looked behind her. The old woman in her chair said nothing, but her eyes had been waiting for Danica's. She moved her head very slightly sideways. No more than that.

You saw?

I saw, zadek.

There was a scraping sound, the chair on the tiles. The empress stood up, easily enough, though she held a walking stick in her right hand. With it, she thumped on a door behind her chair. It was opened instantly by a nervous-looking acolyte.

The empress-mother looked at Pero Villani. "Signore, attend upon us. We would speak privately."

A command. Pero followed the old woman through the door. The acolyte went after them and closed it.

Another brief silence. Filipa di Lucaro smiled again. She said, "I do have words to share with you, Signora Miucci, after we share a cup of wine, the three of us. Might I request you to have your guard withdraw, after, perhaps into the gardens?"

"There is nothing," Leonora said, "I do not share with Gosparko Gradek. I owe her a great deal."

"I have no doubt you do, but our guards do not, surely, know everything about our lives."

"This one does," Leonora said. "Everything that might matter here."

The other woman's smile remained but Danica thought there was effort to it now.

Leonora added, "She knows, for example, that Doctor Miucci and I were never married."

The Eldest Daughter's smile faded.

She shouldn't have said that.

Probably not.

Be careful, Danica.

I will try, zadek. Should I leave? And ask Leonora what happened after?

There may be danger for you out there.

And not here?

Here, as well. Watch her.

And watching, Danica saw.

There was a heavy, handsomely made oak cabinet against the wall beside the writing desk. It had a panel that dropped to make a flat surface. Filipa di Lucaro used a key from her belt to open and lower this. She took out a flask of pale wine from inside. She claimed two silver goblets—and then a third, reaching farther back in the cabinet.

That one will be yours, child. Do not.

Danica felt suddenly cold. There had been a sense of danger, but nothing immediate, not the feeling she could die here. That had changed.

She looked at Leonora. The other woman was already gazing at her, brow furrowed. Their host was pouring the wine.

Filipa di Lucaro put the flask back down. She brought their wine on a silver tray, smiling again. She placed it on her desk, nudging cups towards each of them. The third, the one from the back, was indeed Danica's.

Danica removed her bow and quiver and set them down. Leonora came over to the desk and took her wine, also smiling. She walked across the room towards the terrace with the gardens and the vines beyond.

"You can see all the ships coming in and out, it seems."

The other woman strolled after her.

"We can. In good weather it is a pleasure to be out here. And we know who has returned or arrived before anyone else. I enjoy that."

"I imagine you do," Leonora said.

The two of them stood together, looking at grass and trees, sea and clouds.

Danica reached across and took the cup Filipa di Lucaro had intended for herself. She left hers on the tray.

You know what she did?

I think so. Poison already in the cup so she didn't have to put it in?

That must be it. A vicious woman. You may have been right, Dani.

That she is from Seressa?

It makes too much—

He stopped. The other two were coming back. Leonora had known exactly what to do.

Filipa di Lucaro said, "I hope you will let this serve as my apology and that you might now . . ."

She stopped, staring at her writing desk.

"I am happy to," said Danica. "Shall we drink to the triumph of Jad and virtue? And of course I will leave you to talk, after. I am only a guard." She gestured towards the cup that had been meant for her, which remained on the desk.

Filipa di Lucaro's smile was gone. She was polished, however, immensely experienced. A long time doing this. She said, "I never actually drink wine in the morning, myself. But I will touch cups with you and—"

"In Senjan, it is an insult not to drink with guests when the wine has been poured by oneself."

"I am fortunate not to be in Senjan, then, aren't I?"

Leonora was pale now. She was prone to that, her face showing her state of mind.

Danica said, "You are. But if you don't drink with me I will be offended and will also draw a conclusion about that cup."

"Why would I care what conclusions—?"

"Drink it," Danica said. "It was meant for me. Drink it down."

"I cannot imagine taking instructions from someone such as you!"

"Ah. The apology is withdrawn?"

"I simply do not allow barbarous behaviour here."

"Only you are allowed?"

The other woman turned to Leonora. "Forgive me, your servant is unspeakably ill-mannered. It is not acceptable. I must call my guards to escort her out."

"I don't think so," said Leonora.

And she put her own cup down and took the one remaining on the desk. She strode back to the terrace.

"Drago! Gospar Ostaja! I have need of you!"

Drago was out there, as promised, within earshot. They heard him reply. An immensely reassuring man.

"Signora?" he said, coming around to the terrace.

But another man could also be seen approaching, almost running. Big, young, broad-chested.

Leonora said, "Take this cup, please, gospar. Handle it carefully. I have reason to believe there is poison in it. We need it kept safe to take back."

"That is beyond an insult!" cried Filipa di Lucaro. She looked at the other man coming through the garden. "Juraj, I command you to stop this."

Danica said, "He will die if he tries, Eldest Daughter."

"*What?*"

"If the cup is blameless our contrition will be real. If it is not, the rector and council will be informed."

Leonora was still holding the cup. Filipa di Lucaro moved suddenly towards her, a hand drawn back to strike it.

Her life ended.

A thrown blade. The same knife that had killed Vudrag Orsat in the council chamber.

It was an awkward angle. Danica's dagger caught her in the heart, slightly to one side.

Oh, child.

I had no doubts, zadek.

There came a wordless scream from the man in the garden. He had no tongue, Danica realized. He did have a short sword at his belt. Not very usual for a gardener. And he was running now.

"Back!" she said to Leonora. "Quickly!"

It wasn't necessary, in the event. Drago Ostaja, burly and stocky and happier by far on sea than on land, was nonetheless extremely quick himself—and no good sea captain was ever without his own blade.

He met Filipa di Lucaro's tongueless assassin as the man approached the terrace. The bigger man turned to face him, still making that high, unholy-sounding noise. Blades clashed. Danica was turning for her bow when she saw it end.

He was good, Drago, and he didn't fight with anything that might be called gentility. He kicked the other man in the kneecap as he parried a swing. Then he stabbed him in the midriff as the other man stumbled. A straight, short sword thrust. Efficient, you could call it.

The screaming ended. It was suddenly very quiet out beyond the terrace. They could hear seabirds calling from the dock where their boat was moored. The birds were darting and diving in sunlight. The waves sparkled in the breeze from the west. The air was bright, the world was bright, the god's sun was rising through the sky.

So many people I've killed now, zadek!

Child, stop counting.

How? she asked, in pain.

She was trying to kill you, Dani.

I know! But so many. And not one of them was—

Child, stop.

They heard a door open behind them. Danica whirled, reaching for her second knife. She stopped.

"It is past time someone killed that one," said the empress-mother Eudoxia, coming forward to where light from the terrace fell on the tiles. "It is acceptable that it was you."

Pero was behind her. He had stopped by the desk, put a hand upon it for support. Not a man, Danica guessed, who had lived a life that contained much violence. He was looking at Leonora, who still held the cup of poisoned wine.

HE HAD SEEN DEATH SO MANY TIMES.

Everyone saw death, the plague made certain of it, and the gallows, and Seressa was dangerous at night.

But in the past few days he had seen people slain in front of him, or newly dead. Pero Villani thought, *This is much too much. I am an artist. I only want to be permitted to do my work.*

Given the conversation he'd just had in the room on the other side of the door, that might become a challenge.

"You are going to Sarantium?" the old woman had asked, turning to face him. The room was simply furnished, with a narrow bed against the far wall, a sun disk above it. The young acolyte had looked as if she wanted to be anywhere but here. Pero, to be truthful, felt much the same. He didn't correct the empress-mother as to the city's name. He doubted she ever used any other.

"I am, your grace."

"You are commissioned to paint the hound? The enemy of light? His portrait?"

He was quite sure she never used any other names for the khalif, either, unless they were worse.

He cleared his throat. "I am," he said. "I have been honoured by Seressa and—"

"You will paint from life?"

"That is possible, your grace. If I am . . . if he permits—"

"Good. If so, you will use the opportunity to kill him for us."

She said it with calm precision. But you knew, Pero Villani thought, you had to know how much undying fire was here, how much hatred, rage.

He was shaken. He struggled to think what he should say, what he *could* say.

She smiled at him, as if encouragingly. Her hair was white under a purple cloth cap. Porphyry, they'd called that colour in the east—and reserved it for emperors and empresses. She wore a dark-blue cloak over a green robe. Her face was small, wrinkled, her eyes wide-set, blue and brilliant, still.

She said, casually, "They will kill you, of course. You will be martyred in Sarantium, die where so many died. A Blessed Victim in years to come—venerated, prayed to. This is not being honoured, being sent to put paint to canvas or wood. *That* will be the honour that clings to your name with the scent of eternal grace."

"My lady," Pero began, "I am not a man of violence or war. I am—"

"You would never get near his palaces if you were. It is," she smiled again, "perfectly devised to our purpose that you are what you are."

Our purpose.

He opened his mouth and closed it.

She said, "We are not yet so old as to be a fool, Signore Villani. We know this may not be possible. We also know that Seressa will have raised this possibility with you. We know the Seressinis. Yes, you will be searched, and watched whenever you are close to the hound of night. But we lay this upon you as a task any Jaddite, loyal to the god and to the city that is lost, must take up with pride. You *know* what was done there twenty-five years ago. You know what Sarantium was for a thousand years. You may have a chance—how many men have had this?—to make redress for all that pain, for the golden centuries stripped away." She paused. "I ask you to pray in Valerius's great sanctuary—for me and for my husband and son and all the dead—whatever else happens when you are there."

It wasn't a sanctuary any more. The Asharites had turned it into one of their own temples. They had removed the altar, the sun disks, what mosaics had remained. Everyone knew that. *She* knew that.

Even so.

Even so. Pero knelt again before this woman whose unbending, unending pride and remembrance was a reproach to all of them. He said, "I am honoured that you have spoken to me, asked me these things. I will remember. And . . . I will do what I can."

He astonished himself, saying the words.

She smiled at him again. It was not a gentle smile. It had been widely reported that she'd had two of her children strangled by eunuchs in the palace complex to smooth the way for her chosen, youngest child to the throne—the one who had taken the name Valerius XI, and had died in the last assault. Pero felt, disturbingly, as if he had entered into a story that wasn't his own.

There came a scream, an appalling, mangled sound from outside.

"Ah," said the old woman, lifting her head. "It is likely that someone has died. Let us go see. Today becomes better and better."

She gestured. The frightened girl sprang forward and opened the door. They went through into the larger room. There was a dead man in the garden and a dead woman on the terrace.

"Very good," said the empress-mother of Sarantium. "It was past time for this to happen."

SHE WAS DYING on the dark-green flagstones. She'd had these stones imported from Varena, the great quarries there. If you knew where the best things in the world were and you had resources you could surround your life with beauty.

She heard the door open, footsteps, the old hag's words. *Past time for this to happen.* She wished, she wished so much, with her last moments alive in the world, that she'd killed the other woman long ago. But the letters—those terrible letters—had crippled her.

There was considerable pain. She hadn't known there could be so much pain. They said childbirth was very hard sometimes, but she'd never had a child. She wanted to speak, but felt blood bubbling in her mouth. This was what dying by a knife in the heart was, she thought. Killed by another woman. Added bitterness in that. There was! It was so hard, always so hard for any woman to make her way in a brutal world, and now . . .

A bright morning. It seemed to be growing dark. It was dark.

LEONORA WAS STILL HOLDING the cup. It contained what she was certain was poisoned wine. It made her uneasy to have it in her hand. Death on the lips from a silver cup. She looked at the body of the woman who had ruled here, very much like royalty. The flagstones of the terrace were green, some were dark with blood, almost to Leonora's feet. *Third time*, she thought. Blood beside her, and someone dead. She was pleased her hand was steady, she didn't want to spill the wine.

"Are you all right?" Danica asked. She had come out to the terrace.

Leonora nodded. Didn't trust herself to speak. How had her life come to include violent death?

She saw Drago Ostaja coming over. He took the cup from her, gently. "I'll look after this," he said. He seemed uneasy, though. They had killed someone important. Danica had. The wine, the poison in it, that would matter in telling the story.

She heard a door open. The empress-mother came back into the room with Pero. The old woman walked past the writing desk. She looked at them all, at the woman lying dead. She said, "It was past time for this to happen."

Leonora didn't understand that. She turned back to Drago. "They might say we put it in the cup ourselves. Whatever . . . is in the wine."

"They won't," said Eudoxia, who had been empress of Sarantium. She moved forward again, leaning only lightly on her stick. Pero stayed behind. "They will send people here and we will show them where she kept her poisons in vials, and in cups at the back of the cabinet, already poured, waiting."

"Why? Why will you do that?"

It was Danica, who seemed someone unable *not* to challenge and confront, Leonora thought, even if she had knelt and kissed this woman's slipper.

Eudoxia said, gravely, "Because she tried to poison us as well, years ago. She failed. As you see." Such a cold smile. "We achieved an understanding after that."

"She wasn't from Rhodias, was she?" Leonora asked.

"Of course not. Seressini, born and bred. Carefully placed here."

"As their spy?" Drago Ostaja asked. Leonora heard hope in his voice. If the Eldest Daughter had been a spy, then killing her might be acceptable.

The old woman smiled again. "We will wait for the rector to send us someone suitable. For the moment, a different matter needs to be addressed."

"And that is?" Danica again.

"Who follows her as Eldest Daughter. That ought to be the doctor's widow, don't you agree?"

"*What?*" Leonora gasped. She stared. "I have no desire . . . and why . . . why would they *ever* accept me? There must be so many who . . . No! That makes no sense!"

The empress was still smiling. Leonora could see Pero, behind her, looking shaken.

Eudoxia of Sarantium said, "It will make extremely good sense after we have done our part and proposed it to the daughters and to Dubrava, Signora Miucci. And don't you have good reasons for not returning to Seressa? Or Mylasia? We did read the letters sent from the Council of Twelve concerning their passengers on the *Blessed Ingacia*. Including the parts in secret ink."

"She let you do that?" Danica asked.

"She had no choice."

There was a silence. "*Will* they accept her?" Danica finally asked. Her voice was thoughtful.

The empress was still smiling, this time with a hint of genuine amusement. "You don't think we can deal with religious women on an isle in the harbour of Dubrava?"

Danica shook her head. "I am certain you can, your grace. You can deal with Dubrava and Seressa, with us, with this dead woman. With everyone."

"Everyone but the Osmanlis in Sarantium. But we are not dead yet, and prayers can be answered, miracles occur, by the grace of Jad."

She looked, Leonora thought, indomitable, and terrifying. And what she had just said was true. Leonora would not go back west. There was no home for her across the narrow sea. Was there one on this isle? She didn't know, but . . .

"I don't have to be Eldest Daughter," she said hesitantly. "I can just—"

"Yes, you do," said Eudoxia. "They will only agree to this—the Twelve in Seressa—if that is what you become. We have to put it to them that way or they will insist you return, to be used."

To be used. Leonora surrendered. It wasn't so hard to do, after all.

She did feel a need to say, "I have no true vocation in Jad. No real desire to live only among women."

The empress-mother of Sarantium threw her head back and laughed aloud.

"And you think this one did?" she asked, finally. "With people murdered for her by that dead mute in the garden? You will be better for the women here, by far, than she ever was. And this is a place where you might—you *might*—claim some control over your life."

Leonora looked at her.

"You will help me do that?"

"We will, but for our own reasons. Do not mistake us."

Leonora stared at her. She felt her heartbeat slowing. People helped you or they hindered you or they went alongside you for a time, but it was your own life.

"I won't," she said.

PERO'S FIRST THOUGHT, moving forward to stand behind the old woman, was, *She cannot have planned this!* And then he thought, *She's more adept than even the duke and the Twelve.*

His next thought, looking at Leonora on the terrace in sunlight, hearing her exchange with the empress, was: *She is lost to me.*

She had never been his, he reflected later, on the small boat, bouncing back across choppy water to Dubrava. The breeze was behind them, the sun overhead. He was silent; Danica Gradek, beside him, was the same.

Leonora had remained on the isle.

The lives of men and women, Pero Villani thought, had not been shaped or devised to give us what we desire. He had read that somewhere.

Nearing the docks he saw a tall figure waiting for them. Marin Djivo had come down to the harbour.

"Oh, Jad, thank you!" Drago Ostaja muttered fervently.

Pero understood. Someone was going to have to go to the rector and council, to begin the process of explaining what had just happened. Marin was so much a better person for that than any of them.

Pero glanced at Danica on their bench in front of the sail. She was looking at Marin as they approached, her own hair blowing, her features almost expressionless.

Almost. He saw something unexpected there. He was an artist, after all, trained to study faces, seek out the soul in them. His father had taught him some things before he died too soon and left his son to make his way in the world.

A NUMBER OF EVENTS followed upon those of that morning on Sinan Isle. It is a mistake to think that drama is steady, continuous, even in tumultuous times. Most often there are lulls and lacunae in the life of a person or a state. There is apparent stability, order, an illusion of calm—and then circumstances can change at speed.

The wine brought from the isle was given to a trusted alchemist. One of the rector's principal advisers, a pragmatic man, fed some of it to a small dog first. Nothing happened to the animal for a day but it died, convulsing, the next morning.

Later that next day the alchemist determined that there was, indeed, a deadly compound infused into the wine. He identified it as a slow-acting poison, although the dog's death had anticipated this, and by then boats had gone across to Sinan and come back with other vials and wine cups. The alchemist was kept busy. His conclusions, shortly afterwards, added further confirmation.

A certain number of untimely deaths in Dubrava, hitherto regarded as reflecting sudden, tragic illness, were now seen in a different light.

It also emerged that the Eldest Daughter of the Sinan retreat had not been, as she had always said, from a distinguished family near Rhodias. She was Seressini and a spy: that republic's principal source of information (and some deaths) in Dubrava for years.

This was not received with anything resembling delight by the Rector's Council or the merchants of the city.

It was pointed out, by the rector himself, that they had always known Seressa spied here, as it did everywhere, as Dubrava itself sought information in all ways it could. This did little to ease tumult in the council chamber. There was, for many, genuine dismay that a holy office had been abused in this way. It spoke to godlessness, even heresy. Along with a blunt letter sent to the Council of Twelve, another went to the High Patriarch and a third to the Emperor Rodolfo in Obravic, outlining the story.

The world needed to know of this Seressini perfidy, and some might be in a position to offer more than condemnation. Any trading sanctions against the Queen of the Sea could only help Dubrava's merchants, of course.

On a more immediate matter, the high cleric of Dubrava had a meeting with the rector and the latter's most trusted advisers. He emerged proclaiming his support for the idea that the new Eldest Daughter on Sinan Isle should be someone who might not have been expected. She was very young, but had rank and family easily distinguished enough (and easily confirmed, this time) to make the appointment suitable.

The widowed Leonora Miucci of Mylasia, just beginning to mourn her husband's terrible murder, had expressed a willingness to remain on the isle and to make redress in her own pious, wronged person for the evils of her predecessor.

It was understood that the retreat's honoured guest, the Empress Eudoxia of Sarantium, had graciously undertaken to guide and support the new Eldest Daughter in her first months and even years (if Jad was kind).

It was also understood in Dubrava that Leonora Miucci might well send tidings to Seressa, given her husband's origins, but since everyone *knew* this it was not untoward. Better to know than not, always.

Nearer to home, a routine matter for a city of commerce and trade, the Djivos, the well-known merchant family that had been at the forefront of many dramatic events of late, now elected to send a small party with goods (jewellery and finished cloth, it was assumed) to join a Seressini group headed east to Asharias.

There were, as always in spring, rumours of war, but the belief was that the Osmanli campaign path would—as it usually did— lie to the north of the merchants' route towards the great city, and in any case the Osmanlis *wanted* western goods from honest merchants.

The Djivo party was to be led by the younger son, Marin, with servants, animals, and four guards. One of these last was the troubling Senjani woman. It was considered a good thing that she was leaving the city. With luck she might never come back. The full party, fair-sized now, also included an artist from Seressa, one Villani—commissioned, by report, to paint a portrait of the grand khalif himself.

If that was true, the man's fortune was made, it was declared over spring wine in Dubrava. If he knew how to paint, it was pointed out. If he survived, others noted.

THE WORLD IS A GAMEBOARD, an Esperañan poet had declared, in still celebrated lines, centuries ago. The pieces are moved, they do not control themselves. They are placed opposite each other, or beside. They are allies or enemies, of higher or lower rank. They die or they survive. One player wins and then there is another game on the board.

Even so, the rise and fall of fortune for empires, kingdoms, republics, warring faiths, men and women—their heartaches, losses, loves, undying rage, delight and wonder, pain and birth and death—all these are intensely real to them, not simply images in a poem, however brilliant the poet might have been.

The dead (with exceptions impossibly rare) are gone from us. They are buried with honour, burned, thrown into the sea, left on gibbets or in fields for animals and carrion birds. One needs to stand far away, or look with a very cold eye, to see all this roiling movement, this suffering, agitation, as pieces only, moved in some game.

Filipa di Lucaro was one of those who had a proper burial with rites before and candles after, in the small cemetery beside the retreat on Sinan, overlooking the vineyard and the sea. This was insisted upon by the woman who replaced her there. The dead woman's dead servant, the mute, Juraj, was returned to his family, who came for his body in a fishing boat from along the rocky coastline north of Dubrava.

It is not known what they did with him.

PART THREE

CHAPTER XIII

There were demons that sought to claim your soul for darkness. There were ghosts and spirits, frequently malevolent. The dead did not always lie quietly.

Followers of all faiths knew these truths. You walked a twilit country path at peril, and when night fell, with or without moons, it was madness to be abroad. You could die in a ditch of a fall, having lost sight of the road.

You lived your life in intimate proximity to its sudden end. Prayers were more intense because of this. Help was needed, under sun, moons, stars—and some reason to hope for what might come after.

Laughter was also necessary, and found, in spite of—or because of—these close and terrible dangers. Simple pleasures. Music and dance, wine, ale, dice and cards. Harvest's end, the taste of berries on the bush, tricking the bees from a hive full of honey. Warmth and play in a bed at night or in the straw of a barn. Companionship. Sometimes love.

There were reasons for fear in every season, however, in every place where men and women tried to shape and guard their lives.

Autumn brought the dread of a killing winter. If it rained too much, if the harvest failed or was limited, some would die in the coming months as surely as a weak, wintry sun would rise to see it happen.

If storms came and smashed the moored fishing boats to wreckage, or sank them amid lightning and wild seas, hunger followed in coastal villages. If enough firewood could not be found and cut and stacked (and defended), people died of cold in the north.

If wolves came gaunt and howling over hard-packed snow and killed the livestock, assuaging their own desperation, people would also die. Disease found men and women (and always children) made weak by lack of food. Starving mothers had no milk for newborns.

Brigands came down from hills or out of dense, black forests. City walls might be proof against all but the worst of these, but what defence had a farmhouse, a lonely retreat, the cabin of a charcoal burner? The silver moon and the blue would swing up the sky and set, while fires took homes and lives. Stars wheeled slowly above snow.

Even in summer there were terrors. If pirates or corsairs, raiding from the Majriti all the way to the harbours of Ammuz, took the longed-for grain convoys, people starved in cities.

Walls, it was often said, could do nothing against famine.

That same summer sun could kill in the south, drying streams and pools, scorching pastures brown and the mountainsides where sheep and goats were herded in the heat.

Plague came in summer (so many times) on merchant ships or with travellers arriving overland. The wealthy fled their cities. Whole villages were savaged by it, bodies left unburied in the sun. White flags by a boundary stone marked a place you did not go.

Summer could be a hungry season, too, before the harvests were in, the last year's granaries (even where leaders had been prudent) trickling towards emptiness. The whole world knew stories of children dying and being eaten, of unwary travellers murdered in their sleep to answer that same need.

You could be robbed of all you had in any season. Your village could be burned to ash, lost to time, forgotten. Your children could be taken into slavery, sold to the galleys—Jaddite or Asharite. All ships of all faiths needed men to row them, chained to their benches, fouling where they sat. The stench of galleys could be smelled from far across the sea if the wind was that way. You rowed until you died, usually, and were discarded into the sea.

And spring? Glorious springtime when the land quickened and the earth was tilled and planted, when wildflowers returned with all their colours and pale-green leaves showed on trees, when desire rose like sap running and whatever hope one had somehow carried deep inside through the cold months and the long nights struggled to emerge again . . . spring, alas, was the season of war.

ൟ

It was a remarkable letter, the Duke of Seressa had decided. Both the words that were visible and those written in their invisible ink between the lines.

The Council of Twelve was an agitated group this morning. Unsurprisingly. He was bemused by how calm he himself seemed to be. He had slept well last night after reading the letter. Yet none of these tidings were good and some were deeply troubling. Was he becoming too detached from matters of state? Shouldn't he be as disturbed as the others?

He put his spectacles back on. He held the original letter from Dubrava. Copies had been made for the others.

He remembered Leonora Valeri very well, from a late night in this room. It hadn't been so long ago. Jacopo Miucci had been with her, part of their clever devising here. Miucci was now dead. That was openly recounted by the woman.

In the secret ink, revealed by application of the juice of lemons to the pages, she had written: *It is unfortunate, but there can be no doubt Dubrava will now come to know—and others will be informed by them—of the actions of the last Eldest Daughter here . . . and her associations.*

Even in a hidden text she was circumspect. Not writing *association with Seressa*. It revealed a maturity even beyond what she'd shown in this chamber. He reminded himself that he'd meant to learn more about her family.

He read again: *It does appear that she purposed the death of a Senjani woman on this isle, and that purpose was detected, leading to her death. Dubrava has taken possession of concoctions that suggest others might have been similarly dealt with in the past. A trusted male servant of the Eldest Daughter—may she rest with Jad—has been implicated in untimely passings here. He is also dead.*

In short, the duke thought, the world would soon know who Filipa di Lucaro had been, and Seressa's role in a long deception practised in a holy retreat.

The High Patriarch would, very surely, be communicating with them, in thunderous terms. He enjoyed thundering. Money, a substantial amount, would be required to ease this wrath. The good news was that money *could* do that with him.

A loud fist banged the table, halfway along. Lorenzo Arnesti's piercing voice followed it in the subsiding of talk. "It is all too clear," he snapped, "that the Lucaro woman was not capable enough for her position. It was an error, placing her there!"

The duke had placed her there. His detached state vanished. Arnesti could do that to him. He removed his spectacles, cleaned the lenses, taking his time, decided something was now necessary.

He said, quietly, but clearly, "You behave like the son of a donkey and a brothel-keeper, Signore Arnesti. You embarrass us. Remind me why you are permitted in this room?"

Shocking. But it pleased him to say it. The words established a fraught, frightened silence. The councillors were like a sculpted frieze around the table now, the duke thought.

He had a wider intent, given the manœuvring for position taking place of late. Arnesti purpled, so outraged he couldn't speak. For once. The duke was happy with his phrasing. He had never offered that particular insult before. If they had been younger men, there would likely have been a challenge and a duel.

He said, "Signora di Lucaro served us ably for years. From a time before any man here but myself sat on this council. She provided regular, accurate information from reliable sources, even on the rectors' councils. She dealt with people we needed dealt with, and did so with discretion. Does any other fool in this room desire to malign her now that she is dead?"

No one appeared to so desire. Glances were lowered, throats cleared, chairs scraped. One man made the sign of the sun disk.

Only Arnesti spoke again, reclaiming his voice. "You have insulted me mortally, my lord duke! I demand a retraction!"

"Retracted," said the duke promptly. (Some things were too easy.)

Arnesti opened his mouth and closed it. He *was* a fool. Too nakedly ambitious, manifestly thoughtless, all posture and bullying. He might buy a certain number of votes in any election, but he had enemies—and would have more before an election began, if the duke had anything to do with it.

"What follows now?" It was Amadeo Frani, on his left.

Frani was a steady, humourless man. His younger son, who liked boys a little too visibly, had been posted away—to Dubrava, in fact—with the duke's blessing and support. Since then, Amadeo Frani would follow him in anything.

"It will cost money," Duke Ricci said. He smiled, to take away that eternal sting, let them know he had thought this through. The council needed reassurance at times such as this. They wanted the seas as safe as they could be, ports open, profits coming in. Everything else was incidental for most of these men. It was the duke who tried to look to the wider world and a longer stretch of time.

He had grown weary doing so. There was an isle in the lagoon, a small chapel, he saw a garden . . .

He said, "We'll pay Dubrava a sum, and send a gift for their main sanctuary, new windows, something of the sort. Perhaps a Blessed Victim relic. They owe us compensation for the doctor's death on their ship. This can be sorted. We'll also have to make amends to the Patriarch for using a holy office for our own purposes."

"Amends being money?" Frani didn't smile.

"Well, he may demand that one of us be hanged."

"*What?*"

"Or we might have to make a pilgrimage together. Go on our knees to Rhodias."

"My lord duke . . . !"

Humourless man. Duke Ricci refrained from grimacing. "I am jesting, only jesting, Signore Frani. It will be a sum of money, with a letter of contrition. I am sure of it."

Amadeo Frani had paled. It ought to have been amusing. The man swallowed, nodded. "And Obravic? The emperor?"

The others were letting Frani ask the questions. Interesting.

"He won't matter. He owes us for loans. He'll need more. He'll also send a letter, but will wait to see what the Patriarch does. They'll enjoy our embarrassment. We could send him another clock." He saw his principal clerk make a note.

Frani nodded again. If he'd had a little more imagination, the duke thought, he might even have made a competent successor. But he didn't have that, and he wouldn't be.

"And the woman writing us? Signora Miucci, as Dubrava believes her to be?"

"Leonora Valeri seems to have solved that problem herself," the duke said. "We appear to be fortunate in her."

"They will permit her to become Eldest Daughter?"

"You read the letter. They already have. I imagine the empress played a role."

"Ah. Yes, yes. The empress." It was clear that Frani had no idea what this meant. He said, "This woman won't be able to do for us what the other one did."

"No, of course not."

"Then we might give thought to placing someone else in Dubrava."

Duke Ricci smiled encouragingly. Frani did have his moments. "Let us do that," he said.

ʘᴓ

Before setting out from Seressa to take up his post in Obravic, as envoy to the imperial court, Orso Faleri had, of course, reviewed the dossier of letters sent by his predecessor.

He had also consulted, on arrival, with the staff at the Seressini residence, who were, in at least two instances, more acute than ordinary servants would be. They'd be watching him as much as helping him. Seressa trusted few people, including its envoys.

Before leaving home he had also sat through two sessions in the ducal palace with that same predecessor, Guibaldo Piccati.

Unfortunately, the Faleri and Piccati families, equally respected, had a feud going back to a night in a celebrated brothel. A Faleri had been a little too amusing about the dubious parentage of a Piccati in the room, the suggestion being that the young man's father had been the artist commissioned to paint his mother. It did happen on occasion, and there was (alas) a resemblance.

Although it had been fifty years ago, the incident had effects that lingered, including some violence. This made the meeting between the returned and the outbound ambassadors less cordial and useful than it might have been. In truth, this wasn't unknown even without a feud: a dramatic success by a new envoy could reflect badly on the preceding one who had failed to achieve whatever the triumph might be.

His own triumphs had been limited. He'd only had a single cold, wet winter in Obravic, mind you, and spring brought a different set of elements into play, the way an alchemist (*hah*, he thought) deployed new compounds in his attempt to conjure gold, or devise an elixir of immortality, or just one that eased gout.

Obravic was worried about its defences in Sauradia. They expected word, any day, as to whether the Osmanlis were on the move again this year against the great fort of Woberg, key to those parts of Sauradia still held for holy Jad.

And a gateway, in grim truth, to Obravic.

There was no sure way to gauge how far the ambitions of Grand Khalif Gurçu might extend. Could the khalif truly imagine Asharite bells ringing the faithful to prayer right here? Sanctuaries of Jad converted (as they had been in golden Sarantium) to profane temples of Ashar?

Distance had been their ally thus far. And rain. Rain was what they needed, each and every spring. Not here, but to the south and east where the cavalry of Ashar and the infantry—including the dreaded djannis—and the great cannons they wheeled ponderously with them came through Sauradia towards the children of Jad.

There was a certain delicacy to the Seressini position, of course: they traded happily with Asharias. They guaranteed the safety of Osmanli cargo in the Seressini Sea. Their lagoon-bound city stayed afloat (poets had written) on the tide of that trade.

Even so, one didn't want the star-born moving *too* far this way. Power needed to be balanced. If only the khalif would be content with the empire he had, with trade and wealth. With his sumptuous palaces and gardens and (by all accounts) the languorous beauty of his women.

There were so many elements in all this. Conflict brought danger, death, grief—and opportunity. Emperor Rodolfo needed money. Urgently. Fortresses that endured sieges required repair. Seressa, through its honourable ambassador, the esteemed Signore

Faleri, had been pleased to offer additional loans at generous rates—in solidarity, Faleri had said, with the Jaddite cause and faith, and honouring the courage of the emperor's brave soldiers.

He had also seeded his ground in the palace with the usual scattering of bribes. Not for the chancellor: Savko was unimpeachable, a succession of ambassadors over the years had confirmed that. The man disliked Seressa personally, it was believed. No one had been able to determine why.

But there were others with the emperor's ear, carrying less meticulously arrayed scruples. Seressini largesse had found its way over the winter to several of these.

At the same time, this court was working on Faleri, of course. The dance of it was amusing. The yellow-haired girl, Veith, the one from his first evenings here, had become a regular visitor after dark. Over time she had induced him to adjust his views as to the preeminence of Seressini courtesans. She deployed certain accessories that were new in Faleri's experience, and she had not yet exhausted either her devices or her imagination.

He still didn't let her into the room on the main level where he worked. On nights when he let her stay (more often, through the winter) he had a servant posted outside that room in case he fell asleep and she wandered—purely by happenstance, of course—to the desk where the papers were. Gaurio, his own manservant, did some of this guarding, then others in the house relieved him. Faleri's letters were double-masked, she'd learn nothing, but he didn't want it reported back to the Council of Twelve that he was careless with documents out of stupefied lust or some such thing.

She did leave him deeply satiated on the nights she visited, though. Certain women, you might say, *understood* a man.

It was all done to a purpose, and Faleri knew it. Everyone who befriended him here was looking to know more about him, about Seressa. She was subtle when they talked in bed. An intelligent woman. Worthy of Seressa, he had decided.

They didn't actually talk a great deal after lovemaking. He tended to be exhausted, and sometimes in pain.

He had come to enjoy this ceaseless dance of under-the-surface intentions, despite hating to be so far from home. His mistress was no longer his, among other things.

It had always been likely. He had thoughts as to what he might do to regain her on his return. It depended on achieving a seat on the Council of Twelve. Annalisa would like that very much, even more than his wife and daughters, perhaps. His daughters remained unwed, though it was past time. His wife had chosen her tactics the way a military commander might do on campaign. She had made it clear she was relying on his elevation to the council to improve their matches.

There was a great deal riding, in short, on his ability to persuade this court and its absurdly distractible monarch that the pirates of Senjan really did need to be—for once and forever—destroyed.

ఴ

The chancellor to Jad's Holy Emperor had much on his mind that spring. He always had a great deal to contend with, but some seasons were worse than others and this was one of those.

They had needed to borrow additional funds from Seressini banks to repair the great fortress of Woberg and to supply and pay the garrison there. There was no question the garrison needed to be paid. They were the main defence to the emperor's richest lands. Woberg had been the principal target of the Osmanlis for three campaigns now. Mighty as it was, those troops couldn't be left hungry and unpaid *and* expecting a renewed assault.

There was also the problem of being so much indebted to Seressa.

He had asked aid from Ferrieres, pointing out (again) that all the Jaddite world was at risk if Woberg and its environs fell under the Osmanli yoke. The young, ambitious king of Ferrieres sent back eloquent letters of agreement and encouragement—but not money, and certainly not soldiers.

The Jaddite world was more divided and mistrustful than ever, the chancellor thought grimly. And, really, if the siege of Sarantium twenty-five years ago had not been able to unite them, what would do that today?

The High Patriarch also sent encouragement and, when winter ended, he had dispatched fifty of his personal guards to journey by sea and land to Woberg. Not a significant force, but fifty good men did help in a fortress. The chancellor replied on behalf of the emperor with appreciation, and a request for prayers.

They needed soldiers, though. Even more, they needed rain. They required the heavens to turn dark and open and *drench* the roads of Sauradia. They needed holy Jad above to soak the infidel armies. Cold water in their boots, dripping into their tents at night, bringing disease, slowing them in thick mud, and—more than anything— preventing their terrible cannons from reaching Woberg in time.

It was always about time, distance, speed.

The fortress gateway to the emperor's heartlands lay at the very end of the Asharite army's fighting range. The Osmanlis had to delay setting out for their horses to be fed and strengthened at winter's end, which meant giving them time to graze on new grass. Then they had to get across land and rivers (the god be thanked for rivers) a very long way, feeding a very large army (and the horses). And then assemble a siege outside Woberg's great walls (great only if they had been repaired) and invest it closely, pounding with their cannons . . . and still leave themselves time to get back home.

They could not overwinter in northern Sauradia until they controlled it. It was a blessing for the emperor. It was what had saved them thus far. There was no way to feed and shelter so many horses and forty thousand men in winter in the lands south of Woberg when the north wind and the hard cold came.

Distance and time weighed in the balance of the scales of war.

And rain. They prayed for rain in all the sanctuaries of Obravic, and the High Patriarch's letter promised that he and his clerical college would do so every morning and evening. Rain, blessed, saving, necessary rain. The destiny of empires turned on spring rainfall.

It could make a man, thought Chancellor Savko, feel as if all his devising was of limited significance. That was a bad line of thought. He pushed it away when it came. You needed to prepare as best you could for a spring of mild sunshine and dry roads—with the massive guns of Asharias rumbling remorselessly north to blast the fortress walls with a noise like the thunder that had failed to come from heaven.

You could not put all your faith in the god. Jad needed you to act for yourself. So it was taught. Good men had to do what they could, year after year. Savko considered himself a good man, if cruelly limited in his resources.

The winter loan from Seressa would carry—as it always did—strings attached. Money would be needed from them again next year. It might be withheld for evidence of imperial ingratitude. They couldn't let that happen.

Savko needed—he always needed—a weapon, levers, any tool to use against the Seressinis. He had agents there, as they had them here, and he was spying on their ambassador, of course. The woman, Veith, was singularly adept; they had employed her before. The current envoy, the merchant Faleri, was not the incompetent figure they had initially thought he might be, but he didn't appear to be *experienced* in these matters.

Faleri had been careful, for example, to keep the girl out of his working room. She had been careful, in turn, to intimate she enjoyed nothing more than being in his bedchamber all night. The ambassador kept her by him in the dark and, lest he sleep and she

drift downstairs in a silent house, had servants guarding his papers.

And, of course, one of those servants was their man. It hadn't been particularly difficult for someone trained to enter the writing room three nights ago, unlock a chest, and swiftly copy the encoded letters Faleri was writing to his council.

Their man had sent copies to the castle that same day.

And they had not helped. At all. They offered no weapon, no tool. No meaning to be found. They couldn't *read* them.

The emperor had the best scientific minds in the Jaddite world gathered at this castle. Savko had immediately put a number of these alchemists and mathematicians to work on the documents. And the finest thinkers in their world had been able to make nothing, *nothing* of the newest Seressini code.

It was maddening. One might have thought—might have naively hoped!—that the expense of housing and extravagantly paying the wretched figures who trundled to Rodolfo's court and explained to him how they, and only they, could achieve his long desire of alchemical transmutation—well, one might have thought they could break a diplomatic code.

Not so. They were, Savko thought—though he shared this only with his young lover and his most trusted adviser—useless. They were buffoons, parasites. He needed, desperately, a defence against the Seressini demands that were certain to arrive—and he didn't have one.

And then, early this morning, grim tidings had come up to the castle, to the chancellor's suite of rooms. The body of a man named Fritzhof, one of the servants employed at the Seressini residence, had been found by the river and recognized. He had washed up on a sandbar downstream from the Great Bridge.

It would not, in the normal course of events, have been a matter for the imperial chancellor. The death of a man in the serving class? They killed each other too often, for too many reasons.

But this Fritzhof had been their man in that house, in the chancel-lery's pay for years (Savko couldn't recall exactly how many years, he had a note of it somewhere).

Fritzhof was the one who had sent the copied-out sheets of the ambassador's letters. And he was dead two nights later. Savko had no idea how Orso Faleri had discovered the man was a spy but . . . he had done so, and acted upon it. No public accusation, no diplomatic protest, no dance of complaint and denial. A body in the river.

A long knife or short sword, Hanns reported. That was the word of the guardsman who had attended when children reported a dead man on the sandbar. It was a common place for bodies to be found. It had to do with the way the river curved, approaching Empress Bridge.

Savko ground his teeth. He cursed, which he rarely did. There was nothing he could do, of course. The Seressinis had avoided a public squabble about spying, and he would have no way—he knew they'd have been careful—of laying this death at their door. And even if he could, it would be an error. This wasn't worth a diplomatic war—and it would cause one if he spoke recklessly. He had been caught placing a spy, and the man had died for it.

Something occurred to him. He called Vitruvius into his offices. His young Karchite lover had a number of skills. This time Savko didn't need him for killing but to forestall the possibility of another death. The woman, Veith, might be in danger now. If not, well, it could serve as an unspoken punishment for Orso Faleri to be deprived of his nighttime pleasures. He sent Vitruvius to collect the woman and remove her from Obravic.

But then, abruptly, he had another, happier idea. That could hap-pen. You *could* be clever, shrewd, inspired. The chancellor smiled for the first time that day.

He summoned an aide and requested that one of the court art-ists be brought to him. He stipulated that it had to be a man who'd seen the current Seressini envoy to the emperor.

FALERI HAD BEEN CERTAIN the woman was also a spy from the first night she'd come to him. It didn't mean she had to be killed or anything so vulgar. They were civilized men in what one hoped was a civilized world of courts.

No, having the servant knifed while sent out on a fabricated night errand was surely sufficient.

He knew the document chest in his workroom had been unlocked, and knew who had done it. He trusted Gaurio, and Gaurio had reported who'd succeeded him outside the room that night.

It was a little surprising that an imperial spy did not know the very simple trick of leaving a thread on a strongbox to be snapped or shifted if the box was opened. There had also been a disturbance of the dust on the writing desk, where a candle had been set down.

The papers had been put back in the strongbox. Which meant that the chancellor's people would be able to detect nothing at all. Copied-out coded papers would tell you no truths or lies if the code itself was a deception and the real technique involved hidden writing between lines.

Seressa was, Orso Faleri thought, far ahead of everywhere else in these matters. It brought a certain pleasure. Killing the servant didn't, but nor did it trouble him. Messages needed to be sent between powers.

He was fairly certain Chancellor Savko (not a fool, one had to note) would have the woman taken away for a time. Regrettable, but one did suffer sometimes in one's duties. That was what service was all about, wasn't it?

He hoped she'd be allowed back before long. He had petitioned to be brought home when his first year was complete. With Jad's favour—and Duke Ricci's—that might be allowed. Other good things might occur once he was back alongside the canals.

He was standing in the writing room at the window, looking out over Obravic's river on a mild afternoon, when Gaurio entered with a letter from the palace. Faleri opened it with interest.

Then he sat down, heavily, on the nearest chest. He looked again at the document that had come with the chancellor's letter.

It was a drawing, a sketch. It showed him lying on a large bed. He was unclothed. His wrists and ankles were tied to the bedposts. His mouth was open in what one might take to be a scream of pleasure, or of pain. He was shown twisting to one side. His member could be seen to be erect. Standing by the bed, also unclothed, was a woman—and anyone who knew Veith would recognize her. She held a short, three-tailed whip. There was an embarrassing accessory—a vegetable, in fact—inserted into Faleri's backside. He remembered that night.

He took a deep breath. A few moments to calm himself and think. Then he sent Gaurio upstairs to lay out his court attire. He was going up to the castle, he said. Yes, immediately. He had just been invited for an evening drink with Chancellor Savko.

As he went, walking with an escort up and away from the river (it cleared his head to walk, and he needed that), Orso Faleri realized something. He wasn't embarrassed or afraid. He was angry. On behalf of the Serene Republic of Seressa, someone was about to pay a price.

IT TOOK VERY LITTLE TIME for the chancellor of the Holy Jaddite Empire to realize he had misjudged this matter badly.

He'd been too frustrated by their failure to break the code. And he had, even after half a year, continued to see this merchant-envoy as an out-of-his-depth figure.

Both were errors.

They were in his own inner chamber. All others had been dismissed, even Hanns, and Vitruvius was elsewhere, dealing with the girl.

"I am," Orso Faleri was saying briskly, "an ambassador to this court for only one year, perhaps two. Whatever embarrassment I suffer from this gross vulgarity will affect only me."

"Yes?" said Savko. He was delaying, watching closely, but already uneasy. The other man was calm, precise, not shaken at all. This wasn't proceeding as he had thought it might. Faleri had come in showing controlled anger, not rage. He had refused wine with an impatient headshake, then declined to sit. He was holding the envelope in which they had sent the drawing. He had waited until Hanns bowed himself out. Just looking at the other man now, Savko had a prickling awareness, an anticipation that this was not likely to be an encounter that brought him joy.

"You, on the other hand, are the chancellor of Jad's Holy Emperor. Entrusted with great duties before the world."

"By Jad's grace and the emperor's, I am."

"Your conduct reflects upon this court and Emperor Rodolfo."

"I have always tried to act as if this is so."

"Do you say? Would that include when you are penetrating or being penetrated by a Karchite boy? And in which position would you prefer to be sketched, chancellor? It can be either, of course. Or both! No need for just one drawing. And we have *extremely* talented artists in Seressa, as you know."

"I have no idea what you are talking about. I find it offensive, ambassador, that—"

The other man arched his eyebrows. "Offensive? I am certain you do. You will find it more so when you see the artwork, I assure you."

"You would poison diplomatic relations for such . . ."

Faleri shook his head. "I doubt that would happen. I am certain it would poison your career and cause great amusement elsewhere. Seressa also has the best printers in the world, of course. And our ships go all over the world, as you also know. Chancellor, any humiliation I suffer from this"—he lifted the envelope he held—"will be a soon-forgotten moment. Yours, I fear, will be a thunderous fall."

Savko swallowed. He had made a mistake. Proceeded too recklessly. Had assumed his tastes and habits had remained more private than—obviously—they were. Yes, a few at court knew he had his inclinations in bed, notwithstanding a wife and son at his largest property in the north. He was far from the only one. But it seemed Seressa knew, as well, in detail.

And this wasn't a matter the emperor could ignore if it reached the world, including—oh, Jad!—the High Patriarch, who had . . . views on this matter.

Cursing himself, working to keep his consternation hidden (that, at least, he had trained himself to do), Savko murmured, "But, my dear man, you misunderstand! No, no, no. The sketch you were sent was found in the studio of a scurrilous artist from . . . Ferrieres, a drunken fool with some family hatred of Seressa! You do understand we have a few of those here? The emperor, he invites people to court and . . ."

Faleri said nothing.

Savko cursed inwardly again. He went on, "The man has already been ordered to leave Obravic on pain of whipping!" That, he grimly thought, was an unfortunate phrasing. "This was the only such drawing we found. I had it sent to you to ensure no one else would *ever* see his scandalous slander!"

"It could have been burned."

"Yes, yes. But I judged it best you . . . that you *know* of this."

"Why?"

Curse the man! "Well . . . these girls, the women one might encounter. They cannot always be expected to say nothing about their encounters, or to tell . . . er, truth if they speak."

"Is that so?"

"It is! It is, Signore Faleri! Alas for us all."

"Alas for some of us. This girl, she will be killed, I trust."

This was ghastly, terrible! Savko had a desire to be drinking. He said, "Either that, or such fear as she has never imagined will be visited upon her. As it was upon the, er, artist."

"Dead is better. Seressa will be pleased to attend to both these matters."

"No, no!" Savko said, gesturing a little too widely. "You are our guest here. This is an offence done to an ambassador. It is our *duty* to address such matters."

"And you will do so?"

"I have just assured you of such," Savko said, with what dignity he was able to summon.

A long pause, then Orso Faleri shrugged. "It is possible, then," he said, "that no Seressini artists need ever be given ideas as to how sketches of important figures in Obravic should be rendered."

Savko put his hands on his desk. He was pleased to see they were steady. He was the chancellor of the Holy Jaddite Empire. He said, quietly, "That would, in truth, be for the best, ambassador. Because you are wrong. It *would* become a matter of great diplomatic offence for the emperor. Insulting his chancellor of so many years? You must never, ever imagine otherwise, signore."

And for the first time, with relief, Savko saw a faltering in the other man's eyes.

"Is it possible," said Orso Faleri, "for two men experienced in the nature of the world to achieve an understanding in a matter such as this without involving others?"

"I believe it is," said Chancellor Savko gravely. "Artists are chancy at the best of times."

"Too much imagination, I have found."

"Far too much."

"Undisciplined?"

"A good word, signore. Also, insufficiently aware," Savko said, "of how actions can ripple and stir in a greater world."

"An elegant phrase, chancellor. If I may say so."

Savko inclined his head.

The ambassador from Seressa walked over to the fire, which was going strongly. He laid upon it the envelope and sketch that had been sent to him. The two men watched them burn.

"Exactly the right thing to do," Savko said, encouragingly, when it was done.

Faleri looked at him from the fireplace. "With your permission, I will take my leave. I prefer not to be abroad after darkfall." He crossed the room.

"Wait, signore."

Faleri paused by the door.

Savko said, still behind his desk, "This is not how Jaddite states and empires should deal with each other, is it?" He was now taking a risk.

The other man said, "I agree. And I speak for Seressa saying so. It is a regret that any of this became necessary. It was not caused by us." He glanced at the fire. "Have we burned this now? Put it behind us?"

Savko took a breath. "Other things burn, signore, when the Osmanlis come into our lands." Here it was.

Faleri nodded judiciously. "The infidels are violent and degenerate. Seressa hopes our generous loan will assist Emperor Rodolfo in defending his lands."

His lands. Of course.

Savko kept his face expressionless. "Seressa has already been of great assistance through its bankers. You will extend our renewed appreciation to the Council of Twelve?"

"Of course. And Seressa will hope to have the emperor's support for a matter pertaining to our own needs and purposes. One that I will raise, if permitted, during my next appearance at court."

Savko knew those needs and purposes. There was a walled town on the eastern coast of the Seressini Sea, offering loyalty to this court. They did more than that. They defended imperial lands and people without being paid at all. They raided inland against Asharites, and in their small boats on the sea. Also, sometimes not against Asharites.

"The needs of his Seressini cousins and dear companions in Jad are always close to the emperor's heart."

"And we are grateful for it." Faleri turned again to go.

"You won't stay for a cup of wine?"

"The wine," said Orso Faleri, "is better at the Seressini residence."

He opened the door and went out, closing it behind him.

"Fuck them all!" said Savko, distinguished chancellor to his excellency the Emperor Rodolfo. "Fuck them and drown them in the piss of their canals."

It wasn't his most elegant phrasing but it was as passionate as he ever became.

He sat down at his desk. He put his head in his hands. He stayed that way for a time, calming himself as best he could. You needed to be calm to think. Much depended on his thinking now, and he'd already made a mistake today.

He realized one thing he needed to do. It might not help, but there was a chance it could, and he would freeze among demons in darkness before he let Seressa dictate what Obravic did concerning a town that paid it fealty.

He took up a pen and wrote the necessary orders.

That done, he thought again, this time on matters closer to his own affairs. By the time the expected knock came and Hanns entered, the chancellor was ready.

"Secretary, a word about Vitruvius."

"My lord?"

"Is he discreet? Vitruvius?"

"Discreet, my lord?"

"Would private matters that take place concerning him be kept from others? Others who might . . . who might not be understanding of all our doings here?"

Hanns was an exceptionally intelligent man. Very much ready to be elevated beyond a secretarial post, even one as lofty as this (there were none loftier). He coloured slightly, the chancellor noted. Understanding and reaction preceded speech in most men. If you were observant you could see that happening.

His secretary said, choosing his words (which was telling in itself), "He is very young, of course, my lord. He . . . he takes great pride in his . . . his roles in the chancellery. His being intimately aware of . . . of much."

His roles. Intimately aware.

Savko was very calm now. "And perhaps he might desire others to be aware of his significance?"

"He is young," Hanns repeated.

"You said that."

"Might I . . . might it be permitted to know what the ambassador said that has raised concerns, my lord?"

Careful, Savko thought. He said, "Seressa appears to be aware of matters associated with this office that it would have been better it did not know."

"I see." Hanns cleared his throat. "And they are aware of these matters from Vitruvius himself?"

"I cannot say for certain. If I were certain . . ." He took a breath. "It would be a grave matter."

Grave. Indeed, Savko thought. Buried deep in a grave. Worms devouring a lovely face, a supple body.

"Perhaps," said his secretary, "I might impress upon him the gravity of *all* circumstances associated with the chancellery? The critical importance of discretion?"

But, listening, Savko came to a decision. In truth, what happened was that he realized he'd already come to it while the ambassador had been in the room. He felt a great sorrow, like winter. The burdens of office and of life.

He said, "Hanns, it would be better, all considered, if neither Vitruvius nor the woman, Veith, were seen again in Obravic."

"Indeed, my lord," his secretary said, voice and face unrevealing.

He was such a lovely boy, Vitruvius. Fair-haired, fair-skinned. Clever and quick to laugh. And tender. He was tender. A sweetness.

Savko added, "In fact, it might be best, for the empire as we prepare for war, if neither of them were seen again anywhere."

Hanns went pale this time. He had a right to that, Savko thought. It still distressed him to see it. A judgment without words.

"Anywhere. Yes. I understand," his secretary said. No judgment in his voice. He was too polished for that. "I will look after this."

"Thank you," said the chancellor. He gestured to the darkness outside the window. "It is late. I am sorry to have kept you. You may go. I will see you in the morning. Take this please, Hanns. Have it copied and sent." He handed him the orders he had written, the ones for Senjan.

He sat alone for some time after Hanns left. The room was warm with the fire going. He thought about pouring himself a glass of wine. *Better at the residence*, the accursed envoy had said. Probably true. It was reported he'd brought reds from Candaria. Those were difficult to obtain, even at court, except through Seressa.

He did get up, did pour wine, watered it as he always did. He was the chancellor, he needed to be prudent in all things. Sorrow once more, with that thought. A lovely boy, really, with such promise. So was the woman, though he had to admit she mattered less to him. The way of things. *We can only grieve for so much at a given time*, Savko thought.

He sipped his wine. He thought about Senjan, the orders he'd just given to his secretary to have carried the long way south. They would obey those orders. He knew it. They were fiercely, violently loyal. To the emperor, to the god. To Imperial Chancellor Savko, acting for both.

And in obeying, they would be terribly vulnerable, of course. But, Savko told himself, it was necessary. It was his way of trying to protect them against the demand coming from Seressa here in a day or two. The republic had given the emperor money he needed. And they would need more. You owed someone a debt and it *would* be called, one way or another.

Seressa wanted Senjan destroyed. And though Rodolfo wouldn't want to allow it, would feel strongly (as strongly as he felt about anything not alchemical) about the matter, his chancellor might have the duty of telling him that a town of raiders, howsoever brave and loyal, could not be measured in the scales against Woberg, which *could* not be allowed to fall.

He might buy some time for Senjan with that letter he'd just written. Or he might have killed a great many heroes of that town. You could do that, kill people with a letter scribbled in a palace room, copied and carried across hills and rivers and valleys.

He went up stone stairs, a servant carrying a light for him, to his sleeping room. He had a handsome home in the city below—he had several homes, country estates, he was well-rewarded for his services. He slept in the castle most nights. It was best. The needs of a challenged empire did not obey the hours of the light.

They brought him a meal. He read dispatches at another desk while he ate, listening to the wind. The night was clear, there were stars, and then the blue moon.

He crossed to the window and looked out. Down at the river, at the scattered lights of Obravic at night. He prayed for rain in Sauradia. Rain and rain. He drank a second watered glass of wine. Didn't pour a third. He was as melancholy as if it were autumn, edge of winter, not the god's sweet springtime.

Sweet was a hard word just now.

He went to bed, but was still awake, the fire low, when a knock came and a servant entered to his command, bearing a light and two letters, one under seal, one folded. The folded-over note was from the tower where the emperor's guests were housed. He opened that first.

In a neat hand, one of the newer alchemists, a Kindath, explained that the code of the Seressini letters had not been deciphered because there was not, in fact, any true encryption.

The words had been analyzed by him, the man wrote, and no pattern had emerged. It was his belief that the Seressinis used the appearance of a cipher to mask their true device, which was likely to be invisible ink written between the lines of a letter. Only if they held the actual document could it be subjected to various techniques that might cause hidden writing to appear. He signed with humble respect.

It was, Savko thought, sitting up in bed in a linen nightshirt and cap, almost certainly the truth. The thesis covered the matter perfectly. He drew a breath of relief. This didn't help him immediately, but it explained something, and knowledge was always good. It was coinage.

He opened the other letter, which was under seal, from their envoy all the way south in Dubrava. He looked at the date, he always did. The couriers had made speed—this was obviously deemed important. They had brought it to him at night, as well.

He read it. It *was* important. It was a gift.

He sat in a lamplit room and pictured a relay of messengers carrying this here, in morning light and twilight and night, a boat along the coastline, then by horse through mountain passes to this palace, his high chamber. And reading it again, he understood that he now had his weapon against Seressa. Because Jad *could* show mercy to his overburdened, hard-working children sometimes.

They had behaved very badly, the Seressinis. A false Eldest Daughter of Jad placed in Dubrava. Impiety, murders. Murders! Her connection to the Serene Republic kept secret, until now. She was dead, having tried—the letter reported—to kill a Senjani woman, a guest of the holy retreat.

Senjan and Seressa. Again, Savko thought.

Were there patterns in the world, or did men devise them? Did they try to impose meaning on randomness, striving to come nearer to the wisdom of the god? Was that folly, vanity? Was it even heresy?

He dismissed the servant with the lamp. He lay down again, thinking. He realized that these tidings, this weapon, might mean he did *not* need to send the orders he'd just written for Senjan. They might not need this added protection from Seressa now: the idea that they were heroically fighting for the emperor, who could not abandon them while they were doing that.

He considered it, looking at low sparks arcing in the embers of the fire. He decided that, all considered, he wouldn't recall his orders.

The fortress at Woberg would still benefit from Senjani reinforcements—if they managed to make it there. It was a long, dangerous way. But they were supposed to be fierce fighters, weren't they? Wasn't that what was always said about them?

You performed balancing manoeuvres like an acrobat, the chancellor thought. You did shrewd, clever things; you made mistakes. People lived, flourished, suffered, died because of you, or despite you. The faith of Jad was to be defended as best you could devise, also the empire and its borders. You went to the god, eventually, carrying the reckoning of your days, and were judged.

CHAPTER XIV

It had rained at the beginning of spring in the grazing lands near Asharias. A good thing. The young grass grew. The horses, gaunt as always after winter, were let loose to feed and gain strength for the campaign to come.

Rain there and at that time was needed. Later, on the road, it would not be. It would be destructive, perilous to their purpose. The ka'ids of the khalif's armies conferred with each other (grudgingly) and with those responsible for the well-being of the horses. You wanted to leave as soon as you could, but not too soon, or the cavalry would have tired or even dying mounts when the hard slogging in the rough country towards the Jaddite fortress came.

They were going there, however. That much was known at court.

The restive, rebellious tribes to the east were quiet this year. Some had argued before the grand vizier (for him to carry their words to the khalif) that this was the best time to attack east and decisively conquer those tribes. This had been dismissed, as it deserved to be. The Osmanlis were never going to occupy those empty, deadly lands (broiling in summer, open to savage winds and snow in winter). They only needed them quiet.

No, the prize lands were west and north, around and beyond accursed Woberg and its sister forts behind it. If they could take those, occupy and hold them and the farmlands and towns around, they could pasture horses there, overwinter securely, then expand the next year into the richer Jaddite provinces held by the fool-emperor. They might even take his imperial city—as they had taken triple-walled Sarantium, deemed impregnable, and had renamed it and made it their own, and Ashar's.

And then, truly, might Grand Khalif Gurçu, who had named himself "the Conqueror" and was called by fearful Jaddites "the Destroyer," begin to make true an assertion that went back to the first ride out of the desert so many hundreds of years ago—ruling the known world in the name of Ashar and the stars, all other faiths and peoples subdued.

Two dates for departure were proposed to the grand vizier. An astrologer was consulted, a Kindath (as the vizier was). The khalif trusted his Kindath—excessively, some believed. This one was wise enough not to gainsay the wisdom of the ka'ids, whatever his moons and the stars might tell him. He approved of both dates, with the usual equivocations.

The khalif, who might be ascetic and withdrawn (more so as he grew older), had never been indecisive. He chose the earlier date. Messengers had already ridden from the city to instruct every garrison as to where its infantry or cavalry was to join the main army. Prayers were chanted in the temples of Asharias the evening before departure.

The army of the Osmanli Empire, twenty-five thousand of them—to be joined by as many again on their way—left the city in the morning.

They paraded past the palace complex towards the gates. They always did that. If the khalif was watching he did so unseen. It had been years since ordinary men or women had seen him. The soldiers made their way past cheering crowds, past the ruins of the Hippodrome and the High Temple of Ashar that had once been the infidels' great sanctuary before the city was redeemed by the Conqueror. They passed through the triple walls (still standing, mostly, though Asharias needed no walls) and turned north and then west to join the great, wide imperial road. There was sunshine behind them that day, glinting off the city's domes and the sea and the weapons they carried and the great guns on their wagons.

◌

When Obravic sent an important message to Senjan, the court used two couriers, two days apart, for safety.

The identical messages that arrived (within a day of each other, as it happened) that spring were, indeed, important. You could also call them deadly.

There was never a moment when anyone in Senjan, whether at the meeting in the sanctuary, or privately in taverns or homes, or on the streets, or by the sea, spoke a word about not obeying.

Senjan remained what it always defined itself as being. In their own minds they were the eternally loyal warriors of the god. Hardship and death were always present, always close. They defied both.

If you were summoned to war for Jad, however far away, however hostile the lands between, you went to war.

They had done it before. They had died before, on the walls of Sarantium. Every Senjani hero there had died for the last Sarantine emperor. Not one came home, even as a body for burial. Senjan knew, in blood and sorrow, what it was to fight the infidels.

There were just under three hundred raiders in the town at the time the emperor's summons came. After the breaking of the Seressini blockade they'd sent parties down the coast and, more recklessly, across the narrow sea to raid along the other coastline. And because it was spring, two large groups had gone through the pass towards the Osmanli villages that way. Captives to sell or sell back for ransom, oxen and sheep and goats were the usual coinage of these raids, if fortune favoured the just.

This was different. An imperial request, under seal, for a hundred fighting men to go all the way through lands controlled by Asharites, to defend Woberg Fortress. It presupposed they could even get there, with war headed that way. It meant much more than dealing with hadjuk bands and patrols. It meant the khalif's army of invasion, forty thousand of them, perhaps more. They'd have to beat that army to the fortress—then get inside, to be besieged by it.

And then, if they held out, if the enemy could be caused to retreat as summer turned, it meant getting all the way back here across those same hard, dangerous lands.

It also meant leaving Senjan itself thinly populated with fighting men at a time when they had enemies on the water, too.

They never hesitated.

Three captains were assigned to choose the best men remaining in the town. Those with wounds or with wives expecting children were exempt. Men with small children were not; this was an imperial command. Two of the clerics were quick to name themselves for this journey. More surprisingly, three women indicated they wished to come—following an example set by Danica Gradek, not even Senjani by birth or for long, who had gone to sea with a raiding party this spring.

That party had returned from the far side of the narrow sea triumphantly—but with one of their own men dead, at her hand.

She had not come back with the boats. She had gone to Dubrava to plead the Senjani case regarding a Seressini they'd killed on the raided ship. That death could make for real trouble, given that Seressa wanted them destroyed.

Hrant Bunic, the raid leader, had exonerated her in council of any wrongdoing. He'd praised her, in fact. The Miho family took a different view, predictably, given that it was one of them she'd killed.

There had been words spoken. It remained a matter of tension in the town. Her family's empty house had been assigned a guard. A Miho was lashed for approaching it in the dark with a torch. Expulsion was threatened if such an incident occurred again.

It was interesting that the women who volunteered to go north and fight had their offer considered in debate. Voices were even raised suggesting it would be a further mark of the courage and ferocity of Senjan if they went.

In the end the clerics had their way and the offers were declined, though respectfully. The Miho clan elder made some remarks about not permitting the Gradek girl to serve as any kind of example for good Senjani women. Hrant Bunic had a blunt reply to this, and there had been a moment when it appeared that a fight might ensue. It had not. They had Osmanlis to deal with, by command of the Emperor Rodolfo, Jad's anointed in Obravic.

One hundred men set out three days later. Time mattered. The evening before there was a candlelit ceremony in the larger of their two sanctuaries (it wasn't actually very large).

The youngest of that company was fourteen. The oldest, Tijan Lubic, was about sixty years of age, as best he reckoned or remembered. The young one, a Pavlic boy, was faster on foot than anyone in the town; Lubic was the best reader of weather and routes they had.

It was a long way to Woberg. That company of men became the subject of song and story for a long time afterwards—the nearest most men ever come to enduring after death.

It is not truly courage if there are no risks, either apprehended or real. In this case there were both. They had known, hearing the letter sent to them, that this was a harsh request, and still they went. Let a greedy, slanderous, slack world take an example from Senjan.

Earlier that spring, shortly after leaving Dubrava with a party of merchants headed for Asharias in a wartime year, the artist Pero Villani had come to realize something about Danica Gradek.

She was formally with them as one of the guards hired by the Djivo family, but she was really coming because she wanted to kill Asharites.

He liked the Senjani woman, cautiously. He admired her greatly. He knew Leonora felt the same, even more so. He had no sense he understood Danica. He had no one to discuss his thoughts about her state of mind with, but it felt as if it mattered, or that it might.

They were travelling at the same time as a likely departure of the armies of Ashar. They would be south of the military's route towards the imperial fortresses. He'd been assured of that. They had papers to show and bribes to offer. Seressa was not at war with the Osmanlis, and Dubrava was a favoured tribute-paying city-state.

And the artist in this party was travelling with his documents and in response to a very specific request made to Seressa on behalf of the khalif, who wanted his portrait painted in the western style.

There should be no military danger to them, only the ongoing, obvious perils of the road: wild animals, bad food, weather, brigands, illness. Any official they encountered could be expected to assist rather than hinder them—though there would always be those bribes to be paid. Marin Djivo, leading them, had made this journey before.

It was interesting, even disturbing, Pero thought, how a great war might be underway, laying waste to farmlands, villages, cities, killing large numbers—and some men and women could go about their almost-normal lives around the edges of it.

Given that, his belief that Danica Gradek was praying for a fight, that she was *hoping* they'd be set upon by some band, was unsettling.

Whenever he glanced at her she seemed to be listening for something, or watching for it. She was intent, straining forward, even more than her dog was, he thought. The big dog—Tico, she called it—was amusingly happy, chasing rabbits through muddy fields, returning to the party undisturbed by failure.

She wouldn't be, Pero thought. She wouldn't be undisturbed.

They could expect to be six or seven weeks on the road, Marin Djivo had told him—barring incident. The Dubravae was leading, despite the presence of three Seressini merchants and their goods. Most of the party walked, a few rode donkeys, four of the eight guards were horsed—two of these went ahead each afternoon to alert the next inn that a large party was approaching, with animals and goods. They didn't all get beds each night, though the road was quiet. They tended to have to sleep four or five to a room, at inns of varying cleanliness. Pero Villani, denizen of Seressa's tannery district, was accustomed to rough quarters. Djivo, fastidious, paid extra for a room of his own sometimes.

Travel was not for those accustomed to or desirous of a soft life. The guards slept in the stables with the animals, defending their goods there. An even less-soft life, Pero had said wryly when one of his fellow Seressinis complained at the third inn about rain dripping into the room.

Danica Gradek was the only woman, of course. She had refused to cut her hair, though she kept it pinned under her hat. She was tall, wore men's clothing, carried weapons; those encountering them casually might not even know she was a woman.

She and Pero were both on foot. The days were long, often wet. He tried at times to engage her in talk. She was courteous without being attentive.

They had Leonora in common. He wondered if this woman knew about the feelings he'd expressed to the other one in Dubrava, on the harbour. Probably not, he decided. Leonora Valeri (he wouldn't think of her as Miucci any more) was going to have to become extremely discreet in her new role. Another complex woman, and one, he realized, with every step he took away from her, he would probably love all his life.

Not a good realization, in the circumstances.

It began to rain more the second week. A good thing for the emperor and his fortress, if it was also coming down farther north. It made their own travel more difficult, however. You could enjoy wildflowers blooming, the beauty of the countryside in sunshine. These grey days—heavy clouds, wind, cold rain—made even the worst-equipped inns look appealing at day's end if a fire was lit in the front room.

Pero knew this system of roads and inns went back a thousand years, to Sarantium in its glory. Imperial couriers had raced along, all the way to and from Batiara, changing horses at posting inns, hurrying on. Travellers had been frequent, the inns busy and— allegedly—kept honest and clean by inspections. He wondered if that was more legend than truth. The past seen through a tinted glass that made it seem beautiful. The fallen state of the present world. Well, it was fallen, wasn't it? Sarantium was lost.

The Osmanlis had some commitment to keeping this route accessible. They wanted goods coming to Asharias, and Jaddite silver in exchange for silks and spices and other eastern goods. They didn't have the resources of the past, though, and much of what they did have went to their army. The soldiers likely heading northwest by now, towards Woberg.

You had to pray for rain if you were pious or simply hoping that men in Jaddite castles might not die under Osmanli guns and blades. And if the forts fell, everyone knew the way would lie open to Obravic itself and the possibility of another terrifying, unthink-able change in the world.

And there it was again, Pero thought: unthinkable changes, a vast war, and here they were, a trade party carrying goods to Asharias, with an artist in their midst.

They were still on the more southerly of the two main roads. It had begun slanting northeast, to meet the bigger road that went from Megarium to Asharias.

They passed small Jaddite sanctuaries now and then in a wild countryside. Some were ruined, burned and roofless, but not all of them. They went inside when they came to a holy place still standing. They lit candles (if there were any), made donations in exchange for clerics' prayers. The clerics looked cautious, quiet. *Pinched*, Pero Villani thought.

One of the sanctuaries belonged to a sect called the Silent Ones. Those went back a long way here in the east. They kept night vigils to honour the god in his cold journey under the world before the sun returned at dawn. It made Pero realize, standing with the cleric who remained awake each day while the others slept, how far from his own world he was. He had crossed a border when they came through the pass near Dubrava.

The Osmanlis allowed Jaddites among them. The god's followers in the subjugated lands paid a tax for their faith. Many converted because of that. It varied, how much someone would sacrifice for Jad when the invitation was there to change faiths and pray in a temple to Ashar's stars—and not pay that tax at all.

Pero wondered, walking in rain, what he would have done had he been born in this wilderness instead of along the canals. It was best not to judge, he thought.

He said as much to Danica Gradek the next morning. It wasn't raining yet that day, though the clouds were dark and there was a wind in their faces. She looked at him, then resumed scanning the road and the fields on either side. There was a forest north of them. Pero could see it had once come closer to the road, but logging was taking place even here, pushing the woods back. Everyone needed trees. For ships, for shelter, for winter, for a blacksmith's fire.

He thought Danica wasn't going to reply, but then she said, "We always have a choice. Can we not judge when a bad choice is made?"

"Perhaps only if we feel sure we'd not have made the same choice."

She shrugged. "But I do feel sure. Senjan does, certainly. There are things worth fighting for."

"And some things aren't, maybe?"

She was looking at the field where her dog was running. "Some things."

"And what if you can't really fight?" Pero added. "What if your children are dying because there is no food, it went to the extra tax?"

She didn't answer. He didn't feel he'd won anything, though, because he didn't know what he thought himself. She stayed in step beside him, however, didn't move away. There was that.

At some point he'd become aware that Marin Djivo, up at the front of their party every day, was constantly checking where Danica was. He wondered if there was something more to this. No judgment from him, if so. She was a handsome woman, they were grown people living under the god's sky. He kept thinking about that isle in the bay of Dubrava and the woman who was now Eldest Daughter there, and not his. He was walking beside the wrong woman, he thought. The one he needed was farther behind every day, every step taken in mist, in rain, in pale sunlight on grass and trees.

Their road joined the main one after three weeks, halfway to Asharias, if Djivo was correct. This one was wider, the inns larger, though there was still not much in the way of traffic in either direction.

It was wild, hilly, windswept country. Pero found it unsettling. Not a world he understood. He did some sketching when the weather allowed.

They saw villages and farms south of the road, smoke rising from hearth fires. Oxen in the fields slowly pulled ploughs. The soil looked hard, not rich. On their left, north, there was still the forest, evidence of logging here, too. He saw a woodcutters' cabin, no sign of people. Wildflowers were everywhere now, deeper into spring: white and red, deep blue and pale blue, brilliant yellow, bending under rain. They could see them brightly when the mist or drizzle lifted. When it rained hard they crouched under hoods and hats and kept their eyes on the muddy, rutted road.

One night at an inn rumours became tidings: the khalif's army was indeed moving. They exchanged glances. It was not a surprise, but still . . .

The Osmanli forces were out there, joining into one large force. But to the north of them, Pero reminded himself, headed for the fortresses. A reason, of course, that the road was quiet. Prudent men were not travelling.

They had their papers, had duly offered gifts to the local governors and officers along the way. Asharias *wanted* them, he kept reminding himself.

Pero didn't feel any acute fear, but it would be a lie to say he wasn't uneasy knowing that at least some of the khalif's cavalry and infantry—the southern parts of his army, headed for the main force—might be ahead of them in the rain. When he looked at Danica, what he read in her face made him more unsettled.

And then, three mornings after the roads merged, after a night in one of the largest inns yet, Danica lifted a hand shortly after the sun appeared, and said, "Something's ahead. Guards, around the party, weapons out!"

It was surely an overreaction, Pero thought. Then he, too, heard the drumming of horses approaching along the road.

ળ્જી

He was now a person who had killed someone, in a fight forced upon them by their officers. Damaz had never clearly imagined his first killing, but in his dreams it hadn't been someone from the compound, one of their own.

He and Koçi had been an amusement for others, he kept thinking. He tried to stop that thought, but could not. That night had raised Damaz from a trainee into the ranks of the djannis.

It had earned him praise from his serdar and even their regimental commander, who was only one rank below a full ka'id. That such a man knew his name . . .

Damaz now wore the tall hat and green tunic or coat of their most famed infantry. He carried his sword and a bow. He was going to war.

But the memories of the fight in Mulkar had him awake almost every night, sometimes going outside to look at the moons or Ashar's stars, or listening to the rain from inside the tent.

Was it wrong to be disturbed, still, all these weeks after? Wasn't warfare going to be much worse? Some screaming infidel would be trying to end your life, you had to do that to him first, or die? You'd be doing so for the honour of the khalif, of your faith, of Ashar the Blessed who had found truths on a desert night and shared them with mankind.

He just wasn't sure what honour had lain in killing for the diversion of the garrison at Mulkar. And it was hard to push back the awareness that it could as easily have been his dead body carried away while wagers were happily collected from those who'd thought he would prevail instead of disappointing them by dying.

He hadn't liked Koçi. Plus, Koçi had been going out to murder someone for the pleasure of it. That was why—it was the only reason—Damaz had been waiting for him by the gates. This didn't help as much as he wished it did when he closed his eyes at night.

He'd thought, before they'd left, about talking to Teacher Kasim, and about the strange feeling he'd had before throwing his knife—of receiving *guidance* as to what to do. The idea of throwing the blade as smoke blew past from behind him seemed to have come to Damaz as an instruction, not a thought. It was disturbing. Kasim might have helped.

That chance was gone. His teacher was still in Mulkar. Damaz was going to war, as he'd always dreamed.

He discovered that you didn't necessarily dream the same way once something began. Well, maybe others did. He was awake too much. He'd quietly leave the tent to watch the stars—when they shone. They weren't in the sky enough. A bad thing. Rain always was on a campaign, the veterans kept saying.

He wished it were easier to sleep. The daily marches, even in mud, were not hard for him. They hadn't been in training and they weren't now. He was bigger than many of the others, young as he was. He had long legs and strong shoulders. Their commander had him with the group that helped the animals get the cannon carts out of ruts and mud.

They needed the cannons—they couldn't take a fortress without them—but they slowed the army terribly. It would get worse, he'd been told, at the rivers. They had rivers ahead of them. They'd reach them after joining up with the rest of the army. They'd all be together then. He remember Kasim showing them maps, where the Jaddite fortresses were.

Damaz wondered if his father had been a big man, or the brother he was also remembering now. Did he look as they had? Would he, later? He couldn't find an image in his mind of either of them. Just that they'd been there, when he was small. And his mother, and a sister with yellow hair. There had been another man, older. His grandfather? Probably. He'd been so young when he was taken. Someone lifting him into the air, carrying him away.

He wished he could feel happier about what had happened this spring. He *ought* to, he kept telling himself. What else was there to hope for but promotion into the ranks, marching to war, victory in the field? The djannis had first claim when there was booty, even ahead of the red-saddle cavalry. An immensely valuable privilege. You could do well in the khalif's favoured infantry. End up in the palace complex in Asharias, or retire to the countryside with good land granted to you. You'd have servants, tenant farmers, sheep, slaves.

A wife. You might be granted the taxation collection rights in your district, and grow truly wealthy from that.

What better life was there to imagine?

He might have been gelded as a child when first taken.

Koçi might have killed him back at the compound.

It was raining again tonight. Damaz listened to it on the canvas of the tent. There were three others in here with him. They were veterans, and asleep. He should be sleeping too. The rain meant they'd be helping the oxen with the cannons in the morning. Third day in a row. The farther they went, the worse the roads were becoming.

Night thoughts weren't good for you. You chased memories into dark places, or tried to, or tried not to. He knew he was headed, generally, towards where he'd been born, though he had no clear idea where his village had been or memory of what it had been called. It had been west of the fortresses. A long way west. And south, he thought. Wasn't certain. On the other hand, he now knew what his own name had been. He'd remembered that.

He didn't want to remember. There was nothing good in reaching back to when he'd been small, before those hands pulling him up onto a horse in the dark. *Neven* gave him nothing. It was only a name.

He felt confused. He wondered if a battle would help, if he just needed time to settle into these changes. If this mood would simply pass.

In the morning the rain had stopped but the track northwest (it was hardly a road here) had become sucking, grasping muck under a chill grey sky. Damaz was freed from cannon duty, however. There were new orders.

Fifty of them, half cavalry, half djannis, were to leave their progress towards the rest of the army and go kill some people.

Jaddite brigands had been nipping at their supply train for days, firing flaming arrows at the wagons of food, shooting pack horses and mules, shooting men, then disappearing into the shrouded hills and the valleys. This was good country for such tactics, apparently.

The guards for the supply carts and wagons were adequate to defend them, but there was something insulting, mocking, in these raids, and their serdar had had enough.

They were to find this band and destroy it. Damaz wanted to feel happy, excited. This was another stage in his life as a man, a warrior of Ashar. They headed back south, fifty of them.

Late the second morning their trackers found a trail. The sun came out and there was a breeze. Damaz realized he did feel better, moving quickly behind a capable leader, not trudging alongside cannons, or pulling and pushing them. They came back to the wide road running east and west. Their contingent from Mulkar had crossed it when they'd gone north. This time they followed it west.

There was another new memory in him, now, from the night before. It seemed that if you couldn't reclaim what refused to come to mind, you also couldn't stop knowing what you *did* remember.

His sister had been named Danica.

He hadn't remembered the name, and then, last night, there it was, in his head. He also now thought his father had had reddish hair—like his own. He could almost see him if he closed his eyes.

But why would you close your eyes while hunting enemies? And what good were memories like this? What good could they do you at all?

He heard a horse approaching. One of their scouts came into sight, galloping back along the road. He reined up as he reached the head of their column.

"Thirty of them!" he shouted. "Not more. And not far ahead. We have them!"

Dani, no weapons out! You are a merchant party!

Zadek, I know.

They have no reason to attack. They may not even be—

I know. I'm just being prepared.

You can't be! If this is the army you can only—

I know!

He fell silent. She could feel his fear—though he would hate and deny the word. It was fear for her, of course, shaped of love. She didn't think he'd deny that word.

She looked east. The clouds had broken up today. It was mid-morning, the sun high enough that she didn't have to squint. She saw horsemen, coming fast, about fifteen of them, maybe more. Small horses, tired-looking on a muddy road. The speed meant they were fleeing someone, most likely.

They are fleeing, her grandfather said.

She almost said *I know* again, but didn't.

They were not Asharite. You could see it. Didn't make them a safe encounter, these men might be worse. The Osmanlis had granted their party safe passage; didn't mean brigands from the south—or anywhere else—had to do the same.

But twenty or so mounted men was more than an outlaw band, and they were in the open, on the imperial road, which made no sense, unless . . .

Good eyesight, always, and so she saw yellow, a sash, on the man at the front, riding a big horse. Yellow for the sun god, and maybe something else.

Oh, Jad! Danica, I might know who . . . her grandfather began. She heard wonder.

I see it. Is it possible?

We'll know in a moment. Do not let anyone have a weapon out!

"No weapons!" she shouted. "Hold ground, but no challenges!"

Marin looked at her. She hadn't been taking the lead among the guards.

"Listen to her!" he snapped. And then stepped forward from within the circle of guards, four on foot, four mounted, to stand in the road alone, facing the horsemen approaching.

It was brave, she thought. He could die now, she thought.

She moved forward too. Stopped a pace behind him, hands at her sides, weaponless. He was their leader, she was his guard. Her hair was under her hat; she wore a hemp shirt, leather vest, trousers, boots. People had been taking her for a man, unless they looked closely.

Marin glanced back. He said nothing, turned again to face east. It *was* a yellow sash, Danica saw. And the man wearing it had a red beard.

It's him, her grandfather said. *Child, I never thought to . . .*

"You know who this is?" she said to Marin quickly.

"Jad help me, I do."

They waited, standing in the road. Blocking it, in fact. The horsemen pulled up hard at a gesture from the man in the lead. They were mud-spattered, visibly tired, but bristling with some-thing that might be called battle fury. The man in front, on a big grey horse, was the oldest. There was as much grey in his beard as red, Danica now saw. He had a lean face and a lean body.

He stared down at them, sizing up their party. He spoke to Marin Djivo. He said, "Looking to die?"

"Not for some time, I hope, with Jad's blessing."

"Then get off the road. Into the forest, behind those cabins." He pointed north. "Keep your people quiet. Pray. But do it in silence."

"You are pursued?"

"No, I just kill my horses for sport. Yes, we are pursued. And are about to fight here. You have the misfortune to be in the wrong place."

"How many are chasing you?"

"Not your concern, Dubrava merchant. Not you or the pretty Seressinis with you—or the pretty girl guard you have."

"We can fight with you," Danica said.

No! her grandfather snapped, within.

"No," the man on the grey horse said briskly. "Weak fighters hurt more than they help, and this isn't your quarrel, with your signed and sealed passes."

"It is mine," Danica said. "I'm from Senjan."

The man on the horse looked at her. Someone behind him spoke, she couldn't hear what he said. "A long way from home," said the one with the red-grey beard.

"My home was burned by hadjuks."

"How sad. Get off the road with your merchants. We need to prepare what we're doing here. Don't make me ask again."

Danica. Do it!

"I know who you are," Marin Djivo said. "You may know my father."

"I would expect to be known," the horseman said. "Why would I care about your father?"

"He was one of those in Dubrava who voted to support you twenty years ago. You came for money after the fall of Sarantium, when the Osmanlis moved on you in Trakesia. He was outvoted."

Slight change in a cold gaze. "He was, wasn't he? And his name was?"

"His name remains Andrij Djivo. He is still with us, Jad be thanked."

A nod. "I remember him. You are?"

"Marin, the younger son. I was a child, then. I remember feeling ashamed for my city. I am honoured to meet you, Ban Rasca."

"Ban? No, no title. I am not lord of anything now. We lost that fight. Men call me Skandir."

"I know that," Marin said. "You have been nipping at the heels of the army? Dangerous, I'd hazard."

The man on the horse looked at him for a moment before answering. He said, "Dangerous? Do you know how homes are built where my people come from?"

"No."

"On stilts, set well above the ground. They can only be entered through a trap door, so anyone coming in may be killed if need be."

"I see."

"Do you, merchant? Do you know that there are men who have not left a sanctuary of Jad in Trakesia for a dozen years, while other men—their enemies—camp in rotation outside, even in winter, to kill them if they try to leave? Our feuds run deep."

"I have heard as much," Marin said.

"There are valleys where we have hidden from the infidels, and black forests that go back thousands of years. Still untouched, not like those here or yours on the coast."

Marin smiled a little. "And the old gods dwell there, demanding blood?"

"Some say they do. I have given my blood. Dubrava might not understand."

Marin's smile faded. "Some of us honour courage. May I say that?"

The man called Skandir nodded his head again. "You just did. Now get off the road. Give my greeting to your father if you get home. You may not if you don't move this party."

The Seressinis were already leaving the road. There were three loggers' cabins at the edge of the trees. They had to cross a drainage ditch, but there were plank bridges for the logging carts and a trodden path through tall grass and flowers, sloping up towards the trees. Danica watched them a moment, then turned back to the man on the horse.

Danica, no. Child, don't do this. Please—

Not surprising, that he'd know.

She knelt in the road. This was a man who had spent more than twenty years fighting Asharites in lands his family had ruled. Longer than she'd lived. And he was still fighting them.

"Ban Rasca, if you are planning an ambush, will you not need archers? I am good with a bow. This is no boast."

One of the mounted men laughed, said something to another.

The man called Skandir shook his head. "You'd risk your party. You are a guard for men licensed to this journey. We will do what we are here to do and you should not be in sight. I am being patient. It is not my nature. Go. You are putting people in danger."

Child . . .

Danica stood. She turned, facing the forest and the cabins. They were a long way off. She took her bow, an arrow from her quiver. She nocked and loosed, a very high arc.

"The bird on the chimney," she said as the arrow flew.

The bird died. Victim, truly, to a marrow-deep need to not be on the margins, to make redress for the lost. The borderlands scarred people, and they carried those scars into and through their lives.

The man on the grey horse—another of the scarred—looked at her, thoughtfully now. The one behind him was muttering again. Skandir lifted a hand. His man fell silent.

Then the big, red-bearded one said, changing her life, changing many lives, "You wish to join us? You will leave this party?"

Child, no, this is—

"I do. I will," she said.

"Oh, Danica," said Marin Djivo, who might be in love with her, she'd begun to think.

You had no space for that. Not with what lay behind you.

You met riders on a road in Sauradia, in the wilderness of it, and everything altered in a moment, with the long flight of an arrow, with a question and an answer, with the hard needs of the heart coming home.

CHAPTER XV

It is a day—a morning, and what follows—Marin Djivo will not forget.

Hearing horses' hooves, seeing riders approach, he had thought the army was upon them. There was fear then. There was always fear on this road, even if you had made the journey before. If these were army horsemen they were probably far from authority. There were rules of military conduct, yes. They might be ignored. You bribed governors, carried papers—that didn't always help with bored soldiers in a desolate place.

Then Marin had realized—seeing a celebrated yellow sash—who was coming towards them, and a different apprehension overtook him.

Later he will try to understand how his fear, from that first moment of recognition, was about Danica. His understanding will only ever be partial. We cannot always grasp how we know things, why we fear. *What* we fear.

Rasca Tripon, once ruling a good part of Trakesia, has no status now. He is, instead, the most hunted man in all the lands under Osmanli rule. The swath of Trakesia his family had governed

306 Guy Gavriel Kay

(south of here, north of the city-states of antiquity) was a brutal place in the years after the fall of Sarantium, as the Asharites advanced that way. Those were hard lands, with little profit for the khalif's taxation officers there. But open, deadly resistance by the man the world came to call Skandir could not be countenanced. Forces were sent after him.

They destroyed villages in retaliation for what his men did. They hanged men on branches, nailed them to tree trunks, or plucked out eyes and sliced hamstrings, letting them go free—as warnings.

They took women as slaves, gelded boys and sent the ones who survived east. They did this whenever word came of Skandir making an attack on tax collectors, on soldiers, settlers, when he raided a garrison's cattle or sheep. He was obdurate, unyielding, hard as the ore in the old mines there, and they could never get close to him.

An iron warrior of Jad, and for his family and home—in whatever order of priority one might surmise, and at whatever cost to anyone else, and for a long time now.

The man who halted his horse in front of them is not young. Marin has known this, of course. It is different when you see something for yourself. He remembers—speaks of it—when Ban Rasca came to Dubrava, beleaguered and seeking aid. He remembers the city's fear, and the so-clever arguments that his father reported afterwards at their table, the ones used to refuse him and send him away.

Dubrava was already engaged by then—it was *always* engaged— in weighing allegiances and submissions, preserving such freedoms as it could have among the strivings of the mighty.

They had no choice, it was decided. They could battle for trade with the greatest, with their own ships and shipyard, their harbour, their hard-won acceptance in all ports. But that acceptance was the key. They could not support a rebel. There were some who'd wanted to seize him, hand him over to the Asharites. They'd sent

Rasca Tripon away with gifts (wine, a horse, a fur cloak), with words of praise and encouragement—and nothing else.

At least they'd let him leave.

Then they'd reported to Asharias that he'd come to them and had gone away. South again, was the assumption. Marin still remembers, on a morning in Sauradia, the shame in his father's voice, telling of this long ago.

It has stayed with him. What a child remembers and is marked by is not always what one might think.

Danica kills a bird, a long, astonishing arrow sent towards the forest. She announces she is leaving them if Skandir will accept her. He does so after watching the arrow's flight. It happens right here, in sunlight, other birds wheeling and rising against blue, wildflowers all around.

He wants to tell her not to go. He wants to ask her not to.

Instead, after a very little time, he finds himself taking up a guard post—against objections—in front of her at the edge of the wood north of the road. They are some distance east of the cabins behind which the rest of the party is hidden in the forest now.

His own stubborn folly, on a morning defined by folly.

But an archer, in any proper formation, needs a foot soldier as his guard. Or hers. He'd insisted that he be that guard. And Marin Djivo, who is defiant in his own way, cannot stop remembering his father's shame describing what Dubrava had done to this man all those years ago.

We do what we do for reasons that are often without sense. He thinks that, waiting with her by the trees above the road. There is a darkness to this forest. More than shadow and blocked sunlight. It is very old. He imagines villagers and farmers have tales of these woods.

Or else he is just feeling too raw, exposed, in ways he's had no time to think about. This is a reckless exercise, and not just his role in it. Skandir's. And Danica's.

She says, quietly, "You have no business being here."

Anger comes, then. "Really? And you do?"

"I do, Marin. I am sorry to abandon my post with you. Apologize to your father for me. I need you to do that. You will find another guard, as many as you need, next inn. You know it."

"Of course we will. And it isn't as if we have any claim on you."

Bitterness in his voice. Which he hates.

She says, still softly, "You do have a claim. But there are older ones. I don't really live for myself."

He knows that, in fact. "Did you know you would do something like this, when you came with us?"

He thinks she isn't going to answer, then she does. "I was hoping I might have a chance to kill, at least . . . at least *some* of them. Can you not understand that?"

He hasn't been looking back at her but now he does, behind him to his right. She holds her bow. The quiver is beside her against a tree, with a second one she has taken from a mule and brought up here.

She is looking at him. Not a woman who looks away. The light is good in the sunshine. He sees her pale-blue eyes, and in them something new—a wish to be comprehended, by him. There is that at least. She has touched him in the night. She has fallen asleep beside him. He has watched her sleep.

He says, "I do understand. You are the same as him. Skandir. If you were a man everyone would understand."

"Thank you," she says.

☙❧

It was almost impossible to grasp what had happened to them, especially since Damaz had never been in a battle before.

They had been moving briskly along this wide road west, following a trail left by the group that had been raiding the supply train.

There were fifteen horsemen keeping pace beside the djannis, with ten more riders ahead, out of sight now, scouting for the enemy. Their captain had said he didn't think the Jaddites even knew they were being pursued.

Then the horse beside Damaz went down. It spilled its rider. In the same moment the man running just ahead of him fell, an arrow in his neck.

There was death here suddenly, and it made no sense! They were the hunters! They were here to kill bandit-raiders.

Men and horses commenced screaming and dying in what was—clearly now—a cleverly laid ambush.

Even so. They were the red-saddle cavalry of Ashar, and the djannis of the khalif's army—feared on every battlefield the world knew. The captain shouted crisp, unpanicked orders and started off the road, up a slope to the south. The arrows were coming from a copse of trees between tilled fields.

Damaz hurried to follow. Seven or eight of them were down, men and horses. He didn't know what had happened to those riding ahead. He took his bow, seeing the captain do that. Swords would come later. For now they were running towards arrows and needed their own.

But then he saw that the cowardly Jaddites were fleeing. Already! The bandits could be seen in the muddy field and then— this had obviously been planned—swinging astride horses left behind the trees.

His captain nocked an arrow, loosed it. He was swearing savagely.

Damaz sighted, adjusted for wind, released. A long flight, extreme of the djanni bow's range—their archery was about speed, not distance. But Ashar was with him. He saw his man fall from a horse. Damaz shouted with triumph.

Another Jaddite dropped. The captain was loosing swift arrows, so were three others beside Damaz. They were the khalif's golden warriors. They were deadly as a desert sun.

Damaz didn't know if his target was wounded or dead. He started running. Saw another Jaddite rein in his horse, dismount to help one who'd been struck. Damaz stopped running. Another arrow loosed. And this one, too, found its mark. He'd brought two men down. He was running again, right beside his captain.

"Good man!" he heard. "Dispatch those shit-smeared bastards if they're not dead. Get their heads! We'll carry them back."

Damaz didn't actually want to do that with the heads, but he understood. They came up to the fallen Jaddites. One of his two was dead—the second rider. The first had Damaz's arrow in his thigh.

The captain was faster. He drew his curved sword. He brought the blade down on the man, who was screaming on the ploughed ground beside the horses, and he severed the Jaddite's head with that blow, the sweet, honed blade burying itself in wet earth made ready for springtime seeds.

"You! You can ride?" the captain rasped at Damaz. Blood had spattered his uniform, his face.

"I can."

The djannis disdained horses—they had forged their reputation as lethal infantry—but they were taught how to ride for when need arose. There was a need now. They had mounted men to catch.

Damaz took the reins of a Jaddite's horse and hauled himself astride. Five others and the captain did the same.

"Back to the road!" the captain roared. "Eyes open! We find our scouts and we kill these infidels!"

The others shouted agreement. Damaz didn't, but he rode hard, churning through the field to the road. The horse was well trained. It had a good saddle. These raiders might not be such a rabble. He wondered if he should say that, then decided that if he knew it the captain surely did.

He was thinking about two dead men behind them. Both heads had been cut off. He hadn't done it, but he'd put arrows in them.

His first gifts to Ashar of infidel souls. He had dreamed of this, of the starbright glory of it. And these Jaddites had killed men he knew, men he'd been marching beside, eating with.

Damaz found his anger then. It wasn't buried so deeply after all. He left off thinking about beheaded men in a muddy field and aimed himself, like one of his own arrows, towards the infidels ahead of them, who needed to die today.

MARIN HAS LONG KNOWN, without vanity, that he is good with a sword. He's had years of training, takes pleasure in physical action, wielding a blade.

He is also aware that there is a difference between driving off a would-be thief at night in a foreign port, or a match and wager between friends, or lessons from a hired master—and fighting someone trying to kill you in a battle.

He has never been to war. Dubravae noble families do not send their sons to battlefields. The city survives by avoiding such unrewarding activity. They don't even like to support warlike action by others. They'd sent money (not men) to Sarantium the year before it fell.

Nor had they assisted the man commanding this morning's skirmish in Sauradia when he came to them so many years ago. That, Marin thinks, might even be a reason he is now defending an archer by the edge of a forest.

Another reason, of course, is the archer. Who is leaving, if they carry on living after today. Not a certainty, given that Skandir has made clear he has djannis pursuing him, and red-saddle cavalry.

"But I doubt they'll send too many after ordinary raiders," he'd said. "They'll be too arrogant. And they don't know who we are. If I am right, we ought to be able to do this."

I doubt and *if I am right* and *ought to* did not inspire great confidence in a merchant from a city that avoided exactly this sort of thing. So much uncertainty! No one would send a merchant ship to sea with all those random factors in play. It wasn't as if you could arrange for insurance against there being seventy-five in pursuit, or one hundred. *Two* hundred, if it came to that.

Which made it the more foolish, in all ways, that the younger son of the Djivo family, entrusted with their goods en route to Asharias, is standing where he is, holding a sword.

The man called Skandir has explained what is to happen, if all goes as he intends. He said it with such assurance that one might have believed it had already taken place, this battle, that the Asharites were all dead and they were discussing, after, over wine, how smoothly everything had gone, how brave they'd all been.

The field across the road rises and then falls just enough for concealment. It isn't a coincidence. Skandir's men are over that way. The plank bridges on both sides of the road here have now been broken up. The ditches are deep and there is rainwater in them. They will be difficult to cross: a jump down, an awkward, sodden, scrabbling climb back up.

Just east of them a taut cord is stretched across the road. Marin can see it, but only because he knows where it is. It is, apparently, the third such obstacle. Only the first one was likely to down many horses and riders, Skandir said, but this one will slow the Osmanlis just where they need them slowed.

There had been, evidently, an earlier ambush involving almost half of Skandir's band. Those men will be galloping back, ahead of pursuit, if all has gone well. That is why haste is needed. Their own men know about the cords, of course. They know where they are. This has all been planned. Marin's party had simply arrived at a bad time. The fate of men, clerics teach, is not wholly in their own devising. Jad guards the virtuous.

Even so, men can be wise or foolish as well as virtuous. The merchant party was free to act prudently, moving off the road, hiding until this is over. They had been advised to do this. All but two of them are hidden. They are in the forest, behind the cabins.

He isn't. Danica isn't.

"I hear them," she says.

Then Marin hears it too. Horses on the road again. These should be Skandir's men, unless it has all gone wrong already. Eighteen of them, he'd said. Marin stares east.

Skandir's riders appear, galloping. There aren't eighteen of them. Marin sees them jump their horses over the cord. There is a tree south of the road and a boulder on this side where the rope is tied. Those will be their markers. These are not untrained brigands. Their commander had governed a wide sweep of Trakesia before the Osmanlis came, so had his father and grandfather, and back before those.

"Only twelve," Danica says. "The bastards have killed six."

Marin looks back at her. She looks like a huntress come out of the forest, he thinks. She even has a hunting dog beside her. Marin has no doubt Tico can kill a man.

"Soon," she says, looking up the road. "Marin, you don't have to be here. You have your own tasks."

"You're my task just now," he says. She looks at him (she does) for a moment, and he sees her smile, ice breaking for a moment. He doesn't smile back. There is, he is thinking, a first battle for everyone who has ever gone to war. He hadn't thought he would have one himself. Even so. This is where he is, somewhere in Sauradia. This is the choice he seems to have made.

He turns away from her and he, too, stares east along the road.

Skandir's fleeing men turn their horses to make a stand, just below where they are watching, aligned with where twenty others are out of sight across the way. The riders in the road are taking up their bows. Short bows, like those the Asharites use. Danica is the only one with a full-length bow. That is why she's up here, in range for her, not for the Osmanlis. They hope.

And then, *now*, they are here: the soldiers of the khalif's army of Asharias. They aren't invading this place (they govern this place). They had been headed north, this need not be happening. But Rasca Tripon, called Skandir, has caused it to be so. Because some men (and some women) do not surrender to or accept the truths of their world.

Marin is pleased to find himself steady at this first sight of those who are now—in a way that they never have been—his enemies.

Skandir had smiled at Danica, before, as the merchants were hastening across the plank bridge towards the wood. "You killed a bird at that distance. Can you kill men shooting the other way?"

"I can," was all she'd said.

"An easier target?" He'd seemed almost cheerful, Marin thought.

"It is," Danica said. "You want me by the forest."

"Yes. We engage them here. With luck, the numbers favour us. You are to make them even better."

"I understand. It will happen."

He looked at her. Lean, old, red-grey beard, yellow sash for the god. "I believe you," he said. "I'll post a guard with you. An archer needs to have—"

"I'll be that guard," Marin said.

Rasca Tripon turned to him. "This isn't your fight. Dubrava has always made that clear."

"Today it is. Just for me. Not the others. Is there a tunic I can wear, to make me look like one of you?"

For a long time the older man stared at Marin.

"This is your woman?" he asked.

"No."

"No," Danica said in the same moment.

Skandir smiled thinly. "Then why?"

Marin looked at him. Two very tall men. "She saved me from an assassin. I owe her. And we . . . Dubrava turned you away, my lord."

"I am no one's lord. You can handle a weapon?"

"Yes." It would be pleading to say more.

A nod, an order spoken. A saddlebag was opened, a worn grey tunic tossed towards Marin. He caught it.

"I am honoured," Marin said.

His own tunic is behind them in the trees. Wrapped in it are his rings (he likes rings) and his new Seressini hat. His boots and trousers are nondescript and muddy, clothing for the road. In the tunic of Skandir's man he doesn't look like what he is. If he dies here, it will not—it *might* not—lead the Osmanlis to the others, or to blame Dubrava. He'll just be one more infidel in Skandir's band, killed by the warriors of Ashar. Beheaded, most likely.

PERO VILLANI HAD GROWN to manhood in a respectable home in Seressa, son of an artist judged (his son had known this, even when young) capable if not exceptional. Viero Villani had been good enough to work steadily as long as his fees were appropriate. Minor nobility commissions, smaller sanctuaries. A few times a fresco or a portrait for those of higher rank when artists better regarded had been unavailable. Good enough, in short, to have that home in Seressa and for some people to know his name.

His son had followed his vocation if not, currently, his path. He had not ever expected to find himself in the wilderness, hiding in a forest, awaiting the arrival of Osmanli soldiers and a battle between them and a rebel who was a legend, even over the water in Seressa.

Legends, if you crossed their path, could get you killed.

The guards were trying to keep the animals quiet. One of the Seressini merchants was wheezing and gulping in terror, dragging breath into his lungs. Pero didn't think the noise was a danger, they were a long way back from the road where men had now turned to await the Osmanlis. Skandir was with these.

On impulse, wanting to remove himself from the fear surrounding him, Pero slipped away. He stayed in the forest, moving east towards where Danica was—with Marin Djivo guarding her, with her dog.

He came to a clearing within the wood. He kept low, moved to the edge of the forest, to where he could see out. He crouched behind an oak, the glade behind him, and watched. There was nothing, he thought, for an artist to do here but watch.

Danica and Marin were to his left. They were looking east so he did the same. It didn't take long. There was no loud drumming of hooves on the muddy road, no dust rising in the sunlight. The Asharites came into view, some riding cautiously, others running alongside. He thought there were about forty of them, though he wasn't good at judging numbers. There was a tripwire down there. The lead rider spotted it, alerted the others, bent to one side and slashed the cord with a curved sword.

He straightened, and died.

Danica had already released a second arrow and hit another rider before Pero realized that it was her long flight that had struck the man. The Asharites came on, straight for the raiders in the road.

"Once they are upon us," Skandir had said just before Pero had followed the merchants towards the wood, "you'll need to be careful. I'd prefer not to be killed by a girl from Senjan."

"So would they, I imagine," Danica had said.

She was sending arrows at speed, trying to even the odds before the Asharites closed the gap, but the distance did close swiftly and Pero couldn't tell how many Osmanlis had fallen before the two companies met.

But in that moment Skandir's second group surged up and forward out of the field across the road and through the ditch over there—and there was a battle down below.

He heard shouts, commands, cries of pain and fury, the hard clanging of metal, and he was trembling where he watched within the trees.

He hated this, he realized—playing no role at all. He wasn't a fighter, but he'd never been a coward. So he moved. He kept low and backed up into the glade to continue east towards Danica and Marin. He could watch them, at the very least help defend her. There had been a thought the enemy would send men up to deal with her, that was why Marin was there. Deal with her meant *kill her*.

Pero crawled through the glade, moving as quickly as he could. Down close to the dark earth, he saw some metal objects, half buried, glint dully in the light filtering through spring leaves overhead. He looked at one of them—an amulet, very old, in the shape of a bird of some kind. He lifted it for a moment. He shivered. He put it back and left it there.

THEIR CAPTAIN WAS AT THE FRONT. He slashed the tripwire, and was the first to die.

Damaz had given his mount to an unhorsed cavalryman, he was running with the other djannis alongside. It was their second-in-command—now leading—who snapped the order as arrows kept coming from above the road by the forest.

"Take him out! Up there! There is only one. You, you, and you and you!"

Damaz was the third *you*. Two were horsemen who dismounted quickly, the fourth was another djanni. The riders left their horses in the road and the three of them leaped into the ditch beside. It was half filled with water, Damaz saw. Someone had taken away the plank bridges. Of course someone had. This had been planned to happen here.

This order was, he realized, folly. You could die of a commander's errors, but there was no *value* in that. He dropped into the ditch to the east of the other three. The water reached the top of his boots. It was cold. He saw the others clamber out. They had a long, exposed distance to reach the archer.

In fact, he saw, the man by the trees had now stopped. Battle was joined in the road, men were tangled together. The order they'd been given was needless, wasteful. But it was his order, he was a soldier in battle. He saw the other three start across the field trying to keep out of sight. It wouldn't work. The space was too open.

Damaz stayed in the ditch, worked his way back along it the way they'd come, splashing through rainwater and sucking mud. He wondered if someone would think he was fleeing. That thought frightened him.

He peered over the edge of the ditch. Couldn't see his three companions now or the man with the bow by the trees. He climbed out, stayed as low as he could. The grass wasn't tall enough to conceal a man, but it was what he had. He started crawling towards the woods, angling even farther east as he went.

He needed to get through this space to the trees. He had a bow.

He heard a scream, and a curse. One of the other three had been hit. Damaz moved faster, elbows and knees through wet grass. He changed course, straight north towards the forest. The order had been a mistake, he thought, but this man was killing the khalif's soldiers and needed to die, whatever else happened here.

"THAT ONE ISN'T DEAD IN THE GRASS," Danica says.

"I know," Marin snaps. "You hit him in the thigh."

"Higher, with luck. There are two more."

"I know," he says again. "They are slipping west." Something occurs to him, and with the thought he moves. "Danica, I'm going after them. They will be aiming to come into the trees that way— they'll find the others hiding!"

"No!" she cries. "Marin—these are djannis, you can't fight them!"

She is almost certainly correct. For some reason he doesn't care just now. Can warfare make men mad, as poets have always sung?

"Too many at risk there," he says, starting forward. "Those men are my party. Cover me if these two stand up." He calls it back to her. His eyes are forward, though.

"Marin, *stop!*"

He does. Looks at her this time, from several steps into the wet grass of the field. She is still by the trees, another arrow to string, her hair pinned but without the hat now, since she started releasing arrows at Asharites. Her dream, he thinks: to be doing this.

"You are . . . you are here to guard me!" she says. Her colour is high.

He hadn't expected that.

"I am," he replies, and turns again, moving quickly, down and right, to where the Osmanlis had last been. He can hear the wounded one moaning. He leaves him there. Danica can kill him if she wants, he thinks.

Below him, in the loud roadway, it is difficult to tell what is happening now. A clotted mass of men are trying to end each other's lives. Horses are down and screaming.

He thinks—though he has no experience of judging this—that Skandir is prevailing. Between the men the Asharites lost to his ambushes and traps, and Danica here, and then the flanking attack from across the road, his guess is that this has been well-judged—though there will be losses. Dying men make terrible sounds, Marin Djivo thinks.

And a man can die in a meaningless skirmish on a road in Sauradia as easily as on the triple walls of Sarantium or in the siege of a northern fortress.

Or in a meadow by that same road. He sees the two soldiers. They are ahead of him, working west on their knees as he'd guessed. They will want to go north to the forest and concealment from which to attack the archer.

His sword comes out. He has fought men face to face, driven thieves to flight. He has never killed a man crawling away from him. He does so now. He thinks, *I will always remember this*. He drives his blade into the back of the nearer of the crawling soldiers.

A cry, and a grunt. The one ahead looks back. Rises up, sword out. His face shows fury, no fear. There is even, Marin has a moment to see, a ferocious contempt. Marin knows he can handle a blade. He also sees, from the uniform in front of him, that this is indeed a djanni, and that no merchant from Dubrava can expect—

The man falls where he stands. Marin will dream, on nights afterwards, that he heard the arrow flying past his head before striking the Osmanli in the throat and sending him pitching into the grass. It isn't a true memory. It didn't pass that close to him, you can't hear an arrow that way, but that is what happens in dreams, if not in the life we really live.

He looks back. Sees her across the grass, a tall woman with a bow against black trees, a dog beside her. The two of them stand a moment like that. He lifts a hand, starts back towards her.

He is quite close, in fact, for what follows. For what happens next (there is always something happening next) in the tangle and turn of what men and women do to each other in the world that has been given us, upon earth, under sky, where our brief lives play out, and end.

Close enough to shout a useless warning, even.

PERO, WITHIN A GLADE in a forest, looking out, saw Marin start after the Osmanlis in the grass. He couldn't see them, but he knew they were there. Danica had wounded one; you could hear his moans, nearer than the sound of men fighting on the road.

"*You are here to guard me!*" Danica cried to Marin, something new in her voice. Pero kept moving. There was another man here who could guard her. Viero Villani's son could defend an archer for a space of time, surely he could.

He seized a fallen branch. He left the small metal artifacts and he took a weapon with him. He left the glade but stayed among the trees, passing behind Danica, across to her far side. Marin had gone after the soldiers in the grass. Pero was afraid for him, but that wasn't going to help much, was it? He could try to protect Danica. He didn't think he'd be too useful against soldiers, this wasn't what he *did*, what he'd ever done. Tavern brawls in the tannery district weren't . . . this. But he didn't want to crouch passively in the woods and just watch.

It occurred to him she might hear him behind her and think he was an enemy. He was about to call her name, let her know he was here, when he saw something ahead of him.

He moved then, as fast as he could, running through trees and then out of the forest. Almost in time. Nearly so.

DAMAZ REACHED THE EDGE OF THE WOOD. The Jaddite archer was looking the other way, arrow to string, watching his guard, who had gone after the two soldiers remaining in the grass. The third of their men had an arrow in him down there. He was moaning in pain. Damaz could just see him. His name was Giray. They had shared a tent for two weeks. He had a torn ear and a small son and he told good jokes. He was dying in the wet, bright grass.

The Jaddite guard killed another warrior with his sword. Damaz saw it, a coward's blow from behind. Their last man rose up to engage the infidel, screaming in fury—and the archer killed him, even as he stood.

The Jaddite down there would die, Damaz vowed. But first would be this archer who had ended so many lives. Who *needed* to be killed.

Damaz stepped forward. The archer didn't see him, and his dog was also looking the other way. Damaz nocked his own arrow to his own bowstring. He seemed to be hearing a faint buzzing sound, almost a voice in his head—first battle fears, most surely. That could happen. A man could admit to those, without ever, *ever* yielding to them.

Children! the voice said then, clearly, in his mind. He was no child!

The Jaddite in the grass below had seen him now. It didn't matter. He only had a sword. The man pointed, cried a warning to the archer. Cried a name, in fact. A name Damaz even knew, having remembered it.

Not in time, that cry. Not in time, in so many ways.

The archer wheeled to face him, bow rising. The dog snarled, started forward. Damaz was already releasing. It wasn't far and he was a good bowman, had been from the first time they were given bows and arrows to learn another way to cause an enemy to die.

His arrow struck the archer in the heart, exactly where he'd aimed, having seen that the Jaddite bowman wore no armour. He saw his arrow hit.

Then the shouted name registered fully, and his mouth opened, and in that same moment Damaz felt pain explode like a shattered wheel of bright colours. He pitched forward, having been struck *hard* in the back by someone wielding a club that knocked him flat, his bow flying free.

His head hit the ground. He was dazed, gasping to breathe. There had been a name. Shouted. He *knew* that name. He knew—

A second blow came, and Damaz lost the sense of everything except for—so strange as a last awareness—sorrow. It was sorrow that entered into him, of all things, before the crashing down of darkness under the bright sun, but also Ashar's stars that were always in the sky, as they were taught.

CHILDREN! DANICA HEARD, ringing clear as her grandfather's voice always did, in agony—as he never was.

Oh, zadek! she thought, turning. She had time for that. To see him.

"Neven!" she cried. Or tried to cry, wanted to but failed, as the arrow struck, over her unguarded heart.

IN OLD TALES (and some of these lingered, told to children mostly) of the goddess or god of the hunt—before Jad came, bright as the sun, driving the sun—lovers or acolytes of the gods might be raised from the dead by the deity they honoured. The pagan gods had held such power, or had been believed to do so.

In Sauradia, in the wilderness of it, in the days and years after the fall of Sarantium, in a time of war between the newer faiths of sun and stars, this was understood to not be so any more. Those gods had gone.

Jad guarded his children, yes, battling under the world every night, but someone who died did not come back. Was not caused by an immortal to rise again, woundless, unharmed, alive. After all, the god's own beloved son had not come back when he fell from the sky, had he?

The age of such miracles, or belief in them, was past. It was understood by the thoughtful and the wise that the old tales spoke to longing, and longing was endless. Men and women, lovers, friends, almost-strangers holding a tree branch above a fallen man (fallen boy, it appeared)—all knew they lived in and endured a hard world between their birth and dying. Children slipped away, struggling to draw breath. Fathers and brothers died, lovers were murdered, women passed from the world in childbirth, soldiers fell in war, villagers in raids lit by fire.

If an arrow flew through morning light above spring grass beside an ancient forest and struck you in the breast as you turned to face the archer, you would die.

You would not rise to stand again in that sunlight, however brave you had been, however defiant, however achingly wrong it was seen to be by others that you were gone so soon. The old beliefs, insofar as they were ever thought to have been true, were also gone. They were only stories, told to push back our certain knowledge of the waiting dark.

CHAPTER XVI

It was quieter now, down on the road. Pero made himself look that way. It did take some effort, but if things had gone badly there, they would all be dead, not just Danica. The Asharites would have seen him here, and Marin.

But on the imperial highway the only men still standing or on horseback were Skandir's. They were, he saw, killing the last of the Osmanlis. They were not in a place for hostages or prisoners. This was a lonely part of the world, a road, loggers' cabins, a forest, fields on the far side, a place where death had situated itself this morning.

The carnage on the highway, Pero thought, was not like any of the battle paintings he knew. Those had spears and banners aimed carefully at the vanishing point. Grace and harmony of composition in a crowded, colourful canvas. He had admired some of those greatly. He wondered if he ever would again.

He saw Skandir on his grey horse surrounded by seven or eight of his band. All that were left, it appeared. Even as Pero looked, the last Osmanli, pleading, his voice faint from far away, was killed. There was real stillness then. You could hear birds, the shuffling sigh of wind in the trees behind him, their spring leaves.

He thought he'd heard a voice before. Before death came by the forest. Crying *Children*. And he had no idea if that was a true hearing—or who it had been, if it *was* something true. He was remembering, for some reason, the figurine he'd touched in the glade. They had come to a strange place, Pero Villani thought.

At his feet the Asharite who had made his way up here to kill, and had done so, moved a little and made a sound. Pero didn't have a life on his conscience yet, it seemed. He imagined Skandir or one of his band would deal with this one. Or perhaps Marin Djivo, still rooted like a tree in the field, halfway to the road, looking back this way. Marin held his sword as if he'd forgotten he had it. The point was in the grass at an awkward angle from his body. You could paint that, Pero thought. He looked west and saw the other merchants and their guards and animals now beginning to come out of the woods. Tico was by Danica where she lay. He was urgently licking her face. It was sad beyond words. Pero thought he might weep.

One of the Seressinis cheered, a thin, strange sound. It faded. Birds and wind. The Osmanli at his feet stirred again. *I can't even hit a man hard enough to knock him unconscious, let alone dead*, Pero thought. Bitterness. He had nearly been in time, he had been doing the right thing, rushing here, he just hadn't *done* it.

He had hardly known Danica Gradek. None of them had. It was such a little time ago he'd boarded the Djivos' ship in Seressa. There were others dead here, not just her—on the road, halfway there, three Osmanlis in the grass. He realized that Marin must have killed the wounded man, the one who had been crying in his pain.

In the paintings he'd seen, battle scenes were celebrations. The chaos, the spilling intestines of a life ending did not hang on walls in palaces. You didn't commission a scene where your ancestor died screaming, holding in his guts with both hands. Nor did the triumphant warriors of one's line ever behead pleading, surrendering men. Triumph required artistic balance. A vanishing point. An amount of blue and gold (expensive!) agreed upon in a contract.

He was not, Pero decided, thinking coherently. That was his thought. That he wasn't thinking clearly.

HE IS IN A FIELD. There are wildflowers. He holds a sword. He has killed a man. Others are dead in the road, a great many. Danica is dead up there. He had been guarding her. He has failed. She had been leaving. She'd said that. Was going with Skandir. Whom Marin remembered from childhood. A rebel, hero. In Senjan they called themselves heroes. Others called them raiders. Others called them worse things.

He had been guarding her. Had taken that upon himself. Ban Rasca, Skandir, whom he remembered, had asked if he could do it. He had said yes he could do it. He needs to walk up to her, to where she lies in the grass. He will kill the Osmanli in the grass if he's not dead yet, then the one Pero struck down.

I should want to do that, Marin Djivo thinks. He looks at his sword, which feels strange in his hand. There is blood on the blade. He is a merchant. He looks towards the forest again.

I AM TOO OLD, the man called Skandir was thinking, not for the first time. There were too many dead men among his own. He had never shied away from losses in his long war. There were always losses in a war, even if it was more harassment and defiance than true warfare. They were never going to *win* this. Not in his own time. The Osmanlis had most of Sauradia and Trakesia. Yes, they had difficulties where his family had ruled, but difficulties were only that—and they didn't actually care much about occupying the lands where the Tripons had governed before the fall.

A hard truth, but a truth. It was a harsh, unrewarding place.

It bred harsh men. Independent, yes. Defiant. Implacable. *I am implacable*, was his thought. And he had just killed most of his current band here.

He had made a mistake. The Osmanlis, Jad curse them all to ice and dark, had sent more men than he'd ever imagined they would. Even with his ambushes laid along the highway, even with the archer they'd found, there had been too many.

He had won, yes. The Asharites were dead—the last one just now to his own heavy blade. But a victory could cost too much. He looked around, counting. Seven men standing or on horse, three wounded who might live. One wounded who would surely die, the sword thrust too high, into his groin. You died badly of that. It might not take long, or it might, which was worse. He had dispatched many of his men over the years with wounds like this one. You called it mercy, knew it was, found a sanctuary in which to pray, after. He did pray, often. He felt a heart-deep terror of the god. Also a duty owed to him. A duty and his life, all the days and nights of it. There was no space for love.

He had made an error. An old man's carelessness. Or was it just too unexpected that an Osmanli serdar would send fifty men after a band of raiders being a nuisance with his supply train?

If they had not encountered these merchants and discovered a very good archer—a woman—he and all his men would be the ones lying dead here, their heads being cut off right now. His would have been carried to Asharias. He was a prize. The man who killed him would have his fortune made.

It would have happened this morning if not for the woman sending arrows from the trees. It was hard to be certain, but Skandir guessed she'd killed or wounded eight or ten of the Osmanlis before the two forces met and she'd had to stop. That was the difference between victory here (a kind of victory) and being someone's eternal glory in the Osmanli ranks.

A bad mistake, any way you looked at it. Saved only by great good fortune. You needed luck in war, you didn't want to *depend* on it.

He dismounted and went over to the man with the sword wound in his groin. It was Ilija. Not young, either, that one. Bald, half his teeth gone. One of his band from the beginning, after Sarantium fell. His brother had been with them too, until he died of flux five years ago.

On his back, Ilija looked steadily up at him. The wound was mortal. He was breathing shallowly but not moaning or crying out, though his pain would be massive, vast. So much pride. Their eyes met. More than twenty years, this hard life together. The man lying on the road nodded. Pain was carrying him.

"Farewell, lord," Ilija said. "Freedom," he said, looking up at his leader. Who had done this to him. He had done that to others, through many years of this. It came with what they were, the world they had.

Rasca nodded. "With Jad in light, friend," he said. And killed his man in the road with his sword. It hurt. It always hurt.

He looked towards the trees. The woman, too, was down, he saw. Another mistake, letting a merchant guard her. But he'd needed every man here, hadn't he? Didn't have many left. They would have to go south, take refuge, recruit again. It was harder to recruit every time. He'd be no factor in this spring campaign, not any more.

But he *would* regroup. He was too old to stop. What would he do if he wasn't fighting for the god against infidels? What *were* you, if you stopped? He was very likely going to die in one of these fights. Not yet, though. Not today.

In fact, he was not to die in battle, Rasca Tripon. His severed head would never be a trophy carried east. He would, unexpectedly, end his days lying in a good bed, two women sitting by him, holding his big, scarred hands, a cleric chanting prayers for his soul. He would give one of them his family ring to take away with her. Men, holy and otherwise, would burn his body on a pyre that same night, both moons in the sky, that the infidels might never find his grave to despoil it. He had been a lion in his time.

On a spring morning he looked around him. Fifty Asharites were dead, strung out along on this stretch of road. Word would filter, like water through rocks. It would spread through Sauradia and beyond. It would overtake the army of the khalif, run before it. Not just any infidels beaten, either. Djannis and red-saddle cavalry of the army of invasion. Tricked and trapped. By Skandir. By Skandir again. Destroyed to the last man.

The last man might still be alive up there. The old warrior turned with his sword and started towards the forest. He would do this himself. Down into the wet ditch and up, heavily, leaning on the sword (he was weary, not wounded) and then steadily across the grass, his eyes bleak. Implacable.

He had come up beside the Dubravae merchant, Djivo, when the story changed. Stories do change. We do not understand the world. We are not made that way.

DANICA STOOD UP.

She was aware of each individual movement involved. Of breathing, out and in, and again. Tico was at her side. She reached a slow hand down, touched her dog's head.

She had taken an arrow at short range in the heart and she was standing. The goddess of the hunt was gone from the world, had never been, the clerics taught. A story for children, they said, for the credulous and ignorant, for village hearths on winter nights. And still—she stood up.

There was tremendous pain. It hurt to breathe. She was breathing. The arrow lay in the grass beside her. Danica bent, carefully, and picked it up. She looked at it in her hand. There was blood on it, but only a little. Tip of the arrowhead.

She was standing. Alive. She looked at the artist, Pero Villani, who had seen everything that happened. His mouth was open, she saw. His face was white. He looked as if he would kneel, or fall down. She also felt that way. Her breathing was shallow, it hurt otherwise. There seemed to be more light than before, but that was surely an illusion, confusion. Something of the sort.

Zadek? she said, within. *What just happened?*

There was no reply.

Zadek? she said again. Again, no response.

Zadek!

A cry, that third time, from within the wound of her heart.

But she already understood. Or enough, she understood enough. She was going to weep, and she refused to weep, here in sunlight, among men. She pressed hard at both eyes with the back of a hand. The hand trembled. That wasn't her, either.

Zadek, please?

But she knew now, there was no way to *not* know how it was that she was still alive. She was remembering the ship, the morning of their raid, when Leonora had been walking towards her death at the rail—and had been stopped. Stopped. Danica knew what had pushed her back. She knew from him. From her grandfather. Zadek, she'd called him from earliest memory, from long before the fires and their flight.

And if he had done that for a stranger, a hated Seressini, someone he did not know at all, what wouldn't he have done for her, his grandchild, whom he loved beyond death?

He had died in Senjan. And he had been within her, with her to this day, shelter and guidance and care. Making it so that she was not alone in the world after all.

Now she was. She did not call again. The silence within her was enormous. But an arrow had been stopped. That she might not die. She wiped at her eyes again. Only the artist had seen her fighting tears. Only he had clearly seen the arrow strike, because of where he'd stood.

Well, no. One other had. Danica drew a breath, carefully.

"Is he dead?" she asked, looking at the boy on the ground by the trees, bludgeoned.

Pero Villani shook his head. He looked terrified. How could he not? Truly, how not? And as he stared at Danica—seeing her hold an arrow that had struck her in the heart—the boy on the ground below him stirred and looked up, and saw her there.

The boy on the ground was her brother. She knew it.

He was here and her grandfather—their grandfather—had died almost a year ago, and was only now, only *now* gone from her, and she understood what he'd done, and she knew it was forever.

The world was an inconceivable place, Danica thought. It was vanity to think you could understand even your own life.

"I killed you," the boy said, in accented but clear Sauradian.

She shook her head. She had no idea what to say.

"You . . . you are a woman," he said.

She still couldn't speak. Words felt far away. She heard Marin coming up with the old warrior, Skandir. She felt light-headed, dizzy, afraid. There was a hard, heavy pain in her breastbone. You could say in her heart. It was there, too.

"Danica," Marin Djivo said. "Oh, Jad. How are you . . . ?"

His voice was so strange. He, too, looked frightened. Which meant that he, too, had seen the arrow strike. She remembered a warning: yes, he had cried out. That was why she'd turned to the bowman. The boy. Neven.

She remained silent. What was she going to say?

"I killed you," her brother said again. "I saw my arrow hit."

"Be silent," said Skandir grimly. "Make your peace with your god and stars." He looked at Danica, then at the artist.

"He hit you? With that arrow?"

She looked at the arrow she held. She nodded.

"You wear no armour?"

She shook her head. *Zadek*, she wanted to cry. She wanted to say it aloud.

"I have seen a man survive an arrow when it struck a talisman he wore."

She shook her head.

"This was too close, in any case. That can only happen at the limit of an arrow's range." He sounded calm, but this man, too, was beginning to realize something unnatural had happened here.

Well, it had, she thought.

"You are all right?" Marin asked. More his normal voice.

She looked at him. Such a handsome man, and he . . . she mattered to him. She knew that. Which was unfortunate, in all the circumstances.

"I am," she said. "My chest hurts. There's blood. It is . . . it is on the arrow." She held it up, as if that would clarify something for them.

"I killed you," her brother said for a third time.

"And I told you to be silent," Skandir snapped. "I won't say it again."

"What will you do? Kill me sooner?" Neven was clearly in pain. He'd been struck on the back, then clubbed on the head or shoulders.

He has courage, she thought. And, *Of course he does*, she thought.

"I can do that," the old warrior said.

"Then do it!"

"No," she said.

She knelt in the tall grass by the woods, before the old warrior. "Please, no."

He raised two thick eyebrows. "You will need to say why."

She drew breath again. It was so painful to do that. This was all impossible, she thought.

She said, "I have promised to come with you. To join you. Do you still want me?"

"You killed ten men here. I do."

"Twelve," said Marin Djivo. "She killed or wounded twelve. I counted. You would have lost this battle. You would be dead, Ban Rasca."

"I am not the ban of anything," the old man said, a reflex. "But yes, she is good with a bow. I will take her with me. What does that have to do with this one?"

"He is my brother," she said.

There was no way to not say it, and no way she could think of to make it less blunt. The world didn't allow that, or wasn't allowing it. They were both here.

"*What?*" Skandir exclaimed. He made the sign of the sun disk. First time she'd seen him do that.

"Holy Jad!" Marin whispered. She was looking at him. A moment later she looked across at the other two. The artist still held a branch in one hand. Her brother . . .

"That is a lie!" her brother said.

Tico growled, she silenced him with a gesture.

She stood up again. You should not say this kneeling.

"Your name is Neven Gradek. You may know it, or you may have been too young. Mine is Danica. I don't know if you'll remember me. You were named for your grandfather. You were born in a village called Antunic in the borderlands northwest. You were taken by hadjuks in a summer raid. We fled to Senjan—our mother, our grandfather, me. You were not quite four years old. You . . . you were born in autumn."

There was silence. What could any of them say to this? she thought. Swear, pray, cry aloud?

Skandir cleared his throat. "This is . . . this has always been known as a strange place. There is a glade somewhere back in this forest. People here say . . . there were said to be powers here."

"It isn't so far back," said Pero Villani. His first words. "They have cut the trees up to it. I went through it. I saw . . . I saw talismans there, amulets."

"Did you take anything? Tell me you didn't!" Skandir cried.

Danica looked at him. Saw him make the sign of the disk again.

Villani shook his head. "I touched one. A metal bird. But I put it back. I took a branch." He lifted it a little, as if to show them. He was looking at Danica. "I heard . . . I thought I heard a voice, just before the arrow. It said . . . the voice said, *Children.*"

Danica stared at him. Too much was impossible to explain here.

"I heard that," her brother said.

A different voice this time. He sounded young. *He is fourteen*, she thought. She had always been aware of how old he'd be if alive, wherever he was. Skandir didn't silence him this time.

The old warrior shook his head. "And the world keeps surprising me. I don't like being surprised. There were beliefs about this forest. Maybe that is how this . . ." He looked at Villani. "You touched an offering, you said?"

An offering, Danica thought.

The artist nodded.

But that isn't it, Danica thought. *That isn't how this happened.*

She was looking at her brother. Staring, hungrily. He was fair-haired, more red than she was, freckles, big for his age, broad-shouldered. Their father and brother had been big men. And now she saw something change in his eyes.

She asked, "*Did* you know your name? Mine?"

After a long moment of birdsong and the wind she saw him nod his head, once. He pointed at Marin. "And I heard that one call it, as I released."

She began, appallingly, to weep after all. Furiously wiping tears away, she said, "You were aware of someone, weren't you, this spring, when you fought a man?"

His mouth gaped. "How do you know that?"

"I do," she said. "A knife?"

Fear in his eyes. He was a boy. He nodded again, that same single downward motion. She had carried him through their village, teaching him the names of things.

She said, "You have been loved, Neven. You never stopped being loved."

"My name is Damaz."

"You were named for your grandfather who—"

"My name is Damaz! I am a djanni of the army of the khalif. What you are saying means nothing."

"That last is untrue," said Skandir, but not harshly. "What we come from matters."

"Not to me! Go ahead, kill me, the way barbarians do."

"I can do that," the old warrior said for a second time.

"Please, no," Danica said. "This is my one request."

"It is a large one, even from a good archer."

"Then let it be a large one."

Marin Djivo said, "It might be good if a man survives, goes back to the army to tell them Skandir destroyed those sent after him."

"And if he tells them a merchant party helped?"

"We hid in the woods. An archer from Senjan helped you and rode away with you. If he says it was a woman, their shame is greater. He might not say it."

Marin was, Danica thought, as intelligent as anyone she'd ever met. And courageous, and a good man, and he cared about her and . . . and she was riding away with Skandir, whatever else happened now. Because her life, since the fires in Antunic, had been pointed towards exactly this, killing, revenge, war—just as this old warrior's had been.

She was more like Skandir, she thought, than anyone in Dubrava could ever grasp. It was a sorrow. But that didn't make it false.

"You may go," Skandir said, looking at Neven. "No weapons.

I grant you your life. Ride back to your army."

"I am a djanni. We do not ride."

"You will be hard-pressed to make it on foot, but I am sure a heroic djanni of the great khalif's army has his means."

Neven stood. She saw him wince. She said, she had to say, "You can stay. You are Jaddite-born, you were taken as a child. You can turn your back on those who did that to you. You can fight them. Take your own revenge. They don't get to decide what you are, Neven!"

"No," he said. "Almost every djanni was a Jaddite child. It is what we are. Why would I be the one to betray those who taught me, honoured me?"

"Because they stole your life," she said.

"They *gave* me a life."

"Not the one you were born to, with the family you had!"

"And the faith," Skandir added, quietly.

"I am not the only one this has happened to." He swayed a little, but his voice was firm.

"No, you aren't," Skandir said. "But you are now one who has a chance to return. It is not a thing to turn your back upon."

"Why not? Why would I leave everything I know?"

"To find everything taken from you," the big man said. "Ask me a harder question, boy!"

Her brother was silent, and in that silence Danica said, "Maybe . . . maybe stay because I'm here, too, and asking you."

"*Why* are you here?" he asked. "You said Senjan? Why here now?"

Too hard to answer, too much that would need explaining. She said, "Neven—"

"My name," he repeated, "is Damaz. I am from the garrison of Mulkar, fifth regiment. I am a djanni in the khalif's army." He turned to Skandir. "If you are letting me go, may I leave?"

She wasn't weeping. She wanted to. She reached down again, a hand touching her dog.

"You may," said Skandir. "I said as much. Though if you stay, there is a place for you with me, because of . . . because there is a power in this."

"A power," her brother mimicked, and in his tone she heard their older brother, Mikal, who had died the night of the raid.

"If you leave we will never see each other again," she said. Her turn to sound desperate. She looked only at her brother now.

He shrugged.

"Think, lad! What will they do to the one survivor?" Marin Djivo said suddenly. "They will decide you fled."

"They might," Skandir agreed. He sighed. "If you are wise, you will tell them your leader ordered you back as the battle turned, to report that it was me you fought."

Another shrug, but Danica saw a hesitation.

Clutched by fear, she said, "You think you were made to throw that knife in that fight only to go back now to their army?"

"I threw the knife in a fair fight!"

"And I know about it!" Her voice was urgent. "His name was Neven, too. You were named for him. Neven Rusan. Our mother's father."

She was telling too much, with three others here and the clerics of Jad constantly inveighing against witchcraft, *and* with Senjan said to be a place that knew dark arts, especially the women.

Even so. This was, she thought, her last chance. She wanted to walk across the grass and touch him. She knew she could not.

"Neven, I don't want you to die."

"Why? You don't know me at all."

"But I do. I did. There hasn't been a day when I haven't thought of you, and revenge. That is why I'm here. You asked. That is my answer. It is about you."

She could feel three men looking at her. She kept her gaze on her brother. His eyes held hers a moment. Then he turned away, to Skandir.

"I will not tell about the merchants," he said. "In return for my life, which was in your hands."

"No. In your sister's hands," the big man said. "Without her you are dead here, for the forest creatures to feed upon."

Another shrug. A boy's shrug. She tried to imagine what he must be feeling. She failed. He turned back to her.

"I thank you, then," he said coolly.

And turned. Turned and went away, through tall grass, past flowers, the sun bright above. They watched him go, a well-made boy, back down towards the ditch and then the road. Someone there, seeing him, called to Skandir. The old man held up a hand, staying his men.

Her brother never looked back. Afterwards, days and nights, Danica would see this moment in her mind, clearly, as in that same spring light, and find herself unable to believe he hadn't looked back at her, not once, and that she'd let him go.

The borderlands, what they did to people there.

HE IS AWARE OF DRIFTING, *he is very high. He understands that whatever it is that has held him here, to her, whether his own fierce will or a gift of Jad, or of something else, older, is spent now, is finished. He broke whatever it was when he stopped that arrow. He pushed—and that feels to be the right word—too hard.*

That is why he is floating now, rising. So high on a bright day. Last bright day. He can see them both far below, apart, distance growing. Granddaughter, grandson. The boy, walking stiffly away, is sheathed in pride and fear. Neven. Named for him. He understands pride and still feels fear. For him, for both of them. Even now, even leaving, finally. How long is forever?

He is not a man who had ever offered words of love when he was in the world. He hopes, now, that it has been understood. He hopes they will be all right, as much so as is ever allowed.

He himself is allowed this aching, far, final glance. His last thoughts are their names, the one and then the other, then he is air, sunlight, lost, gone.

CHAPTER XVII

It is Skandir who takes charge after the boy disappears down the road to the east.

He does this effortlessly, an easy assumption that it is his task. There are people who lead, it can be as simple as that.

Looking at Danica as they come down from the trees, Marin wants to comfort her and is afraid to even try. Without a word spoken he has an understanding with the old warrior and Pero Villani that nothing will be said about what happened at the forest's edge. The others were too far away, they will have seen nothing that needs explaining.

Well, one thing. Skandir tells his remaining men that he let the last Osmanli go, weaponless, so he could tell the serdars of the khalif's army who had destroyed them here. If he gets back alive, he adds.

There are no tools in the cabins, but a little farther off they find some buried by the woods. An attempt at hiding them from thieves. There are shovels, axes, woodcutters' saws, in three graves. They set about digging a true grave on the far side of the road for Skandir's men.

Marin is blunt with the Seressini merchants who want to move on immediately—leave these raiders who'd rashly endangered them. He makes clear that if they leave now they do so without Dubravae guards. He invites them to do so. They decline. They actually look afraid of him. He hasn't taken this tone before.

He is uncomfortable with how angry he feels, in fact. Men from Dubrava, he thinks, taking a turn with a shovel in the sunlight, are *so* discreet and diplomatic. It startles people when they are otherwise.

Danica had told her brother that her entire life was about vengeance. Said it was why she was here. She'd said the same thing to Marin, in fact, one night within Dubrava's walls, within his family's walls, in his room.

And he, Marin Djivo, younger son of a merchant? What was his life about? Trade? Clever, profitable dealings? He was from a city-state that flourished by letting no one hate them enough to do anything disagreeable. Where you are situated in the world, Marin thinks, digging a grave in a Sauradian meadow, shapes how you act in the world.

Then he amends that thought: it is *one* of the things that does so. Rasca Tripon and Danica Gradek might frame it differently. Or the old empress living with the Daughters of Jad on Sinan Isle might do so. They are all exiles, he thinks, taken from what they were, where they were.

He digs hard, sweating in the sunlight though it isn't warm. They need large graves, there are many dead. Pero Villani works beside him. When their eyes meet, both men look away.

They'd touched the half-world this morning.

There is no way to deny it. The artist had actually touched something *in* that world. He'd said as much. And they'd both seen a woman take an arrow in the heart—and rise up, alive.

Skandir had said this was alleged to be a spirit-haunted wood.

They have reason now to believe this is so, whatever clerics might declare.

This is a place to leave, as soon as they can, he thinks. They finish laying to rest the dead in the afternoon. Ban Rasca speaks the prayers—he'll have done this many times, Marin thinks. More than two decades of his men dying. It is astonishing, really, that he is still alive, still fighting. They move on, along the imperial road, headed east.

They stop to bury some other men towards day's end—from the first ambush set by Skandir's archers. There are Asharites dead here, too. Marin sees Danica moving about, claiming arrows. Archers never let arrows go to waste. She moves stiffly, is pale and silent. They haven't spoken. He has no idea what words to offer. The boy, her brother—*Neven*—had walked away, returning to Ashar. What did you say?

They leave the Asharites unburied, after taking what can be used from them. Skandir and his men will have done this before, too, Marin knows. You don't leave useful things behind, not in the life these men live. He tries to imagine such a life. He can't, really. It is beyond him. He feels that as a failure on his part. He does notice something, however. He thinks about mentioning it, but does not.

There are six raiders left healthy. There are three wounded they are taking east. One is badly hurt, held on a horse by another rider. Skandir tells them there is a sanctuary with a small village beside it not far ahead. They'll overnight there, have the wounded treated—maybe left behind, maybe left as dead.

In the morning Skandir and the remnant of his band, including a woman from Senjan and her dog now, will go south to regroup in Trakesia. And Marin Djivo, merchant of Dubrava, will carry on with his party as he had been before, in a world that isn't now what it was this morning.

PERO KEPT GLANCING at his left hand as he walked, the hand he'd used to pick up that artifact in the forest.

He had no idea what he was looking to see. Perhaps his fingers would begin to turn black, rot, fall off. Perhaps he was doomed. Skandir, so vividly fearless, had seemed frightened when Pero said he'd touched something in the glade.

He'd put it back. Immediately. He couldn't even remember clearly what it had looked like now, which was strange for an artist. There was a blurring in his mind there. A bird of some kind. Made of metal. An offering? What else *could* it have been?

But to what power? Something strong enough to bring Danica back from death, or let it pass her by? A terrifying thought. He knew what the clerics would say. But . . .

Children, he had heard.

That had not been imagined. A voice in the air, urgent sorrow. And that *had* been Danica's brother there. The two of them, brought together.

Pero could make sense of some things: there had been a raid, and the hadjuks did take small boys. Sold them as slaves, almost always castrated.

But sometimes they became djannis. What the boy had said to Skandir was true: most of those elite soldiers were Jaddite-born. They owed everything to the khalif. Had no division in their loyalties. As they had just discovered here.

But the other thing, Danica rising up . . . Sometimes, Pero thought, you arrived at a moment you could not explain to yourself. He looked at his hand again. Skandir had said that perhaps because he'd put back that object he'd found . . .

Who could know such things? What man far from home, an artist from Seressa's lagoon, could know? Was he accursed now? Blessed? Had he saved Danica Gradek's life by touching something there? Or was he simply a man who had come too late, with a tree branch, out from trees?

He looked for her, at the front of the party again. She hadn't spoken since her brother had rejected her and gone back to find his army, to risk explaining why he was alive and everyone else was dead. The Osmanlis would probably kill the boy, Pero thought.

They went on. Clouds came without rain, moved away, west on the wind. There was no one else on the road now. They didn't stop for a meal: food and drink were taken on foot or mounted. Skandir wanted to reach this village as quickly as his wounded could manage. One of them was in bad condition. Pero didn't know much about such things, but he wondered if a man with a wound like that could live.

His fellow Seressinis were chattering. They always did, but this was different. They'd had an adventure. It would make such a good story back home, Jad willing. The great, wild Trakesian warrior ambushing Osmanli soldiers right in front of their eyes! They had seen it all. Yes, he was alive, Skandir, the legend. Yes, it had been beyond thrilling to see that craggy, bearded figure. A barbarian? Of course he was! The man had swung a sword red as his beard! And killed them all, the Asharites! More wine, please. Yes, it was *very* good to be back in Seressa, queen of cities, Queen of the Sea, where civilized men—and women—went about their lives.

Pero saw Skandir lift a hand, pointing.

There was a small sanctuary, left side of the road. The road itself had curved away from the forest, or the woods had been cut farther back, leaving space behind a small, domed holy building. He saw huts and pens and houses, and tilled fields beyond. The sun was behind them, low, twilight coming. It was colder now.

"I'll go in for the evening rites," Skandir said. He looked at his horseman with the wounded man in front of him. "Take them to Jelena. Tell her it is me. That I'll be there soon."

The man nodded, moved ahead, off the road. The two other wounded ones followed. There were no ditches here. It was quiet, serene. There was smoke rising from chimneys. Hearth fires, the dinner hour soon, animals would be brought in from fields. There was a holy place to pray as the sun went down. Evening coming to Sauradia beside the imperial road that had been here a thousand years. It seemed a peaceful place. That was probably not true, Pero Villani thought.

He went with Skandir. So did Djivo and four of the raiders and all the Seressinis. They left the guards with the animals and goods and walked a worn-smooth path through a gate in a fence.

"There used to be Sleepless Ones here," Skandir said. "Not for some time. Only a few clerics are left. But it is still a holy place, and men died today."

There was very little light inside, only a few candles burning, it was hard to make anything out. A space under the dome, not large, an altar, a sun disk suspended from metal chains behind it. No benches. You would stand, or kneel on a stone floor, to invoke the god here. He saw niches in the wall to his left. They were empty.

From a doorway at the back, behind the altar, a small man in faded cleric's yellow emerged and approached.

"For an offering," he said, "I will gladly lead you in the sundown prayers." He was very young.

"We will offer," Skandir said. "I have done so before. Lead us, please. There are souls to usher towards Jad's light today."

"I am sorry to hear it," the cleric said. "Let me get candles."

Pero looked around again. The walls were bare of art or ornament. Ornaments could be stolen, he thought. Or offend the Asharites who ruled here now. Art might wear away, or be destroyed. This place existed on sufferance. The clerics would keep their presence modest, quiet. He heard a clinking sound, a chip of stone or glass had fallen from overhead. He looked up.

It was too dark to make out clearly what was on the dome. The small windows at the base of it were grimed with dirt. Decades of it. Probably more. Even before Sarantium fell this would have been a too-remote place for attentive maintenance and repair.

There was a mosaic of some sort up there. He made out a single large image spanning the dome . . . Jad, rendered in the eastern way. Of course, given where they were. He could see a dark beard, a lifted hand. The eyes were large. He couldn't see more. Had they come at midday, he thought, he might have been able to discern what some craftsmen had laboured to do long ago. Sometimes you found good work in these remote places, but mosaics needed light. He knew that much, even if no one worked with stone and glass any more.

The door at the back opened and closed again, echoing. The cleric re-emerged from the gloom, carrying four white candles. They'd hold them in reserve for a time when travellers stopped here. Candles were expensive.

He had never prayed under the eastern Jad, the one whose son had died for mankind—bringing fire, in the oldest version of his story. A banned doctrine in the west, heresy. Pero felt it again, how far from home he was. He looked at his hand. It didn't seem to be falling off.

The new candles were lit on the altar, touched to smaller ones burning there, and placed in iron holders. He wondered how many clerics there were. Probably they lived in the village where Skandir's wounded men had gone. Would there come a day when no holy men were here at all? When the faith of Ashar and his stars claimed this sanctuary and that bearded god looked down on the artifacts of another faith? Or when the stone and glass that shaped him were hacked away, not simply allowed to fall?

He stepped on a mosaic piece as he moved forward, a crunching sound. It seemed a sorrowful thing to Pero. Up by the altar and the disk the cleric cleared his throat, bowed, and began the evening chant, familiar words, a different melody. Skandir knelt, and Pero and the others did the same. He felt a tessera under one knee, he moved it away. He felt sad and lonely but there was some comfort to be found in the known invocation. At the proper place he named his father and mother in his prayer.

DANICA SLIPPED QUIETLY inside when the chanting began, staying by the door. She named her dead when the cleric reached that pause in the service—and she added the newest one, who had died a year ago but hadn't left her until today.

It was difficult not to call to him. It was going to be difficult for some time. She added a prayer for her brother, as always, and doing that led her to go back out, before the end of the rites.

It was dark now, colder, twilight upon them in Sauradia. She looked for and found the evening's first star. Her mother, once they had arrived in Senjan, had taught her to name the first star she saw each night for her father and ask its blessing. She still did that. Some rituals were your own, not part of any doctrine. The stars didn't belong only to the Asharites. They shone above them all. She remembered her mother saying that. It was difficult, how alone she felt.

She looked around. No signs of life or movement, but a dog moved past the gate and her own dog stirred from near this door-way and came over to her and pushed his head against her. She reached down and ruffled Tico's fur at his neck. Something, at least, had not left her, she thought—then decided that was weak, self-pitying. Life and the world owed you nothing.

Except sometimes there was a chance of revenge—the chance she was seizing now, riding away in the morning with Skandir. There were unexpected sorrows in that, but sorrow was embedded in everyone's days, wasn't it?

She had come back outside for a reason, she reminded herself, and resumed scanning the fields. The other dog had moved on to the village. Tico stood beside her, alert now, taking his cue from her. She heard an owl call, then the quick sound of its wings before the glide.

A little later the sanctuary door opened and the others came out. The cleric was speaking his thanks, offering further prayers. Someone had been generous.

They went through the gate and started towards the village. Danica fell in beside Skandir, Marin did the same on the big man's other side.

After a few long strides, Skandir stopped, so they all did. He looked at Danica and then at Marin Djivo. He was, she saw, amused.

"You are protecting me?" he asked the merchant.

"Just walking," Marin said.

Skandir laughed. "Both of you? Just walking?" He shook his head. "I am touched. I also saw the missing bow and quiver back at the ambush, and he'll have claimed a horse, after all. But he won't be here."

"You know this?" Marin said.

Danica was feeling rueful. Of course Rasca Tripon would have also noticed what she—and Marin, evidently—had seen.

"He didn't know I'd come this way, had no reason to imagine I would go east, and he needs to get back to his army. He'll be headed north by now, probably ride all night. He is not here looking to kill me with an arrow in the dark." He turned to Danica. "You agree?"

It was difficult to talk. She hadn't done so, she realized, since Neven walked away. She just nodded.

Skandir stared down at her from his great height. He sighed. "I expect my fighters to answer when addressed. Do so."

She looked back at him in the twilight. "Yes, Ban Rasca."

"I am not that. Call me Captain, or Skandir."

"Yes, Captain," she said. "He won't be here to kill you in the dark."

"But you came out to defend me against it? You don't know him very well, do you?"

That was hard, she thought. He would be hard, though. She bit her lip. "I don't, no. I came out to have a look. But I share your feeling, Captain."

"Good." He turned to Marin. "I don't believe I have ever had a Dubravae looking to defend me. It is an odd feeling. Not a bad one,

mind you. Will you allow me to write your father later and com-
mend your actions today?"

"How would I stop you?"

"By requesting as much," the old man said, impatiently. "Why
else would I ask?" He shook his head again. "I hope they have
something to drink here. There is no tavern, but Jelena sometimes
has wine she's made or someone has given her. Come!"

Jelena, it turned out, was the healer.

THE BADLY WOUNDED MAN might possibly be saved if the goddess was kind, but he'd have to stay here for some time and she
couldn't allow that. Not with Rasca's other two wounded men
reporting, proudly, fifty Osmanli soldiers dead along the road,
including djannis.

Fifty! Djannis? It was hard to believe. It was certain the provincial governor would send men to investigate, and a sword-wounded
stranger among them could destroy the village.

Unhappily, but not doubting herself, Jelena poisoned him with
the first healing cup. Best do it immediately since it needed to be
done. It would take him some time to go to the god (his god, not
hers). Late tonight, most likely, and it would be peaceful. Had she
been permitted to, she'd have tried to save him.

The other two she could heal, one easily (cleaning and dressing
a leg wound). The third man would have been better staying with
her a few days, but she'd pack his shoulder where the sword had
slashed, and wrap it, and send him away in the morning with
Rasca, carrying herbs and instructions. He might live, but he
couldn't stay.

They lived a precarious existence here, and word of the presence
of someone like Skandir, if only for a night, could not reach the
Osmanlis. He would know that. He'd concealed himself under a
hat, approaching from the sanctuary, and he had only a few men.
Very bad losses for him, clearly. He'd be suffering, Jelena knew.

She had wine, handed him a cup after they greeted each other. They had been lovers long ago when he was first here. Those days were past. She told him (truthfully) that the gravely injured man was likely to die.

There were merchants with him, headed east. She sent her daughter to arrange with the elders for housing them all for a night. The village could use the money, or whatever the merchants bartered. Rasca denied being injured (she looked closely, decided it was true). He said he had a woman with him, joining his company, an archer. He asked if she could stay with Jelena tonight. She was curious, said yes.

He called the woman in and named her. Jelena looked at this one—and fear stabbed, like a needle or a blade. This happened to her sometimes. It was a part of what she was.

"Is there a spirit with you?" she asked, before she could stop herself.

There were only the three of them here. The wounded were in the other room.

"There was," the woman said, after a moment.

She removed a stained, broad-brimmed leather hat. Held it in one hand. She was very young, Jelena saw. She looked weary, and grieving. "There isn't any more," the woman added.

Jelena took a breath, then said, briskly, "We will have rabbit stew when my daughter returns. Then you will look in on the wounded men with me. And then you must go to the sanctuary."

"I was just there," the woman said.

"I know. But the cleric was inside, doing what he does. You'll go with me when he's gone."

"You can trust her," Rasca said to the young woman.

"She already knows," Jelena said. "You go now. You know where the main guest house is. They will feed you. Do you want something to help you sleep?"

He hesitated, which was unusual. "No," he said, which was usual.

She gave him the wine flask. He went out, ducking his head at the doorway.

Jelena looked at the young woman in her home, a spirit's presence hovering about her. It was fading, though, she could see that now.

"Who was it?" she asked.

This one hesitated, too, and why should she not? Then she shrugged. "My grandfather. He died a year ago."

"And was still with you?"

A stiff nod. "Until today. He's gone. So is my brother."

"He died?"

"No. No. Skandir let him go. For my sake. Back to the Asharites. He's a djanni."

Jelena looked at her. "The sanctuary," she said crisply. "After you eat and after we look at the wounded. There is more to the world than we understand."

"But I know that," the other woman said.

THE HEALER HAD LONG WHITE HAIR. She wore it unbound. It was hard to tell the colour of her eyes in the firelight. She was thin, as if pared down, whittled away. She had very long fingers. Her daughter was Danica's age, small, quick, quiet. They both wore belted brown robes with woollen surcoats over them.

And this woman had somehow been aware of Danica's grandfather. His spirit, ghost, presence, whatever it was. That ought to have been frightening, but she didn't feel afraid. Danica wondered if it was exhaustion or sorrow that was making her so calm.

They ate after the daughter came back from helping the raiders and merchants find beds for the night. Rabbit stew, as promised. Danica chewed and swallowed without tasting her food. You always ate when there was food, you never knew when there might not be. Her grandfather had taught her that.

They didn't speak. The daughter got up once and added a log to the fire after removing the cooking pot. The flames shifted, rose. Danica looked at them. They could hear the wind. No rain.

"Come," the healer named Jelena said when Danica had finished her second bowl of stew. They went through an adjoining door to a larger room. Skandir's wounded men were here, with another raider watching over them. This one stood and went out when the women entered. He bowed his head to Jelena as he did.

One of the men was asleep, the one with the bad wound. The other two were sitting up. They had already been treated, Danica saw—while they were in the sanctuary, it must have been. Jelena went to these two in turn. She looked at their eyes first, setting a lantern down beside each. She held two fingers to their necks, oddly. *But why is it odd?* Danica chided herself. *Why would I know anything about what she does?*

The healer examined the bandages she'd fashioned for them. She said something to her daughter, who went to a heavy table and began grinding herbs with a pestle and bowl. She worked neatly, quickly. Her movements seemed birdlike.

Danica looked at the man who was asleep. His breathing was shallow.

"That one will die," the healer said quietly. "He is beyond me."

"We killed all of them," one of the other men said proudly. "All the Asharites but one."

"We let that one go," said the third man. "Running home like a frightened child. To say what we did."

Jelena looked at Danica but said nothing. The daughter finished what she was doing and brought over two cups. Each of Skandir's men drank.

"Thank you," one of them said.

"Sleep now," Jelena said. "You," she pointed to one of them, "ought to be fine. You"—to the other—"will need to be careful how you move for a few days, and have your shoulder cleaned and repacked every evening with what I'll give to you. Does anyone left among you know how to do that?"

"I do," said the other man. "I'll do it."

Jelena nodded. "I'll look in on you tonight. Come," she said to Danica. She carried her lantern back through the door to the first room and then out into the night. Her daughter remained behind.

There were stars and the blue moon had risen. Clouds moved in the wind. It was cold. Tico detached himself from shadow by the house and came over. He brushed against Danica's side again. He always did that. She spoke his name. *He is still with me*, she thought. Same thought as before—and it still felt weak. She wondered if she might allow herself one night of that.

The path through the village was empty, they seemed to be the only ones abroad. The wind was behind them, whipping across the fields. Houses showed firelight in windows. It was spring, but it didn't feel that way just now.

He'd be north and east in this same dark and cold. She wondered if he'd found a good horse. How he'd explain getting back, if he did get back. If they'd execute him as a coward, or just in fury. She wondered if serdars in the Osmanli army did that, or leaders of lesser rank, wanting to show forcefulness. He'd looked like their father. Already.

She had wept earlier today. It wasn't going to happen again.

They came to the sanctuary gate, Jelena carrying her lantern, and went through, came to the low door and entered.

Jelena set the lantern down on the floor, not far from the door. "We are not here for Jad's disk," she said. "You did that before."

"Why, then?"

Danica cleared her throat, her voice sounded thin. The place was gathered in gloom, she could barely see the disk up ahead, behind the altar. A brittle sound underfoot made her startle.

"Mosaic tesserae," the healer said. "They are falling all the time. They can cut if they hit you."

"Does that happen?"

"Not often." The healer looked around. "Sometimes animals get in. There have been wolves in winter."

"Shall I call Tico?"

"No. We will be quiet and listen."

"For what? Stones?"

Jelena shook her head, the lantern light catching her white hair. She held a finger to her lips. Danica shrugged. It wasn't as if she had a great deal she wanted to say. There was nothing to hear but the wind outside. It was peaceful enough, though cold.

Zadek? she thought, fruitlessly. But she knew he was gone, and fairly certain she knew how, and why. She'd kept Neven's arrow.

Tomorrow everything would begin to be different yet again. She'd ride south with Skandir into a life of war. She'd wanted that, hadn't she? From the time they'd fled Antunic for Senjan. Vengeance *could* be a reason to live, she thought. In fact, it could even be the only—

She heard singing.

No one else had come in, she was sure of it.

A woman's voice. Wordless, as if a prelude to a song.

It came from their left, towards the empty chapels along the wall to that side. There was nothing to see. No one there. She turned to Jelena, who lifted a finger to her lips again. Danica looked up for some reason. Nothing to be made out on the dome, not in this darkness, whatever might be there, crafted long ago, its stone and glass falling through space and years.

Jelena raised a hand, palm out, and then turned it inward, bringing it towards herself, as if welcoming or summoning. Danica was never, after, able to decide which it had been. But the wordless singing became words in the sanctuary dark.

Shall the maiden never walk the bright fields again,
Hair yellow as midsummer grain?
The horns of the god can hold the blue moon.
When the Huntress shoots him he dies.

How can we, the children of time,
Live if these two must die?
How can we, the children of loss,
Hold on to what we leave behind?

When the sun is in darkness under the world
The children of light will cry.
When fear is the master lives are undone.
Time is an answer to sorrow.

Darkness gives way to morning's sunrise,
Winter ends, there are flowers, birds fly.
Honour the goddess, remember the gods.
We are children of earth and sky.

And it seemed she was crying again, after all. The voice ended, the last words floating up, fading like smoke might, towards the dome and the darkness there.

There is more to the world than we understand, the healer had said earlier and, carelessly, Danica had replied, *I know that.*

She did know, and she knew nothing at all. *How can we live?* she wondered. The words of a song, sung by no one. Or, no one alive, she thought. Because no woman or girl (it had been a very young voice) from the village was in this dark space with them, singing those words. A thought came to her. Not one she'd have had a day ago.

"When did she die?" she asked, and the healer looked quickly at her, startled.

"I do not know," Jelena said, after a moment.

"You are showing me that my grandfather was not the only one to . . . remain after he was gone?"

The older woman sighed. "I have no simple messages. Or if they are simple they are difficult for me. I thought you should be here. I didn't know what would happen."

"Truly?"

"Truly. I lie sometimes, but not now."

"And the words of the song? What do they mean?"

Jelena looked at her in the light of the lantern on the floor beside them. She shook her head. "I didn't hear any words," she said.

THE BADLY WOUNDED MAN died in the night. The healer's daughter, awakened by her mother, went to tell Skandir. Danica, who had not been asleep, slipped outside as well. She asked the girl and was given an answer, and with Tico following she went to the house where Marin was. He wouldn't be in there alone, but he could come out, she thought.

She called his name. Did that several times. No answer. She stood in the cold a long time. She couldn't really blame him, she thought, but in a way she did.

She went back to Jelena's house. She helped Skandir and his men bury the dead man by the trees, not in the village graveyard. It was very cold, but it didn't rain.

They left before sunrise.

HE HEARS HER CALLING from outside. The two other men in this cabin, both Seressinis, stir on their pallets. One rises on an elbow and Marin can see him looking across in the darkness. It is Nelo Grilli, the oldest of them, the one who isn't foolish. He says nothing. An unexpected courtesy, Marin thinks. There is bitterness in him, and sorrow.

He doesn't answer, or go out to her. It is, he supposes, wrong of him. She has come to say goodbye, given that her life now is not going to bring her back to Dubrava, and is unlikely to be a long one—taking the morning's battle as an example. She ought to have died today, he knows.

His difficulty is that it matters too much, not too little.

If he goes out now he's afraid he'll plead with her (he is, in fact, certain he will), and you are surely allowed to keep some pride.

She calls his name again. She says something else then, more quietly. He cannot make out what it is. And finally it is silent outside the cabin, except for the wind. He does not sleep, of course he does not sleep.

Their party leaves mid-morning, east along the imperial road as before. As before.

༄

Damaz had found a bow and a full quiver at the ambush place where he'd killed his first infidels.

He'd whistled in a red-saddle horse across the field. They'd had the very best cavalry with them, and still they'd been fooled, defeated. Killed, all but him.

He rode back along the road they'd taken here. It was a windy, bright day. He saw few people—woodcutters, charcoal-burners, farmers in fields. It was ploughing season. He passed a small Jaddite sanctuary with a village beside it. He thought about killing some people, in revenge, and dismissed that as unworthy of a member of the elite infantry of the khalif. These were subjects of Asharias and had nothing to do with what happened this morning.

His task was simple. He needed to get back to the army.

They might kill him when he got there.

His sister had taken his arrow in her heart, and lived.

A voice in the morning air had cried, *Children.*

He had heard it so clearly—and had somehow known this was the same presence that had been with him when he fought Koçi in Mulkar.

She, the woman, Danica, had said it was her—*his*—grandfather. Named Neven. His own name, and he knew it. Just as he knew hers.

Stay with us, she had said.

Terrifying. But you didn't overturn your life like a fruit cart in the marketplace just like that! Stay? Become a Jaddite? After everything his life had guided him towards? After *becoming* what he'd dreamed of being?

He'd expected the old man to kill him.

He'd been preparing to die with what courage he could manage. Jaddites beheaded you. Everyone knew it. They were barbaric, not entirely human. It was necessary and proper they be defeated everywhere, for the glory of Ashar.

They'd let him go. Because the woman—Danica, his sister—asked them to. She'd begged on her knees for his life.

The old man had even told him what to say when he got back: pretend he'd been sent away from the fight to carry word. As if a djanni would lie to his serdar!

You were born in a village called Antunic.

You have been loved. You never stopped being loved.

They don't get to decide what you are, Neven!

And he had said, *My name is Damaz*, and walked away. To find weapons, a horse, his army.

He was in considerable pain: his back, and a pounding in his head that left him unsteady in the saddle. But you could deal with pain, it was what soldiers did, and he did have the horse. He wasn't trying to do this on foot, running.

He was in a hurry, too. He needed to find the path they'd taken down to this road. He could easily miss it in the dark, and he didn't want to be lost out here alone, riding the wrong way. There was food in the saddlebag. Figs, dried meat, a flask of watered wine. Damaz kept the horse moving while he ate.

You never stopped being loved.

How was that possible? Who lived their life that way? Even a girl, a woman?

She had killed more than ten men back there with her bow.

She looked like him. And he'd known her name.

Danica, he thought. He made himself stop thinking it.

His back started hurting more as twilight fell, but he was a djanni (even on horseback) and he made himself ignore it, pay attention to where he was riding, and so he saw the path when it finally appeared on his left—there were marks of boots and hooves where they'd emerged and met this road.

He went that way. He had a considerable distance to cover, since the army would have kept moving north (even if slowly, with the cannons) while they came down, pursuing raiders. He would get there. Who was going to challenge a mounted soldier, even at night? Who would be so foolish?

He never wept, not once, was not even really close to tears, he told himself. Or, if close, not so much so that he couldn't take a breath, swear, keep going. He was scanning the muddy, uneven path as best he could, for the horse's sake. There were woods on either side under emerging stars, and then the blue moon rising on his right, over where Asharias would be.

HE REACHED THE ARMY two days after. Late afternoon, rain. He came up to the supply wagons first—the wagons that had started all the trouble, because they'd been harassed by some local outlaws and fifty men had been sent out to teach a lesson.

He passed by the cannons and saw—again—how slowly they were moving, pulled heavily on their wagons by labouring oxen and men under skies grey as iron. He rode past other infantry—

ordinary ones, not djannis—then he saw some of his fellow djannis, different regiments.

He found his own regiment. He dismounted, handed the horse's reins to an aide. Told him to give it food and water then take it back to the cavalry. It was not his. He was a djanni, pride of the forces of Ashar.

Heart thudding, he went to find his serdar. They were pitching the tents for the night, he saw. There was no point trying to go farther, with the cannon moving so slowly. They'd be dragged up here long after dark, then they'd all start again in the morning. The Jaddite fortresses were still a long way off, and spring was advancing, and there was always a day when they'd have to start home or be trapped by winter in the wild north.

He didn't follow that thought further. It wasn't his place to do so.

He was greeted as he walked. He didn't reply. He found his commander under a canopy erected to keep the serdar dry while his tent was prepared. The space around was open, orderly. Men moved with precision, even in bad weather, performing assigned tasks. The army of the khalif knew how to do these things.

He knelt in the rain beside the officer's canopy and he made his report. He did expect he might die. He had known it was possible as he'd ridden this way.

He was asked why he was alive. Why he had survived.

He said—as the old, bearded infidel had told him to say—that he'd been sent back towards the end of the disastrous fight, so the army of the khalif and its esteemed serdars would know that it had been the hated rebel Skandir they'd found, not some rabble of raiders.

"But why you? Why not a cavalryman on his own horse?"

The next question, anticipated. The serdar had stood up by then, already rigid with fury, had moved close to Damaz. He wore his sword.

And Damaz had said that he had been much the youngest of the fifty and he believed their leader had chosen him because of that.

"So, if you left, you don't know we lost."

"I do not, commander. But . . . but I can say we had only a handful left by the time I was told to report back to you."

"You didn't just flee? Like a coward?"

Damaz, on his knees, looked up. "Kill me, honoured serdar, if you believe this. I am here because I was sent to report. I obeyed the order I was given. I wish only to kill Jaddites, more than ever, for the khalif and Ashar and for my companions who died."

And after a long moment, rain falling steadily, turning the earth where Damaz knelt to thick, cold mud, his commander nodded. "You wouldn't have come back if you'd fled. You'd know I would read it in your face. You did well, djanni. This is information we needed."

"Will we go after them?" Damaz asked. Rain hit his face whenever he looked up, making him blink.

The serdar shook his head. "They'll be long gone, and we have no idea where. Our enemies are north of us. We will take a great vengeance there. Get yourself some food. You are welcome back and will be a part of whatever revenge we take."

Damaz, eating with companions later, vowed that someone would suffer among the infidels for his having been caused to tell a lie for his life—and seeing how easily it succeeded.

When he slept, and he did sleep, exhausted, he dreamed of his sister speaking gently to him, and he woke in the night, cursing aloud, feeling despair. Someone threw a boot at him, snarling, and he fell silent in the blackness of the tent, listening to the misery of the rain.

_____

∞

It was difficult to imagine a time without war. A Sarantine philosopher in the reign of Valerius II, almost a thousand years before, had written that. And offered examples, from the ancients to his own time.

Conflict between faiths was only one cause, he wrote, although he added that it was among the most significant. Sometimes, he noted, religion could mask the ambitions of a king, an emperor, even a holy patriarch in search of a legacy to send his name ringing down the ages like sanctuary bells.

At other times, the zeal of the pure of heart was a strong, true thing, the philosopher added. It rallied armies to fight with ferocity against unbelievers. Terrible things could be done in such conflicts. Had been done.

It needs also to be said that for all the piety of men going to war, or sending others to distant battlefields (or praying for husbands and sons headed there), men and women cannot control the weather.

There have been times when some thought they could. In the years herein chronicled, it was widely believed that the women of Senjan had access to magic. That this specifically involved their ability to conjure winds near their home—winds that destroyed enemy ships and men in wild seas while the Senjani, skillful in their small craft, could ride them through shallows to safety.

Wise leaders of any and all faiths considered it prudent to consult those who claimed they could read the future in the stars and moons, even if their religious advisers called this heresy. They would also, of course, have those same religious advisers offer prayers against storms, drought, heavy rains, earthquakes, floods.

You did what you could when the stakes were high—as they were when the army of Khalif Gurçu set forth from Asharias and the garrisons west of it to take the great fortress of the Jaddite emperor in the northwest.

Both sides did these things. Candles burned in the cities and in towns and villages. Charts were made of the heavens and moons. Shoulder bones of animals were examined. The dead were invoked. In the past, in certain places, there had been sacrifices made at moments such as this. The village where Rasca Tripon, called Skandir, had spent a night along with a party of merchants was near to a place of such rituals, long ago.

It was asserted that these invocations and rites had an effect on the heavens. We have a need to persuade ourselves we are not at the mercy of the world.

That particular spring the rains fell steadily in Sauradia for a time, and then—they ceased to fall. The sun shone, day after day. The roads north and west began to dry out.

It was extremely difficult to determine if this change had occurred soon enough to allow the khalif's great army to reach Woberg in time to assail it successfully. It would be a close thing, men judged, on both sides of that year's war.

Lives continue or they end, empires move forward or are cut off, as with shears, if rain falls or does not.

Part Four

CHAPTER XVIII

Some time later that spring Count Erigio Valeri of Mylasia arrived in Dubrava aboard a trading ship. He had come to confront a wayward daughter and escort her, forcibly if required, back to the retreat near Seressa where he had, in his wisdom and discretion, already decided she would live out her shameful life.

It did not go well.

The count was a horseman and hunter, a trainer of dogs and hawks. He disliked the sea. This blackened his mood further as they crossed the water. He also detested merchants, the sour taint of commerce and its new men, and Dubrava had nothing *but* such people. For an aristocrat of a certain nature, the trade-obsessed republic on the other coast was not a congenial place to visit, and he had never done so. He'd never had a reason.

To make a bad affair worse, he knew of Leonora's disgraceful behaviour only because these greedy merchants had sent him a demand for compensation—regarding a ransom they had paid to pirates to save his daughter from being abducted at sea. They had not troubled themselves to say what the girl was *doing* at sea!

Better, far better, she had been taken by those raiders and they had done whatever they liked with her, then killed her, Erigio Valeri thought. He intended to tell her that, and the rector, or whomever the Dubravae sent to repeat their contemptible demand. As matters stood, the Valeri family shame—*his* shame—was immense, overwhelming, known to the world.

And Dubrava thought he would pay them for this?

If she didn't come with him promptly, he vowed to himself on the damnably unstable deck of the ship, he would kill her, and there wasn't an honourable man in the world who would say a father was not entitled to do so.

The worst of it was there had been a time when he took pride in his only daughter.

He'd seen her as the way their family might rise even higher in the world. Leonora was well-favoured, lively, could handle a falcon and a horse as well as any woman (and many men) in Mylasia. Their fortune (land, of course, no vulgar merchants, they!) was considerable and their lineage long. It had been entirely reasonable to think in terms of marrying her into some even more distinguished Batiaran family, or in Ferrieres, or the imperial court at Obravic. Even the Kohlbergs themselves, that slack-jawed imperial family, were not out of the question. Leonora was an asset.

She had been. Until she got herself with child by one of the Canavli sons.

He never learned a name from her, even with a level of coercion he might have hesitated to use on a man. His oldest son, not the most accomplished but certainly the most physical of his three, had discovered the boy's name in the city through other means, and they'd dealt with that one as he deserved. It meant a feud, of course, but the Canavlis were a lesser family (part of Erigio's outrage), and what strong man feared a fight, in any case?

His daughter had been sent to live out her days away from the world. He still thought he'd been generous. Her leaving that retreat, under whatever persuasion (and he would have words to exchange, it seemed, with the Council of Twelve) was simply not permissible. He had decreed her fate and he would enforce it.

A girl could not simply choose for herself the religious house in which she'd live. He had *paid* for her shelter, infinitely more than Leonora deserved. He had even paid (a small sum, granted) to have the bastard child taken from its birthing to the foundling hospital in Seressa, as was done. And now she was somehow across the water, in Dubrava, and they wanted *money* from him, and she intended to *stay* there?

No man with any pride would tolerate it.

He would leave this ship when it docked, fetch her from whatever corrupt retreat was sheltering her, and take her back to where he had decreed she would live. Otherwise, he would kill her. Then go home and hunt. No ransom money would be given to anyone, and the Dubravae, if they persisted, would hear what an aristocrat from Batiara thought of their money-smeared ways.

They might as well be Kindath or Asharite gold-chasers, he would say—to their rector if it came to that! Everyone knew how close the Dubravae were with Asharias. Face down in bed for them, rumps invitingly hoisted! He spat over the rail, disgusted by the very image.

The sun was up. It was a bright day. Too much wind for him, whitecaps on the water, but at least the crossing had been swift. He saw the harbour and walls of Dubrava. Thick, high walls, formidable, in fact.

His steward stepped to the rail and pointed towards a small island in the harbour. Valeri saw a sanctuary dome, vineyards, outbuildings. "She's there, apparently," the steward said. "The Daughters of Jad on Sinan Isle."

"I need the name? I care about the name of the fucking island?" he said.

"Apologies, my lord!" his man said, retreating.

The count ignored him. He already wanted to be home. The ship had cargo to unload—wine, books, wool, goldsmiths' work— but the captain had promised it would require only a day or two to do that and take on the goods they'd carry back. Valeri had four men with him, in the unlikely event Leonora made a difficulty, or the Eldest Daughter on that island issued foolish demands. He'd pay them a small sum in the name of Jad: they had housed and fed the girl, his shame. He could do that much for his own soul. They could pray for him, in exchange.

This should not, Valeri thought, take much time. One night on board here in the harbour, then, with luck, west and home with tomorrow's sun and tide. Or the next day's, at worst. A burdensome journey but necessary. You did what you had to do, unpleasant as it might sometimes be, for your family and your name.

SHE WAS EXTREMELY WELL PREPARED, the new Eldest Daughter on Sinan Isle, Drago Ostaja thought.

Leonora had requested his presence weeks before. When he'd arrived, she'd asked him to keep an eye out for a ship from Mylasia. Drago had said he'd do that.

He was in the city again after a timber run down the coast. The *Blessed Ingacia* was moored at the far end of the harbour. He was on board early, as always. They were repairing sails and ropes by morning light when a two-master came in on a good wind. They called their origin and cargo in the usual fashion. One of his boys came racing with the tidings: they were from Mylasia.

Drago had thought, in the beginning, that Leonora was taking instructions from the old empress, but as weeks had gone by and clever things happened on the isle, he had come to believe the young woman might not need much guidance. Some people were born to command, and there was no reason why one of those couldn't be a woman. At least in a situation like this, where it *had* to be a woman.

Or even in other circumstances, Drago thought, eyeing the new ship as it docked and ran out ropes and ramps. Women might have to be cautious, discreet, but he happened to know (from Marin, who was east, and might have reached Asharias by now) there were families where the wife or mother was the true power in their business dealings.

On Sinan there was no need to mask who was in control. Although there had been considerable masking by the last woman who had been Eldest.

Seressa had already paid Dubrava a substantial compensation for Filipa di Lucaro's dealings. The wall behind the sun disk in their main sanctuary now held a bronze relief of the god. A gift, a gesture of affinity, from the Council of Twelve to their very dear brethren in Dubrava.

Affinity, indeed, Drago thought. The Seressinis had been caught spying and killing, and were working hard to make up for it. They'd have more work to come. The High Patriarch was furious: a holy retreat had been abused. It was a scandal.

There were pleasures to be found in Seressa's discomfiture, why would you deny it?

Drago Ostaja, with six men, got into one of the Djivos' small craft. They ran up the sail and made their way, tacking across the wind, to Sinan. One man hurried to the religious complex with the news, for the attention of the Eldest Daughter.

Drago and his mariners waited by the dock for the Mylasians to come over. They watched a boat leave the isle from the smaller second dock, headed to the city, two men aboard. He had no idea what that was about.

Time passed. Eventually, one of his men pointed. They saw a craft approaching. "They will come straight here," Leonora had said. Drago looked at the leader. He had real curiosity, though he kept his expression bland. His men helped the new group moor their craft.

Then they politely requested all weapons be surrendered on the holy isle. One of the new arrivals pointed out that Drago and his men still had their swords. Drago smiled and observed that guards were often needed in a remote place.

The burly nobleman in a fur-trimmed cloak, who would be, he understood, Leonora's father, gave a curt nod and his men surrendered their swords. Gently, Drago asked for knives, including the hidden ones. There was some intensity of verbal expression offered, but the Mylasians had already given over their swords to men who remained armed. One tried to keep a stiletto in a sheath on his back but Drago had seen these before and knew where to look.

It was, accordingly, an unhappy group of visitors he escorted up the path past the vineyards. He cheerfully pointed out the herb garden as they approached it. He was, he had to admit, enjoying himself.

He liked Leonora. Admired her courage and her obvious intelligence, thought she was beautiful. And he understood from her that this big, red-faced man in the handsome cloak, her father, had killed someone she loved and exiled her to a retreat near Seressa for life. He would be coming to carry her back there, she'd said when she had summoned Drago weeks before.

"Well, that won't happen," he had said calmly. "Not unless you want it to." A father had his rights, but he was pretty certain an Eldest Daughter at a sanctuary retreat couldn't just be picked up and carted away.

"Want to go back? Not at all!" she'd said. "This is my home now." And she'd added, "Thank you, Gospar Ostaja."

"Captain is enough," he'd said.

Her smile was warming, Drago thought. She had been walking towards the railing of his ship to end her life. He didn't understand what had happened there, but he knew that something had.

ERIGIO VALERI WAS NOT A MAN to be daunted by the unexpected. He had fought in wars when young, as Mylasia was caught up in vicious conflicts among the city-states of Batiara. On the coast with rich hinterlands, their city was a prize. You weren't granted independence in such circumstances, you fought for it. Although it needed to be admitted that it was the High Patriarch's intervention that had ultimately kept them free.

Still, he had distinguished himself in battle, a measure of a man in their society. Endurance, courage, skill, no softness shown—or felt, really.

He was not likely, in short, to feel balked or disturbed by the Dubravae exercising a measure of control in their own harbour. The sea captain who took their weapons was a formidable enough fellow (Valeri made such judgments instinctively, a sighting was often enough) but it didn't matter. They did not intend to *battle* their way home with his daughter.

They were ushered into a room—and there she was, Leonora, right there.

He did feel a momentary check when he saw her. She had been, truly, the only one of his children he could have said he loved. Part of why her betrayal had cut so deeply. She wore a religious robe, which was startling in itself, though he reminded himself that she'd have worn yellow at the retreat by Seressa as well, and it had been *his* decision she go behind the walls of the Daughters of Jad. She just wasn't allowed to be here, across the water. In open, unacceptable defiance.

There had been a story of marriage (an assumed marriage?) arranged by the Seressinis. Who would need dealing with when he returned, and *would* be dealt with, with the clerics on his side.

Leonora looked smaller than he remembered. Her head was high, no sign of apprehension that he could see. Well, he hadn't raised a cowardly child. And it wasn't as if she'd have been pleased with what he'd done. You needed to acknowledge that. You just didn't need to—in any way—yield to it.

He assessed the room. No austerity here, he thought wryly. Those were Ferrieres tapestries on two walls, eastern carpets on the floor, rich furnishings. He saw wine and wine cups on a side table. The doors to a terrace were open to the breeze, heavy curtains moved only slightly. He saw four other women, two of them religious and two servants, no sign of the Eldest Daughter here, unless she was the one in shadow at the back. She might be, but she should be coming forward to greet a count from Batiara, if so.

Only two of his men had been allowed into the room with him. He could have protested but what was the point? You probed weaknesses in a fight, and needed to know your own. Nor was this a battle. He was an aristocratic father with rights over his child. This was a civilized, Jad-guided part of the world, they were *in* a place of the god!

He said, "Good. I see they brought you here. We need not linger. Come, daughter. I will not drag you by the hair, the Valeri are what we have always been. But this disgraceful game is over."

SHE HAD WONDERED how she would feel when her father came.

A lifetime of fearing him and desiring to please him lay behind her. She was reassured to discover as he entered the reception room that she felt calm.

She had been certain he would come, as soon as Dubrava sent the letter requesting reimbursement for her ransom. The council had asked her where it should be sent. She had told them.

Then she had taken thought and written letters of her own that went west on the same ship. Also to Mylasia, but not to her family.

She wondered if her composure today, seeing him shoulder through the door and fill the room with his reality, was a result of the empress's influence through the spring. Or was it simply growing accustomed to authority, to people *listening* to what she wanted done or not done?

She made herself look closely at him. Anger could be controlled, that didn't mean it went away. Her father looked exactly as he did when he'd come to tell her he'd had Paulo castrated and killed, and had ordered her taken north, leaving in the dark of night to hide the shame she embodied. These things did not leave you.

They had taken her child from her.

She knew he would have loathed the sea crossing, would hate being here. Only a fierce desire to deal with her had him in Dubrava. That, and perhaps some wish to still keep this quiet?

Too late for that, Leonora Valeri thought.

She stood behind the large desk that had been Filipa di Lucaro's and was now her own. Her hair was bound up and under a soft hat; her hands were quiet. She looked briefly back towards the empress, but it was impossible to make out her features in the shadows. It didn't matter.

"Good!" she heard her father say, the heavy, remembered voice. A voice for hounds and hunt. "They brought you here. We need not linger. You are coming with me, girl, if I drag you by the hair. This disgraceful game is over."

She looked directly at him. It was, surprisingly, not hard to do. She turned and smiled at Drago Ostaja.

"Captain Ostaja, be so good as to seat Count Valeri in the chair in front of us so we can begin his trial."

"Trial?" her father rasped.

She looked at him again, straight on, in the eyes. She allowed sweetness (false, but a pleasure) into her voice. "For murder," she said. "You are being tried in the High Patriarch's name. You are on patriarchal lands, judicial authority follows. You have also just threatened one of his Daughters with violence in front of witnesses. A crime against faith, though a lesser one, we must concede that."

Nothing on Jad's earth would bring Paulo back, or her child, but you could closely watch a man and see a ruddy complexion pale, and find some small brightness in that, like the sun coming briefly out from morning's eastern clouds.

"More games?" her father snapped. He was quick to regain composure; she couldn't remember seeing him discomfited, until the day he learned she was with child. "Where is the Eldest Daughter here? I have nothing more to say to you."

LEONORA LAUGHED. Looking straight at him, his daughter laughed aloud. He wondered how she dared do so. He heard amusement behind him, too, one of the men guarding them.

And then, because he had always been shrewd, he understood. And astonishment came, even before she spoke.

"If you wish to speak with the Eldest Daughter, I am afraid you will have to address me, father. I did say sit down. Captain, please seat him."

He was shaken, no denying it. But a man, any man at all, he could deal with. He turned to the sea captain. "If you try to make me do anything against my will, you'll have to kill me. Because I will not do her bidding. Do you want murder set against your name before the Patriarch and the god?"

The captain did hesitate. But, to his distress, Erigio Valeri realized the pause was only tactical. The man slid his sword out and swung it expertly, flat and hard, to the back of Erigio's knees. He knew that manoeuvre himself.

You could not remain standing when you were struck that way by someone who knew what he was doing. Valeri was driven to his knees.

"My lady, is it acceptable that he kneel?"

The captain was addressing Erigio's daughter, who was, somehow, Eldest Daughter here, the authority in this room, and who now said, with poise, "I am content to have him kneel before me. Thank you, Captain."

There was a stirring in the shadows. Forward from the gloom came an old woman, using a stick for support. She was tall, white-haired under a reddish-purple velvet cap. She had red paint on her cheeks, wore a heavy gold necklace and rings on many fingers—in some vain attempt at sophistication, Valeri thought. There were brothel-keepers in Mylasia and Rhodias who looked like this.

She stopped beside his daughter. "I take it," she said, a clear, cold voice, "you wish me to sit in judgment on this one?"

"I do," Leonora said. "I would be grateful."

"You? Judge me?" Erigio cried. He was losing his temper. It happened. It tended to frighten people. He rose to his feet, ignoring pain (he was good at that). "Is this a mockery of Jad? An old hag dressed up and brought—"

He pitched forward to his knees again, gasping, for the flat-bladed blow was harder this time, and in exactly the same place.

Behind him, the man with the sword said, "Whatever you might be, whatever rank you claim, it is nothing next to hers. Touch your head to the floor."

"What? Never! Why?"

It was his daughter who answered. "Because you are in the presence of the Empress Eudoxia of Sarantium, widow of an emperor and mother of one. And your judge this morning," Leonora said. "Given that last, it might be wise to pay homage, father."

Count Erigio Valeri began, just about then, to deeply regret having come to Dubrava.

EVERYTHING HAD MOVED SO SWIFTLY, Drago Ostaja thought. That same day, towards sunset, he found himself headed back to the isle, handling their smallest boat alone. He wasn't sure why he was returning, but it was a pull he chose not to resist. He was trying hard to recall the sequence of events, understand what had happened today.

The empress-mother of Sarantium had sentenced an aristocrat of Mylasia to death. He retained a shocking clarity about that.

Her role as judge had been offered and accepted, given that the Eldest Daughter was apparently required to give testimony in the matter at hand. This was, it emerged, the murder of a Mylasian named Paulo Canavli who had been her lover and the father of her child. He had been, evidently, very young, as she had been. It wasn't a new story in the world. The man had apparently been gelded before he was killed by the Valeri sons and retainers.

But before any testimony had been given or read out (there were letters from the Canavlis, sworn before clerics in Mylasia, and from others, who had witnessed the boy's abduction), someone else arrived. With astonishment, Drago Ostaja had seen his employer escorted into the room.

Andrij Djivo, dressed expensively in brown and black, bowed to Leonora, then knelt before the empress. She extended a hand, he kissed one of her rings. His presence, Drago thought, explained the boat he'd seen leaving for the city as they waited on the dock. This had been, it was emerging, a carefully managed sequence of events.

Without speaking to the aristocrat in the room (Valeri had taken the chair assigned to him by then), Djivo sat down to one side. He was here to bear witness, it seemed, *and* his family had paid Leonora's ransom.

A shockingly swift legal process had ensued.

It was swift because Erigio Valeri, clearly not a coward, whatever else he was, said, "I would be shamed to deny anything of this matter and I will not. The Canavli whelp despoiled my daughter and dishonoured our family. He was dealt with in a fashion that has a long history, as everyone in this room will know."

"Indeed. The justice meted out for such dealing has a long history also," the empress murmured. She added, "If the allegations are not denied, we need hear nothing more, and, to be honest, listening to long letters from somewhere in Batiara would be tedious. Keep them for the sanctuary records, send copies when you write the Patriarch, but there is guilt admitted here."

She was looking at Erigio Valeri. "Some believe it is proper to allow an accused person to speak at this time. We see no reason or cause. We never did that in Sarantium. We affirm that the sentence for murder done in this fashion is death. Eldest Daughter of Jad, the means of administering this execution lie with you, and we trust that Gospodar Djivo will consent to witness our judgment and decree."

Andrij Djivo, very grave, stood and bowed. "At your request, your grace," he said. "If need be, and in this holy place."

"There is nothing holy about this!" the man in the chair snapped. "Touch me and there will be consequences that cross the sea."

Still no sign of fear. It was impressive, Drago thought. It suddenly occurred to him that he might be asked to perform the execution.

It hadn't happened that way. One reason he found himself sailing back to the isle at the end of the day.

THEY LEFT DUBRAVA the next morning with the tide. Count Erigio Valeri stood at the prow looking west—not back at that accursed city. He found himself roiled by emotions that included rage and a shameful relief. And something else he couldn't name. He had not slept the night before, here on the ship. He had been politely invited to dine in the city with the rector. He had pleaded indisposition.

Earlier, he had signed what they gave him to sign in that room where—impossibly—his daughter appeared to rule, with people bowing to her. Even the old woman, the empress, had deferred to Leonora.

The empress. He had seen the last empress of Sarantium. He had called her a hag. He winced at the memory. But how was he to have *known*?

She had sentenced him to die. He doubted that he was the first man she'd ordered executed. There had been someone in the room, the ship's captain, a man he was certain knew how to kill efficiently—and would do so when Leonora asked.

She had not. She had let him live.

She'd had the *power* to decide if he lived, which was its own appalling truth. He looked at the waves in front of the ship, blue-green, bright in morning light. He hated the sea.

The merchant, Djivo, had witnessed the documents. In them, Count Erigio Valeri of Mylasia acknowledged that the city-state of Dubrava had done him and his family honourable service in saving his daughter from raiders at sea. Sums had been advanced by the Djivo family. They had been recompensed by the Rector's Council and now, in turn, Valeri undertook to repay this sum, plus an amount (substantial), in gratitude and thanksgiving.

He wasn't carrying nearly so much, of course. This was understood. What man carried that much in coin to sea? There were raiders! No, the necessary sums would be derived from the transfer—without payment from Dubrava—of the goods on the ship upon which he had arrived.

Since these goods were not Valeri's, his steward, present with him, would calculate with Dubravae customs officers what their proper values were. Valeri would sign, in the customs house, witnessed under seal, further documents affirming his debt to the merchants of his own city and of Rhodias who owned those goods, to be discharged when the ship returned to Mylasia. The owners would not be paid by Dubrava. They would be paid by Erigio Valeri.

He also undertook, in his daughter's presence, to build a retreat outside Mylasia to honour the name of Paulo Canavli. And to endow it with funds to shelter and protect thirty Daughters of Jad, in perpetuity.

His steward had been instructed to confer immediately with Gospodar Andrij Djivo as to the sum this generosity demanded. Trust a Dubravae merchant, Erigio remembered thinking, to be able to do such ridiculous tradesman's calculations.

He had signed this, too. Three copies. One would go to Rhodias, to the High Patriarch. It was a retreat and sanctuary being built, after all.

"This act of piety and contrition will," his daughter had said serenely, "undoubtedly endear you to the Patriarch. Not a bad thing. Unless you fail to proceed with it. You might want to note that the document you have signed surrenders to the Canavli family our hunting lodge, and the lands and vineyards adjacent to it, if the sanctuary is not completed within two years. You would do well to build it. I believe that is all we need of you. You may go."

IT GAVE DRAGO PLEASURE that they knew and trusted him on the isle. Arriving again later in the day he was waved on at the dock by the two servants there. He saw three of the younger Daughters in the garden, with baskets, and they smiled at him, one of them quite warmly, actually. His mother, he thought, would be pleased that he was welcome and known in a holy retreat.

He wondered what Sinan Isle would become under Leonora Valeri. She was very young, and she wasn't, evidently, the most pious woman, Drago thought.

He also thought she was wonderful. He would have killed her father for her today, had she asked.

She was on the terrace now, he saw, approaching along the path from the water. His employer, Marin's father, was still with her. They were drinking wine. The empress was not present. Leonora saw Drago and lifted a hand, gesturing for him to come up. He did, stepping onto the terrace and bowing to both of them. She motioned to a chair. He shook his head. He couldn't sit and drink wine with Andrij Djivo. Too intimidating, not their proper roles at all. The son, yes, not the father. He removed his red cap, smoothed his hair.

"I thought you might come back," Leonora Valeri said.

"My lady," he said. He didn't know what else to say.

"You are uncertain about what happened here, and would like to understand. Perhaps write Marin about it? To Asharias."

He *had* thought he might do that.

"If he is there," Andrij Djivo said. He looked thoughtful, but he usually did. He was a good man, Drago had always felt, but not a forthcoming or an expressive one. "We can't know. They may outpace any letters home, depending on how long he stays."

"Well, Signore Villani has a portrait to paint," the woman beside him said. "Would your son leave him there?"

"If he purchased certain goods, and the artist's commission was to take some time, I'd expect him to. They are only travelling companions."

"Indeed," Leonora Valeri said. You couldn't tell what she thought about that. Or, Drago couldn't.

"I did have a letter this week concerning them. To my surprise."

"Your surprise?" Leonora smiled, encouragingly.

It occurred to Drago that women were often expected to say things like this, helping men along with their stories. She poured more wine for her guest.

"From Rasca Tripon, as it happens. Men know him as Skandir."

Drago's eyes widened. He was less skilled by far than either of these two at concealing reactions. It would be good to get better at that, he thought. It was probably too late in his life.

"They do," Leonora agreed. "The party encountered Skandir? How interesting."

"It seems they did. He attacked a good-sized company of Osmanli soldiers. Killed them all. He reports that Marin assisted courageously, as did our Senjani guard. He says he parted with our group the next day, and that Danica Gradek left my employ and went with him. He apologizes for that, and commends my son for integrity and bravery." Andrij Djivo drank. "It wasn't a prudent thing for Marin to do, getting involved with Skandir in a battle."

"You fear for him?" Leonora asked gently.

"Well . . ." Her guest shook his head. "This will have happened some time ago. It is late now to fear."

"A parent who loves his children must always be a little afraid for them, I suppose."

And even Drago Ostaja, not the most subtle of men, as he'd have been the first to declare, could see the line that ran, straight as windbreak trees along the edge of a field, between those quiet words and what had happened here today—and in Mylasia some time ago.

They heard a tapping sound, approaching. All three of them turned. The empress came to the edge of the terrace. She seemed to be leaning on her stick more heavily now. Drago bowed again. Djivo rose and did the same.

Drago thought, *How often does one bow?* And then answered himself: *Every time.* The shame of Sarantium lay upon them. He felt it as a stone.

The old woman was looking at Leonora. Her expression was impatient. "A mistake. You ought to have had him executed," she said. "It would have been better for your power if he died here."

"I don't name that as my highest goal," Leonora said. Her eyes, Drago saw, met the empress's.

"And we have told you it should be. A woman cannot afford otherwise."

"We'll have to see. I did consider your counsel, my lady empress."

"*I did consider your counsel,*" the old woman mocked, savagely.

Andrij Djivo was still standing, a hand on the back of his chair.

He looked uneasy. Not a clash he'd wish to be observing, Drago thought. His own feelings were simpler: he would protect Leonora Valeri against anyone, including a woman who'd worn porphyry in Sarantium.

"I am happier this way," Leonora said mildly. "The ransom paid for me is redressed. A retreat will be built in Paulo's name. And I don't know how useful it would have been to become known as a woman who killed her father."

"Not killed. Executed, with authority. For a crime. You had the law with you."

"Perhaps. The law is slippery, and so are the men at the Patriarch's court. We didn't need further notoriety after Filipa di Lucaro. Or so I decided. Forgive me if you disagree."

"You were afraid," Eudoxia said bluntly. She lifted her head. "Women tend to be."

Leonora shrugged, looked away and then back. "Will you take a glass of wine, your grace?"

The empress stared at her. "You would put us off like that?"

Leonora's expression changed. "I am not putting you off, nor will I ever. I was not fearful. I believe I found a better course. I am grateful for guidance but I will not abdicate from thinking. Would you have me do so? What power would I have then?"

Drago looked from one woman to the other. The breeze was cool from the west but it was still mild on the terrace.

The empress drew a breath. "We are tired," she said. "He called us a hag."

Leonora actually smiled. "He did, didn't he? A terribly foolish man. You do prefer to surprise people with your presence. That sort of thing will happen. The west is not familiar with empresses of Sarantium."

"Sarantium is lost," the older woman said.

"To our shame," Andrij Djivo said, gravely.

The empress stared at him. "Shame? Really? You deal with its conqueror every day, merchant. Your son is there now, trading with him."

Djivo inclined his head. "The world comes to us as it does, your grace. We can die in folly or in courage, or live as well as ordinary men can. We were not all born to be heroes, and peace is better than war for most of us."

Another silence. Into it, Leonora said, as if to change the mood, "I spoke of empresses, and have had a thought. My lady, do you know the mosaics of Varena? There are two empresses of Sarantium in a sanctuary there, across from each other. They are said to be a thousand years old. I saw them once. My . . . my father took me with him there. We could go together one day, you and I, if you had any—"

"Really? Why would we want to see images of a whore and a barbarian woman presented to the world as deserving the purple?"

The words were a weapon. Drago bit his lip. He saw that his employer looked shaken again. Leonora did not. She said (and Drago Ostaja never forgot the moment), "Forgive me, empress, but it is known that the founder of your husband's line was an army officer from eastern lands, and also not the son of his father's wife. Your husband, may Jad shelter him, was famously ill-prepared for Osmanli incursions, and your son, who is surely with the god in light, was brave on the walls and reckless of death, but that recklessness included an indifference to the fate of half a million people in his city. I will never question your anger, my lady, but need it be extended to everyone? Even women dead long ago? I only ask, and I do know you are fatigued. As am I."

It was as if, Drago thought, a cannon had just gone off. One ship hitting another broadside, wreaking devastation. And with words only, spoken quietly, even gently.

Leonora Valeri, he decided in that moment, was unlikely to need his protection, except in ways she requested herself.

He waited for the counterblast. It never came. Instead, to his astonishment, the one who had been an empress smiled faintly at the younger woman. "Interesting," she whispered. "We were wrong. You weren't afraid. Not all of us are fearful."

"Not in all things," Leonora replied. "I have many fears. I would like you by my side for a long time yet."

The empress nodded her head, did so with grace. "We are not leaving you. The length of time is with the god, as all things are. We will retire now, and perform the evening rites and eat in our own chambers tonight." She paused. "In the morning, Eldest Daughter of Jad."

"In the morning, empress of Sarantium."

"Sarantium is gone," the other woman said, a second time.

Drago felt within himself that weight again, years and years of it. He watched her turn and withdraw into the chamber, through shadow.

Not long after, he took his employer back across the choppy harbour waters as the sun set behind them, lighting the red-tile roofs of Dubrava.

THERE WERE TWO WOMEN waiting for her inside, a servant and an acolyte, but she was alone for a moment, finally, for the first time that day. Leonora lingered on the terrace, watching the sun go down.

The Daughters would assemble to pray soon in their small sanctuary: for Jad in his battles, and for themselves through the night to come, and for those they had lost, each one naming her own.

Just now, sitting at the table, feeling the breeze becoming colder with twilight, she was trying to picture Paulo's face and discovering that it was hard to do so. A little panicked, she tried to remember Jacopo Miucci, who had died only at the beginning of spring—and his face wasn't clear to her either. The two men she'd lain with. Shouldn't she be able to hold them in her mind? Shouldn't she?

But no. They were both blurred just now, this evening. What she was seeing vividly was her father long ago. When he'd taken her to Varena (she had no idea why that memory had come to her) and had lifted her up, effortlessly strong, so she could see over the heads of others the two empresses in mosaic on the walls. And then his face, changed and not changed, this morning. When she'd said she'd let him live, and go away.

She did not weep. She could have, no one was there to see, but she did not. She watched the sun slip towards the sea and then, before someone came out to remind her she was needed, she rose and went to lead the others in prayer, as Eldest Daughter of the god on this isle.

CHAPTER XIX

Danica knew she needed to become better on horseback. Also, that she might have to kill or injure one of Skandir's men, as soon as tonight. She was in a mood to do harm, wrapped tightly around grief and anger. Not a good thing, and she knew that, too.

She'd told herself, riding south, that her brother had not been in her life since he was a small child, and her grandfather had only been within her, a part of her, for the short time since he'd died. She ought not to be so bitterly mourning now. She had things to learn, she needed to be *here*, not entangled by sorrow.

For one thing, if another of Skandir's raiders (or the same man again) assailed her with his attentions tonight she would need to make something so clear to him—to all of them—it would never be repeated. She had tried to be restrained about this. She was past that.

She was aware that their numbers were few, that recruiting was difficult, that killing a good fighter would not please Rasca Tripon, who led them. Didn't matter. Not in this. Some messages needed to be unambiguous or she could never be one of his company.

She was not going to lie with anyone if it was not her choice, and if someone persisted . . .

A part of her was unhappy about what might be coming tonight. Another part—if she was honest—was in a mood to hurt someone badly, or even kill. There would be no battles with Osmanlis to assuage that desire—Skandir had said as much. Not for a while, he'd said. There were so few of them riding south. His mood was wintry.

"But you won there!" she had said to him yesterday. "Against djannis and their best cavalry!"

They'd been riding together. He had assigned her one of the captured horses, red saddle, superbly trained. There had been grumbling; they were coveted prizes, and she was new, and a woman. But she had also killed twelve men from by the forest.

"I won?" he'd repeated. "I cannot have another such victory. Think about our dead. They are *your* dead now, Senjani. The khalif will have fifty thousand in Sauradia, more if he isn't dealing with the deserts east. I had forty—forty!—in this band, and perhaps twice that, scattered, that I can summon at any time. And not all are trained. If we lose as many as they do in any fight . . . we lose." He looked at her. "There will be women and children grieving when we get back with this tale."

"If you don't want anyone grieving because of you," she'd said, "stop fighting. Why not do that, Ban Rasca?"

He swore. "Am I going to regret bringing you with me?"

"No," she'd said.

Then she undermined that assurance.

It was the same man again. Skandir had told them on the first morning that she was now one of them, a Senjani raider, battle-tested—not to be harassed as a woman, for fear of his wrath.

Certain things, it seemed, overrode fear of a leader's wrath. Some felt the need to test willingness, or might decide they could accept some punishment for pleasure seized in the dark.

They were sleeping outside, near a stream east of the path. There was some fear of snakes, but no ready alternative in sparsely inhabited countryside. They were already well south of the road that ran west to Dubrava. Two were on guard at a time. The man who felt entitled to her body was one of them. He came to her when the white moon rose. He wasn't especially quiet. Perhaps not feeling a need to be silent, perhaps he thought she'd be ashamed to cry out. Or that her having been discreet before in rejecting him was an invitation to try again.

Danica was awake. Her thought had been that one or two nights of sleep might have to be sacrificed to this. Had her grandfather been with her, she thought, he'd have told her the same thing—she was sure of it. She felt loss, and anger.

Even so, she didn't kill the man.

She waited until he knelt beside her, she lay as if asleep. He whispered to her, face close, then laid a hand on her breast (which still hurt, from her brother's arrow). She gave him until that moment.

"Tico," she said.

Her dog was a hunter, and would die for her. He had been restrained the previous time only by her order to stay. He was released by his name, like an arrow in the dark.

Tico took Skandir's man in the shoulder, not the throat. Perhaps because her voice had been calm. Probably that, she thought. He knocked the man flat, teeth sinking in, as the raider cried out in terror and fury. He called her a Senjani witch. She saw him grapple for his dagger to stab her dog, so she put her own blade in his other shoulder and called Tico off.

She didn't kill him. She had told herself she would not. She stood up. He was on both knees, cursing in pain. Tico had backed away, not far. He was still growling, rigid, ready to spring back at a word. She had tried being discreet. That was over.

She said, loudly, so that no man could ever say he'd slept through this, "Again? You shame yourself and our leader. It would shame me to kill a worm on legs, but I will do so—you or any man who tries this again. Do not ever doubt me."

Men were stirring where they lay. One stood up, came over. The white moon was nearly full. She saw that it was Skandir.

"Niklas? After what I said? Stand!"

The wounded man scrambled awkwardly to his feet, both arms hanging.

"The dog attacked me! Then the bitch stabbed me!" he snarled.

"Did she? And what were you doing? To cause her to do that?"

A silence.

"Answer!"

"My lord, you can't expect a man to—"

"What? But I do expect! I said as much. I gave a *command*."

"Some things are not natural! A woman in a fighting company. You cannot tell us—"

Danica winced. A foolish man, she thought. Skandir had carried his sword and scabbard here. He drew the blade.

She stepped forward. "Please, my lord. No. You need fighters. This is a fighter. I don't want his death on me."

He stared down at her, his bearded face grim in the white moonlight. He said, "It is not on you. That is presumption. I gave an order. I cannot *expect*, Niklas? I am mocked! Someone can ignore me? The offence is to *me*!" he shouted, looking around in the night. But he hadn't ordered her to stand aside. If he did, she would have to do so and the man would die. She knew it.

Skandir sheathed his blade.

He said, "If anyone cares to, treat his wounds."

"I'll take his guard post," Danica said.

Someone relieved her after a time. She went back to sleep, Tico beside her, warm. She laid a hand across him.

Night passed. No snakes were seen. They heard wolves, but wolves were always out there in the dark. They woke at sunrise, said the prayers. They filled their flasks at the stream, ate stale bread, rode south. Niklas needed help to get on his horse with both arms bandaged, but he rode.

It was a blustery day. She caught up with Skandir. She was apprehensive. It might be wiser to avoid him just now, but she'd had a thought. They said nothing for a time. She could feel anger coming off him like heat.

"You need to use your legs more, riding," he said, looking straight ahead.

"I know it. I'll learn. I deliberately didn't kill him, you understand."

"And I deliberately intended to. It was a direct command I gave them about you."

The land was flat, occasional groves of pine and oak, the river to their left. The sort of path farmers would use taking products to a market. Somewhere south of here Sauradia turned into Trakesia, she wasn't sure where, didn't think anyone was sure. Another shifting border in men's minds.

He said, "You need to know something everyone fighting with me knows. If there is a battle where I am about to be taken, I am to be killed first. Do you understand? I must never be captured by them."

Danica looked over at him. A very tall man, not young, greying hair and greying beard. Easy in the saddle after so many years. He looked back at her this time, the blue eyes, a darker shade than hers. "Do you understand?" he repeated.

"I will kill you if I need to," Danica said.

He grunted, nodded. A small, necessary matter addressed.

She had her own small matter.

She said, "As to the other thing. Last night. There is a way I can stop your men, these and those we are riding towards, from causing that trouble."

"Leaving us? You can do that any time. No one is ever forced to stay with me."

"Not that," she said. "I am here because I choose to be." She looked straight ahead. "If I pick one man and he's strong enough, the others will accept it, won't they? Respecting him."

He said nothing. She concentrated on using her legs with the horse. She needed to be better at this, she told herself.

"It is your choice," he said finally. "I am prepared to kill any man who disobeys my order."

"I know you are. It isn't . . . the best thing, is it? Truthfully?"

"No," he said. "Truthfully, it is not."

"My way would be better?"

She looked at him again. He didn't meet her gaze, kept staring ahead, where they were riding. But he nodded. "It is likely better, yes. Your choice, though. I mean that!"

"Good," she said. And felt an unexpected amusement—and something else. "I accept your offer. My choice. I will sleep wherever you are tonight."

He flushed crimson. She refrained from smiling, but did feel an impulse to do so. Small pleasures life could give.

"No, no!" he cried. "I didn't . . . that isn't what . . ."

Danica permitted herself to smile, after all. "My choice, you said. Why would I choose anyone else?"

A glance at her. She had genuinely disconcerted him, she saw. He said, "Because I am old and broken down." He returned his gaze to the road.

"No you aren't. I saw you fight."

Another silence. The wind was from the west, there were ripples in the tall grass. He cleared his throat again. He said, "If you truly wish this. I will . . . I will always be gentle."

Danica smiled again. "I won't always be," she said. And let her horse slip back among the others, riding with them.

Three were injured now. Niklas rode with both hands low, refused to meet her eyes. Some of the others would say this trouble was because of her. How did you sort that out in a fighting company? Was it hers to sort out? It seemed to be, fairly or otherwise. And why did men or women ever invoke *fairness* in the world? That was foolish, really.

She could hear her zadek saying that.

She looked for her dog. Tico was loping along beside them on the right, keeping up.

Riding away from everything she knew, Danica thought about her dead and then, suddenly, about Marin Djivo, who was still on the road to Asharias and who had not come out to say good-bye when she'd wanted him to. That had been harder than she'd expected, his not coming out to her.

A little later she thought she saw something up ahead. She moved forward beside Skandir, looking again, then was sure.

She told him.

"You are certain?" he said. "Don't point! Don't do anything but ride."

"I am certain," she replied. No raider from Senjan would ever have pointed, but she didn't bother saying that.

She had her bow, and she wanted to kill someone. It was why she'd come with him, wasn't it? It was, she had told Marin, what her life was about.

Farther along they reached the point where she'd glimpsed two men guiding their horses off the road, through the scrub into a grove of trees. One of them, at least, also had good eyesight, she thought, though a larger mounted party was easier to see.

"Here," she said.

Skandir ordered a search.

They found them in the trees. The Osmanlis were dragged back to the road, pushed to their knees in the dirt before Skandir. Neither was a soldier. One was weeping, shaking with fear. She thought he might soil himself.

It was not tax-collecting time, not in spring. And there would have been guards and wagons for that. These two were only checking the household rolls in farms and villages here, in preparation for the harvest tax.

Danica expected they'd kill them. She wanted to.

Instead, Skandir ordered them stripped and sent on their way on foot, naked as at birth.

He took their satchels and records. Make someone do it all again. These two, even, if they survived. They might not. Someone might murder them.

Others would come, if so.

Humiliation, he said—laughter shared in a village, among the farms—was sometimes a better weapon than killing insignificant men.

He had been doing this a long time, Danica thought.

She was still unhappy, trying to gain control over this desire to kill any Asharite she saw.

She told Skandir that later, alone in the night.

They were in a village—the one the taxmen had just left. They had offered the sundown prayers outdoors (no sanctuary here) and had been fed. The two of them had a cabin to themselves. He had been here before, she understood. He had sheltered in many places over the years.

He didn't make love to her. He undressed in the dark, then turned on their pallet and made as if to sleep. She lay beside him for a time, then came to a decision. She aroused him, and herself in doing so. She mounted him. He wasn't so old and broken down after all, and she whispered as much, mouth to his ear. He had many scars. She could feel them, hands on his body as she moved.

She heard the wind blowing, an owl hunting. They were in a village somewhere near Trakesia, or maybe in Trakesia. She didn't know its name. This wasn't how she had seen her life unfolding.

But this man was fighting Osmanlis and had been doing that from before she was born, and he intended to die doing so.

This was, Danica told herself, the proper place for her to be. She might be wrong, but how could you be sure of not being wrong?

"Thank you," he said unexpectedly in the darkness, after.

"Thank you," she said. Then she slept.

A day later, still going south, Niklas's wound, where Tico had bitten him, became inflamed. He couldn't move that arm. It began to make a crackling sound, weep pus. He died in pain, feverish, two days after that. She hadn't intended to kill him, but what you intended didn't always come to pass.

০০

Shortly before they reached Asharias, Marin Djivo ordered a halt for a midday meal and said he wished to speak to all of them.

It was a beautiful day, a high sky, late spring now. Birds called warnings to each other. Pero looked up and saw why: a hawk was soaring. It was strange, to feel sunshine and see blue skies and understand them as a threat. He knew the weather here didn't tell them anything about what was happening to the north. They needed rain there, and had no idea if it was falling. Neither would the khalif and his advisers, he thought. His thoughts had, in truth, turned more and more to Grand Khalif Gurçu as they journeyed. He'd also begun praying more.

Djivo cleared his throat. They'd gathered away from the road. The Seressini merchants might be arrogant (of course they were) but Marin Djivo had been here before and none of them had. They'd be growing nervous, would listen.

No one could overhear him where they were. There were people on the road, a great many of them now, including soldiers going both ways. They were very near the city, after all.

City of Cities, Sarantium had been called.

Pero was nervous himself. He had reason to be, didn't he? He was the one who would be separated from the others and expected to achieve a likeness of the khalif that pleased Gurçu the Destroyer. Not a man one desired to displease. He had heard that no one spoke—no words at all—in the presence of the khalif.

That would be a problem for a painter with his subject. One of many problems. He was also expected to gather whatever information he could, to share when he returned home. That return was, Pero Villani thought, not remotely a certainty, given the other task he'd been given. Should the opportunity arise when he reached Asharias, the council's clerk had said, smoothly.

He forced himself to pay attention to Marin Djivo. "We will receive an escort tomorrow or the next day, that happens with Jaddite merchants, so I thought I'd speak today. We will, as you likely know, go our separate ways in the city."

"What? Why?" said the youngest of the Seressinis. He wasn't, it appeared, one of those who likely knew.

Djivo said patiently, "You'll be escorted across the strait to the other shore where Seressinis and other Jaddite merchants have their warehouses and reside. Dubrava has a . . . different relationship. We are permitted to remain in Asharias itself."

"How convenient for you," said the young one. His name was Guibaldo Ferri, and Pero didn't like him.

"It can be," Djivo agreed equably. He grinned. "You'll find pretty women on your side, too. But the guards do watch you. They watch all of us."

"So I've heard," said the oldest of the merchants. "How closely?"

Djivo looked at him. "That's what I wanted to talk about. I do this as a courtesy, you understand. What happens to you doesn't really affect me or my goods, but we have travelled together."

"We have," said the older merchant, one of the Grilli family.

"And so I urge you to say nothing at all, even when you think you are among friends, of what happened on the road. And impress this on your servants, if they want to get home."

"Oh. Skandir, you mean?" Ferri's voice was too loud. Pero looked quickly towards the road.

Djivo kept his expression grave. "Yes, that. Please understand. They will imprison you, and torture you for information, and then kill you if they learn you were present when soldiers died."

"Kill Seressini merchants? Travelling with safe conducts? I think not."

"Trust me," Marin Djivo said. "It is worth your life."

"And yours?" Ferri grinned.

"And mine," Djivo agreed. "And your family will never trade with Asharias again. Think on it, signore."

That had an effect. Marin Djivo, thought Pero, was an impressive man. He'd be sorry to part with him, but his own journey would continue differently now.

"Was there anything more?" Nelo Grilli asked. He was paying close attention.

Djivo hesitated. "One thing, yes. I offer this as another courtesy, signore. Please believe me, I imply nothing at all. Understand that they will search us carefully, our persons, our goods, our rooms. If it has occurred to any of you that you might secret some trade items to avoid the tariffs, I urge you to think otherwise. The tariffs are high, but Osmanlis punish our people heavily for offences— and more so in wartime."

"I have no such goods," Grilli said. "But I understand what you are saying."

Djivo looked briefly at Guibaldo Ferri and at the last merchant, of the Bosini family. Ferri shrugged, Bosini nodded.

They dispersed to their meals. Pero was turning to do the same—he saw that Tomo had set out food—when Djivo called him back.

HE LIKES PERO VILLANI, and is fairly certain the artist will die here.

He doesn't think that means that he will himself, but there are no certainties in Asharias. They are far from home, and whatever Dubrava might do to stay safe and accepted, they are among enemies here, and there is an army in the field. It is, in fact, why these journeys can be so lucrative. Profit measured by risk. Skirting around the edges of a war.

The two of them are alone. Marin says, in a grassy field by the road, amid purple and yellow flowers, "I am uncertain if we will see each other once inside the walls."

"I understand that. I am grateful for your guiding us here."

He hesitates, still. You can like a man and be wrong about him. Then he decides he isn't wrong. He says, "Signore, I am leaving this party tonight. I'll be going ahead with my servants and goods. We will reach our next inn before sunset. I will leave in the dark."

Villani stands very still, thinking. In Marin's experience, Seressinis tend to be quick, too sure of themselves. The artist isn't. Eventually, he says, "Why are you telling me?"

The right question. Marin says, "Because I am inviting you to come with me. I believe . . . I have no knowledge, but I believe that at least one of the others will likely be in difficulty once Osmanli guards arrive as escorts."

"Hidden goods?"

He nods.

"You warned them."

"Yes. Merchants try to avoid tariffs. Sometimes it succeeds and foolish men hear that and decide to risk it. I think you may be endangered if you are with them when you enter the city, given your own tasks."

He says *tasks*, deliberately. He doesn't say *painting*.

"Going into the palace, you mean?"

"To the khalif. And . . ." He needs to say it, Marin realizes.

There is no point to this conversation otherwise. "Perhaps with a purpose beyond a portrait?"

Villani goes pale. Not surprising, really.

Marin says, "I mean you well, signore. I have no knowledge, only some understanding of the Council of Twelve, and perhaps the world . . . and from observing your servant."

"Tomo?"

"Yes. It is possible he has his own tasks. Is not just serving you. And that you might also be at risk because of those. I am sorry to say it, but I am not certain the council would value your life over . . . other things."

Villani looks shaken but not, Marin judges, entirely surprised. "The life of the khalif, for example."

"The end of that life, yes." He does lower his own voice, saying those words.

"And Tomo . . . ?"

"Is he a true servant?"

Villani frowns. "He knows what servants do, but he is . . ."

"More?"

"Perhaps. Yes. How much more, are you thinking?"

This is *such* a dangerous conversation. He shakes his head. "I am not the one to say."

"Shall I?" asks Pero Villani. He smiles faintly.

"Not to me. I don't matter."

Villani shakes his head. "Are you not also at risk if someone you journeyed with tries to kill the khalif?"

Marin can't help it: he looks quickly around. They are still alone, far enough from the road and from the other merchants.

"I might be. But I am not Seressini."

"You could even warn them."

"I could. I won't. It is not how I see myself."

Villani nods. "Thank you. Again."

Marin clears his throat. There is another thing he needs to say. "They will search your paints and supplies, Signore Villani. Before you are anywhere near the palace complex. Signore, you should understand that in Asharias they know . . . they are very familiar with poisons."

The man grows pale again. He says, "I only desire to do a portrait, as best I can. And then go home. What you suggest . . . it is not how I see myself, either."

Marin says, "I imagine that is so. Others might have placed you in such a role?"

They hear laughter from the road. The birds are singing now. There had been a hawk. It must be gone. Marin doesn't look for it. He watches the other man.

Villani says, "I will come with you tonight. I will be . . . I am honoured that you have offered this."

Marin nods, manages a smile. "Perhaps you'll paint my portrait one day, if we both go home."

"Another honour, gospodar," the other man says. "Let us both contrive to go home."

"Let us," Marin says.

Inwardly, regretfully, he still doesn't believe the other man will do so.

PERO VILLANI WAS NOT AN INNOCENT. You couldn't live in the tannery district of Seressa among the cutpurses and the canal-side poor, the artists, the whores of both sexes, the particular friends he had, and remain sheltered in your view of life.

Still, he was shaken by the conversation with Marin Djivo. It was as if he'd come all this way through Osmanli-ruled lands and not considered certain things at all. Which, at this moment, seemed foolish beyond words. Djivo had been calm (he usually was), not judging, only . . . being a friend, it seemed.

And putting Pero to a difficult decision. Not about leaving in the night. That he had known he'd do the moment the offer was made. He was Seressini. If he arrived in the company of others from that widely mistrusted city and they did, indeed, try to conceal goods from the officials, his own fate could easily be bound up with whatever happened to them, and it was unlikely to be pleasant.

No, his decision concerned his servant, and the paint pots they'd carried across Sauradia, carefully wrapped, on one of the pack animals. One ceramic pot, in particular. He was bringing lead white paint with him, already mixed—it was used for undercoats and sometimes to alter another colour's intensity. He had three full containers of it. Well, two full ones, in truth.

The third had a sealed alchemist's vial of white arsenic hidden in the thick paint. The outside of that jar had two scratches on it, not quite parallel to each other, very faint.

It had not been suggested, by the clerk to the Council of Twelve who'd advised him on this added dimension to his mission, just *how* Pero was to place poison in the food or drink of the Grand Khalif Gurçu. Evidently, assassins deployed by Seressa were expected to use initiative in such matters. And to accept the near certainty of their death. It was hinted (delicately) that Pero might wish to save some of the arsenic for himself if he proceeded with this. Should such an action come to pass successfully, he was told, his name would long reverberate with honour in the republic and his family be supported by the state for generations.

"I have no family," Pero remembered saying.

He'd asked why Seressa would want the khalif dead. And, to be fair, the clerk did answer. When khalifs died there was chaos in Asharias and among the army leaders. Successions were never smooth if more than one son was alive, and sometimes even if there was only the one. Others might think themselves better suited to the throne. The djannis often rioted in the city and in garrison towns, demanding extravagant gifts from whoever succeeded, in return for continued loyalty. Rebellion might also emerge among restive tribes in the east, chafing under rule from Asharias.

There was, in brief, extreme disruption. A new khalif's siblings, the ones who lost any power struggle, were invariably killed. Living brothers were a bad thing for khalifs. Various wives, viziers, and eunuchs would also need dealing with, or disposing of.

Trouble in Asharias tended to mean peace in Jaddite lands. No Osmanli army of forty or fifty thousand pushing northwest in the spring. That interlude might end when the new khalif felt a need to show his prowess. But in the interval, trade was safer by land and sea, and for Seressa it was always about trade. And it was entirely possible that whichever son (there were two alive, it seemed) followed the Destroyer might be less ferociously bent on conquest in the west.

Which would be good for Jad and his children, wouldn't it? Pero remembered the privy clerk asking him that. And thus: two nearly parallel lines marking one of his paint pots.

Pero had noted that nothing was said by the clerk about vengeance against the man who'd conquered Sarantium and had the last emperor and his family in the city killed, heads displayed to rot on pikes by the triple walls.

His own city, Pero Villani recalled thinking, was many things, but those in or near power had limits to their pious sanctimony. You could call it a good trait if you wanted to.

In the meantime, right now, as they came to a large inn late in the day, Pero needed to decide what to do. What his father would have done—which was how he often dealt with such moments. Although there had never been a moment like this in Viero Villani's life, he was quite certain.

In the end—the thought came strongly—he was a painter, not a man who killed. Even if killing someone might save lives, or avenge, in some small way, the thunderous fall of Sarantium. Even if an aged empress had spoken to him of that, as well.

It wasn't cowardice, he told himself. And that felt to be true. It had to do with how one wanted to walk under the sun, through a life. Rasca Tripon could not *live* without his battles. Neither, Pero thought, could Danica Gradek.

He was not such a person. And if what Djivo said was correct, he was never going to be anywhere near the khalif without everything he owned being *very* carefully inspected.

No westerners ever stood in the presence of Gurçu. It was known. They never even entered the palace complex. But Pero would be there, it seemed, and soon. So this inexplicable commission for a western-style portrait would put every guard and palace official into a panic-stricken state of vigilance.

Pero Villani, artist of Seressa, son of an artist, was not an assassin. And would never be allowed to become one here. Both were true things, he thought, and he made his decision outside a roadside inn.

He sent Tomo to prepare his room. He asked him to supervise hot water for a bath and a change of clothes. That would take time. He called Marin Djivo over and walked the man away from the others, towards the stables where their animals were being taken. They stopped outside. Djivo looked at him. A tall man, neatly bearded, even after this long journey. Pero said, "I needed a reason to linger a moment here. Thank you. When do I meet you tonight? Where?"

"Right here," the other man said, his voice betraying nothing. "At blue moonrise. Is your servant coming with us?"

"No," said Pero Villani. "I will enter Sarantium with you alone."

"Asharias," said Marin Djivo.

Pero looked at him. "Sarantium," he repeated quietly.

Djivo frowned. "I understand. But only in your mind and heart. If you want to live." He turned and walked away.

Pero went into the stables, found the donkey with his supplies strapped to it. Artists knew how to deal with ropes, knots, sealed pots, canvas. There was light from the open doors, the smell of animals, dung, straw. He unwrapped his gear, found the kiln-fired paint pot with two scratches on it. He lifted it out. Rewrapped everything else, carefully. Tied it back on the donkey. Made himself move slowly. There was no danger here, he told himself.

There was, probably, but he'd be awkward and rushed if he let himself think that way. His heart was beating too fast as it was.

He walked back into the stable yard and then away towards poplar trees and a stream behind the inn. To the west, a willow dropped its leaves towards the water. The sun was going down. It was pleasant, warm at the end of spring. Flowers on the riverbank, drone of bees. He saw a fox run past on the far side.

He pretended to be relieving himself in the stream. He heard birdsong, and someone's servant shouting off to his right. Smoke rose from the main chimney of the inn. Dinner being prepared. He heard laughter over that way.

Pero took his knife and pried open the pot. He hesitated, then began pouring the thick paint out into the water. White lead was not expensive, this was not especially wasteful.

Jad's dear love. I really am a Seressini, he thought. As if the cost of the paint mattered in any way at all.

The apothecary's tube, tightly wrapped, stoppered, appeared at the neck of the jar. Death in a vial. His own death, most likely. He thought about lifting it out, opening it, spilling it in the grass by the willow tree. He realized it wasn't necessary, could even be dangerous. Arsenic could kill on touch, he'd heard from someone. He didn't remember who had told him that.

He poured the rest of the jar's contents, including the sealed poison he'd carried all this way, into the rushing water at his feet. He saw the vial for an instant, then didn't see it any more.

He tossed the empty paint pot in as well and went back to the inn.

TOMO KNEW HE'D been deliberately sent away with those instructions as to clothes and a bath. He had a pretty good idea what the artist would be doing, after his conversation with Marin Djivo. The exchange they'd thought no one could follow.

There were difficulties coming now. For one thing, Guibaldo Ferri was not only foolish, he was dangerous—could get other men killed.

Ferri was carrying twenty small gold-plated sun disks in the false bottom of a clothing chest. His principal servant, a talkative fellow, had told Tomo as much early on their journey.

The duty on Jaddite religious artifacts brought into Asharias for sale was forty percent. You could still make money, but you could make a *lot* of money if you dodged that tax, and Ferri had evidently decided that if others could, by report, so could he and his family.

There was a ready market here (on the far side of the strait, where Jaddites were allowed to live and trade) for such items, and people paid handsomely so far from home. Distance equalled profit, if you didn't get undone by the taxes.

Or death, Tomo thought. He really didn't want to pass through the city's walls in the company of a man smuggling goods. *Religious* goods. In a time of war. Yet he now knew, being rather more than an artist's servant, that his own man and the clever Dubravae intended to slip away tonight—leaving Tomo with the Seressinis.

Not a good development. He had his own assignments here. There had been an awareness within the Council of Twelve that he was unlikely to have any chance to perform some of them. But if Villani was permitted, or required, to dwell inside the palace grounds and allowed to have his manservant with him (unlikely, but . . .) then Tomo Agosta would be the first trained spy in there since the fall of Sarantium.

It was worth a great deal to the duke and the council, and so to Tomo—in silver and gold—if that happened and he returned to the canals with whatever he'd observed. He had his ambitions, did Tomo Agosta. What man of spirit did not?

He was also someone with diverse ways of killing people, and Guibaldo Ferri was on his mind as he offered two coins to a servant in the inn's kitchen to heat water for his master's bath. He wished he had a chance to confirm what Villani was doing, but it wasn't really necessary. He knew. Villani was doing what Tomo wanted to do himself: achieve a measure of safety as they neared Asharias.

He'd be getting rid of the poison. And he'd be planning to be rid of Tomo tonight, leaving him to enter the city with twenty hidden sun disks and a vain, foolish man who would—very probably—begin talking about Skandir the moment customs officers seized hold of him.

Which *would* likely kill them all. Including Villani and the Dubravae.

He wondered if those two had thought about that. Probably not. They weren't trained in these matters. Seressa prepared its spies extremely well. The woman on their ship, Leonora Valeri, had been different, an impulse of the duke's, opportunity seized. Women, attractive ones, could be useful, even without knowing how to unlock doors or coffers, or kill.

He had to think swiftly. There were two different problems. He needed to go ahead tonight with Villani and Djivo. And those hidden sun disks were a danger, and so was Ferri. Tomo agreed with Marin Djivo about this. The disks were *not* going to get into the city undiscovered.

Tomo felt agitated and was trying not to show it. He was leaving the kitchen to sort out the bedroom when Guibaldo Ferri's servant, the talkative one, came bustling in with two coins of his own and a loud request for a bath for his man. And so it was that a light dawned for Tomo Agosta, like Jad's sun rising over the lagoon on a midsummer morning.

"Let him go first," he said to the sweating kitchen servants by the fire. "His master is more important."

THEY WOULDN'T HAVE to meet by the stable, Pero realized.

He and Djivo were sharing a room, with the three Seressini merchants in another. That was a small, useful thing. The other things that happened before the dinner hour were less obviously good.

Tomo, his servant, whom he knew to be a spy (they had told him in Seressa), came in to take his boots for cleaning. Djivo was also in the room, dealing with his own, his servants dismissed for the evening. Pero knew where they'd be, and what they'd be doing in preparation for tonight. Blue moonrise.

Tomo closed the door, which was normal, then he knelt in the middle of the room, which was not. Pero had been sitting on one side of the big bed they'd be sharing. Djivo, on the other side, stood up, looking at the servant. Pero stood up, too.

Tomo said, "Forgive me. I was trained to be able to follow conversations at a distance by watching the movement of lips. I know you intend to leave tonight. Please—let me also come."

Sometimes you really couldn't think of what to say. Pero stared, he waited. Marin Djivo, he noted, was doing the same.

Tomo met Pero's gaze. He was a spy, trained—you needed to remember. Then, abruptly, remembering that became easy.

"I have arranged for Guibaldo Ferri's death," his servant said quietly. "Gospodar Djivo was correct. He would have been discovered smuggling and he would have talked. About the battle. Who fought there."

Pero opened his mouth and closed it.

Marin Djivo said, also quietly, "You killed Ferri? It will be investigated. We will never—"

"I arranged for his death, gospodar. He will die tomorrow, in the morning most likely. It will appear to be a seizure of the heart.

You will be—we will be, I dare hope—gone before that."

"More poison?" Pero found his voice.

Tomo nodded. "In his bath. It penetrates through the skin. It was devised in Esperaña where they know much about such things."

"And what about whatever he is smuggling?" Djivo asked. Pero wondered how the man could be so calm. If he'd ever be like that himself, hearing things like this. If he wanted to be.

"Sun disks. At the bottom of a chest. If Grilli takes over his goods, to deal with them for the Ferri family—and I expect he will—he'll have them closely examined. He knows Ferri. He won't want to risk his own life. I think he'll look."

"And if he doesn't?" Pero asked.

Tomo shrugged. "This is the best I could devise. Ferri would have been caught, he would have talked about the fight on the road. We would have been arrested."

"You keep saying 'we,'" said Marin Djivo.

"Because it is true, gospodar. Servants are tortured first." Tomo offered a wry smile. "I respect Signore Villani greatly, but I would not protect him if they squeezed my balls in a vise."

Pero Villani stood in a room in an inn far to the east, on the imperial road to what he'd have to call Asharias, and he felt his life to be suspended very strangely. He realized, belatedly, that violence was possible now, right here.

Marin Djivo said, "And we trust you why? You have admitted murdering one of our party."

"To save all our lives, gospodar. You know this is true."

"And if you are caught in the city yourself? Identified as a spy?"

Tomo smiled a little. "Gospodar, they *know* I am a spy. Every one of us is when we come east. I do not expect to be allowed into the palace when Signore Villani goes there."

Pero managed words. "But if you do enter with me, would you be looking to kill . . . someone more important than a merchant?"

Tomo's expression turned grave. "Seressa might expect me to try. I have no intention of doing so. Just as you have chosen not to. I believe Gospodar Djivo to be correct: nothing we bring in will remain hidden. My own . . . devices will be discarded tonight, as I take it yours was just now. I would also like to return home, signore, gospodar."

"This is," said Marin Djivo, "much to take on trust." He had spread his feet, Pero saw.

Tomo nodded. "I understand. I . . . gospodar, I believe you are skilled with your sword, and might try to reach for it and kill me now, as a solution. I have no sword, of course, but I have knives on my person and I am trained. I would not accept being murdered, gospodar. I will shout, scream. And I might kill you. It would be better to take me with you. We are, I believe, destined for that now."

"*Destined?*" Pero said.

"Jad has his designs for all of us, signore."

Pero stared at him. "And right now that means Guibaldo Ferri dies and you come with us?"

"I believe it does," said Tomo calmly. "I pray that it does."

Marin Djivo laughed aloud. "This is not," he said, "how I thought the story would play out. I don't believe this is destiny, but I don't see why you shouldn't come with us. We can't really stop you. If we accuse you of a murder you'll tell them about Skandir."

He really did seem amused, Pero thought.

Tomo nodded seriously. "I would do that. For an easier death and having no reason to be loyal."

And with that, both of them turned to look at Pero. Something occurred to him. He shook his head, because amusement, unexpectedly, now overtook him as well—even with a travelling companion about to die, murdered, in the morning. *Because* that was about to happen.

"Yes, come with us. But we aren't going anywhere tonight."

"Why?" Tomo asked. Pero saw Djivo's brow furrow.

"You don't see it?" Pero felt an unexpected pleasure. Too long being the least-adept person here? He said it. "And I am supposed to be the inexperienced artist, guided along the road?" He shook his head again. "First reason: we don't need to go on ahead, with Ferri no longer with us. Signore Grilli will take the sun disks from hiding and declare them to the officials and pay the duty. Tomo will help him find them if he has to. He will say Ferri's servant told him where they are."

"He did tell me," Tomo said.

Pero smiled. "How convenient. You are able to tell the truth."

Djivo laughed. "And is there another reason?"

Pero looked at him. "Think about it. A merchant dies suddenly, unexpectedly, and two of his companions and their servants have slipped away in the middle of the night?"

"Oh," said Djivo.

"Oh," said Tomo.

SIGNORE GUIBALDO FERRI OF SERESSA was found dead when the sun rose the next morning. He was discovered so by Marco Bosini, with whom he had been sharing a bed in their room. Young Bosini's cry of alarm woke Nelo Grilli in the other, smaller cot, and the next shout brought others rushing into the room.

Attempts to revive the merchant were unsuccessful. It was judged that his heart had given way in the night, perhaps in the always dangerous hour before dawn when—it was known—death drifted close to men. Prayers to Jad under the world in the night were made in fearful awareness of this.

It seemed that death had found Guibaldo Ferri here, only days from Asharias and the end of a long journey.

Grilli, the most senior of the merchants, undertook to arrange for the burial and rites, and to supervise the sale of the merchandise Ferri was carrying, when they reached the city markets. There was no questioning Grilli's integrity, and he asked the other merchant,

Bosini, to review all his actions and affirm their rectitude. There were precedents. This did happen when men travelled a long way to trade.

After the burial—in a grave by the stream west of the inn—Nelo Grilli, advised by Ferri's badly shaken servant, and assisted by the artist's man, Tomo, opened a particular chest. He removed from a hidden drawer a number of small sun disks, of considerable value here, even after the tariff on religious artifacts was paid.

On the advice of Tomo Agosta, offered diffidently, Signore Grilli placed some of the gold coins Ferri had been carrying in his purse into the hidden compartment, to make it appear he had been secreting some of his money. That was hardly illegal. It could be called prudent. The money would be found, of course. The customs officials of Asharias would have seen boxes of this sort before.

They would undoubtedly steal some coins, but not—one might hope—all of them. The khalif did want trade, there was an administration supervising foreigners' rights.

The party remained another night at the inn and Grilli led evening prayers by the stream on a mild evening, with the sun of Jad going down. He was assisted by the Dubravae merchant, Djivo, who had a pleasant singing voice.

They left together in the morning. They were met towards evening by an escort. The next afternoon they saw the triple walls and the water and the enormous dome of what had once been the Sanctuary of Jad's Holy Wisdom and was now consecrated to Ashar and the stars. As so many had been through centuries, they felt humbled as they passed through the gates.

The City of Cities had been built to do that to visitors, and it still did.

Men and women cannot know—it is in the nature of our lives—what would have happened had another road been taken, other decisions been made, a life continued instead of being cut short. Nonetheless . . .

Guibaldo Ferri, had he lived, would have had his secreted sun disks found by customs officers. It was true—they were familiar with such contrivances, howsoever intricate. It was also true that officials paid with their own lives if they missed goods that were later found by the *second* careful inspection.

Pero Villani's paint pots were examined, twice. His arsenic would have been discovered. The entire party would have been taken to an unpleasant location and interrogated, and more than one of them (not just Ferri), seeking the mercy of death, would have volunteered the information that Rasca Tripon, named Skandir, had ambushed a company of red-saddle cavalry and djannis. And that he had been assisted by the Dubravae, Djivo, and also by the artist, Villani.

They would all have been tortured for further information in a spirit of very great anger. There would have been no swift deaths. There would have been no portrait of Grand Khalif Gurçu, the Destroyer.

These events did not occur because Guibaldo Ferri died and Pero Villani discarded his poison—as did his servant, Tomo Agosta.

Several of the hidden coins in Ferri's chest were taken by customs officers, both the first and the second searchers, but all was judged in order, and appropriate stamps and seals were provided after the assessed duties were paid.

The two remaining Seressini merchants, Bosini and Grilli, were escorted across the strait to the residences and warehouses allowed to Jaddites there.

Marin Djivo made his way, having been here before, to Dubrava's permitted residence, not far from the ruins of the Hippodrome where, centuries ago, men had raced in chariots behind horses for the delight of enormous crowds and in the presence of emperors.

The artist Villani was escorted to the palace complex. It was alarmingly irregular and the officials there were duly alarmed, but he had been awaited and their instructions were exact. His servant did not accompany him. Servants, the artist was told when he inquired, would be provided him.

Events proceeded in the city and the world.

Eventually, Tomo Agosta did, in fact, find his way home to Seressa and its canals with a tale to tell. He would live a long life, unusual for a man of his profession. He never went to Asharias again. He remembered it, however. Few who journeyed there did not.

CHAPTER XX

As spring churned muddily towards summer, with a calculation of distance and food and health and time to be made, the supreme serdar of the army of the Grand Khalif Gurçu began to endure troubled nights on the road to Woberg Fortress.

It was raining. Almost every day, every night.

Men and horses were wet, weary, mud-stained, dispirited. He looked at the cavalry mounts and he thought even they looked disheartened. He had been a cavalryman. His love, all his life, had been for horses. It pained him, seeing them this way, and there were broken legs happening in the slack, treacherous footing, which meant shooting them, or slitting throats to save a bullet.

The stars were not shining upon him, the serdar thought. And now the heavy wagons that had been trundling two of their largest cannons had both broken.

A bitterness occupied the serdar's spirit. They had done the latest river crossing so well this morning with the temporary bridge the engineers assembled, even in rain—only to have the wagons both crack (loudly!) as their guns were reloaded on the slippery northern bank. He could almost hear that sound again tonight, over the drumming of the rain.

They were not far now from the line of Jaddite fortresses, but they were so very far. And deathly distant from home and safety, where they needed to be before autumn arrived and became winter and men and horses began to die without a blow being struck, by them or against them.

He didn't mind losing soldiers in battle. It was expected. He also, from experience, anticipated that disease would take a certain number. But if he turned back too late and winter came early and only a starving remnant of almost fifty thousand made it home . . . well, he would do best to end his own life on the road, because it would be ended for him, badly, in Asharias.

The serdar had seen that happen.

And so, given all this, how should a man fall asleep in the night? He thought of calling for a woman or a boy to ease him, but these anxieties were not the sort that could be physically assuaged.

Instead, the serdar ordered a lantern lit and roused himself to look, again, at the dates that had been presented to him this evening. He knew what they said, what they imposed, he really did know what he needed to do. But he didn't *want* to do it. He wanted to be the man who took Woberg for the khalif. To return to Asharias in glory, as the one who'd done what no one had ever been able to do: crack open the gateway to the Jaddite emperor's rich lands.

Conquered fortresses were also gateways for those who took them, opening wide upon power, wealth, fame. Perhaps even an avenue to the throne when Ashar took Gurçu the Destroyer to the stars. If the son—whichever one emerged—proved weak, unworthy, less glorious than the brilliant serdar who'd taken Woberg, was this not possible?

He fell asleep on his camp stool over the desk they had set up for him, his head dropping onto dates and numbers. Either his slave or his adjutant must have blown out the lantern, because it was dark in the tent when the serdar woke. He was stiff and unhappy, and none of the numbers had changed while he slept.

Slowly a wan light filtered into the tent. Dawn coming. With rain. He could hear it. He pushed himself to his feet and pissed in his chamber pot. The slave came forward from his corner and carried it out. He lifted the flap to do so and the serdar glimpsed greyness and mud, was hit by a gust of the wet wind blowing.

It was the thought of the horses, slopping forward in that slippery footing, that ended it for him. A cavalryman from the beginning, promoted to red-saddle when not much more than a boy. You cared for your horses, you loved your horses. He looked at the numbers in front of him, but he decided because of the horses.

He sent his adjutant to summon the serdars serving beneath him. It might be the last time he did this. You weren't normally given more than one opportunity to command the assembled army of Asharias. Unless you conquered. And he wasn't doing that.

He gave the order when the eight men had gathered in his tent. No one challenged him. No one would do that here. It would be different back in Asharias. He was hardly the only ambitious man in the army. They would lie, some of them. They would say the rains hadn't been so bad, that the supreme serdar of the khalif's great army had been overly cautious. Even, perhaps, cowardly.

The serdar of the cavalry cleared his throat and made a proposal, based on word that had come in the night from scouts he'd sent ahead.

It was a good suggestion. It involved killing Jaddites without delaying the withdrawal of the main army or trying to get the massive guns north through this accursed mud and the rivers ahead.

It also, as it happened, involved Senjan, that notorious seaside town that vexed the western borderlands and merchant goods at sea. The serdar wasn't sure why there were Senjani here, making their way towards Woberg on their own and in the open. It was an absurd trek for them. Surely the Jaddite emperor had reinforcements available that didn't have to journey so far?

On the other hand, Senjani had died in Sarantium when the walls were breached and the city burned—so they clearly did not mind covering distance to find death.

He gave the order to gratify this desire of theirs. He phrased it that way. There were hard smiles in the tent, on the grey morning with rain when they decided to turn home.

There were a hundred Senjani or so, he was told, on foot, with pack animals, not much more than a day ahead, across the next river. He sent eight hundred djannis and two hundred red-saddle cavalry. Too many, but why not? It would be a small triumph, close to a meaningless one, but he instructed the serdar of the djannis to take some of the raiders alive for him to parade through the city. The court could decide how they died.

He needed something to bring home. These infidel raiders from the coast weren't the only ones at risk of a bad death.

HRANT BUNIC HAD not put himself forward to command the Senjani party headed towards the fortress. That might have been a part of why he had been chosen as leader when they'd set out weeks ago—when they'd been a hundred men, not the ninety-three still alive and moving east on another rainy morning.

Yes, he was an experienced raid leader, but there were others like that among them. This was, he thought, one of the best companies ever to set out from Senjan. That *might* keep them alive long enough to be killed in Woberg. He didn't share that thought, but found it privately amusing. He was that sort of man, at this point in his life.

They were a larger party than hadjuks would ever engage, but that didn't mean archers or spear-throwers couldn't pick off men in rain or at twilight, especially in territory the Asharites knew well, where the Senjani were strangers and at risk if they pursued.

They'd destroyed three small villages and a number of farms. Bunic didn't much enjoy doing that, since they couldn't *take* anything of value while headed north, but he also knew that if anything might deter attacks on them it was the affirmation that there would be consequences. He'd made that clear to the handful they spared in each raid.

Leave us alone. Make sure the hadjuks know.

Of course, in his experience hadjuk militia didn't much care about the lives or deaths of farmers or villagers—hereabouts, or anywhere. The hadjuks lived their own kind of life on the mountain slopes or in deep woods, and sometimes they were commanded by soldiers. They were *offended* by villagers, it often seemed. Contemptuous of them. There were reasons beyond religion for conflicts in the world.

It was not, Hrant Bunic thought, a good time in the unfolding of Jad's creation to be a farmer or village-dweller anywhere. And in these parts of northern Sauradia, with a huge army approaching (he didn't know yet how far the Osmanlis had come), people were likely to have everything they possessed confiscated soon. Armies needed servants or slaves, food and firewood, women for various reasons.

Ordinary folk suffered and died in the places where empires met.

You couldn't really hide when war came to you, especially not if you had a house, land, elderly parents, small children. It didn't make him sorry or anything like that for the infidels here, but it did make him lift his voice more urgently in prayer with the two clerics at sunrise and sunset. He sometimes wondered if the great emperor in his palace in Obravic had any idea what he'd asked them to do when he'd sent messengers to Senjan.

Hrant Bunic had lived thirty-three hard years that spring. He had a father and a wife and a five-year-old son at home, and a woman he loved on Hrak Island. He didn't expect to see any of them again. He was at peace with this. Life did not offer you many kindnesses, and it didn't last long. You hoped for light with Jad after, against the dark.

Two of his scouts—one of them the boy, Miro—came back towards midday. They were exhausted, having run through the night. They reported that the evening before, at sunset, they'd seen—and possibly been seen by—mounted Osmanlis. The riders had been well armed, on good horses with red saddles.

Bunic knew what that meant. They all did. The army was upon them and they were exposed, in the open. He nodded slowly. He smiled at the boy. Some things were clear: they couldn't outrun cavalry to the fortress, still two weeks away, probably. And there were too many of them to hide in this countryside. They had destroyed villages. They would be reported. An ending of this sort had always been possible, from the morning their journey began.

He ordered a halt to allow himself a chance to think. He sent four men across the river to try to find and assess what might be coming this way. Their scouts might not have been seen, though if they thought they had it was likely to be so. Best assume as much. He set about assessing the terrain (not good here) and considering alternatives. He was calm. They were all calm. They were warriors of Jad, those they might soon be fighting were infidels, and there was a price to be exacted from anyone encountering the heroes of Senjan in battle, even far from home.

They were on the north side of a river with usefully steep banks. There was forest cover to the north. It ran back west only a little distance, he wasn't sure about east. None of them had been here before. The river was high and swift with the rains. They had passed a waterfall and rapids coming this way. They'd been working uphill for days. South across the river was open land, then hills, mostly lost in greyness and rain now. Somewhere out there, an army.

Everything depended on how many came after them. Even if they had seen and followed his own scouts, the Osmanlis might decide to ignore a group of men on foot and push towards the fortress. It was late in the season and they hadn't reached Woberg yet. Indeed, it might already be too late for them, if Jad was being kind. The Osmanlis needed their cannon to batter the fortress into submission before they had to turn for home or risk starvation when autumn came—and they were surely having trouble getting the gun-wagons through the mud and across rivers.

That gave him an idea. It might be foolish, but they weren't here for ease and safety, were they? They were marching to defend Woberg, and you didn't have to wait for enemies to come to you. When had Senjan ever done that? The god might offer mercy, but men needed to act for themselves.

They knew the sea and all waters—better than any people alive was the boast. Bunic asked for volunteers for something danger-ous. Every man raised a hand, including the scouts who had just returned, including the boy. Some raised both hands.

He felt, not for the first time, a pride that went bone-deep and had been lifelong. Whatever the world might think or say, in envy or fear or failure to understand, Senjan was what it was.

"This is ours, Hrant, whatever it is you have in mind." The eld-est of the Miho clan had stepped forward.

He nodded. One way to choose, an offer worth honouring. There were six Mihos with them. He picked four. He explained his thinking. He saw them smile, all four of them. He would remember that. They looked like wolves preparing to hunt, not men being pursued. There were no farewells, even with their kin left behind. You didn't do that. Why say farewell? They expected to return, in triumph.

The four of them went farther east, upstream, then swam across, the current bearing them back this way. They carried the necessary equipment in packs. The river was fast but narrow; the steep bank was a problem in rain but not impossibly so for good men. He watched them scale the bank and stand on the far side, directly opposite. He'd had his troubles with some of the Miho clan, but they knew what they were doing, these men.

Ropes were tied to arrows and sent high across the river. The four men on the other side untied them, then deployed small wheels from their packs and made knots and loops, while the same thing was done on this side, and a contrivance was made to pull wooden boxes and other things across the water. They knew how to accomplish these things. Their grandfathers had known how.

The men on the other bank took the boxes when they came. Two of them picked up a box between them. They each raised a free hand to those on the north side of the racing water. They turned and went into the rain and disappeared.

The other two Miho cousins remained, blurred in the mist. Bunic watched them place three crates in the ground there, half-buried. They took the last crate between them and they, too, turned south and ran off. They would need to avoid any Osmanlis searching this way. They would do that, he knew. The rest was chance and the god.

One thing done, two things made possible. He had other thoughts. He shared these. Agreement was reached. Time mattered, choices were limited, life was short. They turned back west, the way they'd come. Not far. They reached the place he'd had in mind by day's end. The rain had stopped, though the world was sodden and grey, no sign of the sun. The flowers in the meadow towards the woods seemed leached of colour. Sound was muffled.

He had left eight men behind in the trees, by the place where they'd sent men across the river.

He didn't expect anyone tonight, and probably not tomorrow. They set about preparing, much as their grandfathers might have done, or their fathers on the way to Sarantium twenty-five years ago. He hadn't told his second set of scouts, earlier, which way they'd be going, where they'd be. It didn't matter, the scouts would read the tracks, find him here.

They did do that, sooner than he'd expected—mid-afternoon the next day. The Osmanlis were close behind them, one said. Would be at the earlier stopping point by sunset, very likely. Many were on horseback. Bunic saw a hint of apprehension kept under control.

There were about a thousand djannis also coming, a second man added. His voice was calm. Bunic didn't believe that number at first, then he realized he needed to and that, accordingly, they were very likely dead, after all, standing here with rain beginning to fall again, between the river and the trees in Sauradia, far from the sea.

AS HE'D LAIN in a troubled sleep the last many nights, Damaz kept dreaming of his sister by the woods. She should have died—of his own arrow. He knew where he'd struck her, he'd seen she had no armour.

Then she'd spoken of his fight with Koçi. There was no way— not in the world as he understood it—for her to know about that. What did you *do* with something like this? Just live your life not understanding? For the rest of your days?

He was with the party sent after the Senjani. They were off the rough track north, crossing rain-soaked fields. The cavalry ahead were tracking the second set of Jaddite scouts they'd spotted, keeping a careful distance, expertly, because these scouts didn't matter except to lead them to the infidels.

Their own commander—the serdar of all the djannis in the army, not just Damaz's regiment—was with them, running as they were, doing so easily. A tall, fit, pale-haired, pale-eyed man, Karchite almost certainly. He had elected to come to this kill, for whatever reasons had seemed good to him. It might be the only fight they'd have, someone had said.

That was because, behind them, the army was leaving. Even as he ran, Damaz was aware that in the camp orders were being given. The army of Ashar was turning back, in shame and in rain, because they could not besiege Woberg and take it and get home in time. So it had been decided.

There had been muttering for days around campfires and on the march. Some of the older men had survived a retreat that had begun too late in the year. It had been, they said, beyond terrible. A good part of an army bigger than this one had died, and most of their horses had starved and been eaten.

You wanted to earn glory for Ashar and the khalif and for yourself—for the good life you might have when warring ended for you. But there would *be* no life after, the old soldiers had made clear, if you shat your guts out in frozen fields and died.

Every campaign in this direction, coming this far, was a war against the Jaddites and their fortresses but also against the weather and the seasons. You could defeat the accursed infidels but not always what came down from the sky.

The rivers had been deadly, high and swift with spring rain. And the guns, the cannons that were their pride and their curse . . . men and animals had been broken getting them this far, and they would break getting them home.

There had not been, Damaz thought, running steadily with a yearning to kill inside him, very much in the way of glory this spring. They had a chance now, though the numbers made this an execution more than a fight. Even so, he might soon slay infidels. He was mindful of the fact that their honour had been badly damaged some weeks ago, back south, by the man named Skandir.

And by Damaz's sister. Who had called him *Neven*. And invited him to come with her. The thought came again: what did you *do* with that recollection?

You ran with your fellow soldiers, until you saw through the evening mist and rain another river, with the red-saddle cavalry massed, holding torches, waiting for them near the bank. One of them was galloping back, torch held high, and Damaz was near enough to hear his report: some of their men had crossed upstream and sent word back. The signs were obvious, the Jaddite band had been there earlier today. They had started back west, fleeing like the cowards they were.

He understood that much before the loudest explosion he'd ever heard deafened him and knocked him to the ground.

There was too much light. Red and orange, towering, and a strange blue amid a stranger absence of noise. Men were shouting, he could see their mouths open, but sound came faintly from far away. Damaz smelled burning and realized it was flesh—men and horses. He was still on the ground, dazed, uncomprehending. All around him were others, also down. He saw his serdar struggling to stand. Damaz forced himself upright and stumbled over to help him, but his leader appeared to be swearing savagely and he shrugged off assistance. Damaz really couldn't hear anything clearly—not even the two bigger blasts that came in that moment, knocking him flat again, beside the serdar.

Later, he understood it had been fire-arrows loosed by the Senjani from across the river, striking explosives placed on the ground here, half buried, close to the riverbank, where the cavalry had stopped. They had also, it would emerge, killed the three men who had crossed the river.

There was a maimed and mangled chaos of soldiers and horses around him in the dark. Damaz could see men screaming through blood and the earth was churned and roiling. There were limbs lying on the wet ground, unattached to anything, and his leaders were shouting frantic orders, but he couldn't hear them for a long time.

THE WAY THE BIG CANNONS had been dealt with by those responsible for them was a very great mistake, though perhaps an understandable one, if you were at all inclined to be understanding.

Such an inclination was absent from the mind of the commanding serdar of the invading army of the khalif.

It appeared that once the order had been given that they were turning back, the artillery commanders responsible for bringing along the great guns had decided to cease bringing them along to link up with the infantry. Why do that at day's end, in rain and sucking mud, only to turn them around (not easy in itself) and drag and push them back the way they'd just come?

Accordingly, as matters would later be understood, on the night of the disaster, the cannons, including the two massive ones, were still some distance removed from the main body of the Osmanli force.

The guns were still guarded, of course. Or, rather, they were supposed to be. But there were more than forty thousand soldiers here—who would ever come near them with dark intent?

This particular question was answered by two detonations that lit the night sky with fire and death and strewn terror, and would have hidden the stars had they been shining.

Then, alas, it became even worse. Their own explosives were, of course, always brought along in wagons with the guns, under the authority of the artillery commanders and engineers. These, too, went up. Appallingly. Again and again and again. The sequence of blasts was seen and heard a long way in the heavy night, even across the swiftly racing river ahead of them. The one this army would never now cross.

OVER IN THAT DIRECTION, north and west, Hrant Bunic looked at a distant, deadly brilliance in the night, accepted a flask of wine, and drank. He did not smile. None of them smiled, in fact. You did what you did in war and sometimes it succeeded. They were still going to die, he expected.

That would not occur now without a very great price having been exacted. Nor were they likely to be forgotten.

ABOUT HALF THE CAVALRY were able to mount up again. A large number of djannis were wounded, though not so many, and only some of them had died—they'd been farther back when the explosives by the riverbank had been detonated. The leader of the red-saddle cavalry was dead. He had been, as was proper, at the front when they'd reached the river.

Damaz was still deaf in the first hours after the explosions. His ears kept ringing as if there were temple bells in his head. He was afraid this would never pass, but it did, during the time they spent killing injured horses and tending to wounded men as best they could in the dark, carrying torches through carnage.

There came a point when he could hear the cries, not just see men with open mouths and understand they were screaming. There had been bodies—and parts of bodies—in the river. They had also seen by now the sequence of blasts far behind them, a distant fire was burning in the night. They all knew where those blasts had come from, why there had been so many explosions, one after another.

Damaz had friends among the artillery and the engineers. He'd been assigned to help with the guns. Pulling a cannon's wagon through mud with other men, you had suffering in common, as a start. Damaz looked at the fires to the south again. They were lighting the cloudy night. There might be no cannons at all any more. He wondered if any of those he knew back there were still alive.

Men had been sent across the river and had returned with a report. By then he could hear again, through the ringing sound and the light-headedness. The Jaddites had left a banner, planted to be found on the northern bank. One of the advance party had brought it back to show the serdar. The man was soaking wet from the river, and crying tears of rage.

Damaz, standing near again, heard his serdar say, grimly, "We will chase them as far as ever they flee. To the walls of Senjan if need be. They will die the worst deaths men have ever died."

Soldiers shouted and gestured approval of that as it was conveyed through the ranks. There was fear and fury, both. Damaz
tried to shout too, but his throat was raw and gritty and his
thoughts seemed as roiled as the earth had been when the explosions had gone up.

In the event, the Senjani were found the next day.

Most of the Asharites were on the northern bank by then,
crossing at sunrise. They left men behind to deal with the dead
and wounded.

The serdar sent eight scouts west with instructions to be swift,
and careful. Two came back. One was wounded. A bullet in his
thigh. The others were dead, or taken. But their enemies hadn't
gone far, it was reported. They didn't need to be chased to the walls
of Senjan.

Fewer than a hundred of the Jaddites, the two scouts reported.
They outnumbered the infidels easily, and they were among the
best fighters in the khalif's army.

They will die the worst deaths men have ever died.

ONLY ONE CRATE of explosives left, and the Asharites coming after
them would be even more cautious now. Six of their scouts had
been killed this morning.

They had brought all the explosive material they'd had in
Senjan when they set out. All of it. That hadn't been a discussion,
either. The intention was to write to the emperor and say they'd
done so, and ask for more to be sent to defend the Holy Emperor's
most loyal town, which was always under threat.

There had been some sour amusement as to the likelihood of
any supplies coming to them, since it never happened, but the
letter had been duly sent with both imperial couriers.

Bunic now had the remaining explosives divided into two
smaller boxes. Again, he asked for volunteers; again, every man

raised his hand. To do the greatest damage, they'd have to be detonated with the Osmanlis right there. That meant an extreme likelihood of dying, either in the blast or after.

He had explained, earlier, his thinking as to what should happen now. Why he didn't think they could escape from here, even if they separated to try to make it back south and west. They were too far away, on foot, in enemy lands, where they'd be seen and informed upon, and with mounted men and djannis after them.

No one disagreed, no one even considered the notion that a company from Senjan would flee before Asharites. Bunic placed men in the forest at first light, implementing one other idea he'd had, more a gesture than anything else. Gestures could matter, if anyone ever learned of them.

They were all aware that their deaths would be bad if they were taken. This had become clear after the night events by the river and—spectacularly—far to the south by the enemy cannons and powder. They had done something legendary there, Hrant Bunic told his company. They all knew it, anyhow.

He refused to pick the two remaining Mihos for this next task; they had done enough as a clan here. Glory and loss should both be shared among heroes. He didn't pick the boy, either, of course, but Miro, intense and excitable, insisted on going with the two men chosen, so that he could run back with word of what happened.

"They have horses to chase you down," Bunic had said repressively.

"I am faster than any infidel horse," Miro had replied, to laughter.

How did you refuse a boy who could say that? This was warfare, for the god and their own souls yearning for light. Miro Pavlic went with the two men, each of those carrying a box of explosives. Bunic made him promise to keep a distance, stay in the trees, watch, and run back through the woods to report.

"What else would I do?" the Pavlic boy said. He took one end of one of the boxes, helping the smaller of the two men. Bunic watched them till they were out of sight.

THEY DIDN'T TAKE either of the two Senjani alive. Another failure.

It was an expectation that they would, an order from the serdar, but the Jaddites killed themselves, crying the name of their god, when cornered in the trees. The explosives on the path this time had been seen and avoided, the infidels seen and chased. They were djannis, weren't they? And red-saddle cavalry. How many times could someone expect to succeed with the same device of explosives and fire-arrows? Really.

But Damaz had to admit he was shaken when both men plunged daggers into themselves after he and others chased them down in the forest.

The serdars would be extremely unhappy: their own here north of the river, and the commander who had turned the army around and wanted captives to carry back.

This company, this *band*, really, of Senjani had done terrible damage. Word had reached them by the river. *All* the big guns were destroyed, and most of the engineers and artillerymen were dead or horribly maimed and burned. There hadn't been much doubt as they'd looked back at those vast fires in the night. The leader of the cavalry here, a much-admired man, was also dead— in the first detonation by the river. There would be consequences for their commanders back home from all of this.

Mostly because of the guns, though. Men died in war, it was expected, acceptable, but the great cannons, when they worked, were precious—because they were so necessary and so often failed. It was almost intolerably difficult to cast big guns that held their shape and purpose, that didn't crack. It was the lost cannons more than anything that might lead to deaths among the leaders. Even Damaz, young as he was, understood that.

He heard a sound. He had shouted an alert and was sprinting after someone through the trees almost before he realized it.

He was a fast runner. Even so, this Senjani—it had to be one of them—was faster, twisting like a deer or a rabbit through the woods. The sound he'd heard had been a choked-off wail of grief. Foolish man! Giving himself away like that. He redoubled his efforts. The other man might stumble, fall, the forest was dense with roots and fallen branches and branches that might hit you in the face. The light was dim.

The other man might also turn and loose an arrow at him if he found a place to do that—a glade, say, where Damaz would have to run into open space in pursuit. He thought about that. They were alone, ahead of the others. Damaz heard them shouting and labouring behind. He wanted to take this raider alive, they had orders to do that. He needed to survive, first.

There was a clearing. Damaz left his feet, diving forward and to his right, rolling, as he came into it. There were oak trees, in leaf now, it was thickly shaded, no flowers grew. He saw mushrooms and moss, and he heard—never saw—an arrow strike a tree trunk behind him.

How did you take a bowman alive when you were alone? He thought of Koçi, remembered the inner voice he'd heard in that fight. It seemed long ago. He grabbed for his knife, rolled hard a second time—another arrow flew past where he'd been, hit the earth. Damaz came up, surging forward, and threw, hard as he could. You couldn't aim to wound, not from this far, you could only hope.

And sometimes hopes were rewarded. He hit the Senjani—a small man—in the shoulder. Shouting, unsheathing his sword, Damaz sprinted forward. There was enough light for him to see . . .

That this other man, this infidel warrior, was younger than he was, truly a boy. And with a horror that clutched, and would stay, Damaz saw the boy draw a knife and plunge it into his own neck, and dark blood burst from the wound.

He didn't cry the name of the sun god. He just died. Right here, in this glade, edge of a small clearing in some Sauradian wood far from anywhere that mattered.

A place in the world where nothing like this ought to happen. Not to a boy. Damaz had no idea where that thought came from.

He stood above the Senjani. He was breathing hard. He heard men crash into the glade behind him.

"Fuck!" someone growled, striding up. "This one too? Why didn't you stop him?"

Damaz didn't answer. He didn't even turn to see who it was. He was looking down at this death, a young face, someone near to his own age with his own fair hair.

"Shut up," someone said to the swearing man. "They aren't letting themselves be taken."

Damaz didn't look back at this one, either. He bent and retrieved his knife from the boy's shoulder. You always retrieved your weapons. There was a lot of blood from the neck wound. He wiped his blade on the earth, then turned and headed out of this forest, towards whatever light there was today.

I didn't kill this one, he thought. But that was foolish, of course he had. And there were others to kill up ahead, or be killed by.

Senjan, his sister had said. Danica. She had gone to Senjan when their village burned. With his mother, with his grandfather, after he was taken as a child.

CHAPTER XXI

The tax assessors, the two they had discovered hiding off the road and had stripped naked and sent away, had been killed. Someone reported it to Skandir's band in a village farther south. They'd been torn apart, it was said, left in a field.

There might be reprisals if it was discovered. There almost always were, but this was a wild, remote place to the south and west, and the Osmanlis were concentrating their attention north just now. To a certain degree the star-worshippers had accepted that this part of the world, where Sauradia became Trakesia, was not an easy or a likely place to subdue. Not worth much, either.

Danica searched in herself and found no weakness. No sympathy for those two men, even in the memory of seeing them stumble naked down the road. One had been weeping. *Good*, she remembered thinking.

They set fire to the barn beside a small garrison after a long ride east along a stream. They had six new men with them by then; they needed exposure to fighting. So did Danica. Asharite soldiers came hurrying out through the fort's wooden gate, carrying guns, which was foolish in the dark. Danica and the two other archers cut them down, by the light of the burning barn. The guns were fired, harmlessly. Skandir sent men to claim them, after. Guns had their uses, just not in a fight like this.

But as they were doing that, two people, young ones, perhaps fourteen or fifteen years old, came running from the barn, half clothed, crying in fear, hands in the air. A boy and a girl. They'd found a place to be together at night. While Danica was watching, uncertain, Skandir and another man rode over and killed them both.

They spent what remained of the night some distance back west in two adjacent farmhouses and the barns attached to each. One Jaddite farmer and his wife gave Skandir their bed, so Danica had that with him. He always accepted, she had learned by now, when such offers were made. He also knew where shelter might be found. It allowed people to feel they were playing a role, he'd said. That they, too, were resisting conquest: in Jad's name, in the name of their fathers and mothers, children, grandparents living or dead.

She said, in the dark, "Those were children, in the barn."

"I didn't notice."

"Yes you did."

He was silent in the bed beside her. A big man grown old, scarred and seamed, lean with the road and war through twenty-five years. He was slow to get up some mornings when it was damp.

"Yes, very well, I did," he said finally.

"That girl died for sleeping with a boy?"

"A boy? An Osmanli soldier!"

"That was no soldier, Rasca."

"You know that? Do you?"

"I do. So do you. That was some farmer's or miller's son, or—"

"An *Asharite* farmer or miller, then, or a fucking smith come to dispossess our own! Tax our faith or kill us for it! Rot them all, girl! What would you have me do?"

He was fierce, Danica thought. He was undyingly fierce. She could feel his rage like heat beside her.

The farmer and his wife could hear them from the other side of the single, partitioned room. She wondered what they'd think. She said, softly, "The girl had yellow hair. She might have been their daughter, these two."

He didn't reply. In the silence she thought about how many people would die, one way or another, in this long war. How many had already died. That girl should not have gone with an Osmanli boy into the barn. She told herself that.

Eventually, she fell asleep. You needed to sleep when you could, and there was little of the night left.

They saddled up at sunrise. They went south. The intention was what it had been from after the battle with the djannis and the cavalry, where her brother had been: regroup, train new men, then go back north. Raid and run, kill as many as you could. Make the infidels regret the day they'd come, and every day after. Live this way, do exactly this, endlessly. Or to an ending.

She was all right with that. She was here for that.

Far to the north her brother was encountering a company from Senjan by another river, and the army of Ashar had been ordered to turn back.

ೲ

They might be facing the best warriors in the khalif's army, Hrant Bunic told his band, but their leaders could make mistakes, and they had never fought Senjan. The heroes waged war differently. They could do things here, between forest and river, that would not be forgotten.

He didn't know if that was true, but he said the words. When you led people they needed to hear certain things from you, and you needed to say them in a way they would believe. He did think some of them would have to live for this to be known and remembered.

There had been no more explosions east of them, and the boy had not come back. Bunic had a bad feeling. He kept that to himself, although the others could hear the silence as well as he could. Birdsong, wind in leaves, and below them the low roar of the river approaching its rapids and then a cataract.

Waiting, brooding, coming back (again) from checking the progress of the work he'd ordered among the trees, he had another thought.

He sent six men with crossbows to climb trees farther east and stay hidden there. There were enough leaves to screen a man now, if he knew how to keep still. It was a milder day, no rain. Overhead you could even see the sun trying to push through windblown clouds to be seen. They had prayed at dawn, led by the clerics. *I have lived*, Hrant Bunic thought, *a mostly good life*. He did want to see his son again, and the sea.

Late afternoon a man came running back. The Asharites were coming: cavalry at the front, djannis behind in formation. They were not yet strung out, not as they would be when they came nearer, because there was only a narrow space between water and wood here. Of course there was only that: was he a fool, the captain of the Senjani?

Better, or less confident, or perhaps less angry leaders of the Osmanli force would have had men on the southern bank with arrows and guns, shooting across, forcing the Senjani into the trees. He took mild, brief hope from this failure. They might still do it, but he didn't think they would. They were too sure of themselves, in their numbers. And enraged. You could fight savagely in that state, or make mistakes. Or both.

It was important, Bunic reminded himself, not to be taken alive.

And just then, on that thought, came two explosions, one and then another immediately after, shattering the day's stillness, and this time he smiled.

AGAIN! AND ONCE MORE Damaz was knocked flying and hit the ground hard, and *again* he couldn't hear anything at all. He had tears in his eyes, was fighting not to sob, which was shameful. Men around him were moaning, he could see it, but he couldn't hear.

An arrow struck someone beside him and the man died. Like that. He had been sitting on the ground, dazed, a hand to a bloodied cheek, and now he was dead, a crossbow bolt in his chest. Alive, not alive.

Damaz flattened himself behind the dead body, trying desperately to make his thinking work properly. He was hearing bells again, ringing and ringing.

How had this . . . ? They had been *watching* for buried chests on the path! Surely they hadn't missed any! And then he knew. The mistake. They had done something desperately foolish. They'd carried the two chests they'd spotted before, the ones that had led men into the trees to chase down the archers ready to explode them. It hadn't worked twice, not against *this* company.

But they'd *carried* them! And crossbow bolts could trigger an explosion as easily as an archer's fire-arrow. And there were trees here, where a man might hide.

Damaz looked at the forest. He wiped at his eyes. Not tears. Blood. He was injured. He couldn't see well enough to spot where a crossbowman might be hiding in the trees. Then another man was hit, just ahead of him, and Damaz pointed, and he screamed "*Up there!*" And their own archers began loosing arrows that way, dozens of them, and then more, and a moment later a man fell from among the leaves, and then another did, and a third came spinning down, so slowly, it seemed not quite real.

Rising to his feet—you couldn't cower behind a dead man!—Damaz hurried to help the wounded around him. A cluster of men had gathered just ahead, and as Damaz came up he saw that their own serdar of the djannis was dead in the blast, his body mangled horribly. You could tell who he was only by the charred shreds of his uniform. Damaz felt a sickness in himself.

Both leaders! The cavalry serdar and now their own. Killed by an accursed band of raiders they outnumbered vastly.

More arrows were flying into the trees. Someone had spotted another crossbowman. Damaz saw this one fall, too. He ran that way. The man might be alive! They were to take them alive, to parade for the khalif. To show their triumph here.

He wasn't alive. Two arrows in him and a broken neck from the fall, his body twisted strangely. They were still loosing arrows, the archers among the djannis, and he saw the flash of the occasional musket shot, which was foolish at this distance. Damaz didn't have a bow, he was marching with a sword now.

He still couldn't hear. He'd been too close to the detonations again. He could have died, so easily. Alive, not alive. He wiped at his eyes and again there was blood. He'd need to have a wound tended, but that wasn't going to happen, there were others much more badly hurt. He needed to help. He didn't know who was giving orders.

He couldn't have heard them anyhow.

He saw that the cavalry was pushing west again, towards where the Senjani had been reported to be. There were enough horsemen to destroy the enemy themselves. That, Damaz thought, would be a disgrace for the djannis! He looked around wildly and saw men running in the wake of the horses. Yes. There'd be enough here to tend the wounded. Someone had to fight and destroy in the khalif's name and for the honour of his best-beloved infantry.

Damaz ran. He didn't draw his sword yet. That was an error they'd been taught to avoid from the start of their training. You waited until you saw who you were to fight. He kept wiping at his head, though, because blood kept dripping into his eyes. Eventually it was too much, he couldn't see. He went towards the riverbank to clean himself with water but when he got there he saw it was even steeper here, a ravine, a gorge, the water far below.

He used his knife and cut a strip from his tunic near the bottom, and started to tie it awkwardly around his head. Another man saw him and ran over and did it for him. He said something, but Damaz shrugged and touched his ears and shook his head. The other djanni nodded and pointed forward, grimly, and Damaz nodded, and they ran together.

ONE OF THE THINGS Hrant Bunic had learned through years of raiding was that if you could provoke an enemy to rage he was more likely to make mistakes.

He hadn't had a lot of time, but they'd rigged tripwires between the woods and the riverbank with archers placed to strike at the fallen, and then more bowmen for when the cavalry slowed, having seen horses fall. Horsemen moving slowly made easy targets if you felt no compunction about shooting the horses.

They didn't. Feel compunction. They had little expectation of leaving here alive. The thing was to take as many with you as you could. He just didn't have enough men, and sending some forward was pretty much sending them to die right now. He told them to loose arrows quickly then get back here through the trees. A few did manage that.

By late in the day, despite having picked off—it seemed—forty or fifty of the Asharites and their horses, an appallingly large number of Osmanlis had reached the narrow point between gorge and forest that Bunic had picked for their last stand. Better to die here, though, than chased down by horsemen. There were no legends about men killed in flight.

They had planted stakes angled outwards, and contrived a barrier of branches, axes ringing in the woods from the moment they'd started setting up here. They needed more arrows, but they needed more of everything. This was not a battle he was going to win.

The narrowness of the space helped. They fought back two assaults, one right after the other. It was good that there was no obvious leader of the Osmanlis now. It seemed as if some of them had simply ridden and run to get here, to hurl themselves upon the

Senjani. Bunic decided they must have killed another serdar with the last explosions, which was a pleasing thought. He had little time for reflection, however. They were fighting. Men were dying beside him. He needed to make men die in front of him.

They went for the horses whenever they could. Bodies of dead or thrashing horses in front of their barrier were an added bulwark. So were slain men. He knew of a fight where those under assault had plugged gaps with their own dead.

He wasn't going to do that here. Jad judged men by all they did in life, and he wouldn't use a companion that way. Some fell in the front and you didn't move them—you didn't have a chance—but that was different. Goran Miho was on his left and the old man, Lubic, was on his other side, and the three of them stayed at the front. The sun had broken through behind them, setting. Another small good thing—it was in the eyes of the Osmanlis now. Even so, this was a place to die under the god's late-day sun, not to triumph. They had done triumphant things, sometimes you paid a price for that.

He saw a horse stumble approaching the barrier, stepping awk-wardly on the body of a dead man. Bunic leaped forward, across the low wall. Goran Miho was right beside him with the same thought, no words spoken, and Miho drove his blade up into the horse's belly as Bunic, on the other side, killed the rider as he struggled to leave the saddle. And so there were two more in front of them, bodies making that other kind of wall, and the raiders hurried back between the stakes and behind the branches.

They were good, quick, strong fighters, the heroes of Senjan. Their methods were those of brigands, raiders. They *were* raiders and brigands. They'd scout a village or salt mine office, find a merchant ship in the narrow sea, come up in the night or as dawn was breaking. That was what they did.

They couldn't match swords and guns and arrows with red-saddle cavalry or the best infantry in the Asharite world, not out-numbered as terribly as they were.

It was, accordingly, a bad time, defined by death. The sun made its way down behind them and the light was turning red and beginning to fade. Bunic watched men die around him that he'd known all his life, men who had come here without hesitation—to their end. He was unwounded so far. His sword was bloodied. They were lucky in another way: the press was so tight in this narrow strip of land that the Osmanli bowmen were kept largely out of the fight.

Lucky. Not really the word for what was happening, he thought. He stepped sideways around a stake, then forward again, two quick steps, and buried his sword in another horse's belly and withdrew. One of their archers sank an arrow in the rider as he tried to free his legs from the stirrups. The man screamed. There was so much screaming. Warfare was loud, Hrant Bunic thought. He remembered, suddenly, sunsets over the sea at home, the sounds of waves, wind in sails.

He'd had about seventy men here, after those sent ahead to do what they could, and the four Mihos who had gone south and destroyed the cannons. Only twenty or so of the enemy could assault them at a time, but at some point they'd figured out that they could send archers and guns into the woods for an angle on the Senjani. Bunic had some archers there, too. Or he'd had them there. Dead by now, it looked like. There didn't seem to be any of their own arrows flying as darkness came.

The attackers called a halt when night fell. Someone had taken charge by then. There was almost always a pause at night for armies in battle (not for raiders). A fear of killing your companions in the dark was part of it, but the Asharites also knew they had the Senjani trapped here, and it was clear that they wanted the last ones alive.

That wasn't going to happen, Hrant Bunic thought.

He watched from behind the barrier and the piled-up dead as the Osmanlis brought up even more men, some with gear for tents, some with food. They began gathering wood for fires. Another leader arrived. He was giving orders, staying out of arrow range. The Senjani also had food and drink, but only because so many of them were dead. There were—he counted twice—sixteen of them left. Sixteen.

They would be overrun in the morning, clubbed down and disarmed, bound and taken away, stumbling on foot or in prison wagons, to be paraded and mutilated and killed for the glory of Ashar and the stars.

No glory for any of you on this campaign, he wanted to shout across the space between himself and—how many were there?— five hundred Osmanlis, probably more. He saw their fires burning now.

Miho came over, limping with a thigh wound. He reported that the enemy had—as expected—sent men to circle behind them through the forest. They had cut off any retreat west in the dark, would attack from both sides when there was light enough to see.

All predictable. If you fought long enough you could anticipate most tactics that would be used against you. It didn't necessarily help. Not if you had only sixteen fighters.

"Is it time?" Miho asked.

"Not yet. Full dark, middle of night," Bunic replied. "Say at moonrise. Ropes are tied?"

"They are." In the first starlight Goran Miho smiled thinly. "Needed to double them."

"Long way down?"

"Yes. This is mad and foolish, Hrant."

"I know it is."

"And wonderful," Miho added. "It is how we should die."

"I don't propose to die, Goran."

"I know. But . . ."

"But . . . yes."

They left it at that. He didn't like Goran Miho, but he'd fight proudly next to him anywhere and die with him now, and face the god's judgment beside him. You didn't have to be a pleasant man to be a brave one.

He drank, ate some dried meat, waited for the blue moon. He saw it rise. He gave the order.

Four men went towards the woods, including the old tracker, Lubic. If you could track like a wolf, you could be silent as one, too. It was unlikely they would get through, but if they did, if even one or two of them could slip past the Osmanlis in the forest and away, it would be such a good thing. No one said farewell. They just went.

The twelve men remaining went down two ropes in blackness under moving clouds and the stars. They went over the cliffs of the chasm there to the small, light boats they'd made in the woods in a day, knowing exactly how to do so, having done it many times before.

Some axes they'd carried (they always carried axes), and some they'd taken in villages they'd attacked coming here. They could cut and sharpen spikes for a barrier, and cut down and carry logs and branches for a wall. And they could make boats. They knew everything about boats.

Two rafts for a dozen men. Frail, open, not enough nails—they were mostly lashed together with cord. Not the best wood for a boat hereabouts, either. You used what you had, including memory and pride.

The last man down, Zorenko, was the best climber. He untied the ropes and tossed them and the spikes over and down, then he descended that cliff in the dark. Bunic wouldn't have ever wanted to try that. Zorenko did it easily. It was impossible down here to see if he was smiling at the bottom, but odds were, Bunic thought, that he was.

With luck, with any kindness from fortune at all, the Asharites would not know where they had gone, or how. They would think they'd fled through the forest, would pursue—and not find them.

Chase them for days in that direction, perhaps, past the wood's ending, into the fields. If they'd caught any or all of the four he'd sent that way, they'd guess the others had slipped through. That had been part of his thought.

There was a thin margin of wet earth here beside the river, which was fast, racing, loud, rushing towards what lay ahead to the west.

What lay ahead were rapids and rocks between cliffs on both sides, then a waterfall. The land sloped down, gently to the south of the river, more steeply on this side. The river in its gorge dropped faster.

They had seen the falls coming this way, looking down in rain. *How we should die*, Goran Miho had said this evening. They were children of the sea and a long way from it, but this river was headed towards salt water and seabirds.

And the Asharites might never know what had happened to the captives they'd intended to take in the morning. They could become a mystery. An enemy failure. If anyone was ever able to tell the story.

If any of them survived this, Hrant Bunic thought, they'd have *such* a tale to tell in the world.

"Wait for first grey," he told his men, this small cluster left from the hundred who'd set out through the gates of Senjan. "We need to be able to see *something* to have a chance." He had to speak loudly, to be heard over the river.

Someone laughed. "Hah! And what chance would that be?" But he shouted it with amusement, not fear, not any kind of yielding at all, and there was answering laughter by the rushing water in the dark.

Hrant Bunic felt so much pride he thought it might burst his chest.

A little later someone said, "I can see your ugly face, Bunic," and a few moments after that he gave the order to get into the boats and push them from the shoreline, and the river took them all.

THERE WAS A STILLNESS AT SUNRISE.

Damaz had been awake for some time, waiting, disturbed by something he couldn't name. Not apprehension. This wasn't going to be a battle. They were only about fifteen of the infidels left and they had five hundred men here. Their only challenge was to capture, making sure not to kill—that was why they were waiting for daylight. He probably wouldn't be at the front of this, and it wouldn't take long.

They had men in position on the far side of the Senjani. He had hoped to be one of those but the new serdar, coming up late in the day, had sent experienced djannis there, through the woods.

Taking a prisoner earned you honour, so veterans had priority. The serdar had decreed that if anyone killed a Jaddite today he'd be executed. There was a great deal of anger—and fear—among their leaders, Damaz thought.

He didn't see a great deal of honour in this coming fight, but that was a private thought. He'd killed that other boy in the forest, and killed or wounded at least two men at the barrier yesterday. He didn't know if anyone had noticed him fighting bravely. They hadn't had any leaders with them for those first assaults.

At least he could hear again. Birds were singing, the sky was brightening. There would be sunshine this morning. Now there would be, after they'd been forced to turn back, after the cannons had been destroyed. By these infidels, he reminded himself. Respect or sympathy were errors, weakness, shameful. The Senjani trapped here had killed companions of his.

Except, it turned out, the Senjani weren't trapped here.

There was no one beyond the barrier, past the dead horses and men.

Word rippled back, uneasily. Someone shouted from the far side. No one there, either. Had they slipped through the woods in the night? There had been a hundred men at a time, in shifts, posted among the trees to stop that.

It turned out three of the Senjani had indeed been found in the forest trying to escape. They were dead, though, not captured. It had been too hard to overpower and take someone in the blackness of the wood. Six of their own men had been wounded, four were dead.

"How do we know there were only three?" asked the man next to Damaz, the one who'd bandaged his head and fought beside him yesterday.

"We fucking don't," said someone else.

The men on the far side of the barricade swore that no one had gone past them. The new serdar looked frightened now. Commanders were going to be executed as a result of these events, Damaz's new companion had said last night.

The serdar ordered the dead pushed aside, including their own, and the makeshift barrier, and he sent cavalry galloping west along the river. If the Jaddites had fled on foot they'd be hunted down like the animals they were, he shouted. And if they *had* escaped that way, even if briefly, the leaders he'd posted on the western side would be decapitated right here.

"We need to check the forest, too," someone said near Damaz. "We know they tried that. There are only the two possibilities," he added, uncertainly.

Damaz thought about that. He walked towards the cliff and looked down. Then he made his way forward, past those carrying away the dead from by the barrier now. There was no order or routine here among the army of the khalif. No one stopped him.

He stepped over the fence, past bodies already beginning to smell, with flies at men and horses. There were carrion birds overhead and waiting in the trees, he saw. He stood where the Senjani had been and he looked around. Some of their own men were going into the wood. Veterans again.

He walked to the forest's edge. He saw where the Jaddites had cut down trees to make their barrier. A lot of trees, he thought.

Then he remembered that there'd been sharpened stakes, too, in front of the fence. He kept looking for something, a hint, a clue. He didn't see anything, he didn't know what he was looking for.

He went back to the cliff and looked down at the river (fast here, approaching the rapids). Something was bothering him. They couldn't have got down there, could they? And why would they? Why would any men choose death that way?

The thought came to him, swift and hard: *better than being captured and taken to Asharias.* He was sure, in that instant, that he was right. And with that thought his life changed. As if a key had turned in some lock in his heart.

He stood there, terrified, unsteady on his feet so near the long drop, above the roar of water. And now he thought: how could the world bring you to your sister the way it had, back south, and have her know you, and have it mean nothing in a man's life?

It couldn't, he thought, his heart pounding. It couldn't mean nothing. Not if you then encountered others, magnificently brave, from the town where she'd fled with your mother and grandfather—whose name you bore.

If you tried to make it mean nothing, what were you denying? Everything?

My name is Neven Gradek. I was loved, and stolen away, and I do not have to accept that as my life.

That thought came to him, it was in him, by a cliff in Sauradia as a rising sun defined the arriving day. His mouth was dry. His head throbbed from the wound he'd taken and the explosions. But—and this was the astonishing thing—he had no doubts. None. Not from that first moment, or after, with all that was to follow.

He closed his eyes. Roar of water below, birds calling above. *My name is Neven Gradek.* He opened his eyes. He turned and joined the men going into the trees. No one had posted him to that company but there was so much chaos that morning, he just went. He caught up to those searching the forest and stayed with a group of them all morning, and then some of them made their way out to the west, into a meadow.

"Come on," he said to the three men beside him. "If they came through, this will be where they went. We can't go back without finding a sign."

They followed him. It seemed, he thought, that if you were decisive when no one else was, you could lead men, even if you were very young.

He led them all day. Late in the afternoon one of the others said, "This is too far, we're exposed. If they came this way and we find them, they'll kill us."

"Go back then!" said the boy whose name had been Damaz when he woke in the dark and watched the morning come. "I'm not! We need to stay out here so we can look for a fire when it gets dark. They won't imagine we came this far after them."

"Do what the fuck you like," the other man said. "Get yourself killed, boy." And he turned and started back. A moment later so did the other two. "Come on!" one of them said to Damaz. They obviously expected him to follow.

He didn't. His name wasn't Damaz any more. He didn't follow them back towards the wood and the river and the army of the khalif.

Neven Gradek went west, instead, alone in a sunset world, then alone under stars as darkness came on the first day without clouds or rain in a long time. He didn't see campfires. He hadn't expected to.

He came to a farmhouse in the night as the meadow turned into cultivated land with low stone walls. He called a warning of his presence. Dogs barked and were called to heel. He told them, keeping a distance, that he was a djanni, one of many out here searching for fleeing Jaddites. Had they seen anyone pass by?

A lamp was brought out from the small house. The old man holding it, with a younger one beside him clutching a spade as a weapon, saw someone standing there in the uniform of a djanni.

They ducked their heads in fear. The older one knelt in his own yard. They invited him in. They were terrified, he saw. They fed him and gave him a pallet for the night, and the young one and two even younger boys went out, taking turns, to watch for any campfires that might be lit through the night.

He left before dawn, accepting food (you needed to take any food you were given) and continued west and, later, across the river south, and away. Away.

Maybe, possibly, he'd get home, he thought. He didn't expect to, but you could try.

TIJAN LUBIC, THE TRACKER, oldest of the Senjani who went east in Hrant Bunic's company, wasn't even certain how old he was. What did a number matter? Jad sent you into this world (there were other worlds, his mother had taught him) and brought you home when it suited him. In between, you did what you did for as long as was allowed.

Lubic was one of the four who went into the forest in the night, trying to escape that way. In truth, there was no expectation they'd do so, but neither was there any belief the frail crafts they'd built would survive the rapids, let alone the waterfall that came after.

But any men found in the forest might conceal the existence of the boats, in the event that some miracle of Jad occurred and one of the two, and some of the men in them, survived.

In the event, Tijan Lubic became the miracle.

He wouldn't have put it that way, even devout as he was. He'd have said (he did say) that being a tracker meant you were also good at hiding. The skills were mirrors of each other, reflections in a midday pool. He wouldn't have gotten away at midday, of course.

He'd put on a dead djanni's uniform at darkfall, over his own clothing. The other three disdained doing that, the three who had volunteered with him to try to slip past the soldiers in the forest.

Lubic disdained nothing when it came to raids, battles, escapes. Disdain, he felt, was a luxury few men could afford. He would have said this was a reason he'd lived so long. Add a lifelong belief that there was nothing, really, that a Senjani hero could not achieve in the service of his god. Silence when he moved, endurance, and cleverness—those helped.

He went last of the four. He crawled along the edge of the trees alone, not entering the forest. He went east, not west, right along the margin of where the Osmanlis were camped between wood and water. He was there to be seen if anyone walked to the wood's edge, to relieve himself, to fetch more firewood.

There were campfires, but none cast a glow that reached this far. Those soldiers sent unhappily into the forest (there would be bears here, hungry after winter, and wolves, and very likely snakes) were farther west, near where the remnant of the Senjani were. That was what Lubic had realized. He kept going east, silently. He passed tethered horses. Those were dangerous, they could become restless, but they didn't.

He entered the forest, on knees and elbows, belly to wet earth, only when he was midway along that line of campfires and tents under the stars. It was easier from then on. He did hear shouts later, and from the triumphant sound he guessed that at least one of his companions had been found, probably trying to climb a tree and go west overhead. He had told them it would be too hard to move through late-spring branches, tree to tree, in silence.

Safer on foot, on the forest floor, away from the soldiers, and with a tread you learned through decades, light and quiet, even among the debris of a wet woodland. Hearing and smell mattered more than sight in this heavy dark. He did smell bear, judged it not recent, not close. It frightened him nonetheless. He had three gouged scars on his back from a bear. Must be thirty years ago. Lucky to have survived. You needed to be lucky.

Home was south and west. A long way. He went north.

It seemed the obvious thing, though when he'd mentioned it to the others they'd given him looks he'd grown accustomed to over the years. A man who preferred to live in and off the land in a coastal town that prided itself on skills at sea. Men who tended against the grain were often regarded strangely. He was used to it, for a long time now. He'd had a wife who liked him well enough. That was a long time ago, too.

Still, it really did seem natural to him, what he was doing. They'd been headed for Woberg, hadn't they? That was the summons they'd accepted. They were far closer to the fort than to home. Better to go that way, then, take your chances with patrols, scouts, villagers, whatever passed for hadjuks here. If he couldn't slip through the likes of those, Tijan Lubic thought, what had he lived this long for?

He did slip through. The uniform got him food twice at farmhouses chosen for their isolation. He had simply shown his sword, then grunted and pointed (his voice would have given him away), and frightened people in remote places had assumed he was too lofty and arrogant to bother speaking to them. A real djanni might have been that proud, he thought. Some of them might also have taken their pleasure with the second farmer's wife—or his young son.

He'd have been able to kill in both places if he'd needed to, but it was best, when you wanted to leave as little trace as you could, not to have dead bodies behind you. Bodies were a trace.

There were two small rivers, neither swift, as the land levelled north. Once, he encountered three scouts on horseback. He heard them coming much too late (he'd been tired that evening) but it had been raining again and the scouts were unhappy and indifferent.

They probably knew their army had turned back by then, he'd thought after. They hadn't seen him, though he was barely hidden in a gully of rainwater where they passed. You needed to be lucky.

After the second river he began looking about, and on a cloudy night he stole clothing from a farmhand asleep in a barn alone.

He had to knock him out of course (you couldn't take the clothing off a sleeping man!) but he didn't think a case of theft would make any kind of trail to follow. He discarded his own clothes and the djanni uniform a day away. He was well north by then, and from the maps they'd had (he always looked at maps) he believed he was close to the borderlands here. Borders changed, mind you. Maps couldn't tell you about that.

He listened carefully now when he hid from people: farmers bringing their oxen in at twilight, girls washing clothing at a morning pond (pretty girls, one or two, but he was old, mostly past such thoughts).

Then one day Tijan Lubic heard the god named and thanked in the accents of the empire, of the north. He gave his own thanks to Jad then. Silently.

He went another day north to be sure, to be very certain. You could die if you didn't make yourself certain of some things. Sundown that next day he saw the small dome of a sanctuary in a village by another pond and heard the evening bells summon men and women to the god's rites and—dressed in stolen clothing, no longer an enemy uniform—Tijan Lubic went into that sanctuary and knelt before the altar and the sun disk, and he prayed with the ten people there and a very young cleric, lifting his voice to be heard by those around him, and by Jad.

Only after did he ask for food and drink and a pallet for the night. Only after did he tell them, cup in hand near a fire, where he had come from—alone, yes, alone—and what had happened there, and request directions to Woberg where he was bound, to tell the tale of the one hundred heroes of Senjan who had answered their emperor's summons, and what they had done to the army of the khalif before they died.

And in this way did that story—of serdars killed along with so many djannis and cavalry, and above all else, of that invading army's great guns destroyed in explosion after explosion on a spring night—come to the great fortress of Jad's Holy Emperor. From there it went on: to Obravic itself and the court, to Ferrieres, Seressa, Karch, Esperaña, Anglcyn, Rhodias and the Patriarch—to the world. To those who record the histories of the world.

To Senjan itself, by the islands and the sea.

He reached home that autumn, amid wind and blowing leaves and the first cold bura winds after the wine harvest, did Tijan Lubic. The only one from that company. None of the others made it home alive, none was ever found.

THE SMALL ENGAGEMENTS of a war kill as surely as do mighty sieges and sea battles or armies engaging each other, tens of thousands on each side, on a celebrated field.

Hrant Bunic did, in fact, navigate the rapids and the moonlit rocks, and he lived through the vast, wild roar of the waterfall, all of them tumbled out of their boat like chips of wood, smashing into the foaming chaos at the bottom. He actually made it to shore, pulling himself up, alive. But his leg was broken in several places and no one else was there to set it for him, even temporarily, and eventually the wolves found him, and they are not merciful.

The wife of the serdar of the djannis killed by the last explosion on the north side of the river took a knife to her wrists when the news reached her of his death and the manner of it. He had been a good and decent man from childhood and through his days.

Hrant Bunic's small son, much loved, grew up hating the Osmanlis with a fierce hatred, vowing vengeance in his father's name. He enlisted in the army of the next anointed emperor of Jad and died in a later war. There are always later wars.

We are children of earth and sky.

CHAPTER XXII

"We believe we will die soon," said the last surviving empress of Sarantium to the Eldest Daughter of Jad on Sinan Isle.

They were on the terrace. They were often there when the weather permitted. Late spring now, a mild day, little wind, the sea calm. Three of the younger women were in the garden working under the supervision of the older one who managed their herbs. They could hear bursts of laughter like birdsong. The labourers were beyond, in the vineyards sloping towards the water.

In the days of the previous Eldest Daughter the men had worked shirtless on warm days. Leonora had instructed that this was no longer acceptable. There had been regret expressed by some of Jad's daughters. Chastity and pure thoughts were an ideal of the retreats, but honoured in varying degrees from one to another.

Leonora was privately unsettled by how little she herself regretted the imposition of decorum. Desire seemed not to be a part of her any more. She couldn't find it, didn't feel any . . . wanting. It had been so important once, and not long ago.

Passion had changed her life. It had mastered will and obedience, led her to exile near Seressa—brought her here. She had loved Paulo Canavli with a need that reached past hunger. Later, she had lain with Jacopo Miucci in his home and on the ship, and now . . .

She did think about Pero Villani occasionally. Wondered if he'd reached Asharias. If he would live to return. He had spoken to her of love. From this terrace she could see the place on the harbour where they'd talked.

So there was that: she did think of him. *I am not an inconstant man.* But it couldn't be said that her nights were restless with these thoughts, or his absence. It disturbed her. Where had passion gone?

On the other hand, she couldn't find any ardent piety within herself either. No longing for that purer communion with the god that defined the truly virtuous.

It was possible, Leonora thought, that she'd had too much change too swiftly. She needed time to grow into what she was now, or *decide* what she was now.

It had occurred to her to confide in the empress, but Eudoxia was not someone who inspired intimacies. Fear, rather, an extreme sense of caution. She had been someone with very great power once.

"Surely none of us really knows that," she said now to the older woman. "As to our dying. Unless you are ill. Are you?"

She kept her manner cool. It seemed necessary with this woman. Weakness was not to be shown. They heard laughter again. The sun was on the terrace at this hour, warm and healing, summer coming.

"It is a feeling, not a god-sent knowing, girl. We said *believe*, didn't we?"

"You did. We are all dying, aren't we?"

Eudoxia made the sound Leonora had learned was her laughter. "You're a cold one," the empress said.

A little near the bone, given her thoughts. Leonora shook her head. "I am careful with you. You have taught me to be so."

The other woman looked at her. Eudoxia had a shawl over her shoulders, even in the sun. But her eyes were clear and her colour was good. She didn't look like someone dying.

They heard girls' voices rise and fall from the garden. A man shouted an order in the vineyard.

"We wish to be buried at Varena," said the empress. "Beneath the mosaics of which you spoke. The two empresses."

Leonora felt a chill. "You said they were . . ."

"A whore and a barbarian. We did say that. And you told us we were unjust. And you were right."

"I don't under—"

"You can be cold and be right, Leonora Valeri." A thin smile. "We often were. Sometimes it is the only way *to* be right about the world." She looked away, towards the sea, which was bright and blue and white in the sunlight.

"They were empresses," she said. "We will be content to lie with their images above us."

She died five days after. No signs of illness, no distress the evening before. She simply did not wake in the morning for prayers, was found lying in her bed, hands folded on her breast. Had lived twenty-five years too long, she would have said.

Leonora wept that night as if her heart was breaking piece by piece, the way she imagined a fortress or city wall might slowly crumble under the thunder of cannons drawn up close. She wasn't *a cold one*. She wasn't cold at all, she thought. And would never now have a chance to say that, in reply.

DUBRAVA DID SEND the body in a small coffin within a larger one, of sandalwood and silver, on a ship across the water and then by road to Varena. The Djivo family's *Blessed Ingacia* was in harbour and carried her. The rector and Gospodar Andrij Djivo (widely

seen as a likely successor) were on board, along with other dignitaries of the republic that had sheltered her for many years. The
ship flew two lowered flags, Dubrava's and Sarantium's.

The Empress Eudoxia was laid to rest in a small chapel in
a ceremony of considerable majesty, attended by high-ranking
clerics from Rhodias, accompanied by emissaries to the High
Patriarch from across all Jaddite lands. She lay, as she had
requested, beneath mosaics made by an unknown artist almost
a thousand years before—works that included two other women
who had worn porphyry in Sarantium.

They prayed, that glittering company, that her soul might rest
with Jad in light, and they spoke of the lamentable fall of the City
of Cities, and then they left and went about their days and duties
and pleasures—as men and women do.

Afterwards, when the chapel was empty again, still and silent,
with late-day sunlight coming in through high windows, one man
returned.

He knelt beside where the empress had just been interred, and
though he'd been only a child twenty-five years ago, he spoke
above her body an apology, through grief he had not expected, that
the terrible fall had been allowed—by all of them.

Then Drago Ostaja prayed, alone in that place, to the god of
light, but also to his beloved son Heladikos, who had been worshipped in the east once, that mercy and grace be extended to the
woman lying here. It mattered to him that Heladikos be named
today. He had not known this would be something he needed to
do. We do not always know.

Then he rose and made the sign of the sun disk above where
the body was, and again before the altar, and then he left and was
never in Varena again in his life.

But there were three empresses from that day forward in the
simple chapel beside the larger sanctuary. Two rendered in tesserae
on facing walls (one with love), amid their glittering courts, and

one under red-and-grey marble in two coffins, no longer enraged and sorrowing, no longer remembering.

☙❧

Danica woke from a dream of her mother. That didn't happen often. It was as if that time was walled off in some way. On the other side of a barrier in her mind.

She was young in the dream. They were still in the village. She had Neven's head in her lap. He was two years old perhaps, falling asleep, and their mother was telling them a story at darkfall. Danica's father and older brother and grandfather were still in the fields but due back soon, and the small house would become loud and warm with their presence. With luck, young Neven would be asleep by then.

But in the dream it was quiet and their mother was telling them a story of Esperaña long ago: about the brave horsemen who had conquered the Asharites of Al-Rassan and reclaimed the western world for Jad and light. Taking cities back one by one until they had them all, led by their great hero, Fernan Belmonte, son of a great father.

Danica could hear her mother's voice in the dream, see her face, hands gesturing, though shadowed, as it was growing dark but was still too early to light a fire. Firewood was precious and would wait on the three men. Their own heroes.

When she woke, Rasca was still asleep beside her. He badly needed rest. They'd had a violent few days. Danica lay waiting for the light, and remembering. Memories, she thought, were tangling things. They brought you ease and they brought you sorrow, and the same images and people could do both.

They had burned a village the night before. Twenty-five of them were riding with Skandir now. The raid had been partly a test for the newest recruits. Here in the eastern part of Trakesia the

Osmanlis had been settling people, building temples to Ashar and the stars or converting sanctuaries, to achieve a long-term change.

Jaddites were still allowed to live among them, paying the head tax for their faith, but it had been judged by the Osmanlis that security was better when good star-worshippers occupied the best land.

Unless it should happen that security was undermined, or destroyed, by the demon Skandir and his band ranging, swift and unseen, to attack them.

Danica and three new archers (she'd been training them in their usual tactics) had been stationed at the edge of the village to shoot those fleeing the fires. Skandir never took hostages to ransom. That wasn't his way. It wasn't why he did this, why he lived.

It had been a savage, brilliantly successful raid. The night had been smoky and red behind them when they left.

They had ridden swiftly, so that little trace of their presence would remain—that they might be seen as avenging spirits who could appear anywhere under the stars, and kill.

He had spoken to her here, in a room together, before they slept. He was a watchful man, in the way leaders of men needed to be, Danica had decided some time ago. Hrant Bunic in Senjan had been like that.

"You are all right?" he'd asked. "First time we fired a village like that."

She knew what he meant. She'd told him her story, hadn't she?

"This is what I joined you to do."

"Is it? Not for a life of pleasure and ease?"

"No." She hadn't felt like jesting.

He'd looked at her. "What will you say to the god when you go to him for judgment?"

Well, that wasn't a jest.

She thought about it. His face looked drawn after three days of hard riding either side of the night raid.

She said, "I'll ask Jad why my family and village had to suffer and die, and depending on the answer I'll accept his judgment of my soul."

"Accept? That isn't very pious."

"No. But I believe I am, in my way."

He really was tired. His expression was odd. "Maybe so. We live a certain kind of life, Danica."

"I know it," she said. "I don't expect to live very long."

He had offered a small, wry smile she could picture now, lying beside him. "Neither did I," he'd said.

He slept, heavily. She was awake in the dark before dawn. Of course she'd dreamed of her own village tonight, after what they'd done.

A certain kind of life.

ଔ

He had been born in Seressa, hadn't he? Amid sophistication and music by the canals, and the muscular presence of power, even if they had never been wealthy themselves. Pero had also seen Rhodias—several times!—taken there first as an apprentice by his father to view the palaces and ruins and the art. They had met with aristocrats and important clerics who'd treated his father with some respect (not overmuch, but some). He *knew* great cities. He had even felt a little superior, walking the smaller elegance of Dubrava before beginning the journey overland.

He didn't feel superior now. He understood that they wanted him afraid, daunted, awed—and he was. He was prone on a green-and-yellow tiled floor, hands extended before him in urgent suppli-cation. And the khalif was not even in the room yet.

He was an infidel, permitted unprecedented entry into the Palace of Silence. Such a one awaited the supreme ruler of the Osmanli people in a position of uttermost submission. If the khalif never came, the Jaddite could remain like this all day, all night. Hostility was in the air around him like a vibration.

Some of the men in this room would, Pero understood, be delighted to kill him. Some of them—the djanni guards with their tall hats—had swords with which to do so.

He had been briefly happy, even excited, following the vizier through an unlocked gold-and-silver gate and along the pathways of a perfected garden to this room—to begin his work.

He had entered through an open pair of doors, and had been immediately struck hard across the back of his knees by the flat of a sword, so that he fell forward to the floor. Anger, briefly. He had already been *told* the rituals here, he had been prepared for them, they hadn't needed to strike him.

On the other hand, he thought, the guard had likely not wished to deprive himself of the pleasure.

So Pero lay face down, heart beating fast. He couldn't really see anything. Only booted or slippered feet. He tried to calm himself, to think about the green leaves on the orange trees in the garden, how he might use them in the background of a portrait, but as they waited, in silence, his mind kept going further back.

This impossible city of present and past did that to you: it sent the mind back in time. He had discovered this over the past days, ever since they'd passed through the triple walls.

He had tried to grasp Asharias as it now was, superimposed upon what had been Sarantium. There was immense richness here for an artist, a colourful, cacophonous splendour to the Osmanli city, from the canvas-roofed markets to the harbour food stalls and shops, to the gardens everywhere. Asharites loved gardens, because of their faith's origin in desert sands—or so it was said.

But all these had been, for Pero, like an overlay on an already painted canvas: added to, superimposed upon the City of Cities that the Emperor Saranios had built long ago, and named for himself.

In those first days, waiting for an audience so his commission could begin, Pero had walked the city, leaving the palace complex. He'd been assigned quarters among other artisans in a cluster of buildings and workshops but he was allowed to wander freely outside. There was no fear among the Osmanli lords of this city, certainly not of a Jaddite painter. He saw that they hadn't even entirely repaired the walls by the harbour, the ones they'd shattered with their cannons. What danger was there, truly, under the holy stars, for Asharites here?

Well, they might fear each other, and defend their khalif with ferocity. There was extreme caution exercised within the palace grounds. Pero was housed in the outermost part of the complex, near the gates to the square outside. Tomo had not been permitted to attend him or even to enter when they'd arrived. Pero had protested politely; he had been rebuffed (politely).

In the palace complex, only those they had chosen and trained (and usually gelded) could attend and serve. It was not a matter for discussion with a Jaddite. Besides, the official assigned to him had said, Signore Villani's man, he of the name Agosta, was not an art apprentice, not a necessary assistant for the portrait, he was only a servant. They had much better servants, Pero was assured. Women would also be made available, of course, at his request.

Pero hadn't requested. He'd wondered how they knew these things about his servant. And what else they knew. Tomo had been escorted to make his way by ferry across the strait, to where the Jaddite merchants had their rooms and space to trade. All, except those from Dubrava. The Dubravae were allowed a residence, trade halls, and warehouses within Asharias itself—a gesture of extreme favour. (Their lowered tariff rates were an even more valued gesture.)

Pero had met Marin Djivo outside the palace gates one morning after receiving a message from him. They walked across the square to the vast Temple of Ashar's Stars—which had been, until twenty-five years ago, the Sanctuary of Jad's Holy Wisdom, built for Emperor Valerius nine hundred years ago to be a wonder of the world.

It was. Djivo had been inside before. He actually warned Pero as they approached the colossal doors, looking at the side domes and up at the one great golden dome above them all.

Even with the warning he had been overwhelmed. It was as if something had begun squeezing his heart like a fist, making it difficult to think, even to breathe. He had known this was here, of course he had. He had read of how travellers were undone, shaken by its grandeur. He had just this moment been *warned* . . . and none of that mattered. Some things you could not be ready for, Pero Villani thought, and wished, with a hard inward ache, that his father had lived to come here with him and see this.

Pity and sorrow and wonder were threaded in him: as a worshipper of Jad (the god now lost here), as a man who aspired to make art that mattered, and simply as someone living in the world, moving through his days until they ended. How did one deal with what this place was—now and before?

It was quiet at the hour they entered. The morning call for prayer had come and been answered and the prayers were done before they walked in, two unbelievers in what had been a sanctuary built at the peak of Sarantium's glory to the glory of their god.

The architect had been a man named Artibasos. Pero knew that much. The only name left from all those who had devised and laboured here.

Glory, Pero thought, and it was as if the word kept echoing in his head amid actual echoes of distant sounds in the dim light that ran off into darkness. The Asharites kept their holy places softly lit, to sustain the illusion of a protecting night when the killing desert sun had gone.

Stars hung above them, thousands and thousands of metal stars swaying from chains at varying heights through the immensity of the temple. Some far overhead, some just out of reach. They were beautiful and strange, and only a man walled off in his own faith would deny there was something holy about this place, even so greatly changed.

The colossal marble columns and the marble floor were from the first construction, Pero knew. The doors were new (the original ones had honoured Jad), and there were no mosaics now—or only fragments. But he also knew that most of the mosaic work had been destroyed long before the Asharites, in the years when Sarantium was riven by battles of doctrine. The winners of that fight, for a time, had been those who saw art rendering the god inside a sanctuary (or rendering anything else, according to some) as a heresy worthy of fire.

Men were very eager, Pero Villani thought, looking about, to burn each other.

The faith of Jad had moved on in the centuries between then and now. But the work of the nameless craftsmen on these side domes, these walls, or on the impossibly high dome at the centre, above where they stood just then . . . their art and craft hadn't moved on, not through time, not to be seen today by Viero Villani's son, or by anyone.

They would have been works of the heart, Pero thought, with certainty: of training and skill and faith and love, born of the desire to do something well in the eyes of the god and mankind in a place of majesty. Such things could be, they *were*, so often lost.

His father and mother lay in a cemetery in Seressa under a single carved headstone with a distant view of the lagoon. *I am very far away*, he thought.

He looked up at the high curve of the great dome, itself so far away, receding into darkness, beyond him, and he thought of his own destroyed portrait of Mara Citrani, and he thought, *I am among those greater than me in that.*

There was, strangely, comfort in the awareness.

He walked under the hanging, swaying stars, thinking of mosaics and his father. After a time he said to the other man, who had stayed in stride with him, courteously silent, "Thank you for warning me."

"Did it even help?" Marin Djivo asked.

Pero shrugged. He didn't know the answer. He remembered something, though, a request made, and standing there he prayed in silence for the Empress Eudoxia, and the souls of her husband and son, as he had promised he would do if he came into this place.

They walked out. Djivo took him diagonally across the huge square to see the smashed and looted remains of what had been the Hippodrome, where fifty thousand men and women would gather to watch men race chariots in the presence of the emperors of Sarantium long ago.

Truly long ago. And here as well the centuries had had their way with the works of man. One needed to enter carefully under crumbling arches, over jumbled paving stones, through a dark, covered space that led from twisted metal gates to open, grassy ground. Wildflowers and weeds grew, untended.

No Asharite garden here. The Osmanlis seemed to be leaving it a ruin, perhaps in memory of conquest, what they could do.

What time could do, Pero thought.

The stands of the arena were crumbling stone all the way around, pale amber in the morning's light, beautiful in their ruin, he thought. He wondered if he could paint that colour, the one just there, where the sunlight was falling.

There were toppled statues in the long inner oval around which the chariots would have run. He tried to imagine a race day, the loud, excited crowd, the emperor and his court up in that box—Djivo was pointing to it now—come to watch men and horses wheel and run like thunder amid the thunder of their cheering. He couldn't.

He couldn't picture it. He had nothing to draw upon. He looked at sunlight falling warm on stone, halfway to gold.

They strolled through a late-spring morning and they were, astonishingly to Pero, nearly alone in there. On the far side, he saw a lightly garbed woman lead a man by the hand from this open space into the covered arcade and out of sight. A transaction would now take place, Pero knew. Probably one that had happened here ever since the racing and the cheering stopped. There had been riots here, too, at times, he knew that.

Birdsong, flutter of wings, bees among the flowers, distant sounds of the city. Pero stopped at one point and tried to read the words on a monument in the infield. It was fallen, broken, and the Trakesian letters were faded where they remained. Someone named Taral . . . or perhaps Taras . . . had won some (unreadable) number of races and been . . . honoured? . . . and . . . a word that looked like exalted . . . with this everlasting . . .

Everlasting.

There was a bas-relief carving on another fallen stone. He looked at this for a long time, unexpectedly drawn to it. A man in profile, long straight nose, curled short hair, beardless chin. A charioteer, doubtless. Handsome, subtle in the details, a craftsman's work, an artist's, and it was lying here broken, lost. No name to this subject that he could see. It might be on another fragment nearby. He didn't look for it. He did look at the sculpted face.

He wouldn't know it for some time, but his life changed in that looking. That can happen to us, too.

They'd gone out the same way they'd come in. The two of them had a companionable glass of wine nearby, with lamb cooked over an open grill on skewers. Then Djivo returned to waiting for his goods to be assessed by the customs officials, so that he could bring them to the marketplace, and sell them, and do his buying, and start home. And Pero had gone back to be searched and readmitted into the palace compound.

A man was waiting for him there to say he was to make his formal abasement and begin work the next day.

The khalif would give him time early each morning and would stop the sitting whenever it pleased him to do so each day, and the sessions would conclude entirely whenever he chose. How long would that be? It was not for the Jaddite to ask questions.

Pero was to understand that if he spoke a single word aloud in the presence of Gurçu the Destroyer in the Palace of Silence his tongue would be ripped out before he was killed.

The khalif valued silence greatly. Everyone knew.

HE HAD BROUGHT ultramarine blue (derived from lapis), which was the most precious. He also had azurite, less expensive, less intense, a green-grey shade of blue, for parts of a work that required less assertion. He had discovered (and was pleased with himself for doing so) an effect that occurred when you used an undercoat of azurite and put ultramarine over it. Expensive, yes, but extremely beautiful.

Pero loved blue, almost a weakness. Smalt was the most affordable undercoat hue, and he'd brought that with him, too.

His principal red was what artists in Seressa called red lake, from the kermes beetle—which was found here in the east, of course, but he hadn't been certain they'd have it waiting for him, so he'd brought his own, along with hematite to grind and make into porphyry, the red-purple of emperors, once.

He had verdigris which, handled carefully, offered a dark, rich green.

He'd brought no yellow he entirely liked, hoped to find a good one here, because his preferred yellow orpiment required arsenic to mix, and he'd dared not carry poison into the palaces of the khalif.

Well, in truth, he'd been daring to do so, a different, hidden vial, until Marin Djivo said it would surely kill him since it *would* be found. He had a memory of himself by a stream west of here, pouring it out into rushing water.

He had gold leaf, most expensive of all, and assumed he could obtain more if he needed it—this *was* Asharias and a portrait of the khalif, after all.

He was going to have to bind his colours with egg tempera. He had decided that even before boarding the *Blessed Ingacia*. He preferred working with oil to bind now, not tempera, but the simple truth was that it took too long to dry, required the subject to sit more often and for longer (Mara Citrani had been happy to do so), and he couldn't risk that in Asharias. Egg tempera it was. The freshest eggs the palace servants could find.

He couldn't glaze properly working with this, or achieve the same effects as with oil, but there were advantages to using the older egg-based paint. One was that he was deeply uneasy here and would be happy to be done quickly, to have done well, and to go home. If he did do well, if they let him go.

He'd been lying in his bed thinking all of this. He hadn't slept much. It was almost dawn, the day after he'd seen the temple that had once been the sanctuary, and had walked in the ruins of the Hippodrome.

The servant they'd assigned him arrived, bringing his breakfast, and he laid out Pero's clothing. His first session of work. The servants would have been told.

There had been, unsurprisingly, considerable jealousy among the artists in the School of Miniatures, none of whom (not one, it seemed) had ever been inside the Palace of Silence where Villani—the infidel, the Seressini—was inexplicably being permitted entrance.

Pero had been assigned a room among the miniaturists at first. It hadn't lasted. Two of his prepared canvases had been found slashed, and though he'd said nothing—he wasn't going to need them, given that he was using tempera—he had been moved the next day to his present room among the enamel-workers. The enamel-workers didn't appear to hate him as much.

The officials of the grand vizier, a Kindath named Yosef, evidently monitored *all* events in the palace compound, even the smallest.

YOSEF BEN HANANON was aware of certain things that had elevated him to his position as the much-feared vizier to the grand khalif, and of some others that had kept him in that position for an almost unprecedented period of time.

Viziers—indeed, most high-ranking officials in Asharias— tended to be eunuchs. Sometimes, instead, they were Kindath, followers of a marginal, often-derided faith. The principle was the same: members of neither group could have any hope of achieving something dynastic. They would owe everything, including their continued existence, to the khalif's mercy and grace.

Beyond this, competence had been the essence of Yosef's survival. He knew what the khalif and the empire needed from him and he was pleased to be able to provide these things. He enjoyed good food, and bodily comfort and the opportunity to converse with intelligent men. For these rewards (and a few others) he offered diligent service. He was not averse to ordering men killed although, to be just, he didn't take pleasure in it, unlike some of his predecessors.

The detailed report on the belongings and companions of the Seressini artist, one Villani (younger than expected, but it didn't appear to amount to a slighting of the court), had been presented to him.

One of the other Seressinis, a merchant, had died only days from Asharias. A matter worth noting—and it had been noted. It appeared to be a traveller's mischance, or possibly a feud among the Jaddites, greed leading to deadly consequence. That was not a matter for the court, nor was it unusual.

The artist's supplies had been (of course) examined. They appeared to be in order, according to the report. One paint pot was missing in the case that carried these, a space for it was empty. But paint pots were fragile and breakage to be expected. The other pots contained what they were said to contain. That is: paints, already prepared or to be mixed, of diverse hues.

The vizier remained uncertain as to precisely why the khalif wished his image rendered in the western fashion, but Gurçu had never been in the habit of explaining himself, and his vizier saw no reason *not* to have this portrait happen.

The artist would be in some danger from others in the palace grounds. Yosef ben Hananon felt a mild curiosity regarding this.

The westerner's servant was of some concern. He was only a manservant, it appeared, not someone trained to work with an artist—which one might have expected.

He had been denied access to the palace. Yosef approved of this. Having their own people attend upon the artist gave them more control over him. The manservant, Agosta, attempted to find a position with the Dubravae trader first but had not been accepted and he was across the strait in the Seressini colony.

He wasn't of great interest, but a man had been assigned to follow him and report. Drink and women, thus far. He sang when intoxicated. Jaddites, on the whole, tended to be lacking in self-restraint.

The vizier, deeply versed in self-restraint, was endlessly aware that his life—which contained luxuries unimaginable to him a decade ago—could end with a word from the throne. It would, of course, be a quiet word, but would never be indecisive, or reversed. His gratitude was extreme nonetheless, and his loyalty unswerving. Eunuchs and Kindath: the best people to be given power. He proceeded that way himself in making appointments.

It was the same principle employed with the djannis in the army, from the ranks of which each of the khalifs chose his own guards. The Jaddite-born djannis also owed loyalty only to the throne. They could be, it was true, dangerous when peacetime extended too long (when there were no rewards to be claimed, east or west), or when there was a change of power in the palace—or even a rumour of change.

This was, in part, why the Osmanli empire was usually at war. It was certainly why a new khalif always had his siblings and any strong-willed family members strangled. There were *reasons* for traditions.

With Gurçu, that had all happened years before Yosef had become a member of the Courtyard of Silence, let alone grand vizier. Gurçu the Destroyer had ruled for thirty years now. He showed few signs of weakness and his two surviving sons (who hated each other for the obvious reasons and a few more) were both infinitely careful—most of the time.

IT WAS THE VIZIER HIMSELF who stood waiting to greet him at the gold-and-silver gate to the inner courtyard. He was clad in black with a crimson belt and hat. Pero had bowed, then did so again, as instructed—even to a Kindath.

When he straightened, he glimpsed a garden beyond the man and the gated wall. The vizier was thin, long-bearded, a man of gravity, close-set eyes and a close gaze. He wasn't old, the beard was dark. Pero had thought that this was a face he'd like to draw or paint. He'd wondered if it would be a transgression to do so in his sketching books.

His palms had been sweating. He'd dried them on his tunic, hoped the other man wouldn't notice, then decided that of course he would.

"You understand how you are honoured?" the vizier had said in Trakesian, without any greeting. His voice was deep, sonorous. There were three other officials with him and four djannis guarding the gate.

Pero nodded. "I do, my lord." His voice seemed to be all right.

And as if that thought had been read, the vizier said, "You also understand that you speak no words at all past this gate." He smiled without amusement. "There is a reason it is called the Courtyard of Silence."

Pero had been awaiting this moment, had lain awake dreading it in the nights.

"That is not possible," he said firmly.

There was a stir. One of the guards slowly turned his head to stare at Pero. A blond man with pale, murderous eyes, very tall.

The vizier had remained expressionless. He touched his beard briefly. He said, "I fear you may not have understood. This is not subject to amendment in any way. The khalif, blessed forever, permits no speech in these gardens or rooms."

A deep breath. "Then I cannot paint his portrait in these gardens or rooms," said Pero Villani of Seressa. "Unless you wish me to gesture without explanation how he should sit, or move, or hold his head. Or use my hands to position his body, which I would not do."

"You would die if you did that, yes," said the vizier. "Or even made to approach more nearly than where you will be instructed to stand."

Pero shook his head. He was very much afraid. There were, he thought, so many ways a man could die. At home, far away, known or obscure, young or old, quietly, violently.

He said, "That, too, makes this impossible, my lord. I must decide myself where I stand, and consider with him where the khalif will be."

The vizier could, after all, look disconcerted. No more than a lifting of the head, but it was there. Artists could be observant too, Pero thought. And were famously difficult. He was remembering the Council of Twelve at night: he had been reckless there as well. What was it that happened to him in situations such as this?

The officials were glaring openly now. The guards seemed willing, anxious you might even say, to use their weapons on the Jaddite right here, end this folly.

Unfortunately for this desire on their part, the folly—though it could never be named so—was that of Grand Khalif Gurçu. Who had made his wishes known and had sent for an artist to achieve them.

Pero said, "Either a portrait is done in our manner, as requested, or it cannot be done. I am content to convey my great respect to the khalif, through you, and return home. The journey has been interesting. But I will not do less than my best work here, it would shame me. And my best work requires that certain things be as they are for all portraits."

"And these would be?" The vizier's voice was measured.

"I must be able to assess the light and furnishings in the chosen room, and adjust or add to these elements—window coverings, wall hangings, a chair, a throne perhaps. I must be able to request that my subject take different positions so that we can, together, decide what is most appropriate for the work."

"You would *decide* something with the khalif?"

"With him, yes. Some artists are arrogant and they decide alone. But for me, the subject's wishes remain paramount. I must know what these wishes are, and advise as a painter what can and cannot be done to gratify them." He looked at the vizier, at the hooded eyes. "I will do exactly the same things with the Duke of Seressa when I paint his portrait on my return, for the council chamber of the palace. This is, my lord vizier, what we *do*, to satisfy our subjects and honour our craft. No one is ever compelled to have their portrait painted. Unless, perhaps, a child made subject to a parent's will."

There was a silence. The sun was rising, it was early morning.

"You will wait here," said the grand vizier.

He turned. A guard unlocked and opened the gate, the vizier went through. The gate was closed and locked. It was magnificent. Silver and gold intertwining, with stars.

Pero waited among men who—he entirely understood—would joyfully see him dead.

He was quite calm now.

A EUNUCH WOULD BE PROVIDED. An older man, of long service, evidently privileged—he had to be, since he was permitted to speak.

Pero would whisper—only when absolutely necessary, and as delicately as possible—into the ear of this man, who would cross the room and whisper the same words (one hoped) to the grand khalif of the Osmanli people.

In this way might the khalif's form or visage be caused to turn slightly to the left or right, his illustrious head be lifted a little higher to catch the light differently.

"This must be acceptable," the vizier said. He actually looked uneasy, as if he *needed* agreement.

"It is acceptable," said Pero.

After a moment, the vizier nodded to the guards. The same man opened the gate again.

Pero followed the vizier into the Garden of Silence and then, past peacocks and orange trees and three small, splashing fountains, into a large ground-level room in a building on the other side, with windows opening onto the garden.

It had been then that the flat of a sword struck him on the back of the knees and he fell forward to the tiled floor. He was still like that, hands outstretched, awaiting the khalif of the Asharites in the Palace of Silence.

A further passage of time ensued. Unearthly long, in the circumstances. Pero was sweating. He heard men breathing above him but no one spoke. Of course no one spoke. He sought an image within that might calm him, anchor him, and what came was Leonora Valeri's face.

He had told her that he loved her. And seeing her now in the eye of his mind he understood this was true, and would remain so.

There might be sorrow in the end, he thought (if he even lived), but there was someone in the world whose existence eased his own. He didn't believe she understood this. He did, however, and his breathing slowed.

A door opened.

Pero lay motionless. The door closed. A footfall, another behind it. A shadow cast in front of him on the floor, sunlight through a window, falling across a man. He did not dare look up. He had no idea how he would know when he could, or should. Would someone kick him? Was that what they did? Moments passed. The breathing of frightened men. He was one of those.

"You had better rise," said a grave voice, in Trakesian, a voice even deeper than that of the vizier. "You can't very well paint my portrait while lying on the floor."

Someone gasped. Would that sound have the man killed, Pero wondered. He did as he was told. He pushed himself to his knees, and he looked up into the eyes of Gurçu the Destroyer.

CHAPTER XXIII

"You also have permission to speak," the khalif continued.

Pero gaped, his heart thudding. He swallowed, he hoped not noisily. He saw that the others in the room—including a handsome, younger man who had entered with Gurçu—looked shaken.

The khalif glanced around. He said, "I weary of empty words, unnecessary ones. I come here to escape this. But if I wish to *learn* things about your western art, and I do, I cannot do so with a silent painter. You will speak with me when we have these sittings. You will answer all questions I ask. It is understood?"

Pero swallowed again, managed to nod.

"You told my vizier we would decide together how the work is to be done. Very well. Let us commence."

Pero opened his mouth. He had no idea what he should say. His mind was blank as a linen canvas. Gurçu held up a quick, imperious hand. Long fingers, three rings, a blue gem, a red, a silver band.

"Wait. Hold. First, everyone else will go."

The vizier startled in dismay. He gestured at his own chest, for permission to speak.

The khalif shook his head. "Lakash will remain as a guard against this obviously dangerous artist. Everyone else leaves. When the painter is to be escorted back, Lakash will summon men to do so. You," he pointed to Pero, "remain where you are, on your feet. I assume we begin today? What are you using to mix your paints? No. No. Wait until they are gone. And prepare thoughts on why rulers in the west desire their portraits done."

He looked around again. A pale face, long nose, eyes almost black, a thin body, that deep voice. It was, Pero thought, as if thunder had swept and rumbled through the room, a godlike storm, shaking all the mortals here.

Someone else spoke. It actually shocked him.

"Father, lord, might I entreat that you permit me to stay? For your protection and my own knowledge?"

Gurçu looked at the speaker, the handsome man who had entered behind him.

"No," he said. "There will be no one at these sittings but myself and my mute and this artist who—for reasons I will learn—was selected by the Council of Twelve for this task."

"Lord, is it not permitted to be as curious about such matters as the khalif?"

"It is. But in your own chambers, with your own readings and visitors to teach you. Cemal, I said no. You will rejoin me when the sitting is done each morning. Wait in the garden."

The handsome man pressed his hands together and bowed. He was an elegant figure, with his father's eyes and nose, and the name identified him. This was the older prince, the favoured son of the two who had been permitted to live.

Beyet, the younger, was alive as a kind of bloodline insurance, Marin Djivo had said, over wine and grilled lamb. Pero had understood: the younger prince was a surety against accident, illness, death in this one. Of course he could also *cause* accident, illness, death. He was, Marin had added, a check on premature ambition as well.

Premature ambition would hardly be unknown among the Osmanlis, any more than it was anywhere else, and this khalif had reigned many years now. His sons would have spent a long time waiting.

He had been instructed to stand. He did so, cautiously. It would be ill-advised, he thought, to move quickly here. The looks he was receiving from the guards and court officials were poisonous—and they also revealed fear. Survival, advancement would be shaped by *access*, and he—a miserable infidel artist—was now to be alone with the khalif every morning, speaking to him, *teaching* him, by request, in a place where no one spoke aloud or they died.

Well, it had always been possible he'd be killed here. It seemed rather more likely at this moment. The son, he noted, as the sleek figure glanced at him, didn't look murderous. Prince Cemal looked . . . Pero couldn't find the word. But it wasn't violent or fearful. Something else.

Not his concern. What would he be using to mix the paint? *That* was what Gurçu the Destroyer wanted to know? Oh, and why Pero Villani had been chosen to come to him.

A more delicate matter, that. He made a decision, standing there, trying to hold his head high without meeting the eyes of the guards, large men who gave every sign of wishing to use weapons on him.

He decided that he would answer with the truth—whenever he could—any and all questions of this hawk-faced man who wielded more power than anyone he'd ever known. More power than any-one alive, in truth.

Men were leaving the room. The vizier turned in the doorway and fixed Pero with a final glance. There was meaning in it, but Pero Villani had no idea what that meaning was. He was too far out of his element. His element was the tannery district of Seressa, or a bookshop across several arched bridges from there. Neither prepared you particularly well for the Palace of Silence in Asharias.

The vizier left the door open—deliberately, of course. Gurçu was expressionless, seeing that. The khalif crossed to a cushioned chair and seated himself. He nodded to his guard, and then at the door. The guard crossed the room and closed it.

"Unless the light is better with it open?" the khalif of the Osmanlis said to Pero Villani.

Pero cleared his throat. "The . . . the windows are the light we will need, I think. Depending on, well, determined by . . ."

"By what? We waste time if you stammer like a child."

With an effort, Pero resisted the impulse to clear his throat again. But really, how would a man not be fearful? He said, "Determined by your wishes and needs, my lord khalif. A commissioned portrait is worthless if it pleases you not."

"Only a commissioned one?"

Pero blinked. He saw a glimmer of pleasure in the other man's face. Gurçu took pride in cleverness, then. Pero said, "If I hire a model, or do a canvas from sketches made in public places, there is no sitter to please. Only myself, my sense of whether I have done well with a chosen subject."

"But here?"

"But here, or with the duke in Seressa, or anyone paying me, the subject has chosen me, lord. Or . . ." he found himself actually smiling a little, "since I was chosen by the duke *for* you, the subject has chosen to have himself rendered in a portrait, and that changes all."

"Because the subject can reject the finished work?"

"Yes, my lord. The subject here also has power of life and death over me. If I fail to please . . ."

An impatient gesture. "I wouldn't invite a man to come to me with the intention of doing him harm."

"Only if I transgressed?"

"Don't do that, then," said the khalif mildly. "How will you mix your paint?"

Pero looked at him. He was studying the features, in fact. The face and also the hands. He was thinking about the quick impatience just now shown again. How could a man with such absolute power *not* be impatient?

He said, "You have found reading material on western art? Have had people advise you, my lord?"

A brief silence. "Better just to answer my questions, Signore Villani."

Pero felt a chill. He lowered his head. Transgression, he thought, was easily accomplished here. Again, he managed not to clear his throat. He said, "I intend to use egg tempera, esteemed khalif. It has certain virtues for . . . for this particular commission and—"

"Because it permits you to work faster? Fewer sittings from me?"

Pero nodded his head.

"But you cannot paint on canvas then, or the paint will crack."

He *had* read a book on western painting, and Pero knew which one. It was astonishing. Pero said, "This is true, lord. I will need to prepare a wooden surface on which to—"

"This has been done. Three sizes for you to choose among, prepared after the manner instructed in your texts. If it is inadequate you are to tell me."

He did clear his throat this time. "I am . . . grateful, my lord."

That hint of satisfaction again. "I had imagined you would choose the method that allowed quicker work. Less demand on the subject, and you go home sooner?"

Pero nodded again. No one had warned him of this sharp intelligence, the curiosity in the dark eyes and lean face.

"Both are true, my lord. I did not presume that I could request as much of your time as oil-mixed painting demands. It dries much more slowly. There is a method some use to do oil-based painting with less demand on the subject but I do not prefer it, myself.

There are . . . there are other reasons I am comfortable with the older way of mixing paint."

"Tell them to me now," said Gurçu the Destroyer. "Then your first thoughts on how you propose to paint me in the western manner. You will show me where you think you want me to be. And before we are done this morning you will explain why you were chosen by Duke Ricci, and why western rulers want these portraits done. You will describe his appearance. And how you will describe me to him, because he will ask you. Then we will be finished for this morning. So. The preparing of paints, the advantages of each method. Begin."

HE BEGAN SHAKING when he was in his chamber again. He hoped the manservant hadn't seen it before he left the room, but when he was alone Pero sat on his bed and looked down at his trembling hands.

Tell him the truth, he repeated over and again in his mind. The khalif was too acute, too versed—all his life, Pero imagined—in mastering men, seeing into them, or leaving the impression that he could do that. Not a man to whom you tried to lie.

"I was chosen because I was judged talented, and also young enough, with little to lose, to be willing to risk the journey here. My father is dead. I have no family to lean upon, only my skills to take me through the world."

"And what skills do you bring, Signore Villani?"

He'd known what was being asked. Of course he did. With absolute truth he said, "None that signify beyond my art, exalted khalif. I know how to bind books, should that be required. I have a memory for faces, gestures, landscapes. That is . . . those are part of my craft, though."

"You will be able to describe for the Duke of Seressa what you have seen here? These gardens? The palaces? This room?"

"Yes. He will want to know. Just as . . . just as you asked me to describe him to you."

"Do that now," the khalif had said.

He hadn't seemed angry at any point. He was . . . attentive, his face betrayed nothing. A lifetime of being that way, Pero thought. Showing little. You needed to live long enough to become khalif. The impatience had probably come afterwards.

He thought of the prince, Cemal.

IN THE DARK of that same night, three men entered Pero Villani's bedchamber.

No lamps were burning and the fire had gone out. One man carried a candle—that is what woke Pero. Another moved quickly, before he could cry out, and placed a hard hand over Pero's mouth.

That one whispered, "Be silent. You will not be harmed. But only if you keep silent." Pero nodded understanding. What else was he going to do? If they wanted him dead he was dead right now.

The man stepped back. Pero saw sheathed blades by the candle's light. He didn't know these men. Why would he? They waited, watchful, while he dressed.

They took him from the room into blue moonlight and wind in the open space between palaces. He saw his manservant standing outside by the door staring straight ahead, seeing nothing—nothing at all untoward taking place in the night.

There was no one abroad at this hour, no guards on the grounds they crossed between the artisans' quarters and the nearest palace. They came to the doors. No one was on guard here either.

They entered and went immediately down a flight of stairs. Pero was terribly afraid. He knew what happened in underground rooms in Seressa to those who displeased the Council of Twelve.

But why would they need to take him anywhere and harm or kill him here? Before he'd even begun his work. For what he knew? For the poison he'd discarded in the stream? That wouldn't have to be done at night—and the khalif *wanted* his services.

That, he thought suddenly, might be why this was secret. Whoever had him now did not want it known by Gurçu. He summoned courage. He said, going down marble stairs, "You know the khalif will punish you if I am unable to do my work."

He received a blow on the back of the head. "You were instructed to keep quiet. Do so."

They reached the bottom and a corridor on that lower level. Pero saw worn-smooth flooring, cracked in places, tiles loose. There were sconces in the walls but no torches, only the lights carried by two of his captors. They were alone down here, footsteps echoing. It was the middle of the night.

They came to a heavy door. The man who had struck him took a key from his belt and turned it in a lock. He pulled the door open. It took some effort, scraped the floor.

"Go," said the man with the key. "We will be here. And will take you back when you come out again."

"Go? In there?" said Pero. "Alone?"

He remembered too late he was not to speak, but no blow came this time. Only contemptuous laughter. "You would prefer your mother came and led you by the hand? There is a tunnel, there are lights, it leads to one place only, a door on the far side. Knock when you reach it. Go."

And Pero was unceremoniously pushed into the tunnel. A hard push. He stumbled forward. The door closed behind him, a grinding sound. The key turned in the lock.

He was entirely alone, in the depths of night, in the depths of the earth, and almost immediately a strange sensation came to him—not the predictable fear.

He looked down the tunnel. There was a bend to the right, he could see by the torches on the walls. But what was strange was the uneasiness he felt—beyond the obvious reasons to be terrified.

What he was seeing in his mind's eye now was the object he'd touched in that forest in Sauradia, crawling through a glade.

He'd touched it, then set it down again. Skandir, after, had been visibly relieved to hear he'd put it back. And now it was as if he were seeing that artifact again, in the palace complex, underground, beneath torches in iron brackets, looking at long-ago mosaics on the floor.

He didn't understand at all, but there was a sense of *something* not natural down here. Not necessarily to be feared, though he was very much afraid of what was happening. No, the sensation he had, as he'd had in the glade, was of age, loss, a span of time.

Well, yes, he thought, trying to gain control of himself: this tunnel *was* old, it would have been built by an emperor long ago. He didn't know where it would lead; they'd said another door, so probably one of the other palaces.

He didn't seem to have a choice. He started walking.

He heard his footsteps, his breathing. It wasn't dark, there were torches all the way along the walls as the tunnel bent one way and then the other. The floor mosaics were chipped in many places, he saw, tesserae scattered. There were patterns, flowers, small birds at a small fountain. The object in the glade had been a bird, he thought. He stepped on mosaic pieces as he went.

At one point, for no reason he could understand, Pero felt a wave of sorrow pass through him. An old sorrow, not about himself or anyone here now, alive now, in the world. He stopped and looked around but saw nothing at all. He walked on and the sensation receded as he went.

He wondered what had happened here through the centuries, who had gone back and forth. Remarkable, that it was as well-preserved as it was. The torches flickered, the air was good. He kept walking as the tunnel bent and twisted sinuously (he had no idea why it wasn't straight), and it wasn't long before he saw the other door that had been promised and came up to it.

He looked back the way he had come. In what had to be an effect of the light, Pero thought he saw something that hadn't been there before, a flame on the floor of the tunnel at the last bend—low-burning, blue-green—and somehow it seemed to be moving. Moving and then gone, begotten of nothing he could see. He shook his head. He turned and, after a hesitation, knocked on the second door.

"*Welcome!*" said Prince Cemal, standing behind the attendant who opened the door. There were others behind Cemal, there were lights.

He was handsomely clad, the prince, in a heavy robe of the colour they called porphyry here. The colour of emperors once.

"I am so very pleased," he said, smiling, "that you have decided to join me."

HE'D HAVE THOUGHT that having armed men burst into his room would be the most frightening thing that happened tonight. It wasn't, in the event.

Pero followed the older son of the khalif, the one expected to be Gurçu's heir, along a corridor and then another. He expected to go upstairs again in this other palace. They did not. They came to a room on this underground level, lit by many lamps. It would have been a storeroom once, he guessed. Nothing was stored here now.

He saw an easel, paints and brushes, mixing bowls, cloths on a table, and a medium-sized wooden surface prepared for paint, already on the easel.

"Your paints have been mixed to instructions in a book from one of your western artists," said the prince. "The one my father read. Cennaro is the name, I believe? I am hopeful they will prove adequate."

Pero looked at him. The prince was undeniably handsome.

Broad-shouldered, tall (not as tall as the father), a full head of dark hair under a black velvet hat. He had the khalif's prominent nose and a neatly trimmed beard. He wore a floral scent, strong in the room.

"Adequate to what purpose?" Pero asked. He struggled to remain calm. "Why have you brought me here in this way, my lord?"

The prince smiled. He had good, even teeth. He gestured. "Surely it is obvious, Signore Villani?"

"I'm afraid it is not, my lord. Perhaps it is fatigue. I was awakened by armed men in my room."

The smile faded. "They were instructed to bring you with courtesy."

"They did not."

"Would you like them killed?" the prince asked gravely.

Pero stared at him. That could happen, he realized. He could say yes, and it was possible the men waiting by the other door would die. It chilled him. And with that, he felt anger stirring, as it had before the Council of Twelve (as it had not with the khalif).

"No," he said. "I would like to know why they were sent. Why I am here. My lord." There was such a need to be careful, he thought. He was too far from home.

The prince smiled again. He smoothed his gorgeous robe. He said, "To paint another portrait, of course. We will do this each night. I trust the room will serve?"

Well, you did ask, Pero Villani thought. It was, as the prince had implied, obvious that he was here to paint.

He said, carefully, "A portrait of you, my lord?"

The smile deepened. "Not quite," said Prince Cemal.

IT WAS NOT a situation in which he had a choice, discretion to decline. Signore Villani would have, the prince murmured after explaining the task ahead, *such* a long road home after finishing his portrait of the glorious khalif, might he live and reign forever.

There were so many dangers for a traveller. Better, surely, to ensure protection for that journey while in the palace complex, brought—much more courteously henceforth—from his room to this one each night.

He is going to have me killed, Pero thought, listening to what was wanted of him. *Either way, I am not going to survive this.*

If he declined, he was being warned he'd meet a regrettable end somewhere in Sauradia, or even before he reached that wilderness. But if he did as requested, he'd be the infidel who *knew* what had been done, and such men surely could not live.

He agreed to paint, to work here by night as best he could. He was an artist, it was what he was here to do, what his life was about. And perhaps Jad would guide him, guard him.

A portrait of you? he had asked the prince.

Only partially so. He was to paint this man in this room, show him standing by a window that would have to be imagined (he had done that before, they all did that). Show him wearing this robe that signified power and royalty by its colour.

But he was to render the face of the subject as Prince Beyet, the younger brother, not Cemal.

He would see the younger prince tomorrow, he was told: there was to be an archery display in the afternoon. This plan, Pero thought, looking at the easel and wood and the tools and paint beside them, had not been casually conceived.

The older son was reputed clever, Marin Djivo had said, the younger one more reckless. Perhaps less trusted because of that. Nothing had ever been announced from the throne, but it was widely believed Cemal was to succeed his father. After which, in a long tradition, Beyet would be strangled by guards.

So why do this? Pero wanted to ask.

In fact, he did ask it. Anger, again.

"It is shared about that you are the heir, my lord prince. Why do you need to—?"

He stopped at a gesture: swift, decisive, a hand across the throat as if to cut it. A gesture from a prince who didn't look at all gracious just then. A face, in fact, that one might paint as a figure in a battle scene, killing an enemy before him.

He lowered his head. "Forgive me," he said.

He looked up. Cemal gestured again—towards the easel and the paints. There were sketchbooks and charcoal, as well. And a basket of eggs. Someone had indeed read Cennaro, *The Handbook of the Art of Painting*. It was impossibly strange.

They began.

IT WAS THE robe that mattered as much as anything. Any artist, steeped in the meaning of symbols, had to know that. The colour, the implication of the colour. And then the features he would impose upon what he did here.

He was being used to destroy someone, Pero understood. It wasn't difficult to grasp. You didn't need to be a courtier, a diplomat, subtle as to eastern ways.

He worked steadily for some time. Three guards and a servant remained in the room. He was offered wine. He accepted. There was no rule of silence here. He told the prince how he needed him to position himself.

It would be a standing pose, more easily done. A profile, also easier, quicker. They had taken some care with what he'd been provided. Someone knew what might be required, had made a point of knowing.

With a charcoal stick he outlined a window to place behind Cemal. Behind Beyet, he corrected himself. He would put ships out there, he thought: water seen beyond the palace. The sea the khalif ruled from here, a prince in porphyry standing before it.

He wasn't tired now but he felt as if he wanted to be sick. There was death hovering, in every stroke he made with charcoal and then brush. He worked. What else was he to do?

"Enough, I think," Cemal said at length, speaking graciously again. "We meet in this room tomorrow night for the same purpose."

The prince had been patient. Taking the poses requested as Pero decided what he needed, remaining motionless in the one chosen, except when he drank his wine. And then he was good at resuming the position he'd held. You could call him an ideal subject. Better than Mara Citrani, who had liked to distract Pero while he worked, for amusement, and then to do other things because it pleased her to do so.

Cemal smiled again. "I need hardly say you will not speak of this, Signore Villani?" His expression was that of one worldly man speaking to another. You could paint that expression, too, Pero thought.

He shook his head. To whom would he speak of it and not die?

"There is," said Cemal, "one more thing. Though I trust you will see it as a reward, not a burden." He hesitated, as if unsure how much to say, then went on. "It is too soon for anyone to know of this room." *Until there is a face on that painting*, Pero thought. "But it may be that you will be seen crossing the grounds at night. Those men with you are retainers attached to my brother's household, not mine."

So they had been bought, Pero thought. He had not yet seen Prince Beyet, had no thoughts about him at all—except that the man was being prepared for destruction, and Pero was part of it.

Cemal's smile was beginning to disturb him. It came so easily. The prince said, "It is necessary, for the moment, to have a story as to why the Jaddite artist is abroad at night, in the event you *are* seen. Stories after dark often involve desire, have you not found this to be so?"

Pero saw one of the guards smile.

The prince said, "It will be put about that someone is rewarding you for your service to the khalif. Later, there will emerge a different tale."

This had been, Pero was realizing again, carefully thought

through. "So your brother is to be offering me a woman?" Anger in him. Again. *Be cautious*, he told himself. Again.

"Nothing so specific yet. But surely you agree it is better for you to be able to tell the truth, should my father ask about your nights?"

Pero closed his eyes. He tried to imagine that conversation.

Cemal went on, "A reward, and a truth you can tell the khalif—in that place where no one else is even allowed to speak."

"And if he asks who is rewarding me?"

"He will not. But if that happens of course you will tell the truth. Of course you will. And then, Signore Villani, you will be safe on the long way home."

Hardly, Pero thought. He kept his face expressionless. "So, there is a woman coming here for me?"

"Here?" The prince looked around at the bright, underground storage room. "No, no. No one comes here at all and—I need hardly tell you—my brother has not offered you any of his women."

"No," said Pero. "He hasn't."

"I have," smiled Cemal.

He turned to the guards. "Take him back to the tunnel. Do so with courtesy. The ones on the other side will lead him to his quarters—afterwards." He smiled again. "One of you go back through with him. Advise them to be helpful. He is likely to be fatigued, after. What Jaddite man will have encountered the palace women of Asharias?"

His guards laughed then, knowingly.

A BLACK ROOM. He was blind in it. No windows, although they were not underground now. He had gone through the tunnel again and once more he'd felt that strange, sharp sorrow (he would feel it every time he passed through). He didn't see the small, moving fire (he would again, other times).

A man had walked with him as commanded, and the others had been waiting when he knocked, as they'd said they would be. They didn't take him to his quarters. They led him up wide stairs in this first palace which was—he now understood—Cemal's, as the other one where he'd painted underground was Beyet's.

He'd understood by then that the younger prince's people over that way were not to learn what was being done in the middle of the night. Or, rather, only those who had been bought could know.

Blackness here, but one could be aware in darkness—intensely aware—of scent, and Pero knew there was a woman in this room, waiting for him.

More than one, he realized.

Desire touched him against his will, as cool fingers did. There was a bed to which he was led by whispers he could not understand, because they were speaking Osmanli. Although, when certain sounds are heard in the dark, close to your ear, and fingers and mouths are touching you, and those same fingers begin to address themselves to your clothes, it is any language and every language that men and women know.

He felt anger again in the midst of this. Even now. He couldn't help it. He was from Seressa, Queen of the Sea, celebrated (notorious!) for both its brothels and its aristocratic women, masked or otherwise, in elegant rooms above the canals. Known throughout the world for the skills of the women (and the men) one could find after dark, and Pero was no stranger to brothels, though not the expensive ones. Besides, in the artists' districts of the republic there were women who had been generous and needful with him out of affection, shaped by their own desire.

He was not, in short, any kind of stranger to lovemaking. He felt as if he was being mocked here in this overly contrived, perfumed blackness. That they imagined the innocent Jaddite painter would be helplessly overwhelmed by the mysteriously skilled, exotically scented women of the east, offering delights unknown in the primitive west.

It was close to an insult, he thought. A crude jest shaped of a lazy fantasy. More than likely men here in Asharias attributed the same secrets and mysteries to women in Seressa, or at the court of Ferrieres. And surely the languorous women under the hot sun of Esperaña, in shaded rooms in afternoons, knew things no man could resist.

What did they think he was? How childlike? How susceptible to foolishness?

And yet . . . who could control what aroused? How could he deny he was hard, excited, even before a mouth belonging to someone he never saw closed over the tip of his sex and moved down, and others found his nipples with their fingers, and then one came to his mouth with her mouth, and then her breast. There were three women. It was dark.

And these were not women one bought for a night in the streets of Asharias. He was in the palace of the khalif's son. These would be Cemal's women. He had heard there were thirty of them. He had heard there were twice that many. Men told wild stories in their folly.

But that was, of course, the real reason it was black in this room, for as surely as Ashar had gone out among the desert stars, no infidel could be with the women of an Osmanli prince like this and live.

He wasn't going to survive in any case, Pero Villani thought, even as someone guided him inside herself with an urgent hand and made a sound he'd heard before. He felt her begin to ride above him, and there were whispers from the others, and yes, through anger—perhaps *driven* by anger—his own desire, his need, was great. He felt shame and hunger both and he believed he was soon to die. There was that, too, shaping a blind (truly blind) impulse towards lovemaking.

They took turns with him, variously, before he left that room. Before he was permitted by them to leave, stumbling into the corridor, blinking in the light of lamps held by guards who led him, finally, to his room. And the same thing happened the next night, and again, each time he was brought back from painting a portrait in the palace at the other end of the tunnel.

This was, Prince Cemal had said, to be the reason—for now—the Jaddite might be glimpsed in the palace grounds in the night. Then there would be a moment when a shocking painting was accidentally discovered and the story would change and people would die.

He thought it might be different women each time. He couldn't be certain. It was impossible to be certain of anything. Except that you could be angry and frightened, feel mocked, yet be enclosed in scent and murmurs, smoothness and someone else's need, and feel a hard desire beyond any words. And even in the depths of that black room there were images he would claim, or devise.

IN MORNING LIGHT after that first night Pero Villani splashed his face with cold water. He drank the steaming-hot morning drink they offered here. Demanded another. An acquired taste. He didn't have it yet but it helped to wake him, burning his tongue.

Then he went with an escort to the Courtyard of Silence and entered through the same gate as before and crossed the garden past the orange trees and resumed painting the grand khalif, which was why he was here.

He answered questions about the west as he worked. About leaders and customs in Seressa and elsewhere, as best he knew, even about the doctrines of Jad. Many questions in that deep voice.

Afterwards, that second day, Pero was taken to view a display of archery skills in a green space at the farthest end of the palace complex, overlooking the sea. This view, he thought, he would use for the night painting he was doing. He was greeted there by Prince Cemal and introduced to the prince's younger brother, Beyet. He bowed twice to the younger prince, who nodded to him.

He watched Beyet during the archery. Studied him. He felt like a man planning an assassination. Beyet looked something like his brother, not as tall, more slender, a fuller beard, also dark.

Fuller lips, too, longer hair, not so long a nose in a thinner face. Both princes engaged in the competition, which was conducted with laughter and high spirits. Both were skilled with bow and arrows. Beyet was better, as far as Pero could tell.

It didn't matter.

CHAPTER XXIV

On a windy morning that spring a boat could be seen making its way from Gjadina Island to the smaller isle of Sinan and the Daughters of Jad retreat. It carried Iulia Orsat, whose condition had been the occasion of considerable violence in the Rector's Palace. She was showing that condition now.

She debarked at the dock with one servant and they were escorted towards the buildings of the retreat. The boat pulled immediately away.

The Eldest Daughter (not old at all, this newest one) had been alerted by an acolyte running ahead. Leonora dismissed her attendants and took the Orsat girl out on the terrace. The day was mild though there were clouds. They were sheltered from the wind.

"This need not take time. I will tell you," said Iulia Orsat, "what I need you to do, and you will tell me if you will, and what your price is."

She was tall, with dark-brown hair, almost auburn, full-figured, more so now, carrying a child. A handsome woman, very young. Anger radiated from her like heat from a hearth.

Leonora said nothing, taking her time. She crossed to a side table and poured wine, then watered it. She walked across and handed the other woman a cup, smiling. She gestured, and Iulia Orsat took a chair. Leonora did the same, her usual seat, offering a view of the sea to the west.

She said, mildly, "Do you wish to have the child here? Or to join us on a more settled basis? Tell me."

Iulia Orsat glared. She had green eyes. "I am not having this child. That is what I need from this retreat. Whatever herbs or methods you employ, I want them. *Then* we can have a conversation about staying."

Leonora sipped her wine, just a little. She had a sense she'd need her wits here. This was not how she'd imagined the Orsat girl when she'd wept for her in the Rector's Palace. A lesson in that, she thought.

"You know this is a holy retreat, gosparko."

The other woman swore. "Oh, please. I know this isle has ended more childbearing than anywhere along the coast. I would expect you to be at least that honest."

Leonora looked at her. "You understand that the last Eldest Daughter is dead? Disgraced? I have a different path in mind for Sinan. You might be a little late arriving with that purpose. Why," she asked, "would you wish to end the child?"

"Why," snapped Iulia Orsat, "would I explain myself to a Seressini woman who stumbled into fortune?"

Leonora smiled at that. "Because you appear to need something from that woman, who is from Mylasia, by the way."

"Just say how much money this requires and we can proceed. I don't really care which city you come from."

"I fear," Leonora said, "you will need to do some explaining before other matters can be addressed. But, if you decline, I understand a desire for privacy. I see your boat has left. Shall I have one of ours take you back to Gjadina?"

She was called a name that would be considered vile in any language. She shrugged. She lifted her voice and summoned her attendant. "Marisa, please escort Gosparko Orsat to the dock and instruct Pavlo to take her to Gjadina. She seems to have intended only a short visit." She stood up. "I'm sorry to lose your company so soon. But perhaps I err in feeling that way."

"I'm not leaving," said the Orsat woman.

"But you are," Leonora said. "We shelter the needful and the sorrowing out of compassion and our duty to Jad. You are only angry, and arrogant. I have," she added, "no difficulty in instructing our sailors and workers to bundle you on board like grapes or a goat if necessary."

For the first time the other woman looked afraid, not angry.

Leonora took her time again, standing beside her chair. The empress had taught her how to do this. Wait, let silence work. At length, she said, "Would you like to begin again, Iulia? I am content to do so if you are. The wine is good, and it is a morning in spring."

Iulia Orsat began to cry. It was not unexpected.

She would not name the father, or why she refused to bear the child. She carried a bitterness beyond words concerning her father and her dead brother, for letting the whole of Dubrava learn her state. "To *defend* my honour? They stripped it from me!"

"They thought Marin Djivo had dishonoured you."

"Marin bedded half the city, including my sister, but I was never with him. Never. I . . ." She drew a breath. "I do *not* intend to discuss this."

"Very well. Do you wish to stay here?"

"Or spend my life serving my parents and sisters like a disgraced servant? Is that what you mean?"

"I suppose it is," Leonora said. She had seated herself again. There was sunshine above the city now, the clouds breaking up that way.

"I will never wed," Iulia Orsat said. "I will never have a house of my own. Or a life."

Leonora considered that. "There are many lives we can have," she said. "I didn't expect mine to be this one." There was no reason to confide further, and reasons not to.

She knew that retreats all over the Jaddite world offered services to women who wished not to bear a child they carried. It hadn't just been Filipa di Lucaro here on Sinan. There were women in villages who did the same.

It was illicit, proscribed, done in different ways, sometimes desperately, sometimes fatally. She'd wondered, often, why she had never considered it herself. Those weeks and months were a blur to her, mostly. Time sliding without thought. The retreat near Seressa would have assisted had she asked. Enough money had been given them. Women died in childbirth so often, it was arguably safer not to carry matters that far.

There was a child in the world she would never know.

Everyone carried their sorrow. She said, "The things you are saying, about the life you feel you've lost—this is a grief you are permitted. It is yours. There are wars, raids, sickness, harvests fail. Cities fall and men and women die there, but our lives are still our lives."

"What are you saying?" The other woman was listening now. That anger, Leonora thought, might have emerged from a balked intelligence.

She said, "Your grief, mine, every girl in a village who has lost her father or seen a man she loves wed another or go away, every child that is hungry or beaten . . . even if they are not the great story of our world, they are not debarred from their sorrow. Or their joy, if it can be found."

The other woman said nothing.

Leonora sighed. "I am teasing a thought out badly."

"No," said Iulia Orsat. "I think I understand . . ."

Leonora smiled. "If you do, you are more clear-headed than I am. I am trying to say that what has happened to you is a hard thing, even if there is war somewhere. Even if emperors and kings die. You are entitled to your rage."

The other woman smiled, for the first time. "I'll be angry whether it is allowed or not, I'm afraid. That much I do claim for myself." She shook her head. "I'm sorry. For what I said before. I would like to stay, if I may. For now, at any rate."

"Of course you are staying," Leonora said. "I can use a friend."

She thought the other woman would cry again, but she was wrong.

"I can be a friend," Iulia Orsat said.

ເຈ⊙

The band of fighters led by Rasca Tripon, known widely as Skandir, executed two more raids in Trakesia that spring, attacking another Osmanli village and a barracks north of it on the next night, while the army of the khalif was in the north.

That army was starting back by then, in fact, undone by rain, though that would not be known in Trakesia for a while.

The band used fire in both raids, as before, with archers, commanded by their Senjani woman, posted to cut down those fleeing. At the barracks they took ten horses, a splendid result. They killed the twelve soldiers there. Three were boys, but they wore uniforms.

Skandir led his company back west, at speed. Their intention was always to appear without warning, as death might appear.

They rested for several days after the barracks raid. Danica Gradek took long walks with her dog. Tico hunted hares, caught one and brought it back to her, proudly. One night she stayed away from the camp, returning in the morning. She was reprimanded for that. She apologized. They moved on. They were always moving.

There was discussion of going back north towards the main

roads across Sauradia, but they didn't know where the army was, and it was decided they'd stay and raid here.

They were still south, accordingly, when word did filter down that the spring rains had stopped the Osmanli advance short of Woberg and the other fortresses.

Skandir ordered them into their saddles the next morning—there were forty of them again by then—and they did start back north. A tired and dispirited army could be harassed. You were at war, resisting and denying, always denying. Refusing, until you died, to accept the change wrought in the world when Sarantium fell.

⚬⚬

The customs officials never ask for gifts but they expect them. There is a fairly precise scale of how much to give at different levels. If you are too generous with someone lower down the ranks of bureaucrats it will often become known, and those higher up will be unhappy. Not only will they expect more themselves, they will be legitimately disturbed that someone is interfering with norms and protocols. It is not for reckless Jaddites to disturb an orderly system.

Marin Djivo understands this, has been amused by it in the past. He is not amused by anything this spring, however, and he cannot adequately explain to himself why he is still in Asharias.

He's had his goods cleared, has sold them to buyers they've dealt with before. He has bought raw silk and gems, and spices from farther east (easy to carry) to take back. He could buy more, hire extra men and mules, but there is a point at which this becomes imprudent, an overreach, requiring the Djivos to borrow funds, and he has reached that point. Yet he lingers.

He has put out word that he will purchase a modest amount of Ispahani pepper, the rarest kind; expensive here, fiendishly so in the west. No one has been able to locate this for him yet. It is early in the year. He has given himself a few more days, after which—he vows—he will join or assemble a travelling party and start home.

It is partly because of the artist. He knows that much. Pero Villani has much to do with why he should be leaving—and why he's still here. What he doesn't understand is why the Seressini should matter to him.

They'd spoken a second time just days ago. Villani had sent a message to the Dubravae residence and they'd met mid-afternoon at the food stall near the Hippodrome ruins where they'd earlier enjoyed grilled lamb.

The artist had looked tired, pale, thin. Not a man in the midst of work that could guide his life to glory. There was an inwardness. Not a quality Marin had seen in him before. Perhaps this was how he was when working? Villani was alone, no servant. He said, quietly, "I am likely being followed. Walk with me to the market, I do need to buy some things."

Marin went with him. He asked the obvious question. "Is there a problem? You weren't followed before, that we know."

"I am painting the khalif now."

"That is what it is?"

Villani shook his head. "It is better that you not know more. But I did want to say something. I'll do it as we go, the market is crowded, people get too close."

Djivo registered the tone, the seriousness.

"I'm listening. I'll help if I can," he said.

"You can't. But yes, listen. So. It would be wise to conclude whatever business you have and leave Asharias. As soon as you can. Tomorrow, even, gospodar. There may be turmoil coming and it won't be safe for Jaddites if there is."

"What do you know?" Marin asked, chilled. How could one not be chilled?

"I can't tell you what I know."

They walked a short distance.

"Will you also be leaving?"

"I have work to finish."

"But if there is danger, what about you?"

Another shake of the head. The artist took a folded letter from his sleeve and slipped it to Marin. "This is for the Eldest Daughter on Sinan. If you would be so kind. There is nothing that will endanger you in it if they search. I swear to this."

He was eerily intense.

"Why do I need to take a letter for you?" Marin asked. But he knew. The other man only looked at him.

"You might warn the Seressinis we came with, as a kindness," was what he said. "And perhaps also Tomo, if you know where he is. It really would be wise to leave, gospodar."

They reached a market then and Villani abruptly changed the subject, asking assistance in finding a place to buy new brushes and a grinding slab. Porphyry stone was best for a slab, he said.

There was no further discussion of any importance at all. They parted at the market, with the supplies obtained. Marin had the letter in his sleeve, and questions unasked.

"Thank you," Pero Villani said. If pressed, Marin would have said he looked resolute—and older.

And despite this encounter Marin is still in the city, and it is surely foolish, after such a warning from a man who means him well and clearly knows something from inside the palace complex.

Perhaps, he thinks, this has to do with the war. Everyone is awaiting news. It is unlikely to be that, however. Tidings from the army would be running through the city, however confidential they were meant to be. No, this will be about something Villani has encountered within the palace walls.

Marin has gone so far as to tell his guards to obtain mules and ready the goods they have for travel. He is still waiting on a possibility for the pepper—which is folly, and he knows it.

But there had been something in the other man's look, and Marin realizes that he does like Villani, very much, and is reluctant to leave him here, even if there is nothing he can do—and there almost certainly *is* nothing he can do. Not every action in a life, he thinks, is entirely sensible.

He sends across the strait for Tomo Agosta. When Agosta comes the next morning, Marin simply says he has reason to believe it might be wise to start back west, and their travel companions ought to be advised.

Agosta seems unsurprised. He is not just a servant, of course.

"Signore Villani told you something?"

"I have learned something, yes."

"From him?"

Marin hesitates. "Yes," he says. "A few days ago."

"But you are still here."

Marin shrugs, irritated now. Sometimes people are more clever than you require them to be. "I will be leaving after a last attempt at buying pepper."

"Ispahani?"

"Yes."

"I can arrange that for you. It might take until tomorrow. But if your counsel is from Signore Villani it is wise to listen."

"Do you know anything?"

"Only about a man who might have Ispahani pepper."

୧୪ର

"Is the Duke of Seressa more feared or loved?"

Morning in the Palace of Silence. Some clouds today, a change in the light when they cross the sun, but he had the lighting and colour he wanted by now, for the garden and trees seen through the window and for the khalif's face. He was nearly done, in fact.

Pero was astonished at his ability to concentrate and work (and answer hard questions). He'd had days and nights of doing two different portraits, one at night in another palace underground, followed by encounters in a pitch-dark room.

There were many things remarkable about desire, he thought. That he should be so aroused, so consumed by need each night. Even knowing—perhaps *because* knowing?—that the prince who was sending him there almost certainly required him dead.

It was a long, often empty road west. And there would surely be great violence throughout Osmanli lands if what seemed likely to happen did happen here: when a vain, reckless younger prince was found to have had himself painted in secret, wearing a porphyry robe.

The artist who painted that portrait was unlikely to survive long enough to *be* on the road west.

So that artist had decided he would do the best work he could in this morning room. Such that, perhaps, this would remain, endure—causing men and women to say, maybe even long after: *This is very good. This one was on his way to becoming a master.* And they might shake their heads and add that it was terribly sad, how the younger Villani's career was cut off so soon.

It happens too often, they might say.

There was a woman in the black room who had been there every night. He had no idea who she was, who any of them were. The others changed, but he had come to know the scent of this one (her own scent, not a perfume), the taste of her mouth. And even as what happened could become fierce with the others on the bed, this one would find and hold his hand—and Pero had begun doing the same with hers in the dark.

He had no notion what she looked like, they could not understand each other's words (there were different understandings in that room). Even so, while others were seeking to excite him, or pleasure themselves, she'd slip her fingers through his, and something else happened, unexpectedly.

There was, it seemed, tenderness to be found in the world, even here. Which meant, really, almost anywhere, didn't it?

He had not been in that room last night. That part of the deception is over. The painting in the other palace had been finished two nights ago. Prince Cemal knows, it seems, exactly what he wants, how this is to play out.

Pero had slept deeply, despite being aware that his life might be tumbling like a chip of wood in rapids towards an ending. The body and mind were strange things. Some thinkers, he knew, had views on that strangeness. He was a painter, though, not a student of philosophy.

He had done strong work here. He knew it. He had shared an unexpected gentleness in the dark. He had slept through last night as if untroubled by anything in the world. He had crossed the garden amid morning sunlight and high white clouds.

The khalif, asking about Duke Ricci and fear or love, held to his pose. He had been an excellent subject. As if, Pero thought, he'd chosen to excel in this as in all else.

Brush in hand, Pero answered him. "More feared, I would say, my lord. The Council of Twelve certainly is." He was working on last details, the left hand, the dark-red ring on the index finger. "But this duke is also trusted, I believe, to guide us wisely."

"And the dukes before him?"

"Duke Ricci is the only one I have known, my lord."

Gurçu thought about it. An unhurried man. "Fear is better," he said. "It follows power and stays with it. Love or trust can change too easily."

"Yes, my lord."

These were words you might hear in Seressa, as well, Pero thought. He didn't say that.

The khalif said, "There was a conqueror in the east, before Ashar's grace came to mankind, who said the greatest joy in life was to slay one's enemy in war, then pillow one's head on the breasts of his wives and daughters."

That, at least, would not have been heard in Seressa. Pero didn't say that, either. "Yes, my lord," was what he said again.

"I used to believe that," said Gurçu the Destroyer.

Silence. Pero Villani was not about to speak to this. He wielded his brushes, his paint. He had come here to do a portrait. It was nearly done. No one had seen it yet. It was covered every time they finished, carefully. He had invited the khalif to look, explained that some subjects wished to do so, others preferred to wait. Gurçu was in no hurry in this, either, it seemed.

The khalif said, "And who follows your duke? He isn't young."

"No, my lord, he isn't."

It was possible to take the view that he should be dissembling with his answers. He had told himself, however, from the first morning in this room, that he would speak truth here and hope it helped him survive.

He said, "There is talk about that. Always."

"That is permitted? Openly?"

"In Seressa? Yes, excellency. But no one knows anything. People make guesses. Start rumours."

"A bad habit in cities."

"Yes, my lord. And others are . . . seeking favour? Attempting to align themselves. It is never easy when change happens."

"Nor here," said the khalif of the Osmanlis, and Pero Villani wondered if he had made a mistake, after all.

He concentrated on the red rings—the real one on the khalif's hand, the one he was painting. Red lake paint, the limited glazing allowed with his material and surface, and—just now—the smallest dab of white with the smallest brush, to show that sunlight sliding into the room through the window had touched the gemstone Gurçu wore.

Pero said, "I have only met the duke once, my lord. When he offered me this commission. But . . . I admired him. I think . . . you might have liked each other, my lord."

Not a thought he'd ever had, or expected to have.

Gurçu broke his pose, turning to look at Pero. Pero was afraid, then saw (he knew it by now) amusement in the dark eyes.

"Is this so? Does this mean you admire me, Signore Villani?"

"That would be too much presumption, my lord! I could never—"

"Do you? Admire me?"

The desire to go to one's knees. This was so appallingly difficult. *Speak truth*, he told himself.

"I do, my lord."

"Why?"

A breath. "The questions you ask me. Your curiosity about my world. All the world."

"That? I am just learning about my enemies."

You didn't contradict this man. You told truth, but you might also be wise enough to keep quiet sometimes.

Amusement, still, in those eyes above the beaked nose he had rendered—Pero thought—quite well. He hoped not *too* well, sometimes that could happen.

"You were about to say something?" Gurçu said softly. He always spoke softly. "Say it."

Orders, you obeyed here. Pero cleared his throat, that mannerism he had almost nowhere but this room. He said, "I have persuaded myself it is more than learning about enemies, my lord."

A sound, and Pero realized it was laughter.

It ceased. Birds in the garden. The mute by the door seemed to grow more alert, as if he had a sense of the khalif's mood. He surely did by now, Pero thought. Then:

"Might another curiosity of mine be assuaged, in that case? As to what you have been doing at night?"

As if a pit had opened. Vipers and scorpions below, in the event your neck wasn't broken in the terrible fall. Pero felt like that.

It was always going to end, he thought. This commission, the secret work at night, the deceptions, his encounters in the dark, hands touching. His life. Everyone's life ended, he thought.

He stepped back from the easel, he put his brush down. The mute was intent now.

Pero made to kneel.

"Do *not*!" snapped the khalif. "Remain on your feet and look at me, Jaddite. I would see your eyes."

And the voice, still quiet, was a whiplash now. It could flay open a man's skin, Pero felt. It could stop a beating heart. His hands were trembling. He clasped them together.

Courage takes many forms. A truth not always understood. Sometimes it is a man managing to hold his head up, control his shaking hands, remain on his feet, when the desire to drop to the ground, head to a tiled floor, is so strong. But the artist Pero Villani, at the edge of the chasm that was his death, changed the world in his time (and for a long time after) by telling truth on a morning of sun and cloud in Asharias.

The khalif was not in his pose now. He had risen from the chair, was gazing at Pero from his great height. He said, "Beyet is reckless and dangerous and will have threatened you. I do know it. But even so—"

Pero interrupted the grand khalif of the Osmanli people. He did that.

He said, "It was not Prince Beyet."

And in that moment, with those words, the course of large events began to change from where they would have otherwise have gone. It can be as simple (and as difficult) as that.

He kept his head up. The khalif had just said *I would see your eyes.* The mute had a hand on his sword, Pero saw. Of course he did.

Gurçu said, "No. I was shown the portrait this morning, infidel. I saw Beyet's face. The vizier wanted you killed immediately. I allowed you to come here to finish this work. Why even try to lie?"

"I am not lying to the exalted khalif. I never have. It was not Beyet."

Rage, barely controlled. It was said that this man had beheaded his commanders himself in his fury when the siege of Sarantium appeared likely to fail. Gurçu said, more softly than ever, "Say what you will now say, infidel."

And so Pero Villani did. "It was Prince Cemal I painted. In that robe. In Beyet's palace underground at night in order to be unseen. So that the portrait would be discovered there. I was presented to Prince Beyet at the archery display and commanded to place his features on the portrait or I would die on the road home. I was taken to Cemal's palace after, each night, to lie in the dark with his women, that this might be an explanation if I was seen abroad before the painting was done. My escort at night were men from Beyet's guard. They were suborned by Prince Cemal. You may have me killed, my lord, but I will not speak falsely as I prepare to meet my god."

And having brought these words into being, into the world, Pero did kneel, after all. Not prostrate, but on his knees. He kept his head high, because the khalif wanted to see his eyes.

And because of that, he also saw the eyes of the other man, the lord of the Osmanlis, and so he knew the moment when Gurçu decided that what he'd just heard was true. When the khalif's understanding, his will and desire for what should be, were changed.

A portrait at night. A man wearing a porphyry robe. Another man telling truth. We do have courage within ourselves. And sometimes it is honoured and sometimes it is not.

The mute had drawn his sword.

THE GRAND VIZIER Yosef ben Hananon was never far from the room where the khalif allowed himself to be painted in the morning—and spoken to—by a Jaddite.

He had not liked this idea of a portrait from the beginning, and he loathed it now. They'd discovered the vile, pernicious actions of the devious Seressini. Executed in concert with the younger prince, Beyet, whom Yosef saw as an unstable force in a world he was endlessly engaged in trying to make stable.

He was, accordingly, only moments away when the two guards posted outside the room where the painting was being achieved came hurrying to say he was required.

It was unseemly for a grand vizier to run. It would be inaccurate to say he did so, but he did walk extremely quickly to the room that was the centre of the world, because that was where the khalif was.

The artist was on his knees (which was proper, though he ought to be dead already). The khalif was in a towering rage. Something the vizier had seen, thankfully, only two or three times but which he recognized because . . . because you *learned* to recognize a wildly dangerous condition in the man who ruled all. And the eunuch had his sword in his hand.

This was still the Palace of Silence. Yosef bowed three times. He said nothing. His heartbeat was rapid. Not good for him at all. He had been prepared to arrest Beyet and the artist this morning, have the prince garrotted and the artist flayed towards a slow, excruciating death. He had been instructed to await the end of this last session. The khalif, he'd decided, wanted to deal with the Jaddite in his own way, and then with the prince. That was proper.

But the Jaddite was still alive and his head was not lowered. The man's hands, the vizier noted, were clasped tightly, but were not trembling.

The khalif spoke, not looking at his vizier or at anyone else. He gave instructions with extreme precision, even within the rage that was consuming him. He could do that. This had also happened the other times he had been in a fury such as this. Commands had been exact. People had lost their lives then.

This time, the Osmanli world changed.

The vizier was made to understand what was required of him. It was, in the event, not difficult to confirm what he was asked to confirm. The guards—Beyet's guards—who had escorted the artist at night were identified. Inducements of an unpleasant sort caused three of them to admit being paid by Prince Cemal (all but one did so, and his suffering, as the first man selected for inquiries, clearly led to the others preferring a kinder death).

It was also not hard to establish that Prince Beyet had been gambling in a brothel in the city (one of the things he liked to do) on two of the nights when he was supposed to have been painted in his own palace by a Seressini, while wearing a porphyry robe.

Some servants in the palace of Prince Cemal also proved unwilling to die terribly. They were able to confirm that the artist did indeed arrive very late at a room where some of Cemal's wives were (shamefully) sent to wait for him at night. In short, it was as the Jaddite said: he had been in an underground room in Beyet's palace with Cemal, escorted both ways through the old Imperial Tunnel, then lying with Cemal's women.

Conclusions could be drawn by a thinking man, and the vizier was such a man. Prince Cemal had, clearly, relied on the infidel being too terrified to speak, or—more likely—not having a chance to do so, with his father acting in violent fury.

Why, indeed, would the infidel ever have been allowed to say anything? He would not have been, had the vizier had his way. Yosef ben Hananon was painfully aware that his own suggestion had been that the man be killed this morning, and he'd urged the immediate death of Prince Beyet, as well. He was also aware (also painfully) that his khalif knew this, and that Cemal would accordingly have succeeded entirely if the vizier had prevailed. Not a good thing for a man seeking the trust of his khalif.

This remained, from the point of view of a pragmatic, prudent grand vizier, an utterly foolish plot, made more so by the clear indications that Cemal was the preferred son, and had only to wait.

It was possible, the vizier conceded, that matters might have changed in this regard if enough time passed. They did not live in a predictable world. It was also possible—a darker thought he would never voice—that having Beyet killed by their father might have been a first step in an even more dreadful plot by an heir grown impatient waiting for the throne.

In truth, that did feel to Yosef ben Hananon to be the best way to understand these events. Beyet to die, and then the sacred khalif. With the Kindath vizier obviously disposed of, if matters went as the prince purposed. Matters had not gone that way, but only by vast good fortune, a blessing from above, the khalif's sagacity. The Jaddite had been useful. His death, accordingly, could justly be made easy.

It was not. The artist was not to be killed. The vizier was caused to understand this later that morning, back in the same room.

Grand Khalif Gurçu added this to a stream of instructions, which remained precise while destroying the stillness in the Palace of Silence. Prince Beyet was to be summoned into his father's presence. He would be spoken to. His status was to change. Prince Cemal was never to see his father again. He was to be blinded, gelded, and his hamstrings were to be severed. When it was possible (if it was possible), he was to be placed among the beggars in the Eastern Market by the walls.

If he wished to profane the laws of Ashar and end his life, that was his choice to make. His father would provide him a begging bowl, and the first copper coin to be put in it.

The portrait painted in the other palace was to be destroyed. The painter would not be. The painter was to be given a guard of djannis

and escorted west all the way to Dubrava. There was some possibility, the vizier was informed, that the older prince—who would
never again have his name spoken in Gurçu's presence on pain of
the speaker having his tongue ripped out—had arranged assassins
on the road, should the artist somehow be allowed to depart.

The artist was being allowed to depart. He even spoke again in
that room, from his knees. He begged that he might send word
to his Dubravae friend and have the man accompany him home.

The khalif's voice, speaking to the wretched person who had
caused all this grief (which was only beginning, the vizier knew),
was unfathomably gentle. Yosef swore to himself that he had never
heard such a tone from Gurçu. Was the westerner a sorcerer? They
did have such men and women.

"You may take the merchant with you, yes," Gurçu said. "You
must leave immediately, however. There is going to be violence
when certain things happen. There always is at such times. A prince
is being disgraced, and an heir will now be named. Some of the
army will have been loyal to—will have been his men, and they will
fear for their lives. Rightly so. They may rebel. People will be frightened and seek those to blame. You do not want to be in Asharias
when that happens."

The Jaddite lowered his head and touched it to the floor. Finally,
the vizier thought. He did so three times, as Yosef had had him
taught to do at the start of all this. The mute had sheathed his blade.

"Now," said the khalif, in a voice closer to his normal tone, "stand,
Signore Villani. I would see the western portrait you have done."

The vizier hadn't given it a thought! The portrait was right there,
on the easel, with paints and implements beside it. The Jaddite rose.
He stepped towards his work. The vizier was on the wrong side to see.

Gurçu crossed the room and stood beside the artist—*far* too
close for Yosef's comfort. He saw the eunuch straining with anxiety, and the other guards were the same. Their world was turning
askew, moment by moment.

It would continue to do so for a long time.

There was a silence. The proper silence, Yosef thought, for this room. Into it, at length, the khalif's deep, measured voice came.

"My nose is quite large, isn't it?" he said.

Surely no sane man would reply to that?

"It suits the khalif's features wondrously," said the Jaddite calmly. "It speaks to strength, and in profile it balances the depth of your eye."

"Does it so?" said Gurçu with an amazing mildness of tone. Then he added, "The orange trees through the window. They are very vivid."

"The richness of the garden suggests the richness of the grand khalif's reign."

"Does it so?" Gurçu said again. And then, after a moment, "Are you pleased with your work?"

And the artist from the west said then, simply, "Lord, it is the best thing I have done in my life."

Whereupon, at the outset of events that would shake the Asharite world from east to west, the grand khalif smiled. He touched the infidel artist on the shoulder (he did that!), and said, "It is well. You have done what I summoned you to do. Go home now. The vizier will provide you an escort and a proper reward. I am grateful. I am also . . . I was pleased by what you said this morning, Signore Villani, about myself and your duke. Convey to him my greeting when you paint his portrait in Seressa. Go with your god, and safely under our stars."

PERO VILLANI AND MARIN DJIVO and the Djivo guards and his purchased goods on mules left Asharias late that same afternoon. It was understood that it would be a mistake to wait for morning.

The Seressini servant and spy Tomo Agosta, by his own great good fortune, happened to be with Djivo when word came to prepare to depart immediately. The day before he had managed to arrange for the merchant a purchase of Ispahani pepper, and he'd arrived for his fee. It was luck, or the will of Jad, whatever one might want to call it, but he was there, and so he did get home.

AMONG THE MANY DEATHS that followed in the succeeding days were those of a large number of Jaddite merchants across the strait. There was rioting, and an uprising among the djannis in the city, specifically those who had been loyal to a disgraced and blinded prince. Even more specifically, those who had been privy to his planning, and so knew their lives were over if they did not somehow end this current reign.

They did not do that. There weren't enough of them, they were unprepared, and the vizier, the devious Kindath, ben Hananon, had already identified a number of them. They had been seized and strangled even before word of the prince's fate left the palace to run through the city.

In the event, the rioting was not too extreme, the deaths, including those of infidels, an acceptable number in the circumstances. Prince Beyet was not disliked in Asharias, was even seen as a romantic figure, doomed to die when his brother succeeded to the throne.

Cemal didn't kill himself when released in the marketplace after the violence in the city came to an end and the loyal djannis and city guards reasserted control, and his wounds had healed.

He had someone else end his life for him, instead, so as not to violate Ashar's law against self-killing.

Matters became bad again, however, because shortly afterwards tidings came that the army of the khalif had been forced to turn back before reaching the Jaddite fortress.

There had been rain, it was said by those sent with the messages. It was also conveyed that the cannons, the pride of the Osmanli artillery, had somehow been destroyed, including the largest ones, by enemy soldiers from a town to the west. Senjan was the name. A name they knew.

The vizier ordered the immediate execution of the leaders of the artillery company, to take place before they reached Asharias. He was informed that the senior ones had died in the explosions that had consumed the great cannons.

The djannis in the city, those guarding the khalif and court, grew restless again at this time. They shared in whatever treasures were obtained from the army's advances in a campaign season, and there would be—evidently—none at all this year.

The grand khalif, following his loyal vizier's advice, disbursed from the treasury a large sum for the troops of the city. It was not a good moment to have his guards unhappy.

MUCH WAS CHANGED by what happened in Asharias at that time. The death of the expected heir and a perception of weakness at the court caused turmoil in the east among the tribes there. For several years Gurçu's forces were engaged, with difficulty, in dealing with rebellion in that direction. No armies went west or north for some time.

Prince Beyet, who became khalif when his father died, was not a good or attentive leader, nor did he choose shrewd advisers after executing his father's, nor did he live long. There were further changes when he died, and more turmoil.

Looking back, it became easy to say that Prince Cemal—his name came to be spoken again over time—would have been a more effective khalif.

Events, destinies, the flow of the river of time . . . these are altered, often, by very small things.

The portrait of Gurçu the Destroyer, who had conquered Sarantium, remained in the palace complex. It survived upheavals and changes, a treasure of the Osmanli people—and the world—for centuries.

BACK IN THE first days of violence in Asharias, that difficult time, investigations were conducted in the palace that had belonged to the nameless prince.

It could not be determined which of his wives had been disgraced by being given to an infidel at night as a part of the prince's degenerate scheme. Because of this it was judged necessary to execute them all by strangling.

There are always innocents who die during times of fear and rage, no matter how gentle hands and heart might have been, how much tenderness lay within a soul under the night's stars.

CHAPTER XXV

She has never been anywhere but their farm. Morning journeys to the village with her parents and brothers in the wagon do not count. She knows that, or feels it, which is the same thing at her age.

She is sixteen and has only a vague idea of the world. How could she have more than that? She understands that much is out there beyond the river and wood, down the road both ways, that large events happen beyond the boundary markers of their fields, but it is difficult to *picture* this.

There is a khalif, there is an emperor. Women are said to wear beautiful clothing. She does not know what this would be. She has never seen silk though she's heard the word. Tidings come at times (to her father and brothers): of war or plague, a flooding of some far river, fire taking someone's barn. There are hadjuk raids. Sometimes those cause the fires. Usually, she has come to realize, news arrives long after an event. A fire will be ashes on wind, the barn rebuilt, a war lost or won before they know of it here, Milena thinks.

None of it really matters, except that to her it does. She can't explain why that is so, but it is. Yes, their lives carry on here—as they have, as she knows her own will—but every so often she has to be shouted home by an angry brother or her mother. She'll be staring into the distance, east or west along the road, or south across it and the stream, when she's only been sent to the well for water again.

They survive. Winters are always hard. Her father is a careful man. She has two other brothers and they went off to join the khalif's army many years back. There wasn't enough to feed so many mouths, even though they'd changed religion long ago. The family had been Jaddite until her grandfather adopted Ashar's faith when the Osmanlis first came this way. Many people around here had done that. Most of them had.

You could cling to your beliefs, her father often said, but what good did that do if the head tax meant your family starved?

They'd paid taxes to the emperor north in her grandfather's youth, they paid them to the khalif now, and those two were—as best a man could tell, he'd said—much the same. Unless you stayed Jaddite and paid the head tax and died because of that.

There are enough Blessed Victims in the world, her grandfather had reportedly declared when he made his decision. Milena has some memories of him from when she was small. A short, strong man, heavy beard, many teeth missing by then, and the tip of one ear. He limped, for a reason no one knew, not even her father. She'd asked, hadn't got an answer. He'd refused to use a stick.

There are four farms here, houses close to each other with the field attached to each stretching out, boundaries marked with big stones. It is safer having them laid out this way—if you aren't feuding with the others. One of the others is her uncle, one is a friend of her father's. The fourth is a family her father doesn't much like, but they have a son a little older than Milena, and discussions have begun. It is, she understands, complex. Land matters are.

Milena is unsure how she feels about this subject. She has unquiet nights, has had them for a while, has explored her body in the dark with a hand she pretends she isn't actually causing to do what it does. And her daydreams can turn towards thoughts that unsettle. She isn't sure what she's looking for across the stream or along the road, but she looks.

The boy they are talking about, Dimitar, is smaller than she is, even if he's older by half a year. Milena is a big girl, strong, her father boasts about it. Dimitar's being smaller doesn't matter, she's told herself. But once, three years ago, they'd been by the riverbank (he was fishing) and twilight was coming, they'd be heading back soon, and Milena had kissed him on the cheek where he was standing with his pole and line above the dark, slow, summer water.

And Dimitar had grimaced and turned away and said, "You smell of onion, foh!" and he'd spat into the water. She'd walked home alone, face burning.

DID PEOPLE FORGET things like that, she wondered now on a warm day nearing another summertime. They'd been young then, she'd forgotten she'd been eating an onion as she'd walked down to the stream where he was fishing. And, the bigger part of this: were there any alternatives for her to marry, live with, lie with, where they were, in the life they lived?

She was carrying the two buckets, the pole across her neck, as she headed for the well. The well had been discovered—all the young ones in the four families knew the story—by a water-finder hired by the grandfathers together. He'd cut a forked branch from a tree in the woods, walked about their lands for most of a day, then stopped at one place and said, *Dig here*.

The well lay near the end of Dimitar's family's land, towards the road and the stream but so much nearer than that rushing water, saving a long walk every time.

Milena was alone, filling the two buckets, thinking about what it might be like to have a man sleep beside her, then thinking about her brothers who had gone away—who had been *able* to go away—when she saw someone coming along the road from the east.

People did come past, it *was* a road, but it didn't happen every day. Their road was lightly travelled, especially this spring. They knew the army of the khalif had been moving, somewhere to the east, headed for the Jaddite fortress. There were numbers spoken that made no sense to Milena. A lot of men was all she understood.

This one was more a boy than a man, she saw as he came nearer. But she also saw that he carried a sword and a bow, though he wasn't in a uniform of any kind. That ought to have caused her to retreat when he left the road and began crossing towards her at the well, but she didn't. It was midday, her brothers were in their field, and Dimitar and his father could be seen on the far side of theirs. They'd have seen this one, he was walking openly.

He stopped at a respectful distance and lifted a hand in greeting, called out, in Asharite, "Is it permitted to take water from your well?"

"You can do that if you like," Milena said in Sauradian. She didn't like speaking Asharite. She thought it made her sound stupid and she knew she wasn't.

"I am grateful," he replied, switching to Sauradian (not smoothly, but he did it, she noted). "It is a hot day to be on the road."

He looked younger than her, but he was taller, a big-shouldered boy-man, and the weapons made him look older, as weapons tended to, she thought. Men with swords or cudgels walked differently in the village, she'd noticed.

On impulse, as he came up, Milena handed him the bucket she'd just filled. "Drink. I'll fill it again."

He had red-blond hair and blue eyes—like her own, in fact, which was interesting. How such an obvious Jaddite could have weapons was a mystery.

Not one she was ever going to solve, of course.

He lifted the bucket to his mouth and drank. She knew their water had a metallic taste, but the boy showed no reaction. He splashed his hands into the bucket on the well rim and washed his face and neck. Then he took a leather flask and filled it.

She saw his gaze go past her. He nodded courteously. "Good day," he said. "Thank you for the drink. I needed it."

"Looks that way," her brother Rastic said. He was the calmer of the two who remained on the farm. Milena glanced back. He was holding his scythe, but easily. This didn't feel like anything dangerous, but she was still a little excited.

"You're well armed," Rastic said.

The stranger said, "Alone on the road. Have to be."

"You know how to use those?"

"I do." He didn't smile.

Milena decided not to think of him as a boy any more. It was interesting, Rastic heard those words but he didn't bristle or become aggressive (Mavro might have, but he was down at the other end of their field). Rastic just looked thoughtful, and maybe, Milena thought, a little bit careful.

"More rain than sun the last while," he said.

The stranger nodded. "All spring. Good for you or bad, here?"

"Mostly good. We'll need it dry come harvest."

"Then I'll wish you that," the stranger said, "and be on my way."

"Safe road," Rastic said, leaning on his scythe handle.

"Do you want to stay for a meal?" Milena said in the same moment.

The two men looked at each other. Then Rastic smiled. "Yes, do that."

"Only if I can cut wood or offer something for it," the other man said.

"We aren't so poor we can't give a traveller a meal," her brother said mildly.

The man with the same colour eyes as Milena smiled this time. "I'll be grateful for it, then. May I at least carry the water back?"

"You can do that," Rastic allowed.

They waited for Milena to fill the buckets, since that was woman's work, then the stranger shouldered them with the pole on his neck, and the three of them walked back to their house.

The stranger's name was Neven. He was headed south and west, didn't say more than that.

He stayed a year.

ၜ

The Eldest Daughter's terrace was good for the breezes, Leonora was learning, as the weather grew warm. If you walked forward, you could see towards the harbour and any boats coming from there to dock at one of their landing places.

Leonora had no idea who was coming now, but she did see a small craft pulling in. She was looking at Iulia Orsat in the herb garden—she was no longer with child but was still here, and had said she wanted to stay.

There were, indeed, methods known—to the two older women who tended their herbs—to cause a girl to no longer carry a child, and Iulia had never wavered in her determination that this one would not be born.

She'd never named the father. It was possible to guess darkly, and it was wiser—and perhaps kinder—not to do so. In addition to which, Leonora liked the Orsat girl, and was genuinely happy Iulia was staying. She was often in the garden, had shown a desire to learn from the older ones. She was healthy, not sad or angry. She had been teaching them songs from Gjadina Island. Some were extremely vulgar and very amusing.

Iulia's arrival had caused some entirely different thoughts as well. They were going to need, Leonora had come to realize, new ways of sustaining themselves on the isle, or life on Sinan would grow significantly less gracious than it had been.

Under Filipa di Lucaro, it was now clear, their comfortable circumstances had been paid for—quietly, and by routes Leonora was still working through in the records—by Seressa's Council of Twelve. For which Filipa had been an effective spy—and assassin.

Not a course available to Leonora, by inclination or opportunity. Which meant pursuing alternatives.

They might need to begin more widely offering the idea that women of good family (and not just those with reasons to withdraw from the world for a while) could find their lives richer here at the retreat. Younger daughters, especially, and perhaps not only from Dubrava. Families paid for this elsewhere, endowing a retreat to ensure their daughters lived in a manner that did them honour, perhaps also preparing the way for prayers when members of the family went to Jad and light.

The isle could also become a resting place for the dead, Leonora thought. The retreat could promise prayers in the sanctuary for ten, fifty, a hundred years, or even forever—at a cost, of course. Forever would cost a lot. Prayers from holy women were valued, though. She would need to learn what the price was elsewhere.

There was room to expand their cemetery, or introduce the idea of people being laid to rest in the sanctuary itself. This was, after all, the retreat where the last empress of Sarantium had chosen to live for twenty-five years in a life of piety. She amused herself a little with that thought. There weren't any people with whom she could share it, though.

A shame, thinking about it, that Eudoxia was laid to rest in Varena. Even though it had been Leonora who had planted the thought. Still, they did have her last belongings: jewellery, books, two sun disks, even the bed where the last empress had gone to the god.

There could be pilgrimages here. Perhaps the High Patriarch would consider making Eudoxia a Blessed Victim? *That* was worth exploring. There were, Leonora thought, possibilities. Life, on a day in late spring—especially after they'd learned the khalif's army was in retreat—seemed more full of promise to her than it had in a long time.

She looked west at the morning sea, whitecaps on a blue that was nearly violet just now. She turned and looked down towards the pier, where that small boat had now docked and was being tied. She saw Pero Villani step out and start up the path between the vines, towards her.

ω

Pero was aware—and always would be—that his being alive was astonishing. You could call it a miracle. He ought to have died in Asharias, or on the way home, at best.

He had been sketching and drawing compulsively since they'd left the city. At every stop for the night, even when they halted by the road for a rest or meal, sketchbook on a table or his knees, charcoal in hand. He was recording memories of the court and the city as rapidly as he could. There had never been anything like this urgency for him.

He did drawings of the khalif. The marketplaces. Cemal, as he had been in that room beyond the tunnel with the quick blue flames. He sketched those flames. The Courtyard of Silence: fountains, orange trees. Stars hanging from the dome in the vastness of the temple. Fallen marbles in the Hippodrome. One of the reliefs he'd seen there he kept trying to capture on paper. But you couldn't do that, could you?

He kept drawing hands.

He didn't speak much, though Marin tried to draw him out in the first days and nights. Pero could read concern in the other man's expression. He had a friend, it seemed. It ought to matter more, he told himself. Perhaps one day it would. Or perhaps, the way lives tended to unfold, they'd never see each other again after he went home to Seressa.

He was alone in the room the two of them were sharing at an inn, upstairs, when the attempt on his life took place.

He was supposed to be guarded. They had eight djannis escorting them—not entirely happily, but it was obvious the soldiers had been given extremely clear instructions that the Jaddites were to arrive home safely. Pero understood by now that failure in this would be a mortal one for the guards.

He was standing at the window late in the day. He had the shutters pushed back against the outside wall. He was sketching again, using the late light, sketchbook on the window ledge. A drawing of the vizier: soft cap and neat beard, heavy, fur-trimmed robe, belt of office, the hooded, watchful eyes.

The arrow hit the shutter beside his head. No one had defended or saved him. He was not a difficult target, framed in an open window. The distance was not so great—only across the courtyard, from near the stables, it seemed. There was no real wind and the light was fine, good enough to sketch by, good enough for killing a man.

The archer had simply missed.

Pero scrabbled back into the room, almost falling. A second arrow—loosed quickly—flew through the window where he had been and hit the far wall. That one would have killed him had he not moved.

He heard shouts below, running footsteps. He stayed where he was. The sketchbook was still on the window ledge, fluttering slightly.

The man was found in the back of the stables, trying to twist through a loose board he'd discovered or created. When the djannis caught up with him, he apparently drove a knife into his throat and died there. The bow, Pero was told that evening by Tomo, was a soldier's.

Prince Cemal had indeed decided that the artist from the west was not to be allowed home to tell a story. He had said as much to Pero in that room in his brother's palace.

That night—and every night after—Marin Djivo kept his sword by him in the other bed and two guards were outside their door.

They continued west. Pero kept making sketches.

This had been expected, hadn't it? You couldn't let fear define you, he told himself. He told Marin that, too, when the merchant asked how he was.

Something had happened to him, Pero now felt, while he was painting those two portraits. One of them would have been destroyed by now and the other he would surely never see again. But he knew they had been strong work. He *knew* what he had done, what he might be able to do going forward, if allowed. He had journeyed to Asharias and had been changed by that. He didn't yet know exactly how, but he knew it had happened. Silence was a way of guarding this feeling, just as the djannis were guarding him.

On the road now he was always bracketed by four men, against an arrow or gunshot from the woods or meadows. The djannis scanned fields and trees all the time.

They didn't save him, however, when the second attack came.

Two assassins that time, as they came up to another inn, late in the day, as always. There was a delay entering. A party of travellers was ahead of them, Kindath merchants, waiting for their mules to be taken to the stables.

It wasn't another merchant party, and they weren't Kindath. Not all of them.

The djannis were checking the courtyard inside and the rooms they were to take. Nodding their heads and smiling, two of the merchants walked over towards where Djivo and Pero were standing. Tomo was attending to their baggage on the mules.

"*Swords,*" Marin Djivo said.

Looking back, Pero wondered at how calm the man's voice had been. It was more a crisp announcement than a shout. But Djivo had his own blade out before the two men did. They pushed back their blue hoods. They were not Kindath merchants: those of that faith could not carry weapons in Osmanli lands or they died.

These two did die.

Pero remembered Marin on the *Blessed Ingacia*, crossing the deck to fight the raider who'd killed the doctor. Later, Drago Ostaja had told him that Djivo would surely have slain the man if he'd been allowed a fight. Which had not been likely that day.

Marin had drawn his sword another time on the way east—to defend Danica as she loosed arrows at soldiers not far from here. Marin had killed men that day, but not in a fight, just dispatching them in tall grass. A man not afraid to end a life.

And, it appeared, skilled at doing so. They were djannis he faced now, but they hadn't expected resistance, and one of them was dead—of a sword in the chest—before his weapon cleared its scabbard.

The other did draw from beneath the deception of his Kindath robes. He twisted away from Marin, turning to Pero—who had no weapon, of course.

He heard Tomo shout a warning from by the mules. He backed towards his voice. He could use the animals as a shield, was his thought.

He didn't need to. Marin Djivo engaged the assassin, forcing the man to turn to him. Djannis were the best of the Osmanli army. Taken in childhood, trained all their lives, only the very best elevated to rank.

This one had to know he was going to die here, Pero realized after. There were noises from the courtyard, the guards would be rushing out any moment. Better to end in glory? Doing your duty? The man did do that, but it had nothing to do with other djannis coming for him. He fell to a sword thrust from an infidel, someone not even a soldier: a merchant from Dubrava. It didn't even take long. It was a difficult thought for Pero Villani, but what came to him outside that inn yard was that dealing death could be elegant.

Later that evening he asked Marin, "How did you know how to do that?"

It had been so smooth, too fast to follow for an eye not trained to combat. Djivo had been breathing quickly when it was over. He'd cleaned his sword, then sheathed it again.

He said, by candlelight, "Two winters in Khatib, waiting for the weather to let us sail. I took lessons, beyond what I'd had at home. Two different masters, different styles. I was young. I didn't want to be a target in the world. I wanted to be one of the others."

"The ones who kill?"

"Almost," Djivo said, after a moment. "Say, one of those who can."

There had been screaming earlier in front of the inn. Their djanni guards had killed the rest of the Kindath merchant party, six of them and their servants. An ugly slaughter. And unnecessary, in the event. Afterwards, the innkeeper would vouch for those merchants, they were often on this road, staying here. The assassins had, obviously, joined them approaching the inn. For safety on the road, they would have said.

But his assigned guards had failed twice now, and people really did need to die because of that. Better that they were only Kindath, Tomo said, later. He said it bitterly.

Djivo was the quiet one that night. Pero left him alone. He did say thank you before they put out their lamps. The other man still had his sword by him. Pero wondered how many times Djivo had killed. Eventually he fell asleep.

There were no other incidents. They didn't stop at the village where they'd spent a night on the way to Asharias, and they didn't leave the road, or slow, when they passed the place where a battle had taken place a little farther west. They had no reason to. None at all.

Their guards took them right to the walls of Dubrava, arriving late in the morning on a sunny day. The djannis did not enter the city with them. Pero was asked to sign a document affirming that he had been delivered safely. He did so. Djivo witnessed it, and affixed his family seal. The djannis turned and started east again, the long road.

Pero Villani and Marin Djivo watched them a moment, then they turned and entered together through the gate, walking along the Straden, past the last fountain. They went into the sanctuary near the walls. It had new frescoes, Pero saw. He remembered being told about these, meeting the artist. They knelt and signed the sun disk and prayed.

"Thank you," Marin said when they stood up. "You saved my life and I will always know it and remember."

"I didn't . . ."

"You did. I'd have died in Asharias if you hadn't arranged to take me out with you."

It was likely true. Others had died. Word of violence had caught up to them, carried by mounted men on their way with instructions for governors and the retreating army. The khalif had told Pero what might be coming. It was why he'd asked to bring his friend.

"Anything I can give you. As long as I'm alive," Marin Djivo said.

Pero found he had nothing to say for a moment, no words came. He was still guarding what had changed, what was still changing within him. He would need to leave that inner space now, he thought, given where they were. He nodded.

"And anything I can give you," he said. "Wherever I am."

Men and women were waiting for them in the street when they came out. They had been seen, of course, and there were loud, excited greetings, and questions. Impossible questions, Pero thought.

He left Djivo to deal with them—this was the other man's home, not his. He told Tomo to take his goods, including his gifts from the khalif, to the Seressini residence. He walked down to the harbour and found a boat to carry him to the isle.

HE WAS CHANGED, she could see it. She felt unexpectedly anxious. A heightened feeling to the morning, as if her senses were sharpened.

She had greeted him, he had bowed to her. They were on the terrace now, shaded from the sunlight. He was looking at the water. He was quiet. He had grown up by the sea, she thought.

She poured wine. She said, "Did you do what you went east to do, Signore Villani?"

He turned to her, courteous, grave. He was dusty from the road. He had come straight here, it seemed. A man who'd said he loved her before he'd gone away. He would be, she thought, dealing with where they were sitting, with what she was now. That was part of what lay underneath this morning.

"I did, my lady."

"And so you met the grand khalif?"

"I did."

"And are you pleased with your work? Was he?" She smiled. "I know the two do not always have the same answer."

She was trying to make him smile. She wasn't sure why. It wasn't like her. She sat down.

He said, "Both are true this time, I believe. He was good enough to say as much. But I . . . signora . . ."

She looked at him. Really not the same man who'd gone away, and he hadn't been such a long time east. Men went back and forth to Asharias all the time from here, didn't they?

"Tell me," she said. "If you are willing to."

A pause. She did feel anxious, there was no denying it. She put her hands in her lap.

He said, "I still love you, Leonora. I told you I was not an inconstant man."

A rush of colour to her cheeks, she could feel it. She hadn't expected those words. Not this way, perhaps not at all.

He said, as if he was carrying a thought forward, "I shouldn't be here. I should be dead. In Asharias or on the road."

And suddenly, remarkably, she didn't feel anxious or doubtful any more. Something became startlingly clear, vivid as the sea beyond him in this light. She felt changed herself, or . . . she felt as if she understood a change, at last.

She said, "I don't believe that, Signore Villani." And as he looked at her, she said, "Pero, you should be exactly where you are. On this terrace. With me."

She saw him smile then, or the beginning of one. She could cause there to be more than just a beginning, she thought. She said, before she could stop herself, "We will take a midday meal, you will tell me what you feel you can share. I want to hear, and I have stories to tell you. Then, but only if it pleases you, signore, we can retire to . . . to my chamber and . . . entrust ourselves to each other." She could feel the colour in her face again. She kept her eyes on his.

"If it pleases me?" he asked.

"Yes."

He shook his head, as if in wonder.

"Beyond words," he said.

A new thing in his voice. Hearing it, she was startled by desire. Yes, startled. That would be the word for today, Leonora thought.

LYING BESIDE HIM, after, she understood that there were many truths arriving swiftly. You could call it (she would call it) a memorable afternoon.

She had wondered if her life had taken her to some place far from certain intimacies. But . . . it wasn't so. It wasn't, she now knew, lying on her bed with him.

Also, it appeared that artists from Seressa, or this one, might be more experienced and attentive in some matters than the boy she'd loved in Mylasia, however wonderfully urgent and ardent, or a doctor known only for days but defined by gentleness, remembered that way.

Then Pero had risen from the bed—she watched his slim, naked form—to claim his bag and sketchbooks inside it, and she rose as well, letting him look at her, and opened a curtain letting in sunlight, and back in the bed she'd looked. And her heart had begun beating hard again, for a different reason.

"Oh," she said. "Oh, my dear. Have you always been capable of this?"

"No," he said. "Not like this. I haven't been able to stop drawing since leaving Asharias."

"I have never," she said truthfully, "seen anything like these." And then, "Pero, I am a little frightened of you now. This is a kind of holiness."

And Pero Villani, who was changed but still loved her, said, "I think I am going to do strong work, if allowed." And what Leonora heard in his voice was pride, yes, but also wonder, even awe, at what seemed to be within him now.

And she felt, startled yet again, pride in him, as well. Already! And also wonder of her own, as she turned pages in the sketchbooks, seeing men and metal stars and fallen statues, fires that seemed to be moving, women selling fruit or silk in a marketplace, and the great soaring dome of a temple that had been a sanctuary when it was made.

And also . . .

"You've done so many hands," she said. She saw page after page. "Why did you come to do . . . ?"

"I'm not sure," he said, and stopped. And Leonora heard something (she'd been so *attuned* that day, she would remember, after), and she didn't ask him to say more about this, then, or at any time after, through all the years.

She put the sketchbooks aside, but not far from her, because she knew she'd need to look again. But first. First there really was, in fairness, in honour, for pride and for caring, something she had to find a way to say.

She propped herself on one elbow and smoothed his eyebrows (she had never done that with anyone before) with her other hand.

She said, "Will you stay the night?"

"If I may."

"We will . . . we'd need to move you to a guest chamber."

"Of course," he said. And smiled again. "Or we might not get any sleep at all."

Leonora felt a warmth within her, and desire, stirring, unsettling, and she said, "I believe I might be able to weary you enough for sleep, signore, given opportunity."

He laughed.

And while he was laughing, Leonora heard herself say, or try to say, "Pero. I cannot . . . I will not . . ."

She faltered.

HE SAW HER struggling for words she clearly *needed* to speak, and so he said them for her. He could do that, it seemed.

Smiling, after laughter, gravely, he said, "Love, you cannot leave here, this isle or this office. This is where you belong, where you are needed. You have been guided to harbour."

She bit her lip. He had seen her do that before.

She said, "You can accept that? You understand?"

"I understand," he said, "that if I tried to take you from this, if I acted in any way to deny it to you, I would be making a lie of saying that I love you."

"You . . . no, it is about your life too, Pero! You are going to courts, to cities and power. To Rhodias and the Patriarch! Don't mock me, don't deny it!"

He shook his head. "We can never know if—"

"*I know!*" said Leonora firmly. "I have seen those drawings. Am I . . . am I the first?"

"You are."

"Good," she said. "I like that."

"You are also the first woman I have ever loved."

"I like that, too. If you can accept . . . if you are . . ."

"I will be content to know you are here and that you care for me. That I am allowed to come to you and be welcome."

"Welcome?" she said. "Stay away too long and see how you are greeted, signore. We . . . we can build you a workshop. Do you think you could paint here?"

"That might be affected by how much sleep I am permitted at night."

Leonora laughed. There was a new taste to the world, a feeling in her heart that might be joy. "The air here is said to be good for sleep. As to other things, we'll have to see, won't we?"

"It is allowed? That we do this?"

She smiled. "I will pray this evening and in the morning for Jad's forgiveness."

"And me? Is it allowed for me?"

"I will also pray for you."

He said, "I should like a studio here, then, yes."

"I might even put you to work," Leonora said, and he could see (because her face was already a holy book for him) something sparking. "Could you paint frescoes for us? In the sanctuary?"

"Could you afford my fees?"

"Oh. What are your fees, Signore Villani?"

He laughed—at himself. "I honestly don't know yet," he said.

She touched his mouth with two fingers, just to do so. Because she could. "You will tell me when you know."

"I have to return to Seressa. To report to the council, and paint the duke, if he honours that offer. Then I will see what follows."

"He will honour it," she said.

"You seem very certain in these matters."

She shifted over and then upon him, above, and kissed him, hands on his chest, her mouth where her fingers had just touched. "I am the First Daughter of Jad on Sinan Isle. I know many things."

SHE COULDN'T TRULY know, none of us can, but, in the event, much of what she told him that day, lying together for the first of many times through the years, shaping tenderness, would prove true.

Villani the Younger, as he named himself to honour his father, would paint three dukes of Seressa for the council chamber in the palace there, and many distinguished men and women of that city. He would paint the new, young king of Ferrieres and live at his court for a year, greatly rewarded. Another half-year in Obravic, painting the celebrated late-in-life portrait of the Emperor Rodolfo, and then his son and heir.

He painted the frescoes behind the altar in the principal sanctuary of Rhodias, and three portraits of the High Patriarch over many years. And then, as he began to change his preferred medium to sculpture and his renown grew even greater in that form, he was eventually commissioned to sculpt the statue of the great Patriarch for his tomb.

When a civic disturbance caused the destruction of the giant statues at the foot of the grand staircase of the palace in Seressa, it was Villani who went home to sculpt their replacements, which still stand. And he fashioned the memorial bust for Duke Ricci when he died at a great age, having lived his last years quietly on an island in the lagoon.

He also, later, created the statue and memorial for Duke Orso Faleri, who had guided Seressa through many serene years—after addressing the troubles that followed an ambassador's unwise assassination attempt on a rival of the republic, in Obravic.

Through the years it was also Villani's habit to go each autumn back to Dubrava, where he had close friends and executed many commissions. He would live, during such visits, in a suite of rooms provided for him along with a workshop on Sinan Isle. The isle came to be known through the Jaddite world as a place of pilgrimage. People travelled to venerate and seek healing from the relics of the Blessed Eudoxia, and to see the frescoes there, called by one chronicler "the immortality of art." Villani had painted these in the small sanctuary of the retreat, around the upper walls.

His first great sculpture was also done on the isle, the celebrated rendering of a woman's hands shaping a sun disk, which was set before the altar, always lit by candles on all sides.

And, years later (but not enough, for we are not always allowed enough) he carved the relief upon the tomb of Leonora Valeri Miucci, First Daughter of Jad on the isle, who was laid to rest in that sanctuary, along the western side, with flowers and light before her. Travellers coming there would often say that her face, in that rendering, had surely been done with love.

SHE HAD MORE than twenty years on Sinan, and a life that she felt—throughout, to the end—had been rich, astonishing, blessed. She was taken by a summer fever, as does happen. Leonora Valeri died among friends on the grounds of a holy retreat she had guided to importance in the world. She went to her god loved and admired, and content with what she had been granted.

She had two sorrows at the end, two absences. One was a child she had never seen and never ceased praying for, each morning and each evening of her life. The other was the man who would be coming here again (he'd written from Rhodias) to spend the autumn with her as he always tried to do—and who would now find her gone.

That pained her, dying. He would grieve so bitterly, she knew, since he loved her . . . as much as she loved him, in fact. Another astonishment through the years, another gift, the richest, even, in a life that at one time, when she was very young, crossing to Dubrava on a ship, had seemed certain to offer her no gifts or grace at all.

We cannot know. But sometimes there is kindness, and sometimes there is love.

CHAPTER XXVI

It is sometimes the case that people with great experience will change a planned course of action—and be unable to explain why they did so.

This can be a chronicler shaping a story, a merchant on a buying trip, a king or his adviser making policy, a farmer choosing when to lay seed or begin to harvest, a ship's captain ready to set out from port who delays, unexpectedly—and then a wild storm comes that would have destroyed them on the sea.

It can also be a military leader, leading his band to harass an army, as he had done many times through the years, as he had just done earlier that spring.

They had been riding north at speed when Skandir woke one morning and walked away from the campsite to piss and spit into the scrubland. He returned to his company as they were eating a quick cold meal and making ready to ride.

"We are stopping," he said.

He was always decisive when giving orders. He had been fighting Osmanlis since Sarantium fell. There were men—and one woman—in his company who had not been born when that happened.

"What do you mean?" It was the woman, their archer, the Senjani. The one who slept with him, which—perhaps—was what made her feel she could ask him questions. None of the others would have dared.

"I had a dream," he said.

"We all dream," she said.

"Danica. This wasn't a dream of fishing in a stream or fucking a whore."

She was silent, but you could see that she wasn't happy. It was not possible any longer to doubt her courage or willingness to kill, her importance to this company. She trained all their archers now. Not everyone liked her, but many of these men disliked each other, so that didn't mean much. Some wanted to bed her, but that wasn't going to happen.

"What did you dream?" she asked, a quieter voice. Some were glad of the question—they wanted to know. Dreams were important.

"Walk with me," Skandir said to her.

That meant, the others thought, that she might be told. She might or might not tell them, after. It was hard to know with Danica Gradek. The men in the camp—forty-one of them—watched those two walk off with the big dog, Tico, which was never far from her.

In fact, years later, when she was remembered in that part of the world, it would most often be for her yellow hair, for her skill with a bow, and for the dog that was always at her side.

"WHAT IS IT?"

They hadn't gone far. It was safe-enough country, though they were well into Sauradia by now. Borders were fluid, but the landscape had changed.

"I dreamed the fight on the road," he said, looking away east, not at her.

"When I joined you?"

"Yes."

"That is a good dream. You destroyed djannis and red-saddle cavalry there."

"And lost almost every man I had."

"They all knew that could happen!"

"No, they didn't. Nor do the men here, Danica. Especially the new ones. They think I am magical, invincible. That I'll shed glory on them like blossoms from a tree."

He was angry and unhappy, she saw. She felt, suddenly, a little afraid. If he stopped now, if they *didn't* fight any more, what was her life? He said, "They believe because we've burned some villages and taken horses they cannot be killed."

"I don't believe that."

"I know you don't! But I've been thinking about that army. The serdars are going to be killed in Asharias if they have nothing to show for what they lost up north."

They had heard by now about the cannons. They didn't know how that had happened, but it was a tremendous thing.

"Good! They are angry, and fearing death. They'll be reckless. Let us *bring* them their deaths."

"The serdars? Danica, don't be a child."

She stiffened. "I don't think I am," she said.

"Not usually. But you are arguing against orders."

"I am trying to understand them."

"Why should you? Why would I need you to understand?"

A fair question. She wasn't a child, but she was young, and new to this, and he was . . . what he was. She shrugged. She was remembering that battle, too, now. Her brother, before he'd gone away.

And as had happened before, her silence caused Rasca to speak. He was, she had decided earlier, an endlessly surprising man.

"The dream is what I am telling the others, Danica. They'll understand a dream affecting decisions—they are from Trakesia. But I woke up feeling this was a mistake. That *something* is wrong about going to that road again, trying to find the army. I think they will be looking to find us, in fact. In numbers, to carry back our heads, my head, as a small triumph."

She looked at him. "Your head is no small triumph."

"No. It wouldn't be."

"And so you feel . . ."

"I do! I will challenge them anywhere and take risks doing it. But I won't throw away forty lives, or give those bastards a chance at a *victory* when they have just been shattered! Let Asharias kill those serdars for us. Does that satisfy you?"

"Not truly," she said, being honest. "I would rather kill them ourselves."

He turned to her then. She felt uneasy under his gaze. She sometimes did, as if she was too clearly seen by him. He said, "Girl, do you want to die doing this?"

"I don't *want* it, but—"

"Then don't chase the dark. Danica, none of us help anyone if we're dead."

"I know that!"

"We aren't heroes if we lead men into battles we will lose. Those battles may find us, but we need not race towards them. This is wrong. I feel it. I was about to make a mistake. Will you trust me?"

Under his gaze she said, "With my life."

His expression became wry. "More likely your death, but maybe not right now."

They walked back to the others and they mounted up and turned back south a little distance, then east again, to raid there through that spring and summer, far from the retreating army of Asharias.

IT SAVED THEIR lives. They didn't know anything clearly, beyond the instinct of someone experienced, but a chronicler can sometimes tell, piecing a story together afterwards.

The serdars of the retreating Osmanli army were, indeed, casting about desperately for ways to appease the court and save their own lives. One remembered that the Trakesian rebel Skandir's band had been roaming the main road east-west, had harassed their supplies, killed a force sent after him. Four companies of two hundred men each were dispatched to ask questions in villages and scour the countryside for signs. To find and kill the man called Skandir, after twenty-five years of failing to do so.

People were interrogated. It was not an army in a state of calm. Some of those questioned died, some survived, though not necessarily in the same condition as before. A defiant Jaddite cleric was hanged outside a roadside sanctuary just east of where the rebel had fought the company sent after him.

No one knew anything. No one had seen him. Skandir had, it seemed, ridden south after that battle. He would be down that way, everyone said. No one would lie for that man, they said. He brought trouble wherever he went.

It was probably true. And the south, Trakesia, was large, wild, empty, dangerous, not yet pacified for Ashar. They were part of an army commanded to return to their barracks, with the leaders ordered on to Asharias.

None of the officers leading the search felt personally at risk. It was the serdars who would be so. Indeed, promotions were likely when senior figures were executed. They turned back, all four companies, cavalry and infantry.

The hanged man was cut down by people from the village and his fellow clerics two days later—when they felt it was safe to do so. He was buried with rites in the cemetery behind the sanctuary, another small person in the world, another victim of the wars.

DANICA GRADEK STAYED with Rasca Tripon until the end, which came a little more than two years later, in that same village, in fact.

He had begun to experience dizziness, have trouble breathing. He had fallen once from his horse. It was autumn, not campaign season, and the Osmanli armies at that time were ferociously engaged in the east in the aftermath of changes at court and rebellion among the tribes there, who had never yielded to being ruled from Asharias.

It was judged safe to bring him north.

Four of them accompanied him to the village where he said the only woman he trusted as a healer lived. She had been his lover once. Danica knew that by then. She remembered the woman, too.

The man known then and after as Skandir died in that house. Not in the treatment room but in the healer's own bed on a morning bright and windy when the red-gold leaves had begun to fall. Two women each held one of his hands, one young, one old, both sorrowing.

"I never thought it would be in a bed," were his last words. "I believe I served Jad. I am sorry for some things."

They made a pyre for him that night, that the Osmanlis might never know he had been there, that no grave might lie anywhere to be despoiled. That people might even believe he was still alive, out in some unassuaged wildness of the world, red-bearded, riding a horse, tall and stern, ferociously unyielding, fighting the changes that had come, in memory of Sarantium.

He gave his ring to Danica before he died.

She stayed another season with what remained of his band in the south. She was an important member of that company by then, but it had been held together by the force and will of their leader and it drifted apart, as leaves scatter, as lives do.

She went north alone with her dog, leaving behind stories and a memory for a time down south. Some newborn girls were named Danica in those years, though it had never been a name known in Trakesia before she was there with Skandir.

ଔ

Neven stayed on the four farms through the winter to let his Sauradian become fluent with use—that was what he told himself. There was also the difficulty of winter travel in this part of the world. The north wind came with a lean wolf's bite. There was snow and there *were* wolves, hungry in the dark. On clear nights the moons and winter stars shone hard and bright. The stream south of them froze over. He had never seen that before. You could walk across it.

The language was not a difficulty. It had been, he reminded himself, the first tongue he'd have ever spoken. He had no memories of doing so, but whatever stories his mother or sister had told him would have been in Sauradian. He wanted to be *perfect* with it now. He couldn't really say why, and at some point began to wonder if he was delaying because he was afraid of the next step.

When he became aware of that feeling, Neven knew it was time to go.

In addition to which, he realized he was becoming a problem on the farm and he didn't want to be. These people had been good to him. He had worked hard, but that didn't always ensure that people were good to you.

"If you ever touch my daughter," Zorzi had said (mildly enough) when the offer was first made that he stay and work with them, "I'll have to kill you."

"I don't think you could," Neven had replied, also mildly, "but I will never touch her. My word on it."

There had been a moment of tension when he'd said it that way, then Zorzi had laughed and said, "That will do for me."

One of the brothers (the older one, Mavro) had given Neven a narrowed look, but over time he'd come to easy enough dealings with Mavro, with all three men.

Milena was different. He never said or did anything that could offend her (or her family), and he was aware, early on, that there were discussions going forward between her father and Jorjo, who owned one of the other farms and had a son named Dimitar.

It was nothing to do with Neven, except that Milena seemed to want it to concern him. He liked her. She was pretty enough, strong and hard-working. She asked him questions about the world, and himself. She wanted to know things, Milena.

He managed to avoid the questions that were about his own life. He just said he came from the east and had "reasons" for heading southwest. He stressed this: that he was going on. Milena asked questions all the time, at the table and in the field, or she'd come find him at workday's end just to talk.

"Do I smell of onions?" she asked once.

"No," he'd said. "And what's wrong with onions?"

"Some people say they smell bad."

"Oh. Well, maybe they do. But you don't."

She'd nodded briskly, as if he'd said something important. He didn't tell her that he'd spent many nights in tents with large, unwashed soldiers.

He'd have had to be more innocent than he was not to see she wouldn't be unhappy if he approached her in the dark, or by the stream as the weather warmed. But he'd made a promise, and he had no wish to spend his life here. Not that it wasn't a good-enough life they lived on these farms, but it wasn't his life. Or, not what he wanted for his life. Though he wasn't yet sure what that was.

But at some point it became clear that plans for a marriage and the union of two farms were being made difficult by Milena, who was being difficult because of Neven.

Not that she'd be able to refuse her father, but Zorzi was an unhurried man and he was being patient. He also appeared to have reservations about Jorjo's family, going back a long way, and so perhaps he might not have entirely minded if the big young stranger had chosen to stay with them.

Neven would never know if that was so. After the snow melted and the first buds and flowers appeared, he said at the end of a midday meal that he would stay through ploughing and planting and be on his way.

Milena had given him the dregs of the broth and half portions of cabbage two evenings running, but never said a word. He did feel a little sorry, but Dimitar seemed decent, and there were reasons for those two to be together. Not everyone could go out into the world chasing dreams and difference, especially a girl.

It seemed to him that people must pass through each other's lives all the time, touch them, be touched by them. Leave something behind, maybe, like a star that fell—you became a memory. Teacher Kasim, for example. Kasim was that for him. And Koçi, too. And Skandir, that day above the road, having his life spared by that man. That was more than just a memory.

He wondered how long he'd remember these farms, the sound of the wind, owls in winter nights, killing wolves with Zorzi and his sons with the moons shining on hard-packed snow. Milena's body curved over the table as she poured soup for all of them, or standing beside the well towards the river at day's end, looking at something in the distance no one else could see.

He left before dawn one morning, the last stars still in the sky. He'd told Zorzi at twilight, coming in from the spring field, and they'd exchanged a farewell. He didn't tell Milena that night, but he did receive her father's permission to leave her a gift: he was going, it was all right.

He had a silver Asharite neck chain with a silver star. He wasn't going to wear it any more. He looped it over the handle of her bedchamber door and left.

He spoke Sauradian like a native by then. He *was* a native, he told himself on the road as the sun rose behind him. And he did know where he was going now, after all. Probably always had, he thought.

HE WAS ATTACKED three days later.

He'd known he was being tracked all morning. You might leave the djannis, everything you'd known, change your life (or try), but you didn't leave your training behind so quickly.

Three men had been moving with him, north of the road. He thought they might be hadjuks; the land kept rising, and high ground was their country. He hoped they were hadjuks.

They came down exactly where he'd thought they might, where the slopes came close to the rough ribbon of road, with scrub and bush and a copse of trees for cover.

Not enough of that.

"Stop there!" he shouted in Osmanli. "Unless you are in a hurry to die."

They didn't stop. He hadn't expected them to. He was one man in a lonely place, and he had, at the very least, a sword and bow they could take. They stood up to be seen and came forward, spreading out. Two of them carried heavy guns. Most people, he thought, would raise their hands in surrender now, or kneel, seeing hadjuks with guns. Hoping to be robbed only, escape with their lives.

"I don't think we'll be the ones who die here," one of them said. He had a long beard and a wool cap.

"Bad thought," said Neven. "I don't like hadjuks, as it happens."

"Is it so? How do you feel about guns, pretty boy?"

"I think they aim badly and misfire often. I think those are old and I doubt you know how to reload at any speed."

They stopped walking. His calm causing that. Then the one who had spoken took aim.

"Let's find out," he said.

They did. Neven really had been one of the best with a bow in Mulkar. A natural eye, the archery teacher had said, not a man quick to praise.

He killed the one levelling the gun first, as they'd been taught, and the explosion of its firing sounded as the hadjuk died, convulsively twitching his finger.

The other two sprinted forward. One fired his gun, which was pretty much a waste of effort if you were running, it would just be noise. Neven didn't even bother to duck down (you were taught to drop, men tended to aim high). He had time for the arrow that took this one, too.

For the third he could have used his bow again—djanni archers were trained to speed, it was *why* bows were still better than guns, usually—but these were hadjuks, and he wanted to engage with one of those, kill him with a sword, see him fall from close.

This was done, this happened.

Silence, after. It could often seem quieter after loud sounds ended, Neven thought. There had been a wing and flap of birds from trees when the guns went off (he recalled that), but there was this stillness now.

It ought not to be so easy to end a life, he thought. He wasn't regretful, they had come down to kill him. But even so: they had been breathing, thinking of a woman, their herds, the brightness of the sun at midday, they were hungry or tired or excited, and now they were none of those things.

It was likely, he thought, that others might come now from the hills, having heard the guns, so he picked up his pace after cleaning his sword and checking if the hadjuks had anything he could use.

There was a little food. His own boots were better than theirs (they were poor men, ragged—not a life of ease, he thought). They had knives, but so did he. He left the guns. They were heavy, and he didn't like guns. He did retrieve his arrows.

The second man wasn't dead yet. Neven looked down at him where he lay fighting for breath beside the road.

"This was for Antunic," he said. He bent and pulled out the arrow. "For my father and my brother." He straightened and watched as the man died.

He carried on. Days and nights. You were careful here, of men and wolves at night. He saw deer at the edge of the trees. Wild boar. A bear once. It rained, there was sunshine. The road turned to the south. He'd hoped it would. He'd have had to strike out off the path had it not. He wasn't entirely sure where he needed to go. He asked people when he came upon them—when they didn't flee at his approach. There were few farms. He'd reached wilder, hillier country as he continued south. Mountains to the west now, in the distance. Sheep and goats grazed. He hunted rabbits and game birds. The road dwindled and disappeared. He walked open country. He suspected he might have to go more to the west at some point but he didn't know where.

IT WAS NEARLY summer when he found it.

He spoke one morning to a brother and sister minding their flock. Caused them to understand he meant no harm, despite the bow and sword. He didn't know if they believed that, but they didn't run away. Or they were defending their sheep, showing courage.

The brother was aggressive, trying to make himself feel braver. Neven understood how men (and boys) did that.

"Don't challenge me," he said to him. "I have no ill intent."

"Do you even know how to use that bow? Did you steal it?"

"If I stole it, I'd have had to do so from a djanni. Look at it."

They wouldn't know a djanni bow here, he realized.

"Show us, then!" the brother said. "Hit that tree." He pointed south. Neven didn't turn.

"I did say don't challenge me. I see where you keep your knife. Don't do it. You can't stab me while I shoot at some tree. You can't.

I can kill you both, and your friends on the ridge. I don't want to. I just have a question, then I'm away."

"Bartol, leave it alone. I think he means it." The girl's voice was surprisingly calm.

Her brother looked at her—there was an obvious resemblance—then back to Neven.

"What's your question?" he said gruffly.

"I'm looking for a village called Antunic."

"Why?" the girl asked, surprising him again.

No reason not to answer. "I was born there."

"Then why don't you know where it is?" she asked.

"I was taken by hadjuks as a child."

"We're hadjuks," she said.

"Cilya!" her brother said sharply.

"He said he wouldn't hurt us."

Neven nodded. "I won't. I just want to go home."

"You won't find much," she said.

It wasn't, as it happened, very far. He arrived towards sunset the next day. There was a west wind, high clouds.

NOTHING HAD BEEN REBUILT. No one lived here. Neven had thought there'd be a new village settled, that some might even be here who remembered his father, his grandfather. Might even remember him as a child. Vuk Gradek's little boy. He had wanted his language skills to be flawless, for when he came home.

He looked around the emptiness left behind and he felt so hard a sadness he wanted to weep.

He swallowed, spat into the grass. This wasn't the way he'd imagined it would be. There were blackened ruins of houses you could walk past and look into. One of these would have been their own. He had no idea which. Ash was everywhere, you'd have thought it would have all blown away by now. Weeds and wild-flowers. The wind blew, he rubbed grit from one eye.

There were sheep grazing nearby watched by another pair of shepherds and their dog. They eyed Neven warily. Asharites, he saw, as the brother and sister had been the day before. This was currently Asharite land, it seemed. He knew the borderlands went back and forth, over and over.

He had left his necklace with Ashar's star at the farm, looped on Milena's door. He knew nothing about the faith of the sun god, but he was going to be a Jaddite now.

That decision he'd made when he left the army. They had taken him away, taken everything *from* him. You could try to find your way back, step by step along springtime roads, muddy fields. He was doing that. Had done that. He looked around. A hawk overhead. The sun—Jad's sun—setting over the mountains.

He tried to imagine—to *remember*—fires in the night here. Or anything from before. There was something, but not enough. Nothing clear, or sharp. He felt terribly alone. There was nothing to stay here for. He had only the one place left he could think to go to now. He might die there, but it was the last link he had.

He wondered if an Asharite army was headed for Woberg this spring even as he stood here. Red-saddle cavalry and new cannons (new serdars for the artillery) and the djannis in their regiments marching towards glory in the khalif's name.

It had indeed been a drier spring. They could have reached the fortresses, in fact, but no army was headed north that year. The forces of Ashar had gone east instead. There was rebellion there. It needed dealing with.

It would take more than a season to do that. Hard fighting in desert places would stretch Asharias to the limit for years. There was no thought of Woberg Fortress, of conquering in Jaddite lands during that time. The disgrace and death of Cemal, the khalif's expected heir, a perception of weakness, these had shaped instability among the eastern tribes.

(The artist Pero Villani, whose words had begun all this, in the

Palace of Silence in Asharias, was painting Duke Ricci of Seressa that same spring.)

Neven Gradek built a small fire in the village where he'd been born, and he stayed awake through the night beside it, as you needed to in such an open place alone, keeping it burning to ward off wolves, watching the moons cross the sky and the wheeling of the stars. In the morning he went west, towards the mountains and a pass through them, headed for Senjan, where his sister had said they'd fled, through the borderlands.

DADO WAS ON WATCH alone by the tower outside Senjan's walls. (His real name was Damir, but no one called him that, however much he tried to make them.) He ought to have been *in* the tower, up top, but he was someone who'd always hated feeling enclosed.

The emperor, may Jad defend him, had offered to send more imperial guards for their defence, and weapons and goods (and payment!) for Senjan's great heroes. They were badly depleted since the events of last spring, and they'd accepted fifteen soldiers. With their own numbers so low, and uncertainty as to the future, it was necessary.

But this year it was said that the Osmanlis were marching east, not west—for reasons he didn't understand. But it did mean that if there were raids on the border they'd as easily be *from* Senjan through the passes. And the Seressinis, may they be cursed to have their limbs fall off (*all* their limbs, including the fifth one, his father always added), were not in any position to make trouble right now.

Not after a hundred Senjani had died in the service of Jad while destroying the khalif's great cannons and a very large number of the best soldiers and officers he had.

Senjan was—for a moment, a springtime, a year—truly a place of heroes, known as such through the Jaddite world. The High Patriarch himself had sent them commendations, with a relic for their sanctuary—and a ship's hold of food! It seemed that prayers were being chanted in Rhodias itself each evening for the courageous Senjani who had died in the far northeast in the god's name and to his eternal glory and their own.

Dado's father had said he didn't know much about eternal glory, but it had been a decent spring, no denying. He'd lost two sons (Dado's older brothers) with Hrant Bunic. There wasn't a family in Senjan that wasn't mourning someone, but they were heroes, those boys and men, and Senjan had always known what Jad needed it to be. That was why they'd marched out a year ago, a hundred of them, wasn't it?

So, on a warm, lazy day, Dado Miho, alone on guard outside the wall, was sitting on the grass, leaning back against the tower, eating cold meat and drinking ale when he saw a man come down from the wooded eastern slope.

He was alone, but he was armed. It wasn't worth ringing the bells for, but a good lookout did report, so Dado hastened back (after assembling his food and drink and spear) to the gate. He reported, dutifully, what he'd seen.

They said he'd done right. For a thirteen-year-old that was reassuring. He watched as four men went and stood in the road, blocking the way into town. They didn't bother to close the gate. Not against one man. That would suggest they were fearful, and Senjan never was.

The man—a boy, it looked like—came up with the long, steady stride of someone used to walking. He lifted a hand in greeting while still a distance away but didn't slow down as he came past the tower and up to the gate. He had a good sword and a bow. He was dusty and muddy from crossing the pass.

He stopped in front of the four men barring his way.

He said, "My name is Neven Gradek. I was taken as a child by hadjuks. I'm looking for my family. I believe they might be here."

From behind, where Dado was, the four men in the road could be seen to shift uneasily. Their heads turned as they looked at each other.

Finally, one said, "There are none of your people left here."

"My mother? My grandfather?"

"Goranka was your mother?"

"She was. And Neven Rusan was my grandfather. I'm named for him. And my sister . . . my sister is Danica." He hesitated a moment, and Dado suddenly felt sorry for him. "Don't tell me she is dead, please."

They let him come in through the gate. They waited in a small group just inside and sent for the person best suited to address all this. While they stood there awkwardly, Dado stepped forward and offered the other boy his flask. He knew his family were supposed to hate all Gradeks, but his cousin Kukar had been a terrible person in Dado's opinion, and this one was alone and had come a long way, and he looked . . . it was hard to say all of how he looked, but thirsty was part of it.

NEVEN WATCHED AS an older man made his way towards where he stood among others by the gate. They'd told him his mother and grandfather had died two years ago—a summer illness had taken many people. They'd been burned with others. That was what they did here at such times, the young one who'd given him a drink said. There was no slight meant in it, he'd added anxiously.

"I know," Neven had said to him.

Other than that he didn't speak. They said Danica had gone away. He knew she had. He had *seen* her.

He had come a long way and there was no one here.

The old man stopped in front of him. He spat in the dust through a gap in his teeth. He said, "If you were taken as a child and are not gelded and have those weapons, you are a djanni."

Neven nodded respectfully. He said, "I was. Not any more. I left after the fighting by the river last spring. I am here because of the courage of Senjan I saw, and because my family are . . . my family were here."

"You were in that fighting?"

"Yes."

"So was I. Should I believe you?"

"I have not come this far to lie."

"How were the cannons destroyed?"

"Men crossed the river with explosives and set them off by the artillery. I was with those already by the river. We saw the flames— people for a long way in all directions will have seen the flames."

"And you crossed the water?"

"Eventually. We'd suffered more losses when explosives in the mud were set off with fire-arrows by your people on the other side."

"This is so," said the old man. "That is how we did it. And then?"

"And then we crossed and the Senjani were barricaded to the west between wood and water, and we killed almost all of them. At night some tried to escape through the trees and they were caught. But . . ."

"Yes?" said the old man.

"I think . . . I do not know this, but I think those going through the trees were distracting us from others who went down the river."

"That is also true," the old man said. He spat again.

"There was a waterfall," Neven said. "I don't think they could have survived, but I hope they did."

"They didn't," said the other man. "I am the only one who came home."

Neven looked at him. "I am sorry to hear it. They were more brave than any men I have known. They did great damage to an army."

"Why are you here?" the old man asked.

Neven looked around. There was a crowd now, men and women. Not friendly faces. He hadn't seen friendly faces since leaving the four farms. He said, "I tried to go home to Antunic. There is nothing there. So I thought I might come here. To find my family, and do what I can to make up for those lost."

"One man?"

"I can't be more than that," Neven said.

"Do you know anything about the sea?"

"Nothing," Neven said.

The old man—he would learn that his name was Tijan Lubic and he had escaped from the slaughter through the woods—spat another time into the dust, then he smiled.

"We'll start by teaching you that," he said. "There is a rumour your sister is fighting with Skandir, bringing us honour if it is true. I knew your grandfather well. You can have your family's house, Neven Gradek, and you will be welcome among us. Come to the sanctuary. We'll pray there, all of us, for you and your dead."

"I don't know how to do that properly yet," Neven said. He was close to tears he realized, which would shame him.

"We'll teach you that, too. But few of us do anything properly here, I have to say."

There were smiles now. It was a hard place, it seemed, but not without generosity to go with courage.

They walked him across the square. The boy he'd seen by the tower stayed by his side on the way and in the sanctuary. His name, he whispered, was Damir, and he said he thought Neven's sword was the finest he'd ever seen in his whole life.

HE STAYED MORE than a year, until the autumn that followed. They did teach him about boats and the sea. In spring he joined a raid (and then two others) south past Hrak Island towards lands held by Seressa on this coast (for salt, for timber). They boarded a merchant vessel flying the lion flag of that republic.

They were careful: looked for goods belonging to Asharites, and there was Kindath cloth. These were free to take. They left

Seressini goods mostly untouched, though their raid leader did allow a cask of wine from Candaria—what men could be expected to not take *any* of that?

Neven discovered he liked the sea. The salt and spaces of it, the seabirds, and the dolphins they'd often see. Sea swells didn't unsettle him, nor did storms when they came.

He taught the younger Senjani archery, starting with how to make bows and string them, and the best ways of fashioning arrows. Two girls joined them for this. There was a shortage of men in Senjan at that time. He had a house of his own, skills, was an obvious marriage prospect, even young as he was. He learned that women in Senjan made their own decisions as to where they'd spend a night, and that having a place of his own, with a way for someone to get in and out through the back, was a useful thing for a man learning the ways of women. He didn't marry, though, didn't allow it to be discussed.

His sister, they told him, had been like that. His sister was remembered.

His sister was why he left when he did. No one had word of her, though they asked down the coast. It wasn't as if Skandir made his location easy to find. Assuming she was even with him, was still alive. The last sure knowledge of Danica was from Dubrava. She'd been employed by a merchant family there.

There were none of them alive but her and him, and he hadn't looked back when he'd walked away in Sauradia. He'd wanted to, but he hadn't.

So he made his decision and moved on again, looking for her. To Dubrava, by boat, in autumn. Some friends (he had friends by then) took him south. He knew how to pray to Jad by then, and they all offered the invocations in the sanctuary, as men did before going to sea.

It wasn't intended to be a permanent leave-taking. He'd said that to two girls, and to young Damir, and also the raid leaders, who'd asked. He was going to see if anyone knew anything about his sister.

He was never in Senjan again. How can we ever presume to know what will come of our choices, our paths, the lives we live?

HISTORY DOES NOT proceed with anything like fairness or a recognition of valour or virtue. Senjan was gone, the walls broken and smashed, on both the harbour and the landward sides, less than a hundred years after this time. Matters of larger politics made the Senjani both unnecessary and a problem. They were scattered among villages and farms.

In later years, long after the shattered pieces of the walls had been carried away by farmers in carts to be used for buildings or stone fences to mark fields, all that remained of Senjan was a round tower near where the town had been. That was described, centuries after, as evidence of the strong, steady presence of the empire's brave soldiers there, defending a vulnerable town.

Dubrava, however . . . Dubrava to the south never fell. Its walls were not breached. The republic by the sea, sowing treaties in all directions, placating and observing, trading, negotiating trade tariffs, dwindled, rose again, dwindled, but never died. There was an earthquake once. They rebuilt.

Three hundred years later the republic did surrender briefly, to an army from Ferrieres (Ferrieres had become very strong in that time). It was said by the cynical, and there are always those, that the citizens opened the gates and let the great besieging general and his troops come in so the claim could remain that the walls of Dubrava were never breached, for all eternity.

Eternity is too long for us. It is not a scale for men and women. We live by different, smaller measures, but there are stories we tell . . .

Their attempt to assassinate the head of the newest bank in Obravic could scarcely have turned out worse for Seressa.

This disaster took place in autumn, two years after Neven Gradek made his way south from Senjan by boat. In that same season of falling leaves, Pero Villani was painting Seressa's newest duke, a former ambassador himself (for two years) to Obravic. It was his successor at the emperor's court who was implicated in what happened.

Obravic would never, of course, take an accredited ambassador into custody or punish him personally, despite confessions obtained, but they did deny the man access to the emperor and his officials—making it necessary for a new ambassador to be appointed. Signore Arnesti returned home in disgrace.

In Seressa he was ruinously punished—financially. His reckless folly would end up costing the republic a vast sum. The events of that day in Obravic would be—were already being—reported around the world, with consequences to their bankers and merchants everywhere, bringing rapture and delight to the enemies of the republic.

The recently elected Duke Orso Faleri would spend considerable time and attention addressing this unfortunate matter. It took years and a flood of money before the effects could be said to have truly receded, making it just another in a list of transgressions—and everyone had those.

ON THE DAY his guards have told him he is meant to be killed, Marin Djivo, head of the newly opened Djivo Bank in Obravic, lending funds to the imperial court itself, is not greatly concerned.

Afterwards, his principal regret will be that he was not able to deal with any of the would-be assassins himself. He is, as is somewhat widely known, adept with a sword. On the other hand, it would have reflected badly on the bank's security should their head have been compelled to draw a blade to defend himself, and so he never did so that day.

The Djivo guards are—and have been for some time now—exceptionally good. They need to be. The family has been making ambitious incursions into the cloth trade north, and now into the world of banking, with a view to vying with Seressa as lenders to the courts of the Jaddite world.

They have started in Obravic. He has been here for some months, and their immediate plans include Ferrieres and the court there. Esperaña is possible, and Anglcyn he has thought about. Emperors and kings always need funds—for wars, and for expanding their reach and esteem in other ways. In the coming world, as Marin sees it, bankers will hold great power, and he has persuaded his father—and others in Dubrava, backing them—that there is no reason why Seressa's dominance in this need remain unchallenged.

The Seressinis always respond badly when challenged. Hence the well-trained guards, and the events earlier this day, Marin is thinking. He is back in his Obravic mansion, receiving a stream of concerned visitors in the front reception room.

He knows—everyone knows already—that this was an ambitious man's personal folly. But an ambassador represents his court or council, and Signore Arnesti's mistake is therefore Seressa's.

Marin has more people here with him in Obravic than is widely grasped. His men learned of the plot quite easily, told the broad details, deducing the secondary ones.

The men who were to kill him were not in any obvious way tied to Seressa. They were to feign a robbery attempt as the Dubravae banker walked through the street. He would be hacked to death. Then the assassins would be killed—by Seressinis—after fleeing to what they had been told was a refuge, where their payment and a secret way out of Obravic would be waiting for them.

The house of refuge had been located by Marin's men. There were to be, he was told, men with guns there on the day, to kill the four street assassins. Then the men with guns would disappear in the throngs. Obravic was expected to be in great tumult after the shocking death of Gospodar Djivo of Dubrava.

It wasn't a badly conceived plan in some ways, Marin had told his men. It was only foolish for failing to consider what might happen if they didn't succeed, and for not realizing that he was guarded exceptionally well.

The street thieves were identified and disarmed before coming anywhere near him as he walked through the cloth market on a sunny autumn day. They were carefully not killed.

Other Djivo guards had earlier made their way to the proposed house of refuge. They had surprised and overcome the Seressinis waiting there, who had not expected anyone for some time. These men were also left alive, trussed, gagged, their guns beside them.

When the assassins confessed to the imperial guard (it didn't take very long) and revealed where they had been instructed to flee after killing the banker, soldiers of the emperor went quickly to that place—and found the Seressinis. Assertive questioning ensued.

The story emerged swiftly as a result, and led straight to the ambassador's residence. The motivation was obvious—the Djivo Bank had offered compelling financial terms to the emperor, and had a persuasive man offering them. The imperial advisers had good reason to reduce their dependence on Seressa.

Trade, commerce, business in all its incarnations, that was what Seressa lived for, and by, and a threat to any of this was not likely to be ignored. Although—murder? Well, yes, murder. The devious republic had done it before, Emperor Rodolfo's chancellor reminded him, sadly.

It was, in short, a disastrous day for the devious republic. For Dubrava and the Djivo Bank (and its backers), it was wondrously good.

Marin was, accordingly, put to some effort to appear shaken and disturbed as officers of the court attended upon him at the house and business premises he'd purchased near the castle.

Their apologies—on behalf of the emperor—were profuse, intense. Rodolfo had already been informed, they told Djivo—and his imperial majesty was outraged. The privileges of the Seressinis in Obravic were to be curtailed. And this ambassador would not remain in the city.

The High Patriarch would be written to.

Marin thanked them for their solicitude and for the emperor's kind concern. He praised their swift actions of behalf of justice and business integrity. He intended, he said, to pray in thanksgiving for his deliverance in the sanctuary down the street, perhaps they would join him?

They did so, of course. The Djivo guards were much in evidence as the dignitaries proceeded both ways at day's end, escorting the handsome Dubravae banker. So were the soldiers of the emperor.

It could not, Marin is thinking, going up to his rooms some time later, have unfolded better if he had been instructing the Seressinis as to what he needed them to do.

He thanks the two guards who have walked him up (there will be one in the hallway all night) and he enters his chambers.

Lamps are lit and the fire is going on a cool night in Obravic. His wine is where it should be.

There is only one cup beside the decanter.

He closes the door.

He says, "I could have poured your cup."

He turns and sees—finally—Danica Gradek, sitting on his window ledge again.

She looks as he remembers. Years have passed.

She says, "I saw two cups. Didn't know when you would be . . . wait! My cup? Were you *expecting* me?"

He crosses to pour himself wine. "Our guards are much better these days."

"I heard that. Someone tried to kill you."

"Yes. They didn't."

"Seressa?"

"Yes."

Her hair is shorter, or tied back, he can't tell from here. She wears dark-green trousers, a blue tunic, belted, a sheepskin vest over it, boots. A ring he doesn't remember. No bow, no sword. She will have knives.

"Well, good that they failed," she says. "Your guards really saw me?"

"Yesterday. I was told a tall woman with yellow hair had been looking at the house from across the street. They said she had a dog. How is Tico?"

"He is very well," she says stiffly. She looks affronted.

He is amused. "I told them it was all right, not to be concerned."

"Did you?" she says. "And had a second cup put out?"

He walks to the window and takes her cup and crosses to fill it and his own again. He turns back to her and from halfway across the room, to have a little distance, he says, "Danica, since I returned from Asharias, more than three years now, I have set out two cups in my chamber every night. Wherever I am."

There is a silence.

"Oh," she says. "Have you?"

"Yes. In the . . . small hope you might come to find me."

She has coloured now, he sees.

She says, "I did, didn't I? Come find you."

"It seems so."

She sips from her wine. She says, "You were angry with me, that last night."

"In Sauradia? I . . . yes, let's say that I was."

"You know why I left, though. Don't you?"

There are changes in her, after all. Of course there are. Time has run. He says, "I do. I did then, Danica. We can still be made angry."

She looks down at her wine. "Two cups every night?" she says.

"Yes."

She shakes her head. "And now you are here? Obravic? A bank?"

"Yes. And you are here because . . . ?"

"Because I heard that this was where you were."

She has always been direct, he remembers.

"I see," he says calmly enough, but his heart is beating faster. "You never came to Dubrava."

"No. I . . . no." A silence. She says, "Did you marry? The clever girl who liked you? Katija?"

"Kata Matko. No." He smiles. "My brother did. They have two children already."

"I see. And . . . you made it to Asharias, then, that journey? With the artist? A success? Have you gone back?"

"It was a success. I have not gone back. I found it difficult to be there, and I almost died."

"Oh?"

"You heard of the rioting? Wherever you were?"

"When the prince died? Yes. I was in Trakesia. Were you . . . ?"

"I got out just before. Pero got me out. He saved my life."

"Oh," she says again. "There is a story?"

"There is." He hesitates. "If we will have time for stories."

And now, finally, she smiles at him, the needful wonder of that. And as he sees this, the room, the northern night behind her, the arc and unfurl of his whole life all grow brighter, it seems to Marin Djivo.

"Why," she asks, "would we not have time?"

And because she is smiling, and there is a feeling within him like balm spreading healing, warmth, and something far beyond, he does not delay what he has to tell her any more and says, "I told you that our guards were better now."

"You did. That they knew I was here."

"Danica, the one who has trained them, made them better for two years now, is your brother."

"*Oh, dear Jad. Please tell me . . .*"

He tells her. "Neven came to Dubrava looking for you two years ago. But none of us knew where you were, where Skandir might be, if you were still with him. So he stayed, waiting for you, with us. My father took him on as a guard, as you had been, and then, when we saw what he was, he was asked to train the others as our needs grew."

Her hands have gone to her face.

"Danica," he says, "remember, we had no idea where you were."

"Say he is all right. Please."

"He is more than that. He is wonderful. Most of the merchants in Dubrava and most of the merchants' daughters want him for their own."

"The daughters? He's too young!" she cries, a reflex.

His turn to smile. "No, he isn't," he says.

"Oh, Marin," he hears her say. "Oh, Marin." His name. Finally.

"OH, MARIN," she hears herself whisper, twice. And arriving at that, at his name again in this moment, feeling whole, entirely here, in this room, in this one night in all the world's nights she also feels—after all the years and journeys—as if she has been granted a blessing. After everything.

She looks at him, the composed ease of his body, the smile she remembers, eyes on hers, his *presence* with her, hers with him, amazingly.

She stands. Places her cup on the window ledge, carefully. She says, "Is it possible, do you think, for you to take me to your bed?"

She sees his smile deepen and she knows there is a home in it, in him, for her, and that she is someone who can live in that home now, finally. They make love by lantern light and firelight.

They marry, not long after. In time there are children, who bring, always, the future with them. There are sorrows and joys, as there are. One of them dies, and then the other does, not long after. They are laid to rest beside each other in the Djivo family plot overlooking the sea, on an island near Dubrava. They are still there, though the graves are hard to find after all this time.

One of her grandchildren would talk to Danica in her mind, silently, for many years, from the first moments after her grandmother died. Another blessing granted, to both of them. This should not happen, perhaps, but it does. We live among mysteries. Love is one, there are others. We must not imagine we understand all there is to know about the world.

ACKNOWLEDGEMENTS

Some years ago I was on a promotional tour in Croatia. Driving towards an event on the Dalmatian coast, my publisher suddenly exclaimed, "I know what you should do! You should write a book about the *uskoks*." In my most suave manner, I replied, "Say what?"

He spoke of pirates, small, swift boats, a ruined town on the Adriatic somewhere not far ahead. We carried on along Roman roads. Years later, again on tour in Croatia, a historian picked up on the *uskok* theme as we talked, then sent me links to a book in English and scholarly articles. The book, Wendy Bracewell's *The Uskoks of Senj*, was compelling, immensely useful.

These conversations are the primal "origin story" of this novel. So my first acknowledgements belong to Neven Anticevic (who has published all of my books in his market) and Robert Kurelic. It took me a long time to get to this story, but I seem to have done so.

A second piece of an emerging book became Dubrovnik. Walking the walls, viewing the harbour, climbing the hill to look down on the city and islands—all helped give me ideas. So did a number of books about that fascinating city-state. I'll mention Robin Harris's *Dubrovnik: A History* as a very well done introduction. I also found useful more narrowly focused works by Susan Mosher Stuard and David Rheubottom.

Venice attracts as many writers, it sometimes seems, as it does tourists. There is no shortage of material on the history of the republic. I'll note a recent, engaging history by Thomas F. Madden (he's a great admirer of the city, there are less sympathetic accounts to be found of some moments and figures). I also want to recommend *Bound in Venice* by Alessandro Marzo Magno, genuinely delightful on printing and books in the Serene Republic.

The history of the Ottoman Empire has also been widely chronicled, also with diverse perspectives. For the general reader, one classic is Kinross, *The Ottoman Empire*, but there are many more recent treatments. Rhoads Murphey's *Ottoman Warfare 1500–1700* was useful. Andrew Wheatcroft has written about both the Ottomans and the Habsburgs—also a component of my story here, obviously. Those who know the history will have noted that I used Rudolf II's court in Prague as an inspiration—backing it up a century or so to the late 1400s. My city of Obravic is an amalgam, but it is Prague more than anything else. A thoroughly engaging book on Rudolf and his remarkable court is Peter Marshall's *The Theatre of the World*.

On Renaissance trade and commerce and so much more, the great resource, to my mind, remains Fernand Braudel's magisterial *The Mediterranean*. I reread it for this novel, taking more notes, without doubt, than from any other book I read. (Mind you, it is longer than any other!) A fine, newer work is Peter Spufford's handsome *Power and Profit: The Merchant in Medieval Europe*.

There are a great many more titles, and writers. I never want to overload these notes, only to guide readers who might be interested to some of the background that engaged me. Michael Herzfeld's *The Poetics of Manhood*, which is about Cretan mountain villages, was unexpectedly illuminating. So were works by Chiara Frugoni on daily life in and around this period. Cennini's celebrated

The Craftsman's Handbook, a contemporary work on the craft of painting, was a delight.

I have written and spoken often over the years as to why I deploy what one writer called "history with a quarter turn to the fantastic" in my fiction. Those curious will find some of my remarks on the brightweavings.com site, created originally by Deborah Meghnagi, and administered also by Alec Lynch. Elizabeth Swainston is present with Alec on the Facebook page on my work, and responsible for our presence on Pinterest (where I often name and recommend books I've found useful—or just wonderful). I am grateful, always, to the three of them.

I had a longstanding editor and friend retire this past year as this novel was in progress, and this feels a proper place to acknowledge the support I received over the years from Susan Allison in New York. I may yet forgive her for retiring. I'm deeply grateful for her editorial commitment to this book, and others, from another dear friend, Nicole Winstanley, and also to Claire Zion, Adrienne Kerr, and Oliver Johnson. Catherine Marjoribanks copyedited with patience and humour—our eighth time around, she says, and she's the detail person. You'd think we'd stop battling over commas by now. Or not. Martin Springett, another old friend, did patient, professional work on the map.

I owe thanks to my agents, John Silbersack, Jonny Geller, and Jerry Kalajian. And—as always, and with love—to Sybil, Rex, Sam, Matthew, and Laura. It may seem as if we write our books alone, but it just isn't true.